Prologue

Guinevere Beach, Florida
July 13, 1899

The locomotive sounded like a terrifying scream in the night, the brakes hissing and screeching as it pulled into the station. Passengers could make out a crowd awaiting the train's arrival. It might have been a protest or a welcoming committee, it was hard to tell. Fifteen-year-old Cordelia Merrigan, returning from a visit with her grandmother in Tallahassee, felt the energy in the compartment grow tense. These weren't women returning from a shopping expedition, there was something more purposeful.

Cordelia let the car empty out before disembarking. The crowd appeared to be waiting for several of the passengers. Cordelia needed to get home, but little out of the ordinary ever happened in Guinevere Beach, so she decided to hang back and watch as the two groups mingled, at first looking as though they might fight each other, then appearing to come to some agreement.

"What ya fuckin' waitin' for then! Light 'em up already!" a burly woman from their midst called out. One lit torch was passed around, lighting the others one by one. Cordelia wondered if it was for some holiday she had failed to register.

"Lead away, Eleanor!" the burly woman yelled, tipping her blazing torch toward a refined-looking woman who looked more like a schoolteacher.

"All right, women, no more messin' about! Reparation time for Mrs. Tidwell!" the one called Eleanor shouted.

Cordelia now took in the full size of the crowd. Behind those carrying the torches, there must have been a hundred or so women.

She recognized the wife of the baker, a neighbor from down the road, and mothers of her friends. All the same, Cordelia kept to the skirt of the throng as they began to parade through the city, yelling and cussing the name Sandy Guinevere. Cordelia had heard the name Guinevere, but only in passing. Her friend's mother had cleaned for her but spoke neither ill nor well of the woman.

As they went, townsfolk only stood by, letting the flock pass. Cordelia wondered if this was what they called a mob or a riot. No one dared to stop them. Whatever menfolk were around ducked into their homes and pulled down the shades.

Cordelia Merrigan followed the large horde to the beach.

From her vantage, in the light given by so many torches, she saw them approach a woman standing at the edge of the water, waves slowly lapping at her feet. The woman, Sandy Guinevere, didn't startle at the crowd. She appeared to even be expecting them. She was beautiful, and perhaps such beauty was all it took to repel the mob. The wind blew her hair, which appeared to sparkle in the ocean mist and torchlight.

"There she is!" Eleanor called, pointing to the lady. "And that's her house! Sear it down!"

"You heard Eleanor! Burn it ta ashes!" a woman Cordelia recognized as Vasa Fionnghuala shouted.

A group with torches broke off and marched toward the house. Cordelia watched as they broke windows and threw torches inside. Soon, a warm light emanated from inside, and a crackling sound could be heard over the waves. Then all of a sudden, the door burst open, and a woman in a maid's uniform came screaming down the front steps. More torches were thrown through the door, landing on the carpet. Soon, the house was totally engulfed in flames.

Cordelia turned her attention back toward the crowd on the beach. Now the women had surrounded Guinevere, who stood impassive. Outraged, silently offering a prayer, Cordelia gathered all her courage and approached, close enough to listen in.

"She thinks she got away with murder. Isn't it so, bitch?"

"I did no such thing," the woman answered.

Ya would lie, wouldn't ya?"

A DARLING OBSESSION

S.R. MURRAY

First Edition

Fulton Books, Inc.
Meadville, PA

Published by Fulton Books 2021

ISBN 978-1-63860-489-1 (paperback)
ISBN 978-1-63860-491-4 (digital)

Printed in the United States of America

"Do what ya must, but I curse ya all ta hell," Guinevere declared.

"Grab her!" Eleanor exclaimed.

Several women grabbed Guinevere by the arms then hauled her into the waves. Only now did she fight to get away. But it was too late. With animalistic shouts, they pulled her under.

Then, suddenly, it was over, and Guinevere's lifeless body surfaced, bobbing in the water.

Ashes from the burning home spread over the sky, and smoke filled the air.

"Murderers and their kind get what they deserve!" the hefty Vasa said proudly.

The mass of women reformed on the beach in front of the burning house.

"We have done Mrs. Tidwell proud! That's justice floatin' in the water along with all else she hath burning to the ground," Eleanor exclaimed. "Now hang the dead bitch for good measure. Then, after all have seen what happens to no good harlots, wrap the body with stones and sink her for the fish to eat.

"What about the other?" Vasa asked, pointing toward the water.

Eleanor stared in the direction Vasa pointed. After a brief silence, she replied, "Stones only." The mob strung up Guinevere's limp corpse.

Nearby, a bright light flashed, and a glass bulb burst.

March 1983
Sandy Beach, Florida

Detective Robert Justice opened the station door for De'Ron Goodman, otherwise known as Goo, and let him walk through. He wasn't going to rush the alleged dealer. The kid was handcuffed and wasn't going to run. Where would he go? The farthest he'd been out of Sandy Beach was likely the Waffle House on the interstate. Local boy, like Justice himself. But that didn't stop Goo from giving him some lip.

"Get these fuckin cuffs off me!" the young dealer yelled, announcing his presence in headquarters.

Now he was making a big display. In Justice's cruiser, he'd done nothing but sulk in the back seat. Justice directed him to the processing desk. "Sit down here, you little asshole," he told the boy. His tattoos and cable-like muscles were animated by sheer bad attitude. Bobby pushed him into the seat.

"What you got, Detective?" Tim "Tick" Tickerrman, the desk officer, asked.

"Selling weed and a bit of blow."

"Is that a crime?" Tick joked. Small-scale possession was usually tolerated if it was a tourist caught holding. It was only right that locals got to enjoy the privilege as well. Blow was different. Suddenly, vacuum-packed bags of it were washing up like seashells. Justice wasn't having it. Not from tourists, not from Goo.

"Damn cops. Always be fuckin' lying. Fuck yo bitch ass!" Goo said.

"Oh, I'm lying, am I?" the detective asked.

"Damn right, muthafucka!"

The detective smirked. "So how's your uncle going to feel about today's little screwup, Goodman?"

"None of yo goddamn business."

"Well, don't you worry. We're going to keep you nice and safe. We'll even feed your skinny ass," Robert Justice said as Goo tried to stare him down, but he soon lost nerve and dropped his gaze to his lap. "Now tell me I'm lying," Justice finished.

Goo was still studying his own crotch when the captain poked his head out of his office.

"Bobby!" Captain Greg Curry shouted.

"Yes, Captain," the detective replied.

"When you get done playing over there, come see me in my office."

"Yes, sir!"

"I got it from here, Detective," the desk duty cop said.

"Thank you, Officer," Bobby stated before giving Goo another long look and heading to the captain's office. Bobby knocked on the half-open door. "So what is all the shouting about?" he asked.

"Where do you make the arrest?" Captain Curry asked, looking at Justice over his reading glasses.

"Not too far from the auto repair shop," Bobby said as he sat.

The captain appeared to suppress a smile. At fifty-two, he still enjoyed his job, and making life difficult for the local underbelly kept him cheerful. "This should piss off the big guy some."

"Is this what you wanted to ask, or do you just miss me?"

Captain Curry pointed toward the pen, where the beat cops and detectives did paperwork.

"The other side of your desk has had an empty chair for quite a while now."

"Barker saw fit to move on."

"Bobby…"

"I don't need a partner, Greg. I mean, Captain."

"Sandy Beach is changing, Bobby. More drugs, more firearms. Drug runners traveling through, fugitives hiding out. This town has always had its issues, but now even more so it seems."

"That's part of what keeps me, I suppose," Justice said, looking over Curry's shoulder to his array of diplomas and photos. Curry kept pictures of his platoon next to his degree. When the door was closed, they talked like vets do with each other—with a foundation of unspoken understanding. But now the door was open. *All business.*

"Protocols are evolving also. Now look, I know you work best alone. I know you prize that, and I respect it. It's just...you can't expect the newer officers to train themselves. No one is transferring here at the moment. Times are changing. The budget isn't."

Bobby prepared himself, knowing there was more to the captain's request. His mind immediately propelled himself forward in time. A cold beer. Maybe with a plate of clams and alligator bites. Why wait for retirement to enjoy yourself when you could do it every day if you lived in Sandy Beach?

"Bobby, I'm recommending you for a promotion to sergeant when we get those spots filled."

"Thank you, sir," Bobby said, mildly surprised.

"Long overdue, Bobby, and you aced the test," Curry said then picked up a golf ball and attempted to spin it on his index finger like a basketball.

"Now until the new detective is prepared to take over your place, you will keep the same schedule. And partner up."

"Well, who do you have in mind?" Bobby asked.

"The young buck, Jack Cutler."

"Who's that?"

"Come on, Bobby. He's been here over half a year. Came to your birthday party."

"I didn't even go to my birthday party."

"Well, if you did, you'd know who I am talking about. He did well on the test. He's a good kid and works hard. Maybe he's still green, but that's where you come in. Once he's ready, he will partner with someone else."

"What about Alan? What about Tick or Pac? At least I know what to expect."

"Jack's spent time in Tallahassee. Knows a thing or two. And, Bobby, this isn't really open for discussion."

Bobby knew Curry hadn't made this decision lightly, so he ceased protesting. "Yes, sir."

A knock came at the doorframe.

Bobby didn't let his gaze stray from Curry until he heard Jack sit down. Out of the corner of his eye, he saw Jack's hand extend toward him. Bobby slowly turned. Jack was not exactly what he expected—a kid the same age as the grunts in his squad in Na Dang. He pictured Jack in a private's uniform. He'd seen kids Jack's age ripped in two as though they'd swallowed the grenade. But there was a scar above Jack's eye that provoked a grudging sympathy. And Curry wasn't going to budge on the order. Bobby knew it wasn't the time to press him. He summoned a smile and reached out his hand. Jack seemed to have been holding his breath because he exhaled audibly, taking Bobby's hand and working it like Bobby was a well pump on a hot day.

"Good to meet you, Detective."

Justice nodded. "You too."

"Officer Cutler, you're being bumped up to detective, and I'm going to partner you with Detective Justice to train. Bobby calls the shots," Curry said.

"Awesome, Captain," Jack said, looking back at Bobby. "Well, howdy partner. Or boss? Whichever you prefer, bud."

Bud. Bobby shook his head, looked to the captain with a smirk, and whispered, "Fuck."

Later that evening, Bobby was sitting at the Snappy Turtle, one of the few Sandy Beach pubs that preferred locals to tourist traffic. It was the type of place that kept Christmas lights strung around the bar mirror year-round. Above the top shelf, a taxidermy turtle wearing a miniature top hat was mounted precariously. Bobby kept wondering when it was going to fall and hit Wanda, the bartender. Like most regulars, he thought it might improve her disposition. Bobby was gearing himself up to take a dry bite of tuna on rye—his doctor's warnings against cholesterol a few weeks ago had him off the establishment's famous calamari burger and fried oysters—when he felt a hand on his shoulder.

"Hey, bud! I mean, boss!"

"Jesus," Bobby said.

"Sorry for sneaking up on you like that. I know you're quick with the trigger." Jack shot into the air with his finger.

Bobby took in Jack as if for the first time. He was taller, more fit than he had looked hunched in his chair in Curry's office. *Jack,* Bobby thought, *looks better in dim light.*

"I suppose I'll have to invite myself to sit," Jack said. Bobby sighed and nodded toward to neighboring barstool. He put his sandwich down, feeling like he'd been caught, though not sure what he had been caught at.

"Bobby Justice. *The* Bobby Justice. Hey, by the way, your—"

"Yes," Bobby cut him off. "I'm aware of my last name and my chosen profession. If you think you have a new catchphrase, let me let you in on a secret—you don't."

"Damn, how did you know what I was going to say?"

Bobby gave him a hard look. The young were exhausting. But then again, so were the old.

"Call it instinct. Go ahead and tell me about yourself, Jack," Bobby said. "If that's what you're intent on doing, let's just get it out of the way."

Jack smiled and picked up a menu. Bobby signaled for another beer and one for Jack. "Not much to tell, honestly," Jack said as he scanned the menu. He ordered the calamari burger when Wanda brought the beers. "I'm from right here in Sandy Beach. I've been here most of my life, same as my parents. Been with my girl a few years, may make it official."

Bobby searched his mind. He guessed he'd stopped noticing people who weren't getting in bar fights or selling weed from the back of their truck.

"Transferred back from Tallahassee not long ago. Thought I'd try the city, but I missed Sandy Beach. Small town. You know, the sand gets under your nails, but the town gets under your skin." Jack laughed at his own joke when Bobby didn't.

Instead, Bobby sipped his beer then called Wanda back and asked her to take the half-eaten tuna away. "So you're twenty-seven, twenty-eight?"

"Will be twenty-eight soon."

"College boy?"

"Um, would that be a good thing?"

Bobby noticed Jack's gaze fall on his faded arm tattoo—Green Beret. His face seemed to relax, and before Bobby could answer, he said, "No, not really. This is what I always wanted to do, but I had to wait a few years. So after high school, I worked at my dad's appliance store. Then I joined the force in '77. Now I'm your partner." Jack lit up a cigarette and held the pack up to offer one to Bobby.

Bobby shook his head. "I hope you don't plan on smoking those in the squad car."

"Nope, not now anyway. Besides, I only smoke when I'm having a cold one or just passing the time. It's not much of a habit for me. I can make a pack last a month or longer," Jack said, as though bragging. "You don't really believe that cigarettes lower your sperm count bullcrap, do you?"

Bobby's gaze hardened. "No. It's just that last year, some kid I picked up for loitering by the arcade pissed himself. Haven't been able to get the smell out. Last thing I need is smoke on top of that."

Jack took a sip of his beer then started to say something before catching himself.

"Out with it," Bobby said.

"I mean, I know you kick ass and all. You do have that reputation. But did you really pick up a kid for hanging out in front of a video game arcade? I mean, that's what they are there for. For kids. To hang out at."

Wanda delivered Jack's burger, setting it down without a smile. Bobby looked at him then picked up one of his fries and put it in his mouth. The kid didn't flinch.

"I mean, I get it. Not much crime here."

Bobby chewed slowly, knowing what was coming. The kid had already had a few drinks, he could tell now.

"Not like the old days."

Bobby knew he was talking about Payne. Bartholomew Payne had brought more mayhem to the town than any person Bobby could remember. Jack must have been, what, six then? Bobby was still in the service at the time, but the crime spree, which had been an aberration for Sandy Beach, was legendary in the station.

When Bobby didn't reply, Jack changed tact. "So has it been a while since you had a partner?"

"It's been about seven months or so since he moved to DC to work for the FBI. The captain and I were partners for a short time after I made detective in '73."

"Hmm. I heard he transferred due to some personal issue. I'm just saying, whatever problem you had with him, you won't have with me."

"Glad to hear it."

"Glad you're glad," Jack responded.

"Now dig into that burger. Nothing worse than cold calamari," Bobby said and signaled to Wanda that his glass was almost empty.

The next morning, Bobby woke up with a start. The conversation from the night before immediately began replaying in his mind. Once Jack realized Bobby would dispense advice if he kept buying him beers, the questions kept coming. Bobby sat up in bed and dredged up what he could remember. Yes, he'd told Jack what any kid would want to hear—detective work was about instinct, elbow grease, about communication. What he didn't tell him, what he would have to learn in time, was that it was also about shutting your eyes to the suffering of others, keeping objective on the job, and getting results no matter what the cost. Something he hadn't done in a while. Shit, Jack was right. Picking up a kid for standing around in front of a video arcade *had* been a bitter, mean thing to do.

Bobby dry heaved in the shower, shaved, fried half a carton of pre-beaten eggs in a pan, then heaped the ugly results onto a slice of white bread, topped it with tobacco, and then ate it in a few bites before he headed out to his cruiser. Only his cruiser wasn't there. In its place was Jack's cruiser. Jack was waiting for him, now holding a cup of coffee up like bait. Yes, he'd left his car in the Snappy Turtle parking lot. Jack must have driven him home. And the wide conspiratorial smile told him he had gotten sloppy with his talk. Probably about his ex, the miscarriage and all. Well, if Bobby had to suffer a new partner, he decided, it might as well be Jack, and Jack might as well know what he's in for.

*****

Lee Earl Elwood watched a squirrel scamper across the patch of knotty grass in front of his trailer home. He considered the squirrels in western Florida odd, misshapen, runty, rusty-colored instead of gray. If he had a gun, he'd shoot it, but as a felon, he was prohibited from carrying one. A cartoon played on the small black-and-white portable TV behind him. He never watched, but the cartoons sparked his imagination. Better than a cup of coffee. He watched the squirrel with a stillness like prayer, knowing even a movement behind the window might startle it. When the animal picked up a nugget, nibbled a little, then fled, Elwood gave his first smile of the day. He had laid out the poison that morning. Feeling like he had accomplished something, he went to see his neighbor, Roy Boutte.

"Roy!" Lee Earl shouted as he knocked on Roy's camper door. "Roy! Wake your ass up! Roy!"

Roy cracked opened his door, peeked around, and saw who it was.

"Oh, hey, Lee," Roy hesitantly greeted him through a yawn. "What's up?"

As Roy opened his screen door farther, Lee Earl got a view of his neighbor's pee-stained jockeys.

Lee raised an eyebrow. "Thinking that I should've called first."

"What can I do for you, Lee Earl?"

"Let's take a ride."

"Ride where?" Roy asked.

"What difference does it make where?" Lee Earl asked while looking at the rotund thirty-four-year-old Sandy Mart stock clerk. He hated fat on a man. On a boy, it was fine and could even be attractive. But Roy was no child. Probably had his childhood eaten up by lines at the food pantry and empty seats on the school bus. He'd internalized failure and rejection so much that he didn't even expect basic kindness.

"Well, are we gonna be very long? I was napping."

Lee knocked Roy back as he shoved open the door. "Napping in the morning is called sleeping late. Now stop asking so many stupid questions and get in the goddamn truck."

"All right, dang. Lemme get some pants on," Roy said, staggering back into the darkness of the trailer.

"Please, fucking do."

As Roy went back into dress, a young boy caught Lee's eye. Blond, like so many in these parts. That strawberry blond hair that would darken as they aged.

"Hey there, Ryan. Why don't you come by and say hi anymore, bud?"

"I can't, Mr. Elwood."

Just then, the boy's mother walked out. She looked surprised for a moment, then her expression darkened. "Ryan, get inside." Once the boy scampered away, she took a step toward Lee Earl. "Elwood, you stay the hell away from both my boys."

"Well, damn, Claire. I was just saying hi," Lee Earl told her as he rested his hands on his hips. "What's got your panties in a twist?"

"You heard me. I'll call the law," the woman said before stalking back toward her trailer.

Roy returned, now fully dressed.

"What's all that about?" he asked Lee Earl.

"Nothing. She is just crazy, is all," Lee Earl answered while flipping off the woman's backside as she shut the door of her trailer behind her. Lee was angrier at himself than the woman. Angry he had again felt the pull in his gut. For him, that's where it started. Not in the mind or imagination, not in the balls, but in the gut. Like some juniper berries fermenting there, waiting to intoxicate him. But he hadn't meant anything by talking to Ryan. He'd made a promise to himself and knew taking it further just wasn't worth it.

*****

Later that morning, the West Central Florida sun beat down on the mangroves and turned asphalt into a warm bed for snakes and other animals destined to be roadkill. Lee Earl Elwood and Roy Boutte pulled off the interstate and headed toward the coast before they arrived at the Sandy Beach Hotel. Lee Earl thought the place looked like some haunted house out of a Disney cartoon. Wooden, built on stilts so its tail end reached over the water of the Gulf, it looked like a great crustacean that was set to scuttle off into the ocean. Maybe it had been built, maybe it had just washed up, spat out by the sea. Even though somebody had given it a new white paint job years back, the sun had already cracked the white into flakes. Lee Earl hoped to sell the proprietor, Ms. Marina Kerrigan, on doing some touch-ups, but she didn't seem too concerned with the appearance. "People didn't come to the Sandy for luxury," she had explained to him. "They come for mood."

"I didn't know you worked here also Lee," Roy said.

"Easy cash. Small stuff, It all helps with the bills."

Roy belched. "They don't have people for that?" he asked, finishing off a beer.

"Yes, Roy, but it's an old ass hotel with lots of needs and a small staff. Fuckin' thing was built in the forties, I think."

"I thought they were going to tear down this dump."

"Nah, not while there's still some money to squeeze from it," Lee Earl said as he started toward the service door around back. After a moment, he looked back. Roy was just standing there. "You coming?"

"Being here gives me the heebie-jeebies," Roy said, looking around. "So much weirdo stuff has happened, and people say it's cursed."

"The only curse you'll get is me cursing you out if you don't bring along my tool kit. That sink isn't going to fix itself."

By the afternoon, Roy had finished half of the six-pack of Olympias Lee Earl had been saving for the end of the job. Lee Earl didn't mind. He didn't want to drink, didn't want to lose control. But over the course of the day, he'd felt like he, too, had downed a few beers. Or maybe there was a carbon monoxide leak. Lee Earl felt dizzy. Not exactly dizzy, just a bit off. Some bad juju in his veins. He put his wrench down and looked behind him from under the sink.

"Roy?" he called. The man had wandered off again. "Roy!" Lee hollered. Then, from the hallway, he heard the creak of a floorboard. *The place has the aches and pains of an old woman,* Lee Earl mused. He looked to the hall and thought he caught sight of a blur of blond hair. A child running by. "Man, what the fuck," he said, stepping from the room. Only the hallway was empty. He thought again of the boy he had seen in the trailer park. Something stirred inside of him, ready to wake up.

Lee Earl silently cursed himself. *He had been doing so well.* Sandy Beach, with its heat and calm waves from the Gulf of Mexico, the stars, kept him focused, kept him grounded. *What was done is done.* He wasn't going to be that man again.

Lee Earl jumped when he felt something against his neck. He turned and saw Roy—simple, dopey Roy—holding a lukewarm Olympia. He took the can, because he wanted to calm the feeling that was rising within.

"Okay, dipshit, let's get back to that damn sink. And leave a fucking beer for me."

Roy grimaced as he picked at the tab on the beer can. "You don't have to get mad at me like that."

Lee Earl took a deep breath. "Hell, I'm sorry, Roy. I know this sounds crazy, but just right here, I decided something."

"What's that, Lee?"

"I need a son."

"A son?" Roy looked at Lee curiously. "Like, a boy?"

"Yes, a boy who could help me do little jobs like this and get me a beer when I need one…fix things for his old man when they break. We could be playing cards right now instead of doing this bullshit."

"I can get you a beer, Lee. I didn't drink 'em all."

"Just get me the damn wrench for now," Lee Earl growled.

Roy picked up the first wrench he saw from the toolbox and handed it over. Lee Earl worked in silence for a moment.

"Well, it's not like you can pop one out yourself, ya know," Roy said.

"I know how it works, dumb ass," Lee Earl mumbled.

"Well, how else then?" Roy sat back at the table. "Adopt?"

Lee Earl contemplated the word before rising from beneath the sink. "Hell yeah, Roy. Exactly. Adopt. That's a fuckin' goddamn excellent way to say it, and that's what we are going to do, bud."

"We?" Roy repeated with a nervous tone.

"Yes, *we*," Lee Earl confirmed, staring right at Roy.

"You can't just go adopt a baby, Lee. Where are you gonna put it?"

"Who said anything about a baby? Don't be stupid, Roy."

"Oh, good, I thought you were serious."

"Eight or nine is about the right age," Lee Earl said as he turned the water on. "Look, see there, Roy? No more leak."

"I think I need another beer," Roy stuttered.

*****

Later that night, Kate Lovell pulled up in her driveway and parked the family County Squire station wagon. At thirty-eight, she still garnered looks from the fishermen and felt lucky to have her big fourteen-year-old with unbrushed shaggy black hair, Hunter, and her undersized nine-year-old, Chase, along when she shopped. She didn't mind the suggestive comments, but only to a limit. Hunter had been embarrassed when she wore her favorite Jordache jeans, but she could still pull it off and sported the tight indigo denim when she needed an ego lift. Hunter walked behind his mother while Chase scampered up to the porch and opened the front door. Her husband, Todd, was probably home, but they never bothered to lock it anyway. *Sandy Beach isn't the kind of place where you need to worry*, she thought.

Kate, with a bag of groceries balanced on her hip like a toddler, found her husband, Todd, sitting on the couch watching TV. The forty-three-year-old handyman smiled up at her. Even sitting, he looked fit. Kate had married him despite the moustache—since shaved—and love of the Buccaneers. Like most residents of Sandy Beach, she was a Miami Dolphins fan. But this being basketball season, they came together over the Gators.

"Hey, Dad!" Chase shouted.

"Hey, hey! Did everyone have a good time?" Todd asked.

"You don't see any tears," Kate answered, and she closed the door once Hunter, a bit sulky and slow to keep up lately, stepped inside. She set her purse down and bent over to kiss her husband. "It would have been more fun with you there."

"Hey, Dad, you going to go with us next time? Huh?" Chase jumped over to his father to give him a high five.

"It's a deal, bud! How was the film?"

"Scary," Chase said.

"Yeah, but wasn't that awesome when he sliced that girl in the shower?" Hunter said excitedly.

His mother guffawed. "That's the last time you get to pick the movie. Horror films have sure changed since my day when the scariest thing we had was the blob or some zombies your grandma could outrun."

"Zombies? Bitchin'!" Hunter said with widened eyes.

"Hunter, watch your language. How many times do we have to tell you that?" Kate reminded him.

"Bogus," Hunter whispered under his breath.

"Hey, Dad?" Chase said, plopping down on the couch, looking up at his father with wide eyes. "Can I stay after school and play basketball in the gym for a little while tomorrow?"

Todd let out a frustrated sigh. "No, not by yourself, Chase. Please, don't make me have to tell you that anymore, you hear me?"

"Yes, Dad," Chase said.

Todd cast a glance at his oldest son. "Hunter, you don't leave your brother after school again. He's not old enough to be there alone."

Hunter lifted his arms in defiance, glaring at his father. "He knows the way home!" he spat out.

"Yeah, can I, please?" Chase asked again.

"You're only nine, Chase. Your brother is almost fifteen," Todd said. "When you get a little older and bigger, you can. Maybe when you're twelve or thirteen, but not now."

"You almost gave your dad and me a heart attack last time," Kate chimed in. "We didn't know where you were—"

"'Till he's thirteen?" Hunter interrupted. "That's like forever!"

"Boy, watch that lip." Todd pointed a calloused finger at Hunter. The skin on his hands was tough as croc skin from working with his tools all day. "Now go upstairs and get ready for bed. Both of you."

"It's only like, eight," Hunter said.

"I ain't saying go to bed. I'm just saying *get ready*," Todd said sternly.

Hunter, pushing his bangs from his face, turned and stomped up the stairs. The slamming of his door echoed through the house. Kate turned to Todd and gave an exasperated look. Before she could complain, she heard Hunter's door open again. "Chase, stop messing with my damn video games!" Hunter bellowed then slammed the door for a second time.

Todd looked up toward Hunter's room. It had been so calm. The Gators. A limp but pleasant hard-on during a shampoo commercial. Then this. "Hunter, calm down!" Todd turned toward his youngest and ordered him upstairs as well.

"Okay," Chase said somberly. With his head down, he plodded up to his room.

"That boy has no mind for his own safety," Kate said once he was out of earshot.

"Ah, he's young. Of course, he doesn't think about what's going to happen. Why should he? He's a kid," Todd said, and he kissed his wife's hand. "It's Hunter and his quick temper that worries me. Not just with us but with everyone. Hell, we can't even keep pets around here. The whole hamster thing—"

Kate put her finger over Todd's lips. For some reason lately, she feared Hunter overhearing them talk about him. Kate sighed, now moving her finger down Todd's shoulder. "I know. Anyway, did you finish up your job today?"

"Well, yeah, but they found some more work for me to do around there. I may have to hire a few guys."

"Oh, okay. But no more weekends, or at least no more Sundays, please. We need a day for family time."

"I'll try, honey. I have to make hay while I can. You know how this job can be—feast or famine."

"I know, baby. Do you want to come and watch TV in bed with me? *Dallas* is on. You can pretend I'm Lucy," Kate said, a gleam in her eye.

"Tempting, but I'm going to finish watching the game then clean my tools." Todd's eyes were on the TV again.

"Well, I guess I'm just going to take a shower alone and go to bed early then."

Todd stood from the couch to turn the volume up on the television while Kate headed to their bedroom.

*****

The first time Rosalina saw Marina Kerrigan, it was through a curtained window of the Sandy Beach Hotel. Her silhouette was lit, a black slick of shadow fringed with light. Rosalina stood a moment looking at the sight until the curtain was thrown back and there was Kerrigan in full view, catching her spying before she started work. Ms. Kerrigan smiled, unsurprised, looking still as a portrait, as Rosalina bowed her head and walked around the deck to the service entrance.

Her sister Isabel had warned her Ms. Kerrigan would be haughty, aloof. Luckily, Rosalina answered to Isabel, who was head of housekeeping, which Rosalina considered a bit much considering there were only the two of them.

Rosalina found Isabel waiting for her in the lobby.

"I think I just met the boss," Rosalina said.

"Don't worry about her. I vouched for you. I'll teach you how to turn a room and everything else," Isabel said. "But first, let me show you around the place." Isabel gave Rosalina a tour of the hotel. Even compared to hotels in Havana, the rooms were drab. Most had a forced nautical theme with fishing nets, seashells, and old photos of sailors and ships on the walls. "Now let me show you the best room," Isabel said, taking Rosalina by her hand and pulling her through a hallway with flame-shaped bulbs and paintings of old vessels. Rosalina was uneasy with the creak of the floor and the sound of the waves from outside, but she followed her sister. They arrived at a room in the back, which her sister opened with a key from a chain of keys.

"This is so great," she said.

The room was worn looking and looked like it hadn't been redecorated in decades. An old boat wheel adorned the wall, and the navy blue wallpaper was frayed in places, the drywall showing through. But in the center of the room, there was a trapdoor which Isabel pulled open. There, in a pit of darkness, waves lapped up at them.

"It goes right into the ocean!" she said.

Rosalina laughed as Isabel reached her hand down to touch the water. But as she did, Rosalina saw her sister's expression change. Isabel pulled her hand back quickly, as if it had been bit. Rosalina thought she heard a whisper.

"What's wrong?" Rosalina asked as her sister closed the door.

"I don't know. I just get a creepy feeling from the sea. I feel cold," Isabel said. Rosalina immediately wanted to be out of the room, out of the hotel, though she knew she needed the job to support her studies.

"Are you okay? You look a bit sick," Rosalina said and pushed the trapdoor closed.

*****

Darling Family Care Clinic
George Darling, MD
Family Medicine since 1950
Sandy Beach, FL

So read the sign out front.

Inside, George Darling finished treating another case of food poisoning. It wasn't a problem with the clams—they were always fresh, but newcomers sometimes overloaded on seafood, and their systems weren't used to it. Hydration. Charcoal pills. A prescription to keep the pharmacy in business.

Sometimes he cleaned and stitched superficial cuts that weren't serious enough for the hospital. Kids liked his Flintstone Band-Aids. For Dr. George Darling, this was business as usual ever since he opened to patients in 1950 at the age of twenty-six. Though gray poked from the hair behind his ears and he contributed to his dentist's retirement fund more than he cared to, he was as spry as ever.

Nurse Bayard, whom Darling was sure had some Seminole blood for the keen way she watched him, let him know his two o'clock appointment was in Waiting Room E. With a curt nod, George wrapped his stethoscope around his neck and began down the hall. He picked up the patient's file from outside the door and stepped inside as he glanced her forms over.

"Hello… Isabel Dominguez?" the doctor confirmed as he tapped the door closed behind him with his foot, like flicking a soccer ball. "So what are we having problems with today?"

"It's my chest, Doctor," the woman answered with an accent Darling placed as Cuban. "It's been hurting."

George nodded as he finished skimming her slim file then tossed it on the counter. When he finally looked up at his patient, he felt the floor beneath him shift. The mane of raven hair and a gingerbread complexion. The full lips and brown eyes, dark and mysterious yet full of light, like glass marbles. For a moment, time stopped, and Isabel Dominguez was all that existed. Like an old love, seeing her felt both fresh and comfortable.

"U-um…" George stammered then cleared his throat. "Yes, let me give it a listen. Please have a seat." He rolled fresh paper onto the examining table and supported her by the hand while she hopped up.

He took his stethoscope and placed the drum gently on her chest.

"Deep breath in for me," he prompted. "And exhale." He placed his hand against her upper back while surreptitiously admiring the curves of her body. "Good. Again, inhale. And exhale. Very good." He hazarded a look at her left hand. No ring. "Is it Ms. or Mrs. Dominguez?"

"Miss..." Isabel answered. He felt her eyes on him as he stepped toward his desk, where he picked up a prescription pad and pen. Perhaps she'd detected too much interest in that question.

"Sounds as if we have a bit of a chest cold," George said as he finished writing. Unlike most doctors, Darling's script was neat and composed and looked boxy, like cuneiform on an ancient crypt. "These antibiotics should help, but please come back if your symptoms don't improve in a week or so." He tore the slip of paper off the pad and smiled as he handed it to Isabel. "We want to make sure you don't end up with pneumonia now, do we?"

Isabel accepted the slip of paper, folding it once and putting it in her purse. Darling liked that she didn't drop her gaze but looked him straight on. She was probably an immigrant, worked service or hospitality. He noted, though, that she carried herself with dignity, as an equal. "No, Doctor," she said.

"Okay, Ms. Dominguez. Unless there is anything else?" Isabel shook her head. The doctor held the door open for her as she grabbed her purse and strode into the lobby to pay her bill. George stopped in front of his office door and pretended to be filling out a form when in fact, he was slyly peeking over at Isabel and listening in.

Kate Lovell, George's receptionist for the past eight years, smiled as Isabel approached the counter. "That's going to be seventy-five dollars today," she said. "Cash, card, or check?"

"Oh my! Seventy-five dollars?" Isabel's brow furrowed.

Kate didn't let her smile fall. "Is there a problem?"

"Do I have to pay it all now?"

"Well," Kate said, finally letting her expression relax. "How much could you pay?"

Isabel rummaged around in her purse for her wallet then fingered her cash. "I could pay twenty-five now."

"Well, let me—"

"It's okay, Kate." George dropped the form to his side then approached the counter and stood next to the woman. "Ms. Dominguez, perhaps you can pay some or all of it when I see you on your next visit," he said. A look of relief washed Isabel's face. He decided at that moment that he wanted to see that face soften again.

"I'm more than grateful for that, Doctor. Thank you!"

"Ready?" a younger Cuban woman said from a reception chair. She closed what looked like a textbook and stood. Dr. Darling watched the pair exit the clinic. Only then did George notice Kate looking up at him, grinning.

"*What?*" he said innocently.

"Nothing. Only she might be a bit young. But I say go for it. You're too good of a man to spend so much time alone," Kate said.

"Nonsense. Plus, I'm not alone. I have my patients. And I have you."

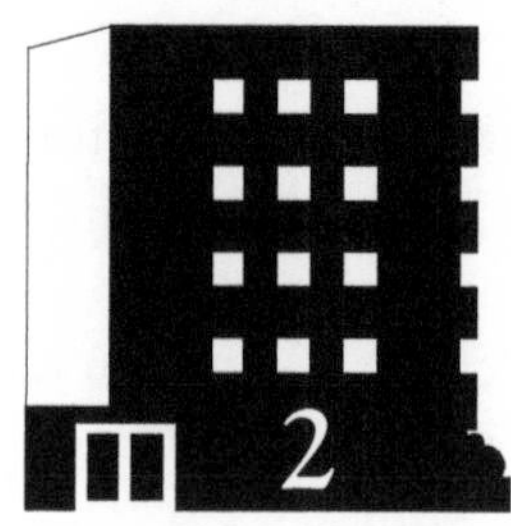

April 1983

Bobby and Jack had taken a call to investigate a convenience store robbery. They surveyed the area, ran some forensics, and spoke with the cashier, the store owner, and some of the teens loitering out front to find out if they'd seen anything. If they had, they weren't telling. And the cashier couldn't ID the robber because he had a mask on, even wore gloves to cover up his hands. One witness did see the robber jump in the passenger side of a gray pickup truck. After getting everyone's statements, the two officers decided to grab some lunch at a nearby food truck before heading back to the station.

"Why the hell is my dog plain?" Bobby grumbled once Jack unpacked the bag.

"I thought that's what you said," Jack replied.

"By plain, I mean no jalapenos or *queso* or whatever crap that's not pig and ketchup."

"Come on, Bobby. Loosen up. It's 1983, for Chrissake."

Bobby plucked a package of Ruffles from the bag. "These yours?" he asked.

"Yes, why?"

Bobby opened the bag and popped a potato chip in his mouth. "Next time, get my dog how I like it."

"Man, what's with you eating my food?" Jack said.

"I like your food a sight better than your taste in music. If I have to listen to that damn Deaf Leper cassette tape again—"

"It's Def Leppard, and I thought you liked it," Jack replied.

"There's a difference between *liking* and *tolerating*. Just ask your folks to illuminate."

"That's pretty cold. I mean, you don't even like Tom Petty."

"Can't say that I do, but he's better than most of these newer singers, I suppose."

"Come on. Petty's Florida as the everglades."

"Glades ain't much to brag on," Bobby said as he crunched another potato chip.

"Man, for a guy who's only holiday was a trip to Ho Chi Minh, you are an awful snob. Is that why we can't turn on the air-con? The heat reminds you of the good ole days?"

Bobby looked at him hard.

"It's Saigon," he finally said. "Only the commies call it Ho Chi Minh."

"Sorry, boss."

Bobby tossed his half-eaten dog back into the bag. Jack had been right about the heat. He liked it against his skin. It was the only thing he cared for in Vietnam, except for the occasional poke in a village brothel. He pushed a Chet Baker cassette into the player slot but didn't press play. Something was nagging at him.

"Something is off about this robbery," Bobby thought out loud as he crumpled up the empty chip packaging.

"Yeah, I feel it too. I can't believe whoever it was would risk years of jail time for less than two hundred dollars in cash, a few packs of cigarettes, and some beer...well, a lot of beer, but still," Jack acknowledged.

Bobby started the car up and pulled onto the interstate. "The beer makes it seem more like a couple of idiots being idiots rather than an act of desperation. Lucky nobody got hurt. Still, for idiots, they're making our jobs tough. Sometimes idiots just do that." he stated.

"Yeah, we don't have shit to go on," Jack said. Sometimes the young detective got overly frustrated. Bobby didn't mind, as it gave him an excuse to explain some things.

"Maybe one of my CIs who lives out this way can give us something," Bobby opined.

"Someone that can help us now?" Jack said and drummed the dashboard in excitement. "That would be fantastic."

"I don't know how things worked in Tallahassee, but round here, you can't be a detective worth a hell without a few good informants." Bobby looked to his partner for a moment before turning his attention back to the road. "A cop is only reliable as his CIs, and that still holds as true today as when Curry told me that ten years ago."

"Curry told you that? That's like scripture."

"I'm sure you have collared a few guys that you felt a rapport with after speaking with them, right?"

"Yeah, some aren't bad people. Just caught up in a bad situation." Jack nodded.

"Exactly. Maybe you can help them with something, then they can help you in return," Bobby continued.

"Use our leverage."

"I guess you can always try and force things, being a cop, but I've found the best way is to do them a favor. Something easy for us to do, and this helps build trust," Bobby clarified.

"Such as?"

"They bring you speeding ticket. 'Okay, we'll take care of it, but what do you have for me?'" Bobby counted on his fingers to illustrate the point. "You catch them buying some weed…well, I don't have to report this, but I'm going to need something from you. Hell, even get them out of jail as long as it's nothing too serious."

"So we trade with criminals?"

"What…you some damn saint over there? You just said the exact same thing a minute ago, and now you get all moralistic on me."

"I'm just asking," Jack said.

"Look, the higher you go in this profession, the bigger the arrest…the ones doing the everyday, ordinary shit are the assholes that give us info on those operating above street level. Think about it, Jack. Play by the book. Just *rewrite* it a little. Okay?"

"I'm with you, partner…loud and clear," Jack said, looking out the window. They were driving into the Trap, an area east of Sandy Beach where cars on cinder blocks were used as lawn sculpture. Beer empties stood in for garden gnomes. "Why the hell are we *here*?"

"For you to shut up and learn."

Bobby pulled up to a beefy man wearing blue oil-stained overalls. His red beard looked like a dull fire against white skin. Bobby cocked his head out the window. "Hey, Country, you been working out? I say you looking like a slim 335 right now, big man."

The man called Country wiped the sweat from his brow, peeking with no little caution around the open truck hood. "Howdy, Detectives."

"Country, want to take a ride? It won't be long."

"No, thanks, Detective Justice. Are you trying to get my redneck ass jumped?"

"Now, Country, you are gonna hurt my feelings. Enjoy the freedom, boy. More than a few in your situation are sitting in jail because they didn't have a buddy to do them a favor."

"Damn it, Detective. I haven't done anything. I've been good, I swear."

"I'll get right to it, seeing as it's a bad time," Bobby said. "What do you know about the store robbery that happened earlier this morning?"

"Not shit!"

"Country, don't let me find out, later on, you are lying to me. I'll start to think we aren't friends anymore." The hefty informant stayed quiet. "This 'I do for you, but you don't for me' type relationship just isn't going to work. Careful, or I may take it upon myself to track down some stolen auto parts."

At this, Country shuffled on his feet like an ox that got skittish in its pen. "Okay," the big man said. He looked around then looked at Jack. Bobby nodded, indicating that he was in safe company. "I heard some young boys at the Coral Trailer Park were having a big party tonight. That's all I'll say."

"Does one of these boys happen to have a gray pickup truck?" Bobby asked.

Country paused then gave a simple nod.

"Thanks, Country," Bobby said, handing his informant a card and a small bag. "If this info works out, you can use that card for a favor. Oh, and I wouldn't go to that party tonight."

Country looked into the bag as Bobby and Jack drive off. "It don't even have chili on the damn thing!" he yelled before shrugging and taking a bite of the hot dog he found there.

*****

As the final bell rang on the campus of the all-inclusive Sandy Public School, home to the Brown Sharks, students rushed through corridors and out the exits. Some found their parents waiting for them in their vehicles while others boarded the buses. Those who lived close enough to the school simply rode their bikes or walked home. Chase found his brother, Hunter, at the bike rack unlocking the metal chain from his wheel. Chase's banana seat Schwinn was locked next to his brother's blue Scrambler, but he didn't bother to unlock it yet.

"What you waiting on?" Hunter said as he stuffed the lock into his backpack. "Look, you better not be thinking about staying."

"Why?" Chase asked. "You gonna tell?"

Hunter mounted his bike. "Do what you want, freakshow. They'll find out anyway."

Chase watched as his brother rode off then turned and headed back toward the school's gym. They'd had basketball in PE that day. The bigger kids hadn't passed to him once, but Chase knew he would be a decent player if he was only given a chance. He strode past a small group of kids who were playing a pickup game to the opposite end of the court then slid off his backpack and tossed it against the wall before grabbing a ball from a bin. He dribbled it and took his first shot, imagining he was jumping over the guard of his classmates. He missed—air ball!—and went to retrieve it. Chase continued to dribble and weave in and out of imaginary players and taking shots.

Meanwhile, a school janitor was sweeping around the bleachers, unnoticed to Chase. As if pretending to check its cleanliness, the man scanned the gym. Nor did Chase notice when his gaze lingered on the boy as he tried to dribble between his legs.

Chase was in the zone. He darted past one imaginary guard, then another, then took a Magic Johnson leap in the air before shooting, though the ball hit the rim and bounced off, rolling until it was stopped by the foot of the janitor. The man picked up the basketball and took a shot himself. It missed, and Chase jogged after the rebound.

"I was better when I was your age," he said as he walked onto the court. "Some things you just need to keep at. So what are you still doing here? We have to lock up."

Chase hugged the ball to his chest. "I don't know."

"Are you waiting for your parents?"

"No," Chase said. "I rode my bike."

"Well, maybe you ought to get home before your folks get worried about you." The man paused. "What's your name?"

"It's Chase."

"Chase? Never heard a name like that. Must be Japanese."

Chase laughed. It was more of a nervous laugh than anything.

"No. My name is just Chase, and I'm not Japanese."

"Ah, my mistake. Well, Chase, I'm Lee Earl, but you can just call me Lee if you want. I have to lock up these doors, Chase."

"Can I take a few more shots?" Chase asked. "We don't have a hoop at my house."

Lee Earl pursed his lips. "Maybe we should call your parents… let them know where you're at."

"No!" Chase took a step closer. "I mean…they know I'm here. I *have permission*." Chase didn't know where the lie came from, but it felt like it gave him a new hidden power.

"Well, you know they only let you play ball in here while there's still kids waiting for their folks. It seems everyone's gone, Chase." Lee Earl looked around the gym, Chase following his gaze, just then noticing it was only him and the janitor left inside. Chase didn't remember him from the previous year. Custodians didn't usually talk to the kids. He figured the man was new, but this was the first time he actually looked at him. The janitor had the same boiled ham color as his old uncle, the one Mom didn't like to have over anymore. "You don't want to get in trouble, do you?"

"Please," Chase said. "Just a few more shots."

Lee stared at him another moment before a grin spread across his face. "Well, okay. I won't tell if you won't tell."

Mimicking his smile, Chase thanked him. But suddenly, he didn't want to shoot baskets anymore. His attention had shifted away from the fantasy, broken by the negotiation, the reality of his mom waiting for him. He made one last feeble attempt at a free throw then tossed the basketball in the ball bin. He didn't look back as he made his way to the door but felt the janitor was still watching him as he left.

*****

Kate arrived home before her boys, as usual, and was heaping Todd's favorite jalapeno meatloaf into the baking tin when she heard the front door slam and the heavy footsteps of what must be Hunter on the stairs.

"Hunter, is Chase with you?" she called out. No reply. She checked the living room. Maybe she hadn't heard him make a stealth attempt at watching the afternoon *Chips* rerun. "Hunter, where's Chase?" she called with more intention this time.

"Don't know!" Hunter shouted from the landing. "He wouldn't listen to me!"

With an agitated sigh, Kate returned to the kitchen to finish getting the meatloaf ready for cooking later then began cutting the potatoes, telling herself Chase was old enough to walk home alone, and it would only embarrass him if he caught her driving around the neighborhood being overprotective. Besides, this was Sandy Beach, not Miami. Still, she breathed a sigh of relief when an hour later, she heard the door open and Chase's light footfalls. Like his brother, he paced straight up the stairs and didn't stop even when Kate called to him.

"There you are! I was just about to come looking for you! Chase? Chase!" she called, but he had already closed his door. How similar the boys were, but how different. When Hunter shut himself in his room, it was like a jail door clanging for some self-imposed sentence. But with Chase, it was like a rabbit fleeing to his burrow. Kate knocked on Chase's door and opened it when she got no answer. "Look, I know you heard me calling you when you came in," she chided her youngest son.

Chase had nothing to say for himself as he looked over a comic book while lying in his bed.

"Fine, Chase. Well, if you aren't going to talk to me, then you can just talk with your father when he gets home." Kate shut his door and headed back downstairs. *Would a daughter have acted the same?* she wondered. She felt a rush of shame when recalling the disappointment at learning Chase was a boy. Maybe she *was* being too soft with him, as Todd had accused her of several times.

Todd arrived home from work later that evening. He walked straight into the kitchen, chasing the aroma of his wife's cooking. He smiled in greeting, but the look on Kate's face couldn't go uncommented upon.

"Hey, baby," he greeted her. "What's up?"

"You might want to go talk to your son again about lingering around the school without permission."

Todd dropped his tool kit in its place by the back door. "That kid. We just spoke to him about that. Where is he?"

"In his room," Kate said. "Pouting. Over what? Who knows."

"It's not like he's off smoking pot or stealing baseball cards. I mean, he's at school, right?"

"I don't like that he disobeys me, Todd. He only does it because he knows you don't care."

"Can I be the bad guy *after* dinner, baby?"

Todd gave her a playful slap on the bottom, but Kate's stern look told him that there was a line. He knew he could stand at the line and crack jokes but not cross it. Todd made for the second floor.

"So, Chase. Anything you want to talk about?" Todd was secretly glad Chase had defied his mother. He needed a bit more backbone, in Todd's opinion.

"I dunno," his youngest replied, keeping his eyes focused on his game.

"Why did you stay after school? Didn't we just talk about this?"

"Uh-huh." Chase still didn't look at his father. The sound of Chase shooting down a squadron of invading aliens filled the room from the game he was playing.

"Want to put that joystick down for a moment? We also talked about no games until after homework's done."

"Bogus," Chase said. Todd had heard that word from Hunter and liked it even less from Chase.

"Okay, I'm taking your bike, which means you have to ride to school with Hunter, or I will drive you, and your mother will pick you up," Todd said, finally tasting a bit of his wife's frustration. If only the kid would rebel in a more aggressive way. Act out, not just passively resist.

"Great. Then Hunter is going to get mad too," Chase remarked. Todd suddenly felt a flush of anger and grabbed the joystick out of the boy's hand.

"Hunter is going to do what's he's told, or neither of you will have bikes or Atari games. Understood? In fact, I'm confiscating this now."

"Dad…"

The boy looked like he might cry. Todd told himself if he could control his tears, he'd give the console back. Chase seemed to comprehend this and held an expression of shocked hurt. Todd relented, putting the Atari console down again. Todd didn't want to deal with unplugging it anyway.

"Okay, well, you come down and get some dinner and then straight back up to your room."

Chase got up from his bed and began past his father.

"This is for a month, maybe two," Todd added before collecting Hunter for dinner with the family.

The next morning, Kate was signing Isabel Dominguez in for another visit. The young woman could hardly speak through her harsh cough. A nurse took Isabel to a room and informed her that the doctor would be there after his current patient. Kate caught him just as he was picking up the file outside of the door for his eight thirty appointment.

"Dr. Darling," Kate said. "Isabel Dominguez is back. She—"

"Oh!" George's tone heightened as he turned to her. "What room is she in?"

"Room D, Doctor."

"She's ill again?" George pondered out loud, and he carefully returned the file to its place. "Maybe I need to go check on her now."

"Maybe so, Doctor," Kate said flatly.

"Hello… Doctor," Isabel said between coughs.

"Morning," George uttered as he looked Isabel over with an intense stare.

"Are you all right, Dr. Darling? Doctor?"

George didn't respond immediately. He had been suddenly apprehended by a vision of his late wife. The baby. Isabel would have been around her age when they married. She had the same innocence that always drew him into a woman. But the baby…how old would it be? *Rotting flesh. A noose, the rest.* It had been another lifetime, what had happened. He concentrated and lifted his thoughts from the darkness and willed the vision to leave his mind.

"Sorry," he said. "Just a brief head rush. I should cut down on the coffee."

"I'm so sorry to bother, Doctor," Isabel said.

Dr. Darling softened as he felt his nervousness dissolve. He was glad she provoked such feelings. It had been so long since anybody had.

"You could never bother me. And my, that cough doesn't sound good. Did you fill the prescriptions I gave you?" he asked then placed his stethoscope to her chest.

"Yes, Doctor," Isabel said. "But I didn't have the money to refill them."

"Well, Isabel, this may be turning into something serious." George took a small step back to fully look her over.

"I don't know what to do," Isabel said, visibly suppressing a cough. "I haven't been able to work much this week…so my sister, Rosalina, has been doing most of the rooms alone."

"Rooms?" George asked. "What do you mean?"

Isabel took a moment to catch her breath after another series of coughs. "My eighteen-year-old sister and I live and work at the Sandy Beach Hotel."

"The Sandy Beach Hotel?" George mumbled. "Lots of history there. It was still pretty new when I opened my clinic. Not all that history's good," he remarked.

"Yes, I have heard this," Isabel said.

"I knew it reopened."

"Luckily, it did for me and my sister."

"Look, don't worry about any kind of payment today." George placed his hand on Isabel's shoulder. Even he wasn't sure if it was a professional or personal gesture. He'd let her take it as she liked. "I'll let Mrs. Lovell up front know and have her find you some free samples to take with you."

Isabel shook her head. "That's too generous, Doctor."

"Nonsense," George said. "Maybe we can find a way to get you and your sister out of that hotel too," he added.

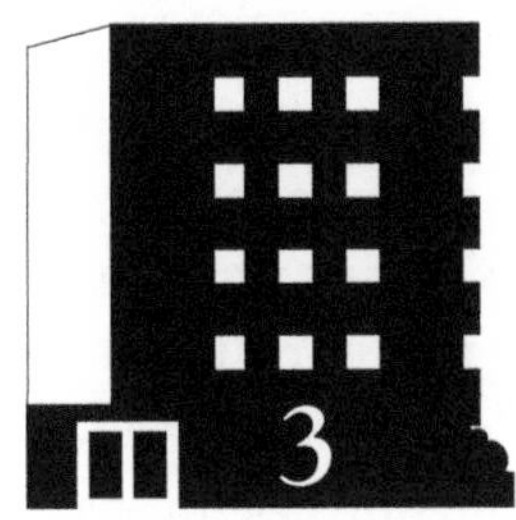

May 1983

Bobby and Jack sat quietly through the sentencing of the pair of eighteen-year-olds who had held up a local convenience store. The courtroom always reminded Bobby of church—greater forces at work, and you had best know your place. With Jack watching the proceedings like a matinee, Bobby offered to get them popcorn, but Jack didn't get the joke.

"Can you believe those guys only got two years apiece for that robbery and won't even serve that?" Jack said.

"Damn lawyers, but with no reliable witnesses other than who saw the pickup truck, it was probably the best outcome," Bobby said. He'd seen it before. Crime was getting worse, and sentences were getting lighter. *Don't get too invested*, he wanted to tell Jack. Like in Na Dang, it's all about choosing your battles. Life's nothing but a triage, deciding who and what's worth saving.

"But they had everything that got stolen from the store plus the truck."

"Jack, we did our job, and what happens after that happens. We don't have to like it."

Jack waved his hand, frustrated. "Do you believe that garbage?"

"They are young enough that hopefully, this teaches them a lesson. Nobody lost life or limb."

"I don't know," Jack said. "It just doesn't seem right, boss."

"It don't have to be right. It just has to be finished."

"Fair enough. We heading back to the station?" Jack asked, changing the subject.

"Yeah. Just need to make a stop first."

Thirty minutes later, they were at the Snappy Turtle. A few others playing hooky from work sat at the bar—a postman, some office types. Even the mayor was on his way out after tucking into a half dozen oysters with just as many tequila shots to wash them down. It was understood that such sightings were forgotten. The Snappy Turtle existed in an alternate universe in that way.

"You sure we should be here, boss?" Jack said.

Bobby took in half a beer with one sip.

"Just a little team building, Jack. We did a good job. Got the arrests and the conviction. We need time to exhale too."

"Understood," Jack said. To him, relaxing would mean getting back on the job, not nursing Bobby's mood.

"How are things with you and Nancy, for instance?"

Jack looked a bit surprised by the personal question. Then he remembered how deeply they got into each other's lives that first night.

"She's still on me about moving in and all that domestic bullshit…having kids, marriage," Jack said as he rubbed his temples.

"Story old as time," Bobby commented.

"You'd know," Jack ventured. The beer put Bobby in a good mood, and Jack looked relieved when he laughed.

"Do you love the girl, Jack?" Bobby asked, his expression suddenly serious.

Jack looked him in the eye. *Was he joking? Bobby Justice talking about love?*

"Yeah, fuck, I don't know. I do, I suppose, yes, hell."

Bobby let out a laugh. "Look, if my opinion matters at all, move in together first."

"Still a big step," Jack said, taking the first sip of the Coke he ordered.

"It is, but having an escape hatch takes the pressure off. If it doesn't work out, then at least you gave it a go."

"Yeah, that makes sense, I guess."

"If she's a good girl, son, it's worth a try," Bobby asserted.

"Thanks, Bobby," Jack said with appreciation. He contemplated the molasses-colored wood of the bar before hazarding his question. "What about you? You're living like some monk."

"Come on, Jack. I'm either at the station or in the field with you. Then I go home. It doesn't seem like there are enough hours in the day for the rest of it."

"It just seems to me that the rest of it follows you into the *rest of your day* anyway. Meaning, if you're happy at home, you bring that in. If you're, well, disconnected, you bring that in. Days are a whole. What's the word? Holistic."

"Don't go all hippie on me, Jack."

"Aw, the hippies weren't so bad in the end. I mean, peace, love, and everything."

"You weren't the one getting spat on, Jack."

Bobby ordered another beer despite Jack's disapproving look.

"So have you talked to the captain about the sergeant thing, Bobby?"

"No, *not* recently, but it's still in the works. We just have to wait till our numbers are back up and you're ready to take my spot."

"I'm ready."

"Yeah, I'm sure you think you are," Bobby said. "But like a pig roast, it takes time."

"Thanks for comparing me to a pig, Bobby."

"I mean it in a nice way."

"I'm sure you do," Jack said. "And for the rest of the day, I'm driving."

*****

Lee Earl Elwood didn't go to work the day after he'd met Chase on the basketball courts. That Sandy Beach middle school shared facilities with the high school felt like a bonus to him. Mostly, it was the high school kids who used the courts after school, but that one boy who like to shoot hoops and keep to himself.

All day, Elwood tried to tamp that old feeling down, taking the last of the Valium skimmed from his stash. But not seeing the boy was worse than seeing him. *That's just the way the imagination works*, he reasoned. Makes things bigger, more attractive than they really are. So he kept that in mind when he returned to work. Maybe talking to Chase again would remedy his fantasies.

Over the proceeding days, he sketched out Chase's schedule, noting his movements until he could predict the path he'd take through the school. Sometimes he'd plant himself on his route, cleaning a floor, refilling the soap in the bathroom. It wasn't long until he found the boy alone with few classmates to listen in.

"Oh, hey, big guy. I haven't seen you in a while. It's Chase, right?" Lee Earl asked, walking past the wing that housed the fourth graders.

"What's up, um, I forgot your name," Chase confessed, looking at Lee Earl as though trying to place him.

"And I thought we were best buds after that day in the gym. It's okay. My name is Lee Earl Elwood, but you can call me Lee if you like."

"Oh yeah. I've been grounded. That's how come I haven't been back."

"Oh no! What happened?" Lee Earl asked as he put his hands on his hips in mock surprise.

"I'm not supposed to stay after alone, and I did anyway."

"Well, maybe you can tell them you had to stay extra because you didn't understand some homework."

"I don't know, maybe," Chase said, throwing his hands up.

"I wouldn't tell, bud. I promise. Then you could shoot some hoops."

"Maybe once I'm not in trouble at home anymore."

"Smart boy. Hey, only one month left of school. You must be excited."

"I'm okay, I guess. I don't mind school."

"I don't hear that often from a kid your age. Anyway, look, school is almost over, so you better come before we lock up the gym for three months."

"Geez, you're right," Chase said then let out a worried sigh.

"So you better get in some hoops while you can."

"All right, I will soon."

The boy's face brightened, and Lee Earl felt the dark energy rise in him again.

"Well, okay, Chase. Have a good day, buddy."

Chase waved goodbye. "You too, Mr. Elwood."

On the same day, toward the end of class, Hunter Lovell was sitting in the back of ninth-grade algebra with a friend.

"Go ahead, man, talk to her. Stop being a pussy," Hunter's classmate, Toby, whispered. Hunter had been probing his friend about his opinion of the girl, as though talking about her gave him some claim on her.

"Screw you, dude. Time's not right," Hunter replied quietly.

"Almost summer, dude, and I'm not sharing my girlfriend. Private stock."

"Whatever, man, fine," Hunter grumbled defensively.

"Don't puss out. Make your move when the bell rings."

"Stop being a dick. I don't even know her name." Hunter thought that confession would let him off the hook. He began to blame her for the crap he was taking. *If she hadn't been there...*

"That's why it's called introducing yourself, pecker-head. Her name is Amber. You should listen to attendance more."

Hunter flipped his classmate the bird and directed his attention back to the front of the classroom. The girl sat twirling her hair in her finger, appearing to read over the notes in her Trapper Keeper, which she snapped closed when the class bell rang.

"All right, man, go get her," Toby said. "Now or never."

Hunter felt tense as he rose from his desk and walked toward the girl. He rehearsed an introduction, which he immediately forgot once he arrived at her desk. Hunter, not knowing what else to do, just stood looking down at her awkwardly. The girl finally noticed someone standing over her and seemed to think he was a student for the next class, waiting for the desk.

"I'm sorry," Amber said as she put her notebook in her backpack and stood up.

"Hi, how are you?" Hunter finally asked.

"Good. Excuse me, please," she said as she brushed past Hunter without even looking at him.

"Ha-ha, man! She didn't even care, dude," Hunter heard from the back of the classroom.

"Fuck you, dude!" Hunter yelled as he stormed into the hallway then kicked the metal door leading to the schoolyard hard enough that it didn't close properly after.

An hour later, Todd and Kate Lovell were at the school speaking with the principal.

"He's suspended for a week," Principal Jones said. "It could have been more if the custodian hadn't been able to fix the door he kicked."

"I swear I don't know what gets into you sometimes. What were you thinking, Hunter?" Kate asked as she put her head in her hands.

"I was just upset about something," Hunter responded.

"What, Hunter?" Todd asked. "Come on, son. You know we've got better things to do than come down here."

"So go do them! It's just a door," Hunter spat back. Kate began to silently cry.

The three were quiet on the way home, but once behind the closed front door, Todd let loose.

"I don't want to hear anything about you fucking up for the next week! You still better make sure your brother gets to and home every day from school. You ride him there then come straight back here. Then you go back to get him after. And when you start classes again, you do the same."

"Fine," Hunter said as he stomped up to his room.

Chase stepped into the house just when Hunter shut his bedroom door. He had heard about what happened that day at school and could hear his father's shouting from the sidewalk.

"Hey, Mom. Hey, Dad," he said cautiously.

Kate looked at her son. A dark thought passed through her mind: *You're my favorite*. It was followed by guilt. "Do you have any homework?" Kate asked.

"No, Mom."

"Good. Then you can get your little butt upstairs also," Todd told his younger son.

Chase walked up the stairs and into Hunter's room. "What did you do now, numb-nuts?" he asked.

"Whatever. They just like busting my balls," Hunter said.

Chase lingered at the door, hoping Hunter would invite him in. Normally, he'd just barge in, but lately, he sensed that wasn't okay anymore. Hunter was growing into something rougher and wilder than he was used to.

"Come on. Get in or get out," Hunter said.

Chase took a tentative step into his brother's room.

"Wanna play Centipede?" Chase ventured.

"That's a baby game. Check this out," Hunter said. He grabbed a video game cartridge and inserted it into the console.

"That's violent," Chase said of the game that consisted of wandering around a deserted building, shooting robots.

"Life's violent. Same difference," Hunter said, starting a game and handing Chase the joystick. Chase let his brother direct him in how to play, even though he already knew. He liked having Hunter guide him, mostly because he could see it made Hunter feel important. They used to play together all the time, but that was also changing. As Chase advanced through the game, he noticed Hunter begin to lose interest, so he deliberately got hit by a shot by a laser.

"Gimmie that," Hunter said, taking the joystick and beginning his turn. Chase noticed that Hunter used the joystick like a weapon, not holding it in has lap like Chase but thrusting it forward, slamming it on the floor when frustrated. It was more fun to watch than the game, which he wasn't very good at.

"Kill the robots, not the controller," Chase joked.

"Kiss my ass, half-inch," Hunter replied, tossing the joystick aside and picking up his butterfly knife. He began to clean his nails with the seriousness of a sculptor.

Chase laughed, picked up the joystick, and went back to the manageable violence of taking out robots on the screen.

*****

Roy Boutte was sitting on his porch, thinking about moving inside to get comfortable on the couch. Might thaw out a Salisbury steak, make some frozen biscuits as well. He sensed that wouldn't happen when he saw Lee Earl pull up in a new brown van. Lee stepped out of the vehicle, the door screeching when slammed shut. Lee Earl walked his way.

"Lee, where's your truck?" Roy asked.

"That truck is for a single man, not for one that wants to start a family soon," Lee Earl said.

"You're serious about that!" Roy called. "I thought you were joking!"

"Keep your goddamn voice down." Lee Earl took a step closer to him. "Don't broadcast it over the whole fucking neighborhood."

"Broadcast what? You're not *doing* anything."

"Yes, we are," Lee said in a low tone. "I have it worked out. I picked out the boy I want."

Roy began to shake his head. "I won't do this, Lee—"

Lee grabbed him by the shirt and lifted him from his chair. Roy knew he weighed a lot, but Lee had picked him up easy as a caddy with a golf bag.

"You listen to me, damn you!" Lee Earl said, anger contorting his face into something inhuman. "Who helped you when you were almost on the street? Huh?"

"You did, Lee!" Roy stammered.

"Whenever you need something, who gets it?" Lee reached into Roy's front pocket. For a moment, Roy thought he was going for his willy, but he pulled out his vial. "When you need a pill to get you to sleep, or to just stop from your mind running like a go-cart? Who!" Lee Earl shook Roy when he didn't answer quickly enough.

"You do! You do!"

"That's right. I fuckin' do!"

Lee Earl released Roy and straightened out his shirt. He held the vial up to Roy's face then gave it a shake. "You get these back once we have an understanding of what's about to happen." Roy nodded then followed Lee into his trailer. He wanted his pills back. The pills would make this situation okay.

Lee Earl kept a clean trailer. Roy respected that, wishing he had the same good habits. *Funny thing was,* Roy thought, *Lee actually would make a good father, if it was fathering he was interested in.*

"What you planning, Lee?" Roy asked.

"Shut up a minute! I'll tell you."

But they were interrupted by the sound of a car door slamming from outside. Lee parted his curtains slightly to look through the window and saw a familiar face. He turned to Roy.

"Don't say a goddamn thing about anything, you hear me?" Lee Earl pointed the finger at him.

"Yes! Yes!" Roy nodded vigorously before taking a seat.

Lee Earl opened the door before his old acquaintance could even knock.

"Well, look who it is, as I live and breathe!" Lee smiled widely. "Otis Redgrave, finally come for a visit!"

"Fuck you, Lee Earl," Otis said with a flat expression. "I don't like havin' to find out from other folks where yo ass been hiding. This a three-hour drive from Miami. If I didn't have more pressin' business, I would have done whupped ya ass before now."

"Hiding? You know where I was. Hell, you're the man that helped me get the job out here."

"Yo ass sure didn't bother to tell me where the fuck you was livin' though, did you? No call, no nothin'. And I'm glad you remember." Otis took a step closer to Lee Earl. "Who the fuck did what for you?"

All the while, Roy kept quiet and looked at the floor, as though that made him invisible.

"Of course, I remember, man. Calm down," Lee Earl said, taking a small step back. "Hell, come in. Roy!" Lee barked at his friend. "Stop sitting there like a damn fat tick on a dog and get the man a beer. Have a seat. Get comfy, Otis," he added while stepping out of the way to let the man inside. Otis sat in Roy's now vacant chair, the springs squealing under his heft.

"I want what you owe me for helping you out. You know damn well that shit wasn't free. I don't do free."

Roy extended a beer, holding it from the top. If he held it from the side, their fingers might touch, and Roy didn't want that.

Lee Earl lifted his hand to his forehead. "Oh, where are my cock-sucking manners. Otis, meet Roy Boutte. My neighbor and a royal pain in my ass." Lee Earl patted Roy's back hard then chuckled. "I'm just fucking with you, buddy. Roy, meet Otis Redgrave, a dear old friend." Lee Earl gestured to Otis, but Otis only continued to stare at him as he cracked open the Olympia.

"I want my shit, Lee."

"I'm going, brother. Goddamn, give me one minute. Making my damn nerves bad. Roy, sit with the man and keep him company, and I'll be right back." Lee pointed to the couch as he began toward his bedroom.

Lee Earl rummaged through the closet in his room. After a moment, he pulled out three paper bags then headed back into the living room and handed Otis two of the bags. Otis peered into each before glaring back at Lee Earl.

"My nigga. Next time, don't make me come looking for yo ugly ass. You got me?"

"Got you, brother," Lee said. "Say, stay for a bit. Let's play some cards and have a few beers. I'd like to talk to you about something."

Otis appeared to think on it for a moment then offered a curt nod. "I can do that."

"Damn right," Lee Earl said, allowing a grin. "Roy, go get some cards."

"The ones from my trailer, Lee?"

Lee turned to him. "No, the ones from up your goddamn ass. Yes, your trailer!" Roy guessed Lee was being so short with him because Otis was there. Otis was somebody Lee Earl wanted to impress. Roy hustled out the door. Now he wanted to impress him too.

The three sat around Lee Earl's table, drinking, smoking, and playing Texas hold 'em. When Roy got up to use the bathroom, Lee took the opportunity to speak to Otis.

"So, Otis, you still got your grandmother's old house?"

"Got some dogs in there now I'm sellin'. Stoppin' by there on the way back."

Lee Earl put the other bag on the table. "How about letting me use the old house for a day or two? Hell, I even got extra for a dog in there."

Otis looked into the bag. It was fat, like the others. "When?"

"Not sure yet, but soon. I'll give you a heads-up," Lee Earl said.

Otis watched him as he contemplated. He decided Lee was to be trusted with simple transactions. Not that he would hire him as a babysitter anytime soon.

"Yeah, fuck it," he said. "A day now. Two at the most. After that, you better have another one of these lil stank-ass bags."

Roy returned from the bathroom and settled down in his chair. "Whose turn is it?" he asked.

Lee Earl smiled and patted Roy on the shoulder. "Yours, bud. Yours."

*****

Isabel fluffed a pillow, reflecting on her situation. It had taken several visits to Dr. Darling and a change of medication, but she was finally back on her feet. The doctor never charged her for visits. George had asked her to return for another checkup in a week. Isabel, although grateful, let the doctor know she didn't feel it necessary, and she needed to work hard to make up for her time off.

Isabel was glad to have the job and was taking extra care with her work. It was low season, and only half the rooms were ready for use anyway. That meant she could take her time turning the rooms, making sure the sheets fit tightly over the mattress, that the bathrooms smelled fresh but not like cleaning products. Plus, she liked the time alone in the rooms. Much better than waitressing, when everybody wanted a piece of you, and you came home every night smelling like cooking oil and oysters. True, there was a spookiness to the hotel. Ms. Kerrigan was distant and strange with her, but Isabel also found that a bonus. She didn't want to be friends with her boss, and the creepy place gave her stories to write about to her mother in Cuba.

She put a mint on the pillow and stood straight to appreciate her work. She was taken by surprise when she turned to find Selma, the day receptionist, in the doorway, watching her. Isabel gave a jump like a cat that stepped on a tack.

"Sorry, dear. You have a visitor."

"A visitor?"

"A man, here to see you."

"Who? I am so sorry, missus."

"Don't be sorry. We like it when people come to our hotel."

Isabel apologized again and looked at the floor when she passed Selma on the way down the hallway. There in the lobby, under the netting that decorated the wall, was her doctor.

"I'm sorry to disturb you."

"Oh, it's you. What can I help you with, Doctor?"

"It's only that I found these at the office." He dropped a handful of blister pack samples on the desk. "Just in case the symptoms return."

"I thank you, but I have to get back to work."

Dr. Darling appeared not to hear her and kept talking nervously. "This is an old building, you know. Some say it's haunted, but I don't think so."

"Why not, Doctor?" she said, taking a moment to indulge him.

"Buildings don't get haunted. It's people who get haunted. That's the misconception. Why some people see ghosts, others don't. The building's just a vessel. But they've done a bang-up job with the place."

"You have been here before?"

"Oh, yes. I lived here for a spell. But that was a long time ago."

"Was it?" she said.

"Lifetimes ago," George said before bowing and taking his leave.

The next day, George showed up at the hotel with flowers.

June 1983

Over the proceeding weeks, the flowers were accompanied by Godiva chocolates, then gold bracelets that were a prelude to a stunning diamond necklace. It became so much that Isabel began passing gifts on to her little sister.

One day, they were cleaning a room on the third floor when Rosalina happened to glance out the window and see George Darling park his car in a secluded area of the lot. Through the car window, she could see him take a sandwich from a bag and begin to eat lunch, something that seemed to have a become a ritual for him.

"He's here again," Rosalina said as her sister collected the pillowcases.

"Hasn't missed a day yet," Isabel said.

"I wonder if he still shows up on your day off?"

"I think he should take a day off himself," Isabel joked.

"He seems so sweet," Rosalina said with a slight smile.

"He's older than father would have been."

"Be nice. I can barely remember our father's face. It might have been similar to the doctor's by now," Rosalina mused.

"You do not think it strange how he comes over so much?" Isabel asked as she smoothed a new sheet on the bed.

"He's just a lonely old man. Let him buy you things. I would."

"They expect something for their money."

"He's probably too old to get it up, Isabel," Rosalina said, winking at her big sister.

Isabel crossed her arms. "And if he isn't?" she asked.

Rosalina started stroking the top of a broom. "Get creative."

Isabel laughed. "You are *so bad.* Maybe. I don't know yet."

Before Isabel had time to stop her, Rosalina opened the window and waved.

"Probably has bad vision and thinks I am you."

George noticed then smiled and waved back. Rosalina blew him a kiss.

"Rosalina! Stop that," Isabel said, swatting her sister with a towel. "It's a little creepy."

"Relax. Now go see what he brought us today!"

*****

As Hunter unlocked his bike from the rack, he scanned the schoolyard for his brother, who was nowhere in sight. He cursed under his breath, shook his head, and headed home, knowing he'd get the blame but not really caring.

With a week a school of left, Chase had other ideas that afternoon. He had been ungrounded by his mom at breakfast, so remembering what the janitor—what was his name again?—had said about summer coming up, he slipped into the gym and got a ball from the bin. All alone, he was posting up and shooting one over Johnson. No, he *was* Johnson.

"Whoop!" he shouted to the empty bleachers when the ball swished through the net.

After he tired himself out, Chase returned the ball and ran out of the gym to his bike. He bent down to undo the lock and groaned when he noticed his tire was flat. He wondered if Hunter did it to get some kind of revenge. *But revenge for what? Just for being Chase?* He put his lock around the handlebars and began to walk the bike home. He was only a few blocks from his street when a brown van slowed down beside him. When Chase looked over at the vehicle, he recognized the janitor in the passenger seat.

"Hey there, Chase!" Lee Earl greeted him from the open window.

"Hi, mister…"

"Why are you walking?" Lee Earl asked. "What's wrong with your bike?"

"It's got a flat tire," Chase said.

"Well, shoot. Don't you have a brother?" Lee Earl asked. "Where is he?"

"I didn't see him before he went home."

"Well, hop in. We'll give you a ride. Won't we, Roy? Don't mind Roy. He's just driving," Lee Earl said with a smile. Chase nervously looked at Lee, and he shook his head. There was something *too nice* about him.

"It's okay. I can walk."

"Oh, c'mon," Lee said. "I can give you a ride, and maybe when we get there, I can tell your parents I'll watch you after school. Then they won't be so worried."

Chase mulled that over and thought it could be cool. He liked the idea of having an audience to see his improved free throw. They'd for sure let him stay if Lee was there, and then he could just ride home. He looked at Lee.

"I guess so."

"Good boy! Roy, slow down. You heard the kid!" Lee Earl said as Roy slowed the van to a stop. Lee Earl got out and ran over to him awful quick, it seemed to Chase. He lifted up the bike and carried it with one arm to the back of the van. Chase stood motionless as he opened the door and placed the bike gently in the hold, all the while smiling over at him. Lee Earl then gave a bow and gestured for Chase to follow, like a doorman. The whole thing made Chase think of a clown in a circus act.

"Come on now, son. We've a bike to get home."

Lee had him sit on a spare tire in the hump seat, as he called it. Looking out of the window, Chase saw his house come up then go by.

"Hey, that was it," he said.

"It's such a nice day though." Lee Earl glanced at Chase through the rearview mirror. "Let's just take a ride."

"But I'm going to get in trouble."

"You don't have to worry about that anymore, Chase," Lee Earl said, smiling. "That kind of trouble is behind you now."

Lee Earl had Roy drive straight to Roy's mother's house, an hour away in Bronson. Suffering from dementia, she was now in a nursing home, and the old decrepit house was vacant. Lee Earl could hide Chase and continue to make further preparations.

"Fuck me!" Lee Earl exclaimed as he entered. "This house smells like if your nose got pinned between someone's shitty ass cheeks all day. Son of a bitch!" He waved his hand in front of his face.

"My mom and those damn cats," Roy said sheepishly.

"She musta had a ton of those little bastards. You'd think with plastic covering the furniture, the smell would not have sunk in so much," Lee Earl grumbled as he toured the house.

"There was seven, and it wasn't easy to get rid of those mean little rascals," Roy said, following along behind him. "That's why I can't sell this dern place."

"That, and it looks worse than it smells," Lee Earl said, continuing with his inspection. Yard sale paintings of sunsets and a black velvet Jesus were still on the wall. There were dollar store rugs.

Lee felt a stab of affection for Chase, who cautiously looked around the living room for a cat.

"Are there any left?" Chase asked.

"No," Roy said, stepping into the living room too. "They weren't the pet'n type anyway."

"Listen, you two," Lee announced. "I have to go back to town and grab something. You all don't go outside for no reason, understood?"

Roy and Chase both nodded at Lee Earl as he walked out the door.

Chase kept thinking to himself it was only a matter of time before they took him home.

"Mr. Roy, is this where you live?" Chase asked.

"Heck no, I live in Sandy Beach like you."

"Then when are we going back home?"

"I guess whenever Lee decides," Roy mumbled.

"Can't you decide?"

"It's best we just don't upset Lee Earl and play along. Then it will be okay," Roy said, suddenly filled with guilt.

*****

Sandy Beach, Florida

The sun had begun to set by the time Todd arrived home. He fretted when he saw Kate's face and could have guessed what she was going to say.

"Big surprise. Your son isn't home yet."

"Lord have mercy, that boy!" Todd growled as he tossed his arms up. "What do you want me to do? It's late already. Has anyone gone to look for him?"

"No," Kate said. "I was waiting for you to get home, and I thought he would have shown up by now."

"Well, I'll drive to the school to see if he's there. Where's Hunter?"

"His room," she said, rolling her eyes.

"You get on his ass too," Todd said, pointing at her. "I'll be back."

When Todd returned, he found Kate sitting with Hunter at the table, the boy pushing a glob of peas and mashed potatoes around his plate with a fork. Kate looked at her husband, each searching the other's face for a sign that indicated Chase was all right.

"Is he in his room?" Todd finally asked.

"What?" Kate said, her eyes widening.

"He's back, right?"

"You didn't find him?" Kate asked, letting her fork fall.

"You mean he hasn't come home yet? I thought for sure when I didn't see him that I had to have just missed him on his way here."

Kate stood from the table. "Well, where did you look?"

"I checked the school. I went around the block a couple of times, looking for his bike. Even the park."

Both Kate and Todd looked over at Hunter, who shrugged under the weight of their glares.

"I haven't seen him since this morning," he said.

Kate shook her head as she rose from the table. "I'm calling the police."

*****

Officer Jane Pac was sitting at her desk, staring at the sand dollar her daughter gave her.

"When you break it, Mommy, there's something inside," she'd said. "A secret."

Jenny was at her father's now, and Jane, for some reason, couldn't stop thinking about what the insides of the sand dollar held. That was when the call came in. *Missing kid.* Happened a lot, but always demanded attention. Captain Curry liked Jane for these calls. She was a calming presence. Before heading to her patrol car, she checked the availability of Officer Jonsey for backup.

"Alan, there is a nine-year-old boy gone missing in North Sandy," Officer Pac stated. "Can you take a ride?"

"Damn it. I was just heading to a domestic situation with Tick," Officer Jonsey replied.

Overhearing, Bobby Justice looked up from his paperwork. "I'll go."

"You sure, Detective? I mean, Sergeant," Officer Pac asked.

"It's still detective for now, Jane. And yes, hopefully, it's nothing. Jack's off today, so let's handle this one together. We'll take my car."

Detective Justice and Officer Pac headed to Bobby's car. "What's the location?" Bobby asked. Officer Pac rattled off the address. She liked riding with Justice. There had been some flirtation between them, but they had both individually settled on it going no further. At twenty-eight, Jane knew she looked good. She had natural olive skin, no hair dye, and used only a bit of lemon juice to keep it streaked with blond. Somebody once described her as Aphrodite's hard-ass sister. She got a kick out of that.

"All right, let's get going," Bobby said. "I'll radio some patrol units to start checking around the area."

"Thank you, Detective. I appreciate this."

"Anything but filling out forms."

Bobby and Jane Pac headed toward the Lovell address, Bobby's speed betraying no panic or urgency. "Ninety-nine percent of the time, we find these kids at the mall, head buried in some video game."

"It's the one percent that keep me awake at night," Jane said, thinking of Jenny. Justice gave her a smile out of the side of his face and sped up a bit.

*****

Bronson, Florida

Lee Earl returned after an hour of shopping to find Roy and Chase in front of the TV, laughing. He placed the bags on the table, tamping down a wave of jealousy. *Roy's just a big child himself,* he rationalized.

"Well, it seems like I'm missing a good time here," Lee said.

"Where have you been?" Roy asked.

"Errands," Lee Earl said, tucking his keys into his pocket.

Chase's body tensed. "Are you taking me back home, Mr. Elwood?" he asked.

"No, I can't take you home today, son. And call me Lee, okay?"

Lee Earl didn't like the doe-eyed way Roy looked at the kid. The man was too soft.

"Why not?" Chase asked.

"We're gonna talk about that later." Lee Earl looked at him, giving him his best smile.

"But I wanna go home," Chase said.

"Don't be scared," Lee Earl said, going to sit on the carpet next to Chase. "Look, tomorrow we're going to go to this house, and it has a whole lot of puppies. Don't you like puppies?" Lee asked as he ruffled the boy's hair.

"I guess," Chase mumbled.

Lee Earl let his hand rest on the boy's head. Roy suddenly rose and looked at his wrist as though wearing a watch.

"I think I'll take in some air. Yeah, that's what I'll do," Roy said.

"Now don't run off so fast." Lee Earl looked at him while handing over a bag. "I've got a project for you. You're staying here tonight. Take my friend here to the bathroom and put this crap in his hair and leave it in till it's yellow."

Roy stared down at the objects Lee Earl was handing him—a box of powder and a bottle.

"What is it?" Roy asked. "Hair dye? I don't know nothing about—"

"Look," Lee Earl said, losing patience. "The chick at the store said to mix that into that, put it in his hair, and wait and rinse it out. Any retard can do it, including you. I'll be back. I have to make another run."

"Chase, I got something fun for you and Mr. Roy to do."

"What?" Chase asked nervously.

"You'll see. It's gonna be neat!"

*****

Sandy Beach, Florida

"Hello, Mrs. and Mr. Lovell?" Officer Pac asked, with Bobby standing at her rear. Bobby was pleased she was following protocol—confirming their identity before proceeding.

"Yes," Kate told the officers.

"Thank you, ma'am. We are from the Sandy Beach Police Department. I'm Officer Jane Pac, and this is Detective Robert Justice." Bobby noticed the woman was breathing easier already. Jane had that effect. People just wanted to agree with Officer Pac.

"Please, come in. Have a seat," Kate said as she escorted the officers to the living room, where Todd was waiting, brooding on the couch.

"Thank you. When was the last time you saw your son?" Bobby asked.

"Chase. This morning," Kate answered, sitting to take Todd's hand. "Before he left for school."

"What was he wearing?" Officer Pac asked. She had her pen and notebook out. Bobby knew her notes would be thorough and, importantly, legible, unlike Cutler's chicken scratch.

"Jeans and a yellow T-shirt," Kate recalled.

"Decal or anything?"

"A...what do you call it?" She turned to her husband.

"A Space Invader," Todd said. "The kid loves video games."

Bobby nodded.

"Do you have a recent picture of him?" Officer Pac continued.

"Yes," Kate said, standing from the couch. She picked up a picture of her son from a shelf and removed it from the frame. "Right here. His hair's probably a bit messier. Takes ten minutes to get a comb through it." She handed it to Officer Pac and sat down again. Jane looked at the picture for a moment before she gave it to Bobby.

Jane smiled. "Can we borrow this?"

"Of course," Kate said.

"So does he have a habit of doing this?" Detective Justice asked. "Taking off for a bit?"

"He does have a habit of staying after school to play," Todd said. "But it's never been this late." His wife squeezed on his hand.

Bobby nodded again. "We are going to need any relatives' or friends' addresses and phone numbers that he might be with."

"There isn't any to give. My mother is an hour away," Kate said. "He'd never go that far. His brother, maybe. But Chase is a good"—she stopped herself—"a shyer kid."

"Mrs. Lovell, we need to cover all bases."

"What about his little friend that slept over for his birthday last year?" Todd asked.

"They moved, dear," Kate informed her husband.

"Even if it's a remote chance, give me the information," Bobby instructed.

"Of course, Detective," Todd said. "I'll get that for you."

"Tomorrow morning, if he still hasn't been located, I will start questioning teachers and faculty at his school," Bobby continued.

Kate shook her head. "I can't believe this is happening."

"Listen," Bobby said, leaning forward. "Once I get his description out there, all our available men will be eyes on the ground. We'll find your boy."

Kate gave a smile, but Bobby could see the fear in her eyes.

Todd returned from the kitchen, and he handed Bobby a slip of paper. "Here is everyone that we know."

"Have you called any of these people yet?" Bobby asked.

"You have been our only call," Kate explained. "As I said, I just don't think he's with someone we know. Todd has searched everywhere he'd go."

"I understand." Bobby stood up. "May I go upstairs and have a look around his room, please? Anything could be of help at this point. Officer Pac will have a few more questions."

"Yes, sir," Todd said. "His room is upstairs and down the hall, second door on the right."

Bobby made his way upstairs. As he walked down the hall, he came upon Hunter, who was standing in his open doorway.

"And you are?" Bobby asked.

"Hunter," the boy answered. "I'm Chase's older brother."

"Nice to meet you. Hunter, can you think of any place Chase might have gone he might not have wanted y'all's parents to know about? The video arcade maybe?"

"No. We've each got Ataris. He liked playing alone."

"Kind of a loner, huh?"

"Kinda. But not 'cause he was weird or anything. Just quiet, I guess."

Bobby lingered. For some reason, he felt it important to get more out of him. "When did you last see him, Hunter?"

"Uh, on our way to school this morning."

"Did you notice anyone different at school he may have been talking to?"

"No, not really. Like I said, Chase doesn't have that many friends."

"Were you his friend, Hunter?"

The boy looked intently at him. "What do you mean?"

"Do you two get along?"

"I didn't have anything to do with this. Dude."

"Okay, Hunter. Just trying to get a clear picture," Bobby said, giving Hunter one last look before he proceeded down the hall. Something about the boy unsettled him, though he couldn't say what.

He opened the door to Chase's room and spent a few minutes rummaging through the items on his desk, poking through the dressers and closet. Typical kid's room, no indication of a secret life or interests outside what his parents already told him. On his way back downstairs, he was stopped by Hunter.

"You're going to find him, right?"

"Yeah, Hunter, I believe we will," Justice said. Maybe he was wrong about the kid.

Hunter nodded in approval before closing his door.

"Well, we have what we need here," he told Kate and Todd once downstairs. "If he turns up, please call us. We'll continue looking for him tonight, and I will be at his school early if I don't hear from you before then."

"Thank you, officers," Kate said sniffling, escorting them to the door.

*****

Bronson, Florida

Roy's eyes were stinging as he ran his hands through the kid's now blond hair.

"Dammit!" Roy said. "My hands are on fire!"

Bored, Chase was reading the box. "The instructions on the package say you need gloves."

Roy grabbed the package from the boy, mumbling as he read. "Son of a bitch!"

"Are you okay, Mr. Roy?"

Roy felt somehow foolish, like he was the one with strange tastes here in the bathroom, performing hairdressing services for a boy. And not very well at that. Not that Lee Earl would notice.

The door slammed with Lee Earl's return. He appeared at the bathroom, beaming.

"Well, look at you. Like a brand spankin' new kid!" Lee Earl declared.

"Why are we doing this, Mr. Lee?" Chase asked.

"'Cause, just look at how much cooler you are now!"

"I need something for my hands," Roy said. "I didn't wear gloves."

"Just fuckin' wash them, Roy. Look, I'm going to make us some burgers. How does that sound, big guy!" Lee looked at Chase, as though this should thrill him, like he never got burgers at home.

"Sounds good," Roy said with a smile. "I'm hungry."

"I was talking to the boy, dumbass."

"Fine, I guess," Chase muttered.

"All right then!" Lee Earl said then addressed his accomplice. "Roy, come here."

"Now?" Roy asked.

"No, next fucking week. Yes, now."

Roy followed Lee out of the bathroom.

"Look," Lee Earl said quietly. "I need you to call in sick tomorrow."

"I can't! I need all hours I can get," Roy said.

"Roy, don't piss me off. Look, I need your help for just another day or possibly two. I have to do something tomorrow."

"Damn it, Lee!" Roy's eyes widened. Roy knew Lee to become vague when it was something seriously bad or dangerous. Or perverted. Lee Earl was always bad to the bone, but Roy saw something new in him since he, well, since he started working at that creepy hotel. He just seemed less grounded now.

Lee Earl stepped forward and patted Roy's cheeks roughly, as though flattening a burger patty. "It's gonna be okay, bud. Just keep doing what the fuck I tell ya too." He winked. "I'm going to start dinner. Keep the boy happy, and I'll leave a gift under your pillow." Lee shook a vial of pills in his pocket. Roy glanced down and swallowed. Then he went to wash his hands.

*****

Sandy Beach, Florida

Bobby and Jack arrived at Sandy Public School before the first bell on that Friday morning. No officer from the night shift had come across the boy, and his parents had already called twice. Bobby had nothing to give them aside from hollow assurances they were working on it.

"Man, I loved this place," Jack said. "Still smells like peppermints and tater tots, right?"

"That wasn't my experience," Bobby said.

"Yeah, you probably kept whisky in your lunchbox instead of milk," Jack joked.

Bobby had a comeback, but it wasn't appropriate for the secretary, whom they were now standing in front of.

"Good morning. I'm Detective Robert Justice, and this is my partner, Detective Jack Cutler. We need to speak with Mrs. Loretta Jones," Bobby said as he and Jack showed their badges.

"Oh, yes, sir. I take it this is urgent?" the secretary asked.

"I am afraid so," Bobby responded.

"Yes, sir. I'll let her know. She is with someone."

The secretary got up from her desk to alert the principal. Bobby took the opportunity to talk with Jack.

"Jack, let me question Mrs. Jones. This isn't an interrogation. But remember, nothing you see or hear will be unimportant, so keep detailed notes."

Jack held up his pen and notepad. "Just like school. Ready to learn."

"Good. Then afterward, we will both question some of the faculty."

"You got it, boss," Jack responded with a wink while pointing a finger-gun at Bobby.

Bobby's face grew stern. "Jack, keep in mind the impact this may have on the entire school," he said.

"So you want me to quit kidding around?"

"Is that what you were doing?" Bobby said with a smirk.

On the other side of the office door, Principal Jones was speaking with a Sandy Public School employee.

"Sorry for such short notice," the man said. "But my mother is very sick, and I need to get there soon. I'm all she has." Lee knew Loretta Jones had a reputation for toughness. Had to be, he assumed, as a Black principal in a mostly White school. He respected that, even as he lied to her.

"Well, Mr. Elwood," Mrs. Jones sighed. "This is short notice, but I understand that it's your mother. So I'll just wave the two-week notice for you. And if you need a recommendation for another job, I'll be happy to help with you that. You've been very attentive."

Just before Lee Earl could respond, there was a polite knock, and the secretary poked her head inside.

"Yes?" Loretta asked.

"Sorry to interrupt, Mrs. Jones, but Sandy police detectives Bobby Justice and Jack Cutler are here to see you," the secretary said.

"Detectives?" Loretta replied, caught off guard. "Give me one minute, please."

"Yes, ma'am."

Mrs. Jones came from around her desk. "Well, Mr. Elwood, thank you for your service. And best wishes for a speedy recovery to your mother."

Lee Earl stood from the chair, noticing the cross that hung on the wall behind Loretta's desk. He forced a grin despite his racing heart. "Thank you. God bless and go Sharks."

Loretta gave Lee Earl a rare smile then opened her door to let Lee out and greet the officers. "Come in, detectives," she said.

Lee Earl exited the office, giving the detectives a quick glance as he passed them. He put his head down and continued down the hall.

"How are you this morning?" Bobby greeted Loretta as he shook her hand. "I'm Detective Robert Justice, and this is Detective Cutler."

"Busy as usual," Loretta said while retaking her seat. "And to what do I owe the pleasure?"

"It's not pleasant, I'm afraid." Bobby and Jack sat down. "This visit is in regard to Chase Lovell."

"Chase Lovell… Chase Lovell…" Loretta looked toward the ceiling as she tried to place the name. "Yes," she said. "He has a brother, Hunter Lovell, correct?"

"Yes," Bobby said. "He usually rides his bike to and from the school. He didn't make it home yesterday."

"Oh my goodness," Loretta said and lifted her hand to her mouth.

"We have his brother, Hunter, confirming he was here before the start of classes yesterday morning. They arrived together. We aren't sure of his whereabouts after that. So I'm going to need to talk to some of his teachers and classmates to confirm that he was in classes all day and maybe get some insight into his behavior."

"Those poor parents. Absolutely, Detective, whatever you need."

"For starters, we need his homeroom teacher's name and classroom. Then we will go from there. May we use your office for questioning?"

"I have an empty classroom that would be much better. Let me take you there," Loretta said.

"Thank you, Mrs. Jones."

They all stood and followed the principal to a room across the hall. Chairs up on the desks and swept clean, with a large wooden teacher's desk, it would be ideal.

"I can't help but think the department must feel this is dire if they already have detectives conducting interviews," Loretta said.

"Well, it's routine, Mrs. Jones. Don't be too alarmed just yet. A missing person's complaint is a case-by-case basis. Nobody's panicking as of now."

Loretta took a few chairs from atop the desks, righting them for interviewees.

"And just how do we know when it's time to panic, Detective?"

"We're ahead of this one. Considering Chase's age, we took quicker action than, say, with a man with a habit of frequenting casinos whose wife had reported him missing. Or a teen who has a history of running away."

"I see," Loretta said. "I just hope this is a false alarm."

Bobby nodded his agreement. He just then realized how good he was at reassuring others when he himself felt uncertain.

"Well, this should be satisfactory," Loretta said. "Let me notify his teachers. I'll send them in."

"Thank you again."

*****

Lee Earl drove the van back to his camper at Coral Run Trailer Park. He whistled along the way. It was a relief, having given into that feeling. Never should have fought it. The feeling always won. And it never caused him any *real trouble*. After hitching his trailer to the van, he drove to a nearby phone booth and made a call.

"Hey," Lee spoke into the receiver. "Can I come? Because I need to discuss something with the big man. I'll be there in fifteen minutes."

Lee Earl arrived at CG Auto Repair shop several minutes later. The sight of the detectives had made him nervous. He resented that. But his reward was waiting back in Bronson. He just needed patience. Lee nodded at one of the mechanics as he passed then knocked on the office door.

"Come in," a deep voice called from within.

Lee Earl stepped inside and waited while the man sitting at the desk continued with his paperwork, not looking up.

"Close the door behind you," he eventually ordered.

"You got it, boss," Lee Earl said, shutting the door with his shoulder and eyeing the nameplate on the desk. *Cordale Goodman.*

"Have a seat, Elwood," Cordale said, having yet to look up from the papers. "Tell me what's so important you felt the need to visit me here?"

"I'm leaving town," Lee Earl said as he sat. "As in, the *not coming back* type of leaving."

Cordale finally looked up, staring through him with a hardened glare. "Anything that involves me?"

"No, of course not," Lee Earl said. "Nothing like that at all, boss. Just time to move on."

"So you just came to say bye?" Cordale asked as he continued to stare at Lee Earl with cold, dispassionate eyes. *The man must have been a shark in a past life*, Lee Earl mused.

"I just really appreciate you, Mr. Goodman," Lee Earl uttered, fidgeting. He just wanted to leave the trailer park, the detectives, and especially that hotel behind. But ole Cordale Goodman, this was the type of bridge that was best not burned.

Cordale sat back in his chair and lit up a cigarette. Menthols, Lee Earl could tell from the smell.

"With that fuckin' knucklehead Goo getting arrested a couple of months ago and now…whatever issues you have. I'm not in the mood for those goddamn pigs again," he said, taking a long drag. Then he pointed at Lee Earl with his cigarette accusingly.

"I couldn't agree more, boss. I'm just here to see how far your contacts reach. I'd still like to do business for you."

Cordale slowly nodded while blowing smoke toward Lee Earl. "You call when you get where you are going, Elwood. Then we'll see."

"Thank you, boss," Lee Earl said, watching Cordale get back to his paperwork. Lee stood from his chair. "I'll just close the door behind me." He waited a moment, but Cordale offered no response.

*****

Bobby Justice questioned Chase's homeroom teacher, who said he was in first period for attendance, and his other teachers confirmed he was there until the final bell. None had anything particularly relevant to say of Chase, other than that he was a good kid, if somewhat quiet. As the last teacher left the conference room, Bobby handed Jack a folder full of documents on all the school staff the principal had gathered for him.

"Start going through these names. I'm going to have a word with Mrs. Jones," he told Jack.

"Roger that. I'm going to go through my notes also," Jack said.

Bobby stepped into the principal's office to let her know they were finished and would be in touch.

"I appreciate the cooperation today, Mrs. Jones."

"We all want the same thing, Detective Justice. I'm sorry no one could be more helpful," she said.

"Learning that he was still here for his final class was helpful. It may seem like a small detail, but it helps with establishing a timeline."

"Oh, I almost forgot to give this to you. These are the rest of the employees at the school, nonteachers," Principal Jones explained, handing Justice a manila folder.

"Has there been anyone you have seen around here lately that may have looked out of place or suspicious to you?"

"No, sir," Loretta said. "Nothing comes to mind. But I'll give it some thought."

"Thank you."

"And tell the Lovells I'll be praying for them."

Bobby stood silent for a moment. "I'm not sure they're the ones that need prayers right now, Mrs. Jones," he said dully.

Jack and Bobby drove back to the station in silence, both lost in thought. Bobby had hoped the school would yield something. A kid's world was pretty small and usually consisted of home and school. He didn't want to entertain yet that he might have met with a drifter. After making a few calls and stopping by the local news station, Bobby headed to Lovells', leaving the school files for Jack to go through.

Bobby lifted his instant Sanka and took a sip of the bitter liquid. Understandable that their minds were on other things than the perfect cup of joe. He continued with his update.

"We know Chase was at school till three thirty p.m., and we know you made the 911 call around five thirty p.m., so it's between those times he had to have gone missing," Bobby clarified.

"Are those details what matter now, Detective?" Todd asked.

"Mr. Lovell, we are collecting all the information we can. Just because something might not seem helpful now doesn't mean it won't be the key piece we need later. That's why if you can think of anything, even if you think it seems like nothing, tell us."

Todd and Kate sat in silence.

"As far as what the timeline tells me as of now," Bobby continued, "if we are discussing an abduction, I think it had to be someone who knew what street he would be on and at what time. Maybe someone he met before."

Kate and Todd looked at each other. Now that the word *abduction* was out in the open, they looked deflated. Bobby was sorry to have had to lessen their hope of an easy resolution.

"So what do we do now?" Kate asked.

"We continue looking. I'm going to have the local news stations run his picture tonight," Bobby said.

"Shouldn't we have done that hours ago?" Todd's words came out in a panic.

"Stay calm, Mr. Lovell. There are procedures. He wasn't technically missing until thirty minutes ago. Anything before that wouldn't have been considered worthy of news airtime."

"So we had to sit back and give"—Todd shook his head—"some *sicko creep* a day's head start?"

"Mr. Lovell, I'm on your side here. It's just that evidence-wise, we still don't have anything concrete yet that points toward a kidnapping. That being said, that's how I'm proceeding."

"I hate sitting around and waiting. Not knowing where my baby is. It's killing me," Kate said, tears forming.

"I can only imagine, Mrs. Lovell. I promise this is our top priority. My partner is at the station now doing background checks on school employees, and we will also check known offenders in the area."

Just then, Hunter pushed open the front door and closed it loudly.

"Hey, any word on Chase?" he asked.

"No!" Todd said. "And where have you been? You know you're not to be leaving the house."

"How many times did I tell you to wait for your brother after school!" Kate said in an intense growl that made even Bobby wince.

"I'm sorry," Hunter said. "This isn't my fault!"

"Just go upstairs, Hunter," Todd said. Hunter stood motionless as he breathed in deep through his nose, making a huffing sound like a wild animal, before heading up the stairs, toppling a lamp off the end table as he stomped past. Kate jumped as it crashed against the floor then closed her eyes tightly when Hunter slammed his bedroom door.

"You really shouldn't blame him for this," Bobby said after a period of silence.

"He knew better," Todd said. "He damn well knew better than to let his brother come home alone."

*****

Bronson, Florida

The two were sleeping when Lee Earl entered the house. He looked at their bodies, at once corpse-like and alluring. He stood over them, gazing at the boy, then reached down toward the platinum blond hair, glimmering in the moonlight like some underwater sea creature. Lee Earl was about to touch the top of his head when the image on the TV news stole his attention. There on the screen was Chase, with shorter darker hair. A class photo. Kids always looked so obedient in class photos.

Gritting his teeth, Lee quickly turned off the television.

"Roy," he said, nudging him. "Wake up."

"Yeah?" Roy rubbed his eyes. Chase didn't stir as Roy rose from the sofa.

"Change of plans," Lee Earl whispered. "I'm taking him to the other place tonight. You can go home."

"Why? What happened?"

"I just saw his picture on TV—"

"What!" Roy shouted. "Aw shit—"

Lee Earl slapped his hand over Roy's mouth and pulled him close by his shirt.

"Shut the fuck up," he growled. "Now listen! Take your mother's car and go home. Don't say a fucking word to no one. If someone asks you where you been, you say to visit your mother. If they ask where I went, tell them I didn't say." Lee Earl waited a moment to let his instructions sink in, then he removed his hand from Roy's mouth.

"How am I going to get her car back?"

"She doesn't need it back," Lee Earl said. "It's like you said. She's not driving anymore. Besides, I sold your car."

"What!"

Lee Earl covered his mouth again. "You say one word about any of this and we are both done. You're in this too, up to both of your chins. Now take your mother's car and go home." Lee Earl shoved Roy in the chest, causing him to stagger backward.

"Why are you hurting Mr. Roy like that?" Chase asked as he woke up.

"No one's hurting anyone," Lee Earl said, his voice brightening. "Okay, you ready to go look at some puppies?"

"I guess," Chase said. "Can I go home after?"

"I done said we're gonna talk about that, okay?"

"I'm leaving," Roy said and quickly grabbed his mother's keys.

"Can I go with Mr. Roy?" Chase asked, tears beginning to well in his eyes.

Lee Earl slammed his fist into the wall, causing both Chase and Roy to jump. "I said no! Watch TV," Lee Earl ordered between gnashed teeth. "I have to talk with Mr. Roy outside."

Trembling, Chase began to cry. Lee Earl turned on the TV and quickly changed the channel to *Tom and Jerry*. Then he took the remote with him outside. He walked Roy to the car in the driveway.

"What are you going to do with him?" Roy asked, already recovered from Lee Earl's outburst, ready again to comply.

"Raise him upright," Lee Earl said with a smile. "He's my son now."

"Yeah, well…" Roy unlocked the car. "Good luck."

"Just remember," Lee Earl said as he took a step back toward the house. "I go, *you go*." Lee Earl fished the vial from his pocket that he refilled with Valium then tossed it to Roy, who bumbled the catch.

"Thanks, Lee. You know best," Roy said, picking the pill bottle up off the ground.

"That's right, and you will do good to remember that."

*****

Sandy Beach, Florida

For somebody who lived on the ocean, Bobby rarely saw the beach. He didn't like the horizon; its openness made him feel uneasy. An ex once told him he was agoraphobic, but to his mind, he just didn't like the idea there was so much water. Like the jungles in Nam, it looked calm but contained unseen dangers. It was uncontrollable, that was the thing. But sometimes, like now, he took a walk along the marshy coast, with more rocks than sand. He tried not to think about the family he lost, the outbursts that cost him all that.

It had been a long frustrating day, and he wasn't able to stand the sight of a sink filled with dishes and laundry he didn't have the energy to do. He pushed back the craving to just hit the Snappy Turtle. The missing kid demanded his attention. In his gut, he knew he was gone, swiped by some pervert or drifter. Maybe drowned in the murky water in front of him. Florida waters were like that. Good for disposing with things. But what the criminals never count on is that the sea delivers back what's not its own.

A cry broke the silence. At first, Bobby thought it might be the gurgle of a manatee or dolphin taking in air, but he didn't see anything on the surface. But it was distinctly from the water. He suddenly felt like he wasn't alone. He looked around and reached for his service revolver before remembering he wasn't carrying it. It was then that he realized he was standing down the beach from the Sandy Beach Hotel. The lights were on. He had heard it had reopened but couldn't believe it was up and running so soon. The place had the source of trouble for decades, before his time as well.

"You going to shoot me, Officer?"

Justice spun around. Before him stood a woman in a long wavy blue dress, which seemed too elegant for the area. It made her appear somehow old-world, along with the black hair and green eyes that made her look like somebody from an Irish Spring soap commercial.

"No, ma'am," Justice said. She continued to look at him, making him uncomfortable. He made the connection now. She was the new proprietress of the hotel.

"Opening up going smooth?" he asked to break the silence.

"Well, we had some trouble last week. You know the sign that hangs over the door?"

Bobby thought for a moment. "You mean the one that reads Rest Your Head?"

"That one. Some kids had some fun and crossed out the *H* and replaced it with a *D*."

Justice chuckled.

"Is that funny?"

"No, ma'am. It's just that Sandy kids ain't usually that clever."

"Well, I'm leaving it up. Tourists think it's funny. Word gets out that we're a haunted hotel, and we'll have to beat them back."

"Having trouble drawing a clientele?" Justice asked.

"Oh, I wouldn't say that. People find what they want with us. And we're not so selective about who we accommodate."

Bobby grunted. They had accommodated a few corpses twenty years ago.

"I know what you're thinking, Officer. But some people are just drawn to us. You should come by some time. Ask for Marina Kerrigan. We can share an aperitif."

"An aper—"

"A whisky, Officer. I like mine neat," Marina Kerrigan said as she turned and strolled back in the direction of the hotel.

Bobby watched her go. It was only when she had disappeared from sight that he wondered just how she knew he was a policeman.

*****

Miami, Florida

Chase threw the handheld digital football game Lee Earl had bought him onto the car seat. He had grown bored of it, finding it too easy. Besides, he needed to get home soon. He didn't blame Lee Earl, figuring he was just dealing with a man who didn't understand how his family worked and that his parents expected him back. Chase wondered if they'd noticed, or if they still only cared about Hunter. If they kept his dinner in a plate with a bowl over the top to keep it warm. He hoped it was Spaghetti-os.

Chase couldn't see where they were going, so he poked his head into the front seat. He thought there was another kid in the van until he realized he was looking at his own reflection in the rearview mirror. Without knowing why, he suddenly burst into tears. Lee Earl continued driving.

"Don't you want a puppy?" Lee Earl asked after some miles flew by. "A friend of mine said we could pick any one of them."

Chase only answered with a sniffle.

"Come on, we're here anyway. Might as well look at those critters."

Once they exited the van, Lee Earl knelt. He rubbed his hands through the boy's hair and touched his cheek, staring at his catch with intense hunger.

"I just want to see my mom and dad," Chase managed.

"Look at me, boy." Lee Earl pointed to himself. "That's exactly what you see now."

"What do you mean?"

"I have all the love of your parents, and more. The world done brought us together. Now let's go inside and look at the nice puppies." Lee Earl stood up, grabbed Chase by the hand, and led him into the grove where the house was.

Lee Earl fumbled with the keys at the door. It wasn't more than a crumbling shack, but it would do for now. No neighbors, just a path beaten down from tires that led to the interstate. Lee Earl lit a lantern and took the boy inside. He used the toilet, washed his hands, and looked in the mirror. This was his reward for getting out of Sandy Beach and whatever wickedness that place held.

He returned to the room. Chase—his son—sat limply on a stool.

"Lift," Lee Earl commanded. Chase obediently put his hands over his head. Lee slowly started undressing the boy.

"Please stop," Chase cried. "I don't want to be here…please." He could hear puppies whimpering, their paws scraping against their cages from somewhere in the back of the abode.

"Shh, shh," Lee Earl whispered. "It's okay."

Lee Earl pulled him close, holding his head down with the strength a man had over a boy. The raw electric feeling coursed through his veins.

"Stop, no," Chase said, lifting his hand to push Lee Earl away. "I don't like this—"

"Shh, stay still," Lee Earl said gravely, grabbing Chase's wrist. "Put your hand down."

"Please! No!" Chase tried to break away. "I can't—stop, stop doing that!"

"Stop fighting. It will all be over soon, son," Lee Earl said as he took the boy from the chair and forced him to his knees.

The next morning, Lee Earl cooked some breakfast inside the small vacant home. All Chase could manage was to stare at the floor. Not even the puppies Lee had released into the kitchen interested him.

"C'mon, son," Lee Earl said, waving a limp piece of bacon in front of Chase in an effort to get him to eat. "This sure does smell good. I bet this dog would like it." He nudged one of the puppies away with his boot. Chase gave no response. With a grunt, Lee Earl dropped the morsel to the floor and leaned back in his chair.

"Say," he said. "Do you like any of these dogs? I bet one would like someone to take care of it."

Chase's eyes moved to a particular brown puppy that had caught his interest—the one lying on its own, away from the frolicsome litter. The runt.

"I like that one," Chase said quietly.

"Don't you want a bigger one? That one looks sickly."

"I like *him*," Chase said.

"Well, son, get him and let's take a ride. What are you gonna name it?"

Chase winced as he stood from the chair and approached the puppy. Once the dog was in his arms, it happily licked his face.

"Scooby," Chase answered. "Why do you keep calling me son?"

"Because you are my son now." Lee Earl picked a biscuit and took a bite.

"But you're not my dad."

"Well," Lee Earl spoke through a mouthful of food. "I wasn't gonna tell you this till later, but I'm your new dad."

Chase held the puppy against his cheek then put it down again.

"What do you mean?"

"Well, what did your parents get mad at you about recently?"

"I don't know."

"Yes, you do. Now tell me." Lee Earl took another bite.

"Coming home late."

"That's right!" Lee Earl said. "And why don't you have your own basketball hoop yet?"

"They said they didn't have the money right now."

"Exactly! So I went and saw the judge, and they said I could have you. So your parents wouldn't have to worry about that no more."

Chase sniffled. "Please let me call them," he cried. "And tell them I'm sorry. I won't do it anymore! I promise!"

"I'm afraid it's too late," Lee Earl said. He finished chewing and stood from the table. "And besides, they changed their number. I don't even have it anymore. And wait till you see where we're going. It's going to be so fun!" He smiled and took a step closer to Chase.

"You can play basketball any time you want now, and Scooby can run all over."

Chase's body tensed. He tried not to look at Lee Earl, but he felt his hand tightly grip his shoulder.

"It's like with Scooby! He's got a dad somewhere, but now you're his daddy. Does his first dad love him more than you?"

"No."

"There we have it! And Scooby loves you too!"

Chase thought for a moment. "But I can send letters, right?"

"Letters? You bet. I'll send them off all stamped up."

"Can we get stamps now?"

"Well, now we have to get a move on. Besides, letters are better if they are sent from far away. It makes them more *meaningful.* Okay?"

"But when we get there, can we?"

"Sure. Send all the letters you want. C'mon now. Let's get going."

*****

Sandy Beach, Florida

"No, it's okay. Momma…please don't drive out here. There isn't much you can do right now," Kate said as she wiped tears from her face. She had wanted to keep the news from her mother, ailing as she was, but with all the flyers around and news coverage, she had gone ahead and told her herself. Now she wasn't so sure that was a good idea.

"I want to be there for you," Kate's mother said from the other end of the line.

"You are. I'll call if anything changes. I love you." Kate was barely able to get her words out. "We will visit soon. *All of us.*"

"Okay, I love you too, baby."

Kate put the bedside phone back in the cradle and looked over to the empty pillow where Todd should be.

"Todd?" she called. She rose, pulled her robe around her, and tiptoed out into the hallway and past Hunter's room. She couldn't say why, but even normal conversations with him lately took on an edge. Kate chastised herself. *The kid should be the one sneaking around, not the parent.*

She found Todd at the kitchen table, a Hamm's beer in his hand. Empties on the counter. Todd would have one after work or out with his friends, but he never drank after dinner, alone.

"What's up, honey?"

"I just can't take it," he said. "I mean the uncertainty. The not knowing."

"I'm here too. I feel this too." She took the beer from his hand and downed a sip out of solidarity.

"Hunter should have waited. Chase shouldn't have been left alone. I just don't understand him. I know he's my son. And I love him. There's just something wrong. He feels like a stranger."

"We'll get through this, babe. Come to bed, okay?"

"Soon," he said and reached into the carton for another.

*****

George Darling showed up at the Sandy Beach Hotel daily until Isabel Dominguez allowed him to take her out on a date. While hesitant at first, his kind nature won her over. She told herself that he would relent once he saw how different they were, in age and background. But after a couple more dates, Isabel accepted an invitation from the doctor to have dinner at his house.

Isabel felt strangely insecure while driving up to his old colonial house in her old Ford, parking next to his shiny Mercedes. *He must have cleaning ladies*, she thought. *What separates me from them*? He had hired a private chef for the night, who served her a French dish she thought was chicken, then a flambé for dessert, which made her gasp. She knew he was only trying to impress her, but it made her feel small and unworldly. Still, it was hard to say no to the gifts. He even found a way to pay for Rosalina's college tuition at South Beach College.

After dinner, George showed Isabel all the paintings and drawings he had made of her over the past couple of months.

"I can't believe you did all these, George!" Isabel exclaimed before placing both hands on her cheek.

George held up his most recent drawing. They were clunky, didn't totally look like her, but it was flattering nonetheless. "I do it to unwind. And I figure, if you are on my mind, you might as well be on my wall. Do you like them?" She nodded with some sincerity. It was easier if she thought of herself as his muse rather than his obsession.

"Yes, of course," Isabel said as politely as she could. "Such a beautiful home, George," Isabel said as she turned to face him.

"Do you like it here, Isabel?"

"Yes. Thank you so much for the beautiful room you got for me at the Sandy Palms Hotel. And my sister loves the dorm and being able to go to school full time now," Isabel said as she lowered her head. What he gave her was too much, but also too much to say *no* to.

"Next, you'll quit your job. The Sandy Beach Hotel has always had a dark cloud over it," George confessed.

"I know I've thanked you a million times," she whispered.

"Isabel." George placed his finger under her chin to gently lift her head and stare into her eyes. "Why don't you come live with me here? You see," he said, indicating the paintings. "You already kind of do."

"Why do you do all this?" she asked. "Are you some kind of angel?" *Perhaps*, she thought, *this was God working mysteriously through the doctor*. She had prayed on the situation, and perhaps this was part of God's plan.

George laughed. "You walked into my clinic then into my heart. You're all I think about and dream of." He guided her to the living room couch and directed her to sit. Like the rest of the house, it might as well have been a museum to Isabel. It had vases from China and bronze sculptures. It was then that she noticed a black-and-white photo of a younger George, his arm around a woman. He was so trim, muscular. The image was faded with time.

"George," Isabel began as he edged closer to her. "I'm fond of you, and I think you are a wonderful man, but I don't know if I feel this way about you."

George was still smiling as he tucked a strand of hair behind her ear. "You may not feel that way now, but I believe in time, you could. Forget about cleaning or living in hotels. You can have any room you want, including mine. Just try it, Isabel. You will see. You will come to feel about me as I do about you. You can have whatever you want from me, as long as I am there to watch you enjoy it."

"Can I think about it?"

"Of course, you can."

"George, you never said why you don't have a family. It's hard to believe."

"I did once." George's smile faded.

"Where are they?"

"I wouldn't dare hurt those beautiful ears with my boring story."

"Please, tell me. It is important for me to know you."

George sighed as he thought back. "It was forty-one years ago, but the memory is just as vivid as yesterday. I was eighteen, married with an infant child. During the war, the military put us medical students on an accelerated three-year program because of a physician shortage at that time. Helen was only three months old when she died, with no explanation. It's a syndrome they call SIDS now."

Isabel took George's hand in consolation.

"My wife, Meredith, was never the same after. She was diagnosed with tuberculosis six months later. It's not like now, with ready antibiotics and such. She died of it not long after that. She was the same age as you are now."

"I'm so sorry, George," Isabel said. "Forgive me for asking that question."

"You can ask me anything you want," George said brightly. "I haven't spoken of them in ages."

"Yet you tell me?" Isabel asked.

"My wife, Meredith, is the reason I'm still a doctor to this day. I couldn't cure her, but I promised to do my best to save others, and my daughter watches over me every night. She put you in my arms." George touched Isabel's hair again. She felt a shudder but couldn't say why. Was it excitement? Fear? Or was she just moved?

"Sweet man."

"I feel reborn just breathing in the same air as you," George expressed.

Later that night, after Isabel consented to a kiss on the cheek and another date, George padded up the shag carpet on the steps to his bedroom. Despite the fact that he was alone, he still closed the door before going into his closet. From behind a rack of suits, he pulled a hat box which had once been his wife's. He opened it gingerly, like it might somehow release a wild animal or trigger a bomb. Inside lay a pile of black-and-white photographs. *The slashes on their bodies precise like in surgery, seeking innocence but finding only blood.*

July 1983

Patrol teams searching around the clock for the missing boy had yielded nothing. Files were spread out on the table before the detectives. Styrofoam coffee cups stood like sentinels over the detectives as they poured through the information collected about the Lovell case—the backgrounds of the teachers plus known offenders who lived near the school and surrounding area. They also reread their interview notes and fed names into the NCIC database. Time had long passed being on their side.

"Damn it, not one goddamn hit on any of these background checks," Jack said, frustrated. "I mean, these must be the cleanest teachers in the world."

"I still feel like it is someone Chase knew but never felt like it was a teacher," Bobby confessed as he rubbed his eyes.

"Who would he know that his parents don't?" Jack asked as he downed a cup of water.

"That's the hundred-thousand-dollar question. All the known offenders who lived around the area were forthcoming. And I must say, in some cases, they were more cooperative than a few of the teachers," Bobby said.

"I didn't like any of the names we pulled for it anyway. Nothing with kids in their backgrounds or at least on their records," Jack stated.

Bobby ran his fingers through his hair. He could bear a drug dealer getting shot, could look the other way with a shoplifter. But a missing kid. "Fuck."

Then he remembered the manila folder Loretta Jones handed him. "Holy hell, we didn't cover the nonteachers," he said.

"Where's that folder?" Jack asked with one eyebrow up.

"On my goddamn desk!" Bobby said, admonishing himself.

"Hey, it's all right, partner. We would have just been getting around to it anyway."

"We don't have time to waste here."

"Take it easy. I'll make the coffee."

After several hours of punching more names into the department's sole computing system, Bobby perked up.

"Jack, we might have a lead," Bobby announced.

"What?" Jack asked.

"I'll tell you in a second."

Disregarding how late it was, Bobby picked up the phone and called Loretta Jones.

"Hello?" a tired voice answered after several rings.

"Mrs. Jones, Bobby Justice here. Did I wake you?" In the background, he could hear a male voice asking who it was.

"Go back to sleep, honey," Loretta said. "That's okay, Detective. Is everything all right?"

"Lee Earl Elwood," Bobby said. "Does the name mean anything to you?"

"Why, yes," Loretta said, sounding caught off guard. "He's one of our janitors or *was*. He put in his resignation the same day you stopped by."

"*Damnit*. Mrs. Jones, did you know he was arrested twice, once in '70 and again in '72 for unlawful touching of a minor with two different young boys in Albuquerque, New Mexico?"

"My God, no! We would never have hired him knowing that. Our background checks only go back seven years."

"That lines up. He was released in '74 and hired at Sandy Public in '82. Hell, he's even got drug and theft charges going back to '65 and '68. His last known arrest was eleven years ago, and all of them were in Albuquerque. He seems to have stayed off the grid since."

"Oh my, this is so horrible."

"There is an address on file for him. It's that trailer park by the old Sandy Beach Hotel. Do you know if this is current?"

"No, sir," Loretta said. "Do you believe that Lee Earl Elwood took Chase?"

"Well, look at the timeline." Bobby checked his notes. "Chase Lovell goes missing, then you tell me Elwood quits the day after. And on top of that, he has a record as a sex offender. It's the best lead I have."

"What can I do to help?"

"I sure didn't want to hear that he quit, and something tells me he's nowhere near this address, but we'll check it out pronto. Jack may be by tomorrow to interview the other janitors."

"Sure thing, Detective."

Bobby and Jack wasted no time speeding the patrol car over to the address on Lee's file, turning the flashers off as they approached so as not to alert him, should he still be there.

They found a vacant area with weeds growing through broken concrete where a small trailer would have sat. It had the look of someone who left in a hurry—a smattering of items laying around now left behind.

"We'll come back tomorrow to interview the neighbors, but he has cut town," Bobby said, agitated.

"Hardly a shock. I sure could use some shut-eye."

"I'll see the Lovells on my own. Feel free to sleep in. We need your mind sharp."

"Don't you ever sleep, boss?" Jack asked.

Bobby gave the discarded items one last look, ignoring Jack's question. His gut told him the two were now far away.

The next morning, Bobby paid the Lovells a visit to update them on Chase's case.

"Do you believe this is the man?" Todd asked.

"Well, Mr. Lovell, of course, we have no way of knowing that for sure yet, but it's a lead that we are going to pursue hard."

"How could the school have hired a person with a record like that?" Kate asked.

"School background checks only go seven years back. He was released in '74 and hired at Chase's school in '82."

"Still."

"People assume new identities, make new driver's licenses. You can get a fake birth certificate, whatever you want. People create new identities more than you think. Also, I am sorry to say, information sometimes just gets lost. Sometimes the system fails."

Kate shook her head as tears spilled down her face. "Oh my god. My baby!"

"That's also why we're going to move fast."

"So when did he stop working for the school?" Todd asked.

"The day after Chase went missing."

"Damn!" Todd swore.

Bobby was sorry to have had to convey that news, especially to a man like Todd Lovell. Todd looked a bit rough on that morning. Bobby was no over-sleeper. Bad dreams ensured that. But Todd's eyes were pits, and the man smelled like stale beer sweat at eight in the morning.

"Unbelievable… I mean, the day after our son goes missing, a sex offender leaves town. You can't convince me that this isn't the guy," Todd said.

"Look, Detective Cutler is at the school interviewing Elwood's coworkers. Officers are talking to other residents at the park as we speak. We were also able to track down his mother's home address in Miami. An MPD detective is heading to that location now. Our chances are good, but I need you two to stay collected for your other boy."

Bobby noticed Todd scoff. Kate nodded her agreement then put her head on Todd's shoulder.

*****

Miami, Florida

People knew Officer Cane Diaz as Snake for the snake tattoo that ran up his chest, which he'd gotten in the Merchant Marines. He liked to unbutton his uniform to show it off, because it either intimidated suspects or acted as an icebreaker with informants. He knocked on the small house door then undid his button. A moment later, an older woman with long braided hair and a flowing floral-patterned dress answered.

"Mrs. Elwood?" Officer Diaz asked, peering at the woman over his sunglasses. "Mrs. Elaine Elwood?"

The snake apparently didn't work its charm this time as Elaine closed her eyes in what appeared to be annoyance, as though he were some utility man coming to check the gas.

"It's Dixon now. Hasn't been Elwood for a few years."

"Apologies. Hello, Mrs. Dixon. I'm Detective Cane Diaz from the Miami Police Department, and I'm here in conjunction with the Sandy Beach Police Department about your son, Lee Earl Elwood. Do you know of his whereabouts at this time?"

"I haven't seen Lee Earl since I remarried, and that's been for the best," Elaine said. "What's this about?" She leaned against the door. "Did he do it again?"

"What would that be, Mrs. Dixon?"

"Selling drugs, stealing, and, well, cavorting with small boys. Lord knows what else," Elaine whispered.

Officer Diaz nodded, a solemn acknowledgment that there was collateral damage to such crimes, and that included her. He felt for the old woman.

"Right now, he's wanted for the disappearance of a young boy in Sandy Beach."

"I wish I could say that shocks me, Detective, but he always did like stealing."

"Hey," a gruff male voice sounded from inside the home. "If that sick fuck comes back around here, you aren't gonna have to worry about catching him." A tall muscular man appeared behind

Elaine. "Because he'll be outside waiting for you dead! I'll kill that son of a bitch myself!"

"Hush, honey. I'm talking to the nice policeman."

Officer Diaz ignored the interruption. "Do you mind if I come in?"

Elaine stepped aside for the officer.

"Is there a name you can give me? Anyone he may have associated with that would have some information on his whereabouts?"

"Look, like I said," Elaine intoned, now with more hesitancy, as though if she spoke it might summon her son. "I haven't seen Lee Earl going on for three years now."

"If you think of anyone, Mrs. Dixon, a little boy's life may depend on it."

Elaine glanced at the head of the snake, looking taken aback for a moment before speaking. "Otis Redgrave," Elaine said timidly.

"Otis?"

"Redgrave," Elaine repeated. Diaz wrote the name down to forward to Sandy Beach PD later.

"I'm going to give you the number of the man in charge of the case along with mine," Officer Diaz said, handing Elaine two cards. "His name is Detective Bobby Justice. Thank you for your time, Mrs. Dixon."

Elaine didn't respond. She merely accepted the cards, looking ashamed, then waited for the officer to exit before pushing the door closed behind him.

*****

Sandy Beach, Florida

Bobby was sitting alone at the Snappy Turtle, brooding. Missing children were usually found quickly in Sandy Beach. There had been a few deaths of children in Bobby's time on the force—kids who swam in unguarded areas and got swept away by the undertow, kids wearing their headphones on the interstate who miss-stepped into traffic. A parent punished a child with too much force, but rarely did they just disappear.

"Hey, space cadet," Wanda said, waving a bottle of bourbon in front of him. "One on the house?"

"Sure."

"Twenty-year curse got ya?"

"What do you mean, Wanda?"

Bobby knew what she meant. Local legend had it that Sandy Beach suffered a crime spree every twenty years. The mayor, when in his cups, liked to talk about it. But Bobby always politely begged off or changed the subject. Superstition, voodoo, whatever didn't mean much when you've collected limbs of your platoon after stepping on a land mine. Crime came in waves, like the ocean they lived on. Curses weren't nothing but swear words.

"Too many kids around anyway," Wanda said. "I wish someone would take them all."

"You know, Wanda, you're just Christmas come early, aren't you?"

"Ha, well, I am pouring free for the next ten seconds." Bobby indicated he'd accept another, his fifth. Wanda poured one for herself too.

"Just don't go spilling over the side. I'm tired of being this town's damn psychiatrist," Wanda said before they downed their shots.

"I prefer your assistants, Jack and Jim. Now hit me again so I can sleep tonight." Wanda gave him a rare smile and put the bottle to work.

It was another rough night, but Bobby was on the radio with Officer Pac early the next morning. They'd sent her around to Elwood's former residence. Trailer park people were cagey, but they responded well to the feminine energy.

"What ya got, Pac?"

"Well, for starters, I spoke with a Coral Trailer Park resident by the name of Claire Hughes, who said she stopped letting her son, Ryan, go to Elwood's place. She lives what would have been three trailers down from where Elwood was parked. She mentioned Elwood using inappropriate language. Ryan complained he spoke of sex lot and would always try to sit close when he was at Elwood's camper."

"How old is the boy?"

"Eight, and her other son is twelve."

"Jesus Christ," Bobby whispered. The phone on his desk began to ring. "Pac, I'll radio back. I have a call coming in."

"Copy," Pac said, signing off.

"This is Justice speaking," Bobby said into the receiver.

"Detective, this is Officer Cane Diaz in Miami. I have some information for you."

"Morning, Officer Diaz. Let's hear it."

"I talked to Elwood's mother, who goes by Dixon now. Claims she hasn't seen her son going on three years."

"Did she give us anything else?" Bobby asked while writing the name Dixon down.

"Yes, sir. Otis Redgrave," Detective Diaz said. "He's someone who's had dealings with Mr. Elwood in the past."

Bobby leaned back in his chair. "Tell me you can locate him."

"Already did. He wasn't hard to track down."

"Don't make me beg, Detective."

"Well, let's just say he wasn't in a helping mood initially, but after asking very nice and encouraging him to act in his own best interest, he politely gave me some solid leads," Cane Diaz said, dripping sarcasm. "Got your pen ready?"

"I do."

"He was just in your neck of the woods. Apparently, Mr. Elwood owed Mr. Redgrave some money. While there, he played a card game with Mr. Elwood and another man named Roy Boutte. Mr. Boutte lives in the trailer across from Elwood. Seems the two have a close relationship."

Bobby bounced his pen off the desk. "Good work, Detective! Did he have any information about the boy?"

"No, but he did seem angry about some property he let Elwood use recently, probably for that purpose. Redgrave said Elwood paid him to stay at the property for a night or two. Mr. Redgrave isn't an angel by any stretch, but I don't get the feeling he knew about the child."

"You've checked the property, I assume?"

"I sent officers to the address immediately, and outside of some small dogs, it was empty. We'll continue to monitor the property for a couple of days."

"Detective, I can't thank you enough."

"Ten-four, Detective Justice."

Bobby, after hanging up with Detective Diaz, radioed Officers Pac and Jonesy.

"Jonesy here."

"Jonesy, you still with Pac?"

"Yes, sir."

"Put her on, would you?"

"Yessir," Pac answered.

"Did you speak with a Roy Boutte while canvassing the trailer park today? His home was next door to Elwood's."

"Sir," Pac's voice came over the radio. "I knocked on the trailer several times and got no response. There were a few of the residents who were out, possibly at work."

"I need both of you back over there ASAP, and I want Mr. Boutte brought in for questioning. If he still isn't home, find him," Bobby commanded.

"Were on it, sir," Pac said.

*****

Pac and Jonesy were knocking on the door of Roy Boutte within the hour. When no answer came, they knocked again. Through the thin particleboard door, Pac heard the floor creak. Then the door slowly opened.

"Mr. Boutte?" Officer Pac asked.

"Yes, ma'am?"

"Sorry to bother you this morning. I need to ask you to come downtown with us and answer some questions."

"I don't know where Lee is," Roy said, shaking his head.

Officer Pac threw Officer Jonesy a look.

"You mean Lee Earl Elwood?" Officer Pac confirmed.

"Yes," Roy said. "He said he was going to Miami to visit his parents."

Officer Jonesy tilted his head. "Who said we were looking for Mr. Elwood?"

Roy stared at him. "I don't know."

"I think you're going to need to take that ride with us, Mr. Boutte," Officer Pac said, placing her hand on Roy's shoulder, as though in consolation. Jonesy stood back to let Pac lead Boutte to the squad car.

*****

Bobby and Jack, along with Captain Greg Curry, watched Roy Boutte squirm in his chair through the interrogation room observation mirror.

"I think he's sat long enough, boys," Captain Curry said. Bobby nodded, his eyes still on Roy.

"He's shakier than my girlfriend's Chihuahua on uppers, crapping out jumping beans," Jack said.

"There's a real feel-good image," Bobby said.

"Feel-good? Didn't know you had human emotions," Jack replied, "other than grumpy."

"You two finished?" Captain Curry said, and he nodded toward the mirror. "Go get him."

"Yes, Captain," Bobby said and glared at Jack as they walked out of the door. "What are you trying to say, Jack?"

"Nothing," Jack said. "You just don't seem too happy, is all, bud."

"Oh, that's just around you," Bobby said.

Jack stopped walking as Bobby stepped forward to grab the door.

"That's just mean," Jack said.

Bobby shrugged and held the door open. "After you."

Bobby could tell if a man was about to lie just by sniffing the air of the interrogation room. Liars, in his experience, gave off a musky odor that he put down to nerves. Like the salt in seawater, it was just under the surface, but you could still smell it.

Bobby wrinkled his nose at the effluvium given off by the man seated at the table. Roy Boutte was about to tell a whopper.

"What can you tell me about the disappearance of Chase Lovell?" Bobby asked. He slid the picture of Chase toward Roy.

"Who?"

"The boy you helped Lee Earl Elwood kidnap," Jack said.

"Anything you want to tell us, Mr. Boutte?" Bobby prompted.

"Lee Earl just said he had to leave," Roy stammered. "That he was going to Miami to see his mom."

Bobby observed how Roy looked down and left when he spoke, a tic that indicated a deceitful statement.

"He took his trailer and quit his job just so he could go see his mom, huh?" Jack asked, smirking.

"He told me she was sick—"

"Or maybe," Bobby began, "he was running from something? Was he taking someone with him to, you say, Miami?"

"I think we all know he's not in Miami, Mr. Boutte," Jack said.

Roy shook harder, and Jack's grin spread across his face.

"Why so quiet, Mr. Boutte?" Jack asked. Roy looked from Jack to Bobby, as though seeking refuge.

"We know you helped Elwood," Bobby said, placing his palms on the table. "And when we catch him, do you really think he's going to protect you the way you are protecting him?" He paused, letting his question sink in. "You could end up doing more time than he does for abetting a kidnapper and lying to the police."

"You're going to feel a lot better getting this off your chest, Mr. Boutte," Jack said. "We know you're no criminal. We just want to clear your name and find the boy."

Roy turned to Bobby again, and then something collapsed behind his eyes. Roy began to talk.

"He didn't tell me where he was taking him! I haven't seen him since he sold my car and we went to my mother's house, and he made me take my mother's car back home, and my mother is in a nursing home and not using it. He's crazy!" Roy raised his quivering voice. "He scares me."

"Taking him? As in, Chase Lovell?" Bobby confirmed. He pointed at the picture while keeping his eyes on Roy. Roy exhaled. Bobby knew he could get anything he needed out of him now.

"Yes."

"Where is your mother's house?" Jack asked.

"In Bronson," Roy said. "Norwood Avenue."

After obtaining the key from Roy and a tense ride to Bronson, Bobby and Jack entered the house.

"Nobody," Jack said, looking around. "Damn."

"Elwood's smarter than that. Garbage been taken out, beds stripped. Dishes were done. But the food in the fridge is mostly fresh. They haven't been gone long."

"Now what?" Jack asked with the despair of somebody not used to dead ends.

"Now we keep doing our jobs. We keep investigating until we find them. Understood, Detective?"

"Yes, sir."

"Come on, Jack. I'll drive."

The next day, Bobby stopped by the Lovells' to update them on the case. He brought along a photo of Elwood.

"This damn ugly piece of shit," Todd said, staring into Elwood's picture. "I swear to God if I ever find this asshole."

"What's next, Detective?" Kate asked somberly.

"We aren't giving up," Bobby said while scratching the stubble on his chin. "We know it's Elwood, and we gave his picture along with Chase's to the FBI. We also have them in police stations all over the states. Eyewitnesses are so important for cracking a case like this."

"What about the other men involved? Redgrave and Boutte," Todd asked.

"Redgrave technically hasn't broken any laws relative to Chase, or at least nothing we can prove yet. Whatever role Mr. Boutte played, he was forced into it by Elwood just like Chase was. Putting him in prison wouldn't do anybody any good. Elwood just may contact either of these men again down the road. He can't do that if they are locked up. Neither man has any love for Mr. Elwood. Better to use them than to punish them. We'll save all that punishment for Elwood."

*****

Isabel decided to move in with George. Though they had yet to be physically intimate, she couldn't resist his kindness and the material comfort he offered. But despite the luxury of his home, the transition wasn't easy. The first day, for instance, he had to tell her to put away the pail and mop she had found.

"I just want to help to earn my keep," she said, wringing out the mop.

"Darling, you are not a maid anymore. Now people will wait on you," George told her. He was too good to be true. "Come relax with me in the living room while we wait for the food to be prepared. And no, you don't need to help with that either. But would you help me drink this wine?" George held up a bottle with a French name.

"Yes, please. The food smells so wonderful."

"I do hope you love it," George affirmed. "From now on, you can eat whatever you want."

A news report of Chase Lovell was playing on the television, which George sometimes left on during meals. Though it dampened the romantic mood, both wanted to learn what was happening with his receptionist's missing child.

"We have an update tonight of missing nine-year-old and Sandy Beach native Chase Lovell. Authorities now believe that a man by the name of Lee Earl Elwood is connected with the disappearance," the news anchor announced as side-by-side pictures of Chase and Lee Earl flashed on the screen. "Elwood, who has had previous run-ins with the law, was a Sandy Public School janitor who had recently resigned. If you have any information on his whereabouts, please get in contact with local authorities or dial the number you see on the screen."

George turned off the television then went to pour himself a gin and tonic from the drink trolley he kept in the dining room.

"Poor Kate. I told her to take off as long as she needs. I will continue to pay her salary."

"Oh my, yes. I forgot I met her at the clinic. That is terrible. It is very kind of you to continue to pay her."

"She's worked for me ever since Chase was an infant. I just hope they find him," George said as he handed Isabel a glass of wine. "But let's not let it ruin the moment. I want to remember this night forever. Isabel, forever."

"Forever," she said shyly and took a sip of the crisp, refreshing wine.

6

October 1983

Four months had gone by since Lee Earl Elwood abducted Chase Lovell. Bobby Justice was sitting with Captain Curry, neither man enjoying the briefing on Bobby's open cases and the lack of progress finding Chase Lovell.

"No new leads or eyewitnesses to place him in any location," Bobby said. "Either they just disappeared, or no one's talking."

"Elwood hasn't tried to contact his mother or other known associates?" Captain Curry asked.

"It's like he dropped off the face of the goddamn earth."

"I know it's frustrating, and I know how personal this case has become for you. It happens to all of us." Captain Curry leaned back in his chair. "Cases go cold all the time. You have to move on because we have no shortage of crime out there. It's heating up lately."

"Tends to as the holidays creep up," Bobby said.

"Or something else," Curry mused.

"Twenty-year curse?" Bobby said, joking.

"Oh boy, there's a can of worms I wouldn't open," Curry said, perking up.

"Townsfolk talking, is all. Seem to think like the sixteen-year cicada, then we get a crime wave every twenty."

"Yeah, I get an earful of that from the mayor every now and again. Personally, I don't believe in curses, but this year hasn't been pretty. I put it down to MTV and these damn video games where you shoot everything you see. Don't quote me on that."

"I wasn't really being serious, Captain."

"I guess this kidnapping threw a monkey wrench into your sergeant promotion."

"I'm not worried about that right now, Captain."

"I am, because you deserve it. Plus, we lost a couple of officers who left to take positions elsewhere. It's going to happen, Bobby, I promise. I just can't take you out of the field right now. Just give me till later next year."

"Thank you, sir. I understand."

"How is Jack coming along?"

"Your instincts were correct. When Jack is focused, he's a natural. We are lucky to have him," Bobby said. He wanted to talk more about the Lovell case, but there was just nothing to say. He hadn't been by to see the Lovells in weeks and felt bad about that.

"Good to hear. Well, get out there and find some bad guys. Something will pop loose on the Lovell case soon enough. In the meantime, you need to look into the prostitution thing at the Sand Beach Hotel and whatever's happening at the auto shop. We know something stinks there. We just have to prove it."

"Yes, Captain," Bobby said on his way out of Curry's office.

Bobby found Jack at his desk, typing up a report on a recent burglary.

Jack looked up from his paperwork. "How did it go in there?"

"Nothing worth talking about," Bobby said as he sat at his desk. "Basically, we don't have shit on Elwood or Chase Lovell's whereabouts. So until we do, we need to move on."

"Move on to *what* exactly?"

"Possible prostitution ring at the Sandy and a drug supplier who I was looking into before all this shit went down."

Jack nodded. "That place is never dull. So did he ask about me?"

"Yes," Bobby said while looking over some old notes.

Jack leaned back in his chair. "Well?"

"Well, what?" Bobby said, still not making eye contact. "I'm trying to concentrate over here, Jack, if you don't mind."

"Well, what the heck did you say?" Jack asked, throwing his hands in the air.

Bobby looked up from his reading long enough to say, "I said you're a pain in the ass, and I can't stand ya."

"Oh, Mr. Funny Guy, huh? But seriously?"

"That was funny to you?" Bobby said. "Interesting."

Jack glared at Bobby for a moment, waiting for him to relate what he told the captain. After getting no response, he started his paperwork again. After a second, he looked toward Bobby one more time.

"No, I don't think you're funny," he mumbled. Bobby waited for Jack to stop looking then chuckled.

*****

Todd started getting up early before the sun rose. He found he enjoyed a drink more with Kate asleep. He could just sit in the dark of the house, listen to the silence, a Seagram's 7 in front of him. The house, the empty rooms, the distant ocean created its own droll soundtrack. He hadn't opened Chase's bedroom door in a month, didn't know why Kate continued to clean it every week. The booze turned him inward, self-reflective, which was something he resisted all his life. He was never comfortable alone with his thoughts, but now he felt he could have a conversation with himself, the glass as the moderator.

He went to sit on a lawn chair in the yard, where he either passed out or fell asleep, depending on your perspective. Upon waking, instead of feeling self-reproach, he sought out Kate, knowing he'd find her in the bedroom. She was in a funk too. But they had the day ahead of them, at least most of it. He stood over her, trying to muster some affection. All that came was a feeling of loyalty and a touch of irritation. Todd shook his wife by the shoulder.

"Hey, I know it's a Saturday, but did you want to get out of bed? It's after one already. Maybe we can do something."

"No, can't I just lay here and not do anything?" Kate asked.

Todd sat by her. Without her need for him, he knew he'd just get a case of Seagram's 7 and call it a year. He tried to get her talking about something other than Chase.

"How are things going at work? I know you mentioned Dr. Darling is considering selling the clinic."

"Dr. Dominic has been filling in for him quite a bit," Kate said, rubbing her eyes.

"Do you like him?"

"What do you mean?"

"I mean, *do you like him*?"

"I like my job, and he's my boss. He's much younger, but he's smart and nice enough," she said, perking up a bit.

"So where is Hunter? He knows he wasn't supposed to leave."

"I have no clue." Kate finally sat up. "Are you shocked he's gone?"

"I'm not shocked by much anymore," Todd said.

*****

Ignoring his parents' commands, Hunter had left earlier that morning through the back door, sneaking past his parents. His mom was shut off behind her bedroom door, and his dad was dead drunk, so who cared anyway? He rode around the neighborhood. Maybe he'd steal some candy from a Stop-N-Go or light a trash can on fire. He ended up just patrolling around, getting bored, and heading toward home. But on the way, he noticed a black cat in a neighbor's driveway. Hunter jumped off his bike and tried to approach it, but it fled between an open fence door and the house.

"Come on, kitty," Hunter beckoned as he walked toward the cat, attempting to grab the animal when he was close enough. It hissed, scratched his hand, and hissed again. Hunter's face turned red with anger.

"Piece of shit thing!" His first impulse was to stomp on it, but then he noticed a metal baseball bat lying a few feet away. He picked it up, turned around, and closed in on the cat, still sitting vigilant in the same spot.

Inside the house, a woman heard the loud commotion, the ghoulish wail only cats can make. She called out, "Oscar! Come on, Oscar! Get in here, you rascal!" She walked into her backyard. "Oscar—oh!"

She was startled to see a large boy holding her son's bat. She stepped closer, ready to tell the kid to leave, when she caught sight of the bloodied mess. There was hardly anything recognizable left but Oscar's purple flea collar and a disjointed jaw full of sharp teeth like fishhooks sticking from the gory pile of fur.

"Oh my god!" the woman screamed, clutching her chest. "No! No!"

She stumbled, backing away before she ran inside to the call the police.

The kill, the splatter of blood, the sound of the bat hitting soft fur and flesh, topped by the woman's horror, all added to Hunter's high. He grinned as he tossed the blood-soaked bat on the grass and calmly began back to his bike, as though he were a batter who had just been walked. He didn't fight when a hand grabbed him by his collar, pulling his bike to a halt. He allowed himself to be walked back to the woman's house by a man. Her husband, he guessed. The cat's *Daddy*, he joked to himself while enjoying the chaos.

*****

Kate and Todd found Hunter sitting in an interrogation room, sipping a root beer with Tickerrman, the arresting officer.

"He'll be transferred to correctional after we process him," Tickerrman said, explaining why the boy wasn't in a holding cell. It's not like he was denying anything.

"What in the fuck were you thinking, son?" Todd yelled. Hunter offered no response.

"You murdered someone's cat?" Kate cried. "First, it's harassing girls at school then kicking in a door, and now this?"

A faint smirk rose on the boy's face. Todd looked like he was going to jump over the table and throttle him.

"What were you doing out of the house anyway? You're grounded. Or did you forget you got suspended from school?" Todd added.

"I've been in that house for a week now!" Hunter said, his voice knotted with anger. Tickerrman set a hand down on his shoulder to calm him, looking at Todd and Kate.

"The owners of the cat he killed are pressing charges," he said.

Todd threw his hands up. "Jesus Christ!"

*****

Hunter felt an odd sense of relief when the court handed him a five-month stay at the Sandy Juvenile Correctional Facility. He could no longer bear the reproachful look of his parents or Chase's empty room. That tiny house with the shitty aluminum siding that was falling off. The place suffocated him. Hunter told himself he'd find ways to make his sentence fun, but now there was a pit of nerves forming in his stomach as he was buzzed into the SJCF and subjected to a full body search. *When somebody puts their hands on you, it changes things.* The feeling grew as a burly guard escorted him to a room with two cots. Hunter was about to sit on one of the beds when someone walked in.

"So you the new dawg?" a boy asked. He was a tall cocky guy, more lean than muscle-bound, but with hair shorn short and a snarl on his face. He comported himself with a swagger and didn't look happy to see Hunter.

"I guess so. It's my first day," Hunter finally let out.

"That's yo fuckin cot on the left, and you gonna have to get yo own shit paper."

"Whatever," Hunter said.

"Don't *whatever* me. Whatever ain't no answer. You give me a yes or no, son."

"How's that?"

"It like this. See, you can sail down the *left* side of the street, or you can sail down the *right* side of the street. That's okay too. Just not the middle."

"Middle lane gets you the middle finger," Hunter ventured.

"Ha, yeah, son. You all right. So what you up in here for, man?" the boy asked.

"Nothing too serious," Hunter replied, for the first time feeling the senselessness of his crime. He wished he had done something to brag about, at least hurt somebody bad. "Something stupid. What about you?"

"Smokin' and sellin' that killer, dawg," the kid said with grin. "I can hook you up if need be."

"Oh…what would I have to do for it?" Hunter asked anxiously.

"Pay for it, brotha. What else?"

"Hell, fuck if I know."

The boy laughed. "Aight, brotha. I can see you got some learnin' to do. You what, sixteen? Seventeen?"

"Fifteen, almost sixteen," Hunter answered.

"Damn!" The kid gawked. "Big motherfucka for fifteen, huh?"

"I guess." Hunter shrugged his shoulders.

"So c'mon, man. Tell me what's up." The kid lay down on his bed. "You kill the neighbor's cat or somethin'?"

Hunter felt a rush of shame, like he had been caught with his pants down. *Did everybody already know?* "No. It wasn't the neighbor's cat."

The kid laughed loudly. "You serious! Oh shit, man! What the fuck did you do that for, man?"

"Felt right at the time, I guess," Hunter said.

"How long you up in this bitch for?"

"Five months. Then I have like one hundred hours of community service."

"Ah shit, man, that isn't shit. I been in here for like six months. Hell, I'll be gettin' out of this shit probably like a month or so before you."

"How old are you?" Hunter asked.

"Be eighteen when I get out this bitch."

"That's cool."

"So what's your name, my man? They call me Goo-Man. That's short for Goodman. De'Ron Goodman."

"I'm Hunter Lovell."

Both boys nodded to one another in approval.

*****

George and Rosalina were sitting at the dining room table, talking while waiting for Isabel to emerge from the bedroom, the scent of George's *melanzane parmigiana* wafting from the kitchen. That was one thing Rosalina liked about George—his taste for exotic and fine foods. He passed that sophisticated taste to Isabel. Her sister deserved it. And for Rosalina, it was like having a father figure in her life again. One who fed her well.

"Thank you so much for doing this, George. I can't tell you how much it means to me," the younger sister announced.

"It's just eggplant and cheese, dear," George said with a grin. "The Italians considered it peasant food."

"Not just dinner." Rosalina giggled. "I mean everything you have done for my sister and me."

"I've never been happier in my life," he said.

"I hope I can find a man that loves me as much as you love my sister," Rosalina said with genuine sweetness.

"You have. You're looking at him," George said, looking playfully into Rosalina's eyes.

"Aww, so sweet. Tell me how you can be this much of an angel?" Rosalina declared.

"I was going to ask you the same question," George asserted. "Tell me, how is school going, my dear?" he asked.

Rosalina was happy to give a report. Now that she didn't have to work odd jobs to make tuition, she was thriving in her studies. "I'm enjoying it immensely, and I have a nice roommate who I get along with very well."

"Excellent, dear! Have you picked a major yet?"

"Almost. I'm still deciding, but I have time since I still have lots of general courses I need to finish that correspond with all majors."

"You will be fantastic in whatever you choose, I just know it."

"Thank you! That means so much coming from you."

"It's merely the truth," George said.

"I can't believe you lived alone all these years, George. You're such a great man."

George's face appeared to go blank, then she thought she saw him cringe. She had forgotten that sometimes, he reacted to questions about his past in a strange way. She put her head down then smiled at him. George smiled faintly back, lost in some memory.

"You have such a lovely neck," George said out of nowhere. He lifted his hand as though to pantomime hug or—if Rosalina were to take it the wrong way—*strangle* her. Then he appeared to catch himself as footsteps approached the dining room, letting his hands drop to the table.

"Sounds like you two are getting along just fine without me," Isabel said as she entered. "And the food smells so delicious."

She embraced her sister and kissed her on the cheek. Then she made her way over to George.

"My darling, George. I love your name in reverse," Isabel stated as she kissed him on the top of the head.

"And I love you, darling Isabel," George reminder her and rose to retrieve dinner from the oven. Moments later, he returned from the kitchen. He let Rosalina serve them each a square of the cheese-laden dish.

"How is Emilia doing? She should be here tonight. I hope she isn't alone," George commented.

"Mother is well and isn't alone. We aren't a wealthy family, but we always have each other. She has her brothers and sisters," Rosalina said.

"My father wanted us to come to America and prosper," Isabel said as she took a sip of wine. "It didn't seem that would be the case for a long time."

"Yes, then my sister got a cold and now look," Rosalina quipped.

"That cold made me happier than any man alive." George took Isabel's hand. "I love you, *Anna*. I love you both."

Rosalina put her hand to her mouth then smiled, embarrassed, while Isabel appeared not to have heard the mistake. Love makes one blind, *and deaf*, Rosalina reasoned.

November 1983

Though he should have been content, Bobby brooded as he looked at the mangrove swamp from his balcony. Between Cordale Goodman bringing large amounts of drugs into the area and mounting evidence of a prostitution ring run from local hotels, he had his hands full. But he couldn't get Chase Lovell off his mind. The kid rose like a phantom in his dreams then kept him awake at night. The less time he had to work on his case, the more he thought about it in his off hours.

Gwen Thompson opened the glass sliding door to the balcony of Justice's apartment. "Are you coming in, sweetie? The food is ready." Gwen had feathered hair and a double piercing on her left ear that made her look younger than her thirty-two years. But she cooked like somebody who knew her way around a family kitchen.

They'd met earlier in the fall. At some point, she'd helped Bobby get home from the Snappy Turtle. He woke up to find Gwen preparing him a greasy hangover cure breakfast and, later that same day, dinner. They began seeing each other with increasing frequency. Even Jack noted Bobby had a bit more zip in his step and was combing his hair more than once a week.

Bobby didn't turn around. "I'll be there in a minute, baby," he said as he finished his cigarette and extinguished it an ashtray. He had all but given up his quest to lower his blood pressure. If a heart attack took him, he'd have a full stomach and nice view with Gwen sitting across from him and a plate of animal cooked rare. He, like so many others, mistook that self-destructive and indulgent feeling for love.

"Okay, babe," Gwen said as she closed the door back.

Bobby took another moment to look up at the night sky before heading inside. It always put him at ease—the emptiness above.

"You were doing so well with the cigarettes," Gwen said from the kitchen as she watched Bobby approach the dinner table.

"It's just now and then and not every day," Bobby mumbled as he sat down.

"What do you want to drink, hun?" Gwen asked.

"I'll have a beer with a beer chaser," he answered.

"Don't you have to work tomorrow, Bobby?"

Bobby sighed. "No, I've been advised to use up some vacation time in the next couple of months. There's a lot going on, but Chief Curry wants to wait on some operations until after the holidays."

Gwen thought for a moment. "Maybe we can go somewhere and get out of Sandy for a few days."

"If you want to, baby. Pick a spot," Bobby told her, unenthused.

Gwen had made Bobby his favorite—a steak and baked potato with sour cream and chives. She noticed he hadn't eaten anything. "Are you feeling okay, honey?"

"Yes, I'm fine. Why?" Bobby answered.

"You haven't touched your food tonight. I got sirloins too."

"Just haven't had much of an appetite," Bobby said as he pushed the plate away.

"Want to talk about it?"

Bobby didn't answer; he just closed his eyes and rubbed his temples. Fucking Chase Lovell. He couldn't let it go—the feeling of failure around it. That he had made this case personal. What's he doing eating a goddamn steak when there are monsters out in the world abducting children? Gwen's gaze implored him to open up, but he didn't want the feelings surrounding his work to corrupt their relationship. She didn't deserve it. The problem was, he couldn't hide anything from her the way he could with Jack. With Jack, he could just crack a joke and laugh it all off. But she had a radar for feelings.

"If you won't talk about it, can you stop looking so gloomy?" Gwen pleaded.

"Sorry. You don't know what it's like to have this kid's parents look at you and not be able to do a damn thing about it."

"You're doing the best you can. If the parents could see the hours and devotion you put into this, there would be no way they could question you."

"They aren't questioning me. I'm the Lovell's lifeline, and I feel like I've let them down."

Gwen took his hand across the table. "You can't keep beating yourself up this way."

"I'm not giving up on that boy," Bobby said. "Not until someone shows me a body or we find him."

*****

For Thanksgiving, Kate decided she would cook the boys' favorite dishes—tacos with the hard shells from the store, turkey burgers, and potato salad. Todd agreed that at Christmas, they would put presents for both boys under the tree and save them until each would be back to open them.

"It's so hard to enjoy anything, much less the holidays, without them," Kate said as she looked at the home version of Pac-Man she bought for Chase to play on his Atari.

Todd cracked another beer. Kate tried not to object unless the hard stuff came out, but still.

"Can you just wait until after dinner, sweetie?"

"What?"

"You know. I don't want to lose another man around the house."

"Sure, but it's just beer, babe."

"Beer in the day, Seagram's at night."

"Hey, if you've got a problem," Todd said. He knew if he threatened to leave, she would cave. Kate was strong but didn't like to be alone. Especially not now.

"Just be polite, honey."

"I am trying."

"I love you. I don't think I could get up in the morning if you weren't here," Kate said. "Do you want to go visit Hunter this weekend?"

"Yes, I think it's important he knows we want to see him, though it is hard to tell if he gives a crap or not. He acts like he is getting abused if you question him at all. Maybe tough love would work better."

"He's always been awkward that way," Kate said. "You're right, though. But he needs to know we are here for him whether he cares or not."

Todd walked up to Kate and wrapped his arms around her. "We could go pick up your mother on the way back. She should be with us for the holidays."

"I'll call her and see what she wants to do. She may stay for a bit." Kate snuggled into her husband's embrace.

"It's always nice to hear what needs fixing around the house and that I don't do it as well as your father," Todd said, laughing.

Kate also giggled. It was like the old Todd for a moment. Confident but self-effacing. "Oh, she loves you. That's just how she is."

"I know. I'm just teasing," Todd said as he offered a rare smile.

"Babe?" Kate said, risking breaking the good mood. "We can't take care of Hunter unless you take care of yourself."

"I know," Todd said. "I'll do better."

*****

George took Isabel to the beach. November was cool by night—sweater weather. Isabel loved the shore, the smell of the ocean, hunting for sand dollars and shells, then tossing them back into the water. The tides were calm as they walked, the waves occasionally tickling their feet. They carried their sandals, holding hands.

"So, my love, are you ready to head home?" George asked.

"Can we walk just a little while longer?" Isabel requested. "It's such a delightful night."

George smiled. "Of course, we can. We can do whatever you please."

As the two strolled in silence, Isabel was reminded of the books in the grocery checkout. The covers of romance novels that seemed bathed in gauzy light, windswept and perfect. That's how life felt with George now. She'd grown so accustomed to the life George gave her that sometimes she feared it would end soon, like all novels end. But those were books. This was *real.* When George idly squeezed Isabel's hand, it prompted her to speak.

"George? Do you love me?" she asked softly.

"With everything I have," George confessed. "You're the only thing I care about and need."

"You overwhelm me with the things you say." Isabel's voice trembled. "I'm not sure what I did to deserve your admiration."

"We have crossed a lifetime together, and I love you more today than when I first saw you."

"You haven't asked me to marry you in a while."

Isabel looked at George when he chuckled.

"I asked you just last night. In fact, I can't think of a night when I haven't asked."

Isabel stopped walking. George stood in front of her. Their eyes met, then he kissed her on top of her head and smiled.

"I don't think you have asked yet tonight, my darling George."

"The night is not over, my love." George pulled Isabel's hand to his lips and gave it a kiss. "I have until you close your beautiful eyes to fall asleep."

"Ask me right now," Isabel gently commanded.

George let go of her hand to caress her face. "Will you marry me?"

Isabel placed her hand over George's. "Yes. Yes, I will."

She smiled when George pulled her in for a kiss. And even though she couldn't meet the passion in his lips, she still felt like she'd made the right decision.

January 1984

Bobby didn't like staking out the Sand Beach Hotel. Being near the property made him uneasy. He never took up Kerrigan's offer of a nightcap, doubted he ever would. The hotel, like a toxic relationship, had a way of keeping the wrong people around. This time, the department had information several rooms were being used in a prostitution ring. Reports of young Latino girls hired out as escorts, exploited for sex. With Jack, he was running an undercover operation from a van parked by a Stop-N-Go that was within walking distance of the scene.

Jack was jumpy and overly enthusiastic for action. But Bobby, being a veteran detective, knew the patience needed for a stakeout like this.

"Man, I will need some more coffee if it's going to keep dragging like this," Jack said.

"Head home for some shut-eye after your shift. Surveillance may seem like low-effort work, but it does actually tire you out."

"Yeah, I'll grab a burger and beer. Or two. Hey, how come you never drag me to the Snappy Turtle anymore?"

"I'm taking it easy, Jack."

"Never saw you as the moderation type. New Year's resolution?"

"Perhaps. You may want to take it slow too, especially if it has anything to do with Nancy leaving."

"I'm fine. We are working things out."

"Good. Then get that damn camera ready, sunshine. The suspects should be pulling up soon."

Jack grabbed the camera bag. "Don't we have enough pictures? It's time to make a move."

"Jack, I know this is your first stakeout, but can you stop bitching? This is the biggest difference between patrol officers and us. We don't just roll up and bust heads. We investigate. We detect. Hence the title *detectives*. This is what that looks like."

"I get it," Jack said as he attached the telephoto lens to the camera. "You act like I haven't been with you for the past ten months. We have done plenty of investigations."

"This is different from a store robbery or…what we were doing," Bobby grumbled. "Patience is our most important skill here."

"I'm just saying we haven't seen anyone trade for sex yet," Jack mentioned.

"Well, I think it's safe to say by now these aren't the usual hookers giving hand jobs on the street corner for a few dollars, so we aren't going to catch them screwing in the hotel parking lot."

"If I didn't know you, I'd think you didn't want to go in there. You believe that creepy curse stuff?"

"What do you know about that?" Bobby asked.

"Same as everybody. Keeps things fun, you know. Every town needs a haunted house."

"I don't know anything about haunted houses or curses, Jack, but that place does have its demons." Bobby looked at the building. "*That I do understand*," he mumbled under his breath.

"That's a hell of a piece of real estate," Jack said. "No wonder nobody wants to live by it."

"It is a bit lonely in this part of town," Bobby mused.

"So when do we take down some scumbags?" Jack asked.

"Jack, let me explain something."

"Here goes…" Jack sighed.

"This is a more sophisticated operation, and for different reasons. Foremost, it's in neither party's interest to report the other. That's prostitution in general. That's why we wait, document, calculate."

"I always guessed you like *to watch*," Jack said. "I get all that, but when in the hell do we go rattle someone's cage?" Jack pleaded. "I can go knock on the door."

Bobby gathered himself then glanced at his partner. "And say precisely what, Jack? You might get us both killed."

"I was *just saying*, damn," Jack whispered, annoyed.

"You're right, though. We have to find a way into one of those rooms," Bobby stated as he looked toward the hotel through a pair of binoculars.

"I know the bosses can't give us a wiretap on the hotel phones unless we have evidence showing the hotel knows what's happening," Jack surmised.

"I highly doubt they are using those room phones for much anyway. I guess it's possible, though. But again, you're correct about getting a wiretap."

"Too many damn rules made to protect for those breaking them."

"There's nothing illegal about renting rooms to assholes, especially if you don't know they are assholes," Bobby said. "We need to roll one of those Johns once they leave the hotel."

"When? Today? What do you have in mind?"

"All right, you have been snapping that damn camera for a week now. Tell me what's on it?" Bobby turned to Jack. "Give me a rundown."

"Regarding the cars that appear regularly, there is a big goatee-faced dude who drives the silver Ford F-250. The pretty blond drives the white Toyota, and there's a blue Lincoln some guy in a suit drives. Then the red '81 Grand Prix, just an average-looking guy, comes in and out."

"I'd say the last two are Johns," Bobby said.

"The employees park in the back of the hotel. Plus they got those ugly green and red uniforms. Not hard to pick them out," Jack acknowledged.

"No, but one or two may know something," Bobby said.

"Can't we ask the hotel folks who may or may not be regulars around here and who's been staying for the last week or so?"

"Not without the paperwork that says they gotta, which is the whole damn point of what we are doing right now. Plus, what if you ask someone who's in on it? They could tip them off."

Jack sighed. "Got it."

Bobby saw another car pulling into the parking lot. "Look, our goatee guy just pulled in with the blondie. And there are new girls on tap for the day so that the others will be heading back to the gated house."

Jack started taking pictures. "Won't be long before some customers roll in. Few hours maybe. Who wants it this early in the day? I mean, work up an appetite."

"Some are sneaking around, and some…who the fuck knows. Maybe that's just what gets them off."

"There goes whiskers and blond arguing again. What do you think that's all about?"

"Goatee seems to be the guy who delivers the money and probably the primary muscle. I wish we could have gotten into that gated area he went. If I had to guess, that's their base of operations."

"I got a few shots of it when we tailed Whiskers."

"Good, and we know there's more muscle in there guarding the rooms."

"Damn it, just ran out of film. I didn't get a chance to snap a shot of the four girls they brought out."

"I think we've seen them from before. If not, we'll get them whenever they come back out."

"Once they are in that hotel, it's like they vanish."

"They are kept hidden. Remember, these aren't just any girls. They are brought in from other cities to work for a few weeks at a time. Then new ones get sent to replace them. They are like livestock to their handlers."

"Hidden where? How many rooms can they have?"

"From what I see on the hotel pamphlet, they offer a deluxe triple-room suite on the first floor and two-room one on the second." Bobby tossed the brochure to Jack.

"Didn't even think about the rooms connecting," Jack said, flipping through the pages of the pamphlet. "What did you do, just walk in and get one from the desk?"

"Tourist office had them. Live and learn, kiddo. Radio the station and get either Pac or Jonsey to run the plate numbers that we have. Then we can pick out the most likely mark to turn."

"Yes, sir!"

"Happy now?" Bobby asked.

Later that day, Jack dropped Bobby back at the station before returning to the stakeout.

"Captain?" Bobby poked his head into Curry's office after knocking.

"Detective Justice." Captain Curry looked up from a report. "Got an update for me?"

"Yes, sir." Bobby placed several photographs on the captain's desk. "We were able to use a friend at the bureau to help us identify these two. Ricardo and Valentina Nunez," he said, pointing to the suspects.

"They look mean as a pair of pit bulls with their tails tied together. What do you know about them?" the captain queried as he examined the photos.

"Not a lot right now. There isn't much information to find on them, at least not in the States. We don't know if they are married or related at this point, although we have seen them arguing a couple of times, so lean more toward married."

"Are these the two running everything?" the captain asked as he removed his reading glasses.

"Ground level, yes. I would say, definitely running things at the hotel."

"That hotel can't catch a break." The captain shook his head. "I know there are still some lovely homes around there, but outside those one or two decent subdivisions, it's a shady area. But it's right by a beach, so it will always have that going for it, despite its history."

"Perfect location for this crew since they aren't trying to bring any attention to themselves or advertise. It's an invite-only operation, and the Sandy Beach Hotel isn't going to turn away business or ask questions," Bobby explained. "Not right now, with so many chain hotels opening."

"Yeah, but it's like that place lives in an alternate zone of creepiness."

"We can close it down," Bobby said offhandedly.

"You know they tried that," Curry remarked with a chuckle.

"Who?"

"My predecessor."

"So why's it open?"

"No grounds, Detective. Doesn't defy any zoning laws. A developer who was set to buy the property died under mysterious circumstances. The previous captain had a heart attack not long after looking into it. With that in mind, I'm going to let it rest. I like my ticker."

Bobby chuckled. "Well, I see your point, Cap."

"What other leads do you have?" Curry asked.

"We tailed Ricardo here." Bobby showed the captain a picture of a big home. "It's about two hours outside of Sandy down the coast. It's gated and protected."

"So whoever lives there is a much bigger fish than Nunez," Captain Curry clarified.

"Yes, Captain." Bobby spread more photos across the desk. "We ran some of the plate numbers and got some names. These two men have been at the Sandy Beach Hotel consistently. Rueben Jennings, a local landscaper, and I shit you not, an out-of-town lawyer named Peter Bright."

"Did you squeeze one of these gentlemen?"

"Mr. Jennings, the landscaper," Bobby said, pointing him out. "We pulled him over like it was a routine traffic stop. I showed him some photographs then gave some friendly encouragement to get ahead of this before his name was in the news, and with his cooperation, we could help make sure that didn't happen."

"Did he go for it?"

Bobby laughed. "Give Mr. Jennings credit for protecting his self-interest. With a business plus family, he had a lot to lose."

"Great work, Bobby. So did he give us a way to contact these people?"

"Yes, sir. You call and ask for Valentina, and you need to know a code word, which we have now."

The captain pointed at one of the photos. "This her?"

"That's the only Valentina I'm aware of right now, so I'm going to answer yes."

"What's the code phrase?" Captain Curry asked.

"You have to use the words *respect* and *discretion* in a sentence or a variation of those words when prompted."

"Not exactly Morse code, is it?"

"I don't suppose it needs to be," Bobby added.

"No, I suppose not. We will want to make sure Mr. Jennings is kept safe. But now that we have the contact info, it's time to send someone in with a wire. And once money exchanges hands, we'll bust the doors down."

"I'm going to update Jack, and we will keep working it."

"I'll start getting the paperwork typed up and signed."

"Yes, sir, Captain."

After more surveillance, it was decided Officer Alan Jonsey would call the given number and pose as a potential customer. Bobby wanted to do it, but Jonsey was in line to be promoted to detective, and Curry wanted him to get some more experience.

"Okay, Jonsey, are you ready, big guy?" Bobby asked. They were sitting in the station conference room. Bobby had coached him on what to say, but Jonsey still seemed nervous. Bobby considered pulling him off, but Curry reasoned a man calling for illegal sex would probably be nervous as well.

"Ready as I'll ever be," Officer Jonsey responded.

"All right, quiet down, people," Bobby told the room of agents and officers supporting the sting operation before looking to his partner. "Jack, ready to go?" he asked. Jack nodded, his finger hovering over the tape recorder. "Okay, Jonsey, let's make a date."

Alan Jonsey dialed the number, and after a few rings, a woman with a Colombian accent picked up.

"Hello, this is Madame Nunez."

"Can I speak to Valentina?"

"Yes, this is the madame, and who do I have the pleasure of speaking with?"

"I'm Theo Mann."

"How may I be of service, Mr. Mann?"

"I'd like a date to visit your offices and make a donation if possible."

"Mr. Mann, are you from Sandy Beach?"

Bobby shook his head no at Officer Jonsey.

"No, I'm just here on business. A mutual friend gave me your card."

"We are happy you would like to contribute to our business, Mr. Mann. And what did our mutual friend say about us?"

"He had nothing but high admiration for your company's professionalism and good judgment."

"Thank you, Mr. Mann. Any special arrangements you need us to make?"

"I trust your good taste, madame."

"There is an appointment open tomorrow evening at four in the afternoon. Are you free then?"

"Yes, I am."

"Excellent, Mr. Mann. We will send you a welcome package based on your contribution."

"Our acquaintance didn't give me specifics on that. What do you recommend?"

"One hundred dollars for a one-hour visit, and you can always add sums to your account. That's cash."

Bobby holds up two fingers to Jonsey.

"Let's start with two hundred and go from there."

"Excellent, Mr. Mann. Are you familiar with our location?"

"I'm not sure of the office number."

"It's number eight, Mr. Mann. Simply knock on the door, and we will have someone there to arrange everything."

"Thank you, madame," Officer Jonsey said before he hung up.

Bobby gestured for Jack to stop the recording.

"Great job, Alan. That was perfect," he said as he patted the officer on the shoulder.

"Thanks, Detective Justice. I appreciate that."

"One more cherry popped."

"Well," Jonsey said, "there *is* a first for everything."

January 13

After a day of prep, the agents were ready to make their move. At the Sandy Beach Hotel, Officer Pac entered undercover to detain Ms. Kerrigan and inform her of the operation. Pac would later relate that the proprietress, who seemed not to know of the illegal activity, also remained calm as the day's scheduled workers were kept sequestered in the staff room. The police team ran the operation from a rented motel room not far from the Sandy.

"All right, Alan, we can only keep eyes on you until you go inside the room, but we will be listening to the whole time you're in there," Bobby said.

"So I'll be paying the money to the male Nunez…correct? Or to the female who comes in?" Officer Jonsey asked as agents attached a wire around his hip, under the suit he'd gotten married in, which he had dusted off as a disguise.

"I'm sure Ricardo will take the money. But remember, once the pro comes into the room, she has to initiate some type of sexual contact," Bobby explained.

"I'll say *money-time* when things start to happen."

"Okay, as soon as we hear that, we will be knocking the door down," Bobby said.

"Got it. You know that dude isn't going to go quietly," Alan Jonsey speculated.

"We got you covered. We aren't leaving anything to chance," Jack said.

"All right, people, let's get these assholes," Bobby said.

Officer Jonsey drove a rented luxury car to the hotel and parked. Bypassing reception, he knocked on the door to suite 8. It was answered by a large man who fingered his goatee as he looked down on Jonsey.

"And you are?" the big Colombian asked.

"Theo Mann. I have a four o'clock appointment."

"Payment before entry," Nunez said, blocking the doorway.

"Of course, Mr…"

"You pay now or no business."

Officer Jonsey pulled out a billfold.

"Stay in here. I'll bring the girl."

The man left. Jonsey looked around the room. With the cheesy marine motifs, there was nothing sexy here. Sex was the last thing on his mind. *What a place.* Without knocking, Nunez opened the door and, holding her by her arm, drew a girl into the room.

"You like?" he asked.

"She's…" Jonsey caught himself before he said something that might make Nunez suspicious. He'd expected somebody young, but this girl might have well just stepped off a school bus. "She'll be fine. Does she speak English?"

"Only Spanish, but I think this is better for you, my friend," Nunez said, crossing his large arms. "Quiet, unless she's fucking," he said with a deep laugh.

Ricardo Nunez then walked across the room and disappeared through the door to the adjoining suite. The girl looked at Jonesy and shrugged, bored already. Jonsey went to sit down. He knew he should have given the signal, but he had been overcome by a strange feeling. Like he wanted to just fuck it all and go through with it. *Damn the assignment, damn his job.* He sat on the bed. The girl walked over and knelt between his legs, putting her hands on his thighs. Officer Jonsey was sighing as though already in the throes of ecstasy when a cry came from the next room.

"Got damn bitch! You fucked everything!"

There were sounds of a woman screaming while being thrown against a wall and glass breaking.

"Al diablo contigo, bastardo!"

Jonsey snapped from his trance, standing from the bed. "Money-time guys! And we have something going down in the next room!"

More screaming and loud Spanish, then two gunshots rang out.

Jonsey heard the door broken down, then the shouted commands of the SWAT team. He carefully opened the adjoined door to see a woman lying on the floor, shot through the eye, with Nunez standing over her, holding a gun.

"Drop the weapon!" Detective Justice yelled.

Nunez raised his weapon, but Bobby was quicker, dropping him with one shot. Nunez lay squirming on the floor, the gun flung out of his reach.

"Cuff that piece of shit," Bobby said to his backup.

"Fucking pigs!" Ricardo Nunez yelled. "Cerdos! My arm!"

After the dust settled, Valentina Nunez was pronounced dead at the scene. Four teenage girls were escorted out of the hotel along with two clients; and Ricardo Nunez was arrested, along with two other Colombians who were guarding the rooms.

Federal agents held Ricardo Nunez at the hospital and began grilling him after the wound in his arm was cleaned. Meanwhile, inside Greg Curry's office, the captain was conferring with Bobby and Jack.

"So the Johns who were detained. We have the local landscaper who I think my parents used…anyway, and my fave, the lawyer, Mr. Bright, who had a bag so full of sex toys, he could have started a porn shop," Bobby summarized.

"Well done, gentlemen," Captain Curry told Bobby and Jack.

"What about Mr. Nunez?" Jack asked.

"The Feds are going take it from here with him, the underage girls, and will work the gated community angle also. We could assist, but we don't have the manpower to run with that right now, detectives."

"Understood, sir," Bobby responded. "It's out of our backyard, so it's out of our hands."

*****

De'Ron Goodman and Hunter Lovell were eating lunch in the Sandy Juvenile Correctional Facility cafeteria. Sloppy joes with a side of tater tots and vanilla pudding. The food generally wasn't great, but nobody was complaining today. Hunter had given his dessert over, knowing it kept De'Ron happy. He was glad that's all he had to give over, hearing what happened in some other rooms.

"Damn, that is some fucked up shit 'bout yo little bro," Goo-Man said. "I'd help you kill that bitch who took him."

"My parents fucking blame me." Hunter shrugged. "Maybe they're right."

"Fuck that yo. You can't be riding that blame solo," De'Ron said, a finger jabbing at Hunter.

"I don't give a fuck. Maybe we can find that piece of shit when I get out," Hunter said.

"Fo sure, man. Fuck these fake niggas up in here. I need someone I can trust that will have my back."

"You got that right, brother. *I got you no matter what*," Hunter said in an intense tone.

"What yo ass gonna do without me watchin' your back for the next month?"

"You mean not having someone talk my fucking ear off every day?" Hunter said with a grin. "I'll try and manage."

"Fa real, you and that crazy temper you have. I'm surprised all you kilt' so far is a fuckin cat." Goo-Man laughed before polishing off the pudding.

"It's not that bad, is it? I only fucked up that one kid last week because he said something about Chase," Hunter said, glad Goo had taken notice.

"You sure did fuck his world up…another reason you lucky had my ass lookin' out for you."

"That's true, my dawg, but I'll be good till next month, bro."

"I know you gonna be straight, and I'm gonna def make sure I leave the word to make sure of it." De'Ron and Hunter gave each other a fist bump.

"You know, you never did tell me why they call you Goo-Man," Hunter said.

"Big man told me that's how I said Goodman when I was small. Goo-Man. It just stuck, I guess."

"I need a nickname," Hunter said.

"I'm just gonna call ya Killa."

"That works," Hunter said with a nod, mentally appreciating the name.

"Look, when you get up out of here, you know where the shop is. Just leave a number, and I'll get with you."

February 1984

A warm breeze from the sea hit De'Ron as he waited for his ride from the facility. The wind never made it into the courtyard where he worked out. He had forgotten it and the feeling it carried, which somehow made him feel small in the world. But Goo was glad to be out, glad to be free. *That wind had flavor.*

As Cordale Goodman pulled up to the curb, Goo-Man pushed away from the chain-link fence he'd been leaning against.

"Well, well, happy new year, free bird," Cordale told De'Ron as he got in the car. The Monte Carlo's crushed velvet interior felt stupidly luxurious compared to the Naugahyde he had grown accustomed to inside.

De'Ron clapped hands with Cordale. "What up, my blood?"

"It's good. You straight?"

"Hell yes, '84 goin' be lots better. Especially now I'm out that fuckin' bitch."

"How's the ass? Still tight, I hope?" Cordale stole a glance at Goo-Man as he turned out of the facility.

"Oh, hell, nah!" Goo-Man said with a laugh. "Didn't no one fuck with me in there."

"Aight, gangsta. Look, you did good keeping quiet," Cordale said in a forgiving manner. "And if yo knucklehead ass gets caught again, you better keep extra quiet then too."

"That shit ain't happening again. Believe dat!" De'Ron proclaimed.

"Yeah, lil nigga. Watch me hold my breath."

"Fa real though!" said Goo.

Cordale snickered. "Aight then, we'll see."

"So what's like the plan an shit? We still gonna run things like before?" Goo-Man asked.

"Look, you need to lay low right now," Cordale instructed while lighting up a cigarette at a red light. "Because for one, that motherfucking Detective Justice is still watching, and he got a partner now."

"Fuck that dumb pig."

"Caught yo knucklehead ass, didn't he?" Cordale said matter-of-factly as he turned his gaze from Goo-Man back to the light turning green. "He got a job to do, and he works hard at it. They just pulled off a big bust at that hotel."

"Busted who?"

"Some midlevel sex trafficker. Too bad. It could have brought some business our way."

"We should just take care of his cop ass and be done with it."

"Good lawd, you scare the hell out of my black ass. Kill a cop, nigga?" Cordale threw his cigarette butt out the window. "What kind of heat you think comes with that? That's an endgame, leaving town play, homey. Put that shit out yo head now."

De'Ron shook his head, feeling like he couldn't say anything without Cordale tearing him down. Couldn't he just let him have his day? "Fuck, bro, look, just tell me what you need me to do."

"You need to get a regular job for the time being. Then I'm gonna have some work for you."

"What the fuck?" De'Ron turned to look at Cordale. "What I do *is* a regular job, far as I'm concerned."

"Naw, I mean *regular* regular."

"What's that?"

"The one I get for yo ungrateful lil ass. That one," Cordale said, sounding annoyed. "It's just till I get shit straight with your probation officer. Which is the main reason for keeping it cool for a minute."

"Aight, I'm good with dat."

"Fuck, I guess you are, nigga. Shit," Cordale told De'Ron with a cross look on his face. "Hadn't even got home yet, and you done got my blood pressure up."

"Damn, I was just sayin' I got ya. Fuck," Goo-Man said, looking out the window at the blur of trees flying by. The man sure had a good way of ruining a ride on a sunny afternoon.

A couple of weeks later, once De'Ron had gotten accustomed to his freedom and even found some time to be bored, he headed to the auto shop to speak with Cordale about the job. Goo-Man gave a quick knock on Cardale's office door then walked in and sat down.

"What ya got for me, big man?" Goo-Man asked.

"I got you a position at that little diner by the Sandy Beach Hotel," Cordale said. "They gonna have you washing dishes."

"Dishwasher?" Goo-Man spat out the word as though it were a curse. "That ain't no position. That's bitch work. I don't want to be cleanin' no fuckin' dishes."

"What the fuck you think you was gonna get? Manager?" Cordale asked, exasperated.

"Damn, dawg." Goo-Man raised his hands. "Why can't I work here? Or a store selling Adidas or some such? Fuck some nasty ass dishes."

"Because this is the job I got for you," Cordale said, writing down the name of the manager De'Ron would need to see. "Besides, it's only for a goddamn minute."

"Which diner did you say?" Goo-Man asked.

"I didn't. I want to know we're good first."

"Yeah, we good."

"Surf Side Diner. Burger and seafood joint." Cordale handed De'Ron a sticky note with the address on it. "Ask for that manager when you get there."

"I need a ride," Goo-Man stated, as though still negotiating.

"Spoiled ass lil nigga." Cordale threw a set of keys on the desk. "Take the truck. You payin' for the gas."

"So when do I start?"

"Tomorrow."

*****

Bisbee, Arizona

"I want to call my mom and dad! I hate you!" Chase Lovell yelled inside the live-in RV. If there were anybody around, they would have thought it a family spat. But only the desert, with its vast desolation, its dry empty air, was witness to the conflict. During that argument, Chase felt his voice had deepened just a bit. He knew he could shout without getting hit—that Lee Earl, despite being violent, was lazy enough to let him get away with talking back.

"I am tired of hearing that shit!" Lee Earl Elwood yelled as he grabbed a beer and slammed the refrigerator door shut. "How many goddamn times do I have to remind you they don't want you!"

"You lie about everything!" Chase screamed, as though his voice could obliterate the man who thought he was his father. "I don't believe anything you say!"

"Eight months of you bitching and moaning. I'm about ready to throw your ass in a ditch somewhere."

Lee spat in the sink before he took a sip of beer and a deep breath. He knew it wasn't the boy he was mad at. He was mad at himself for keeping the kid around, for his whole stupid plan. But now he couldn't turn back.

"Do it! You always say you will, so do it!" Chase kicked the coffee table, upending it, causing Scooby to bark.

"You act like you got it so damn hard," Lee Earl said. "All you have to do is pick up the packages I tell you to and hand over the packages I tell you to then shut the fuck up and watch TV."

"I fucking hate this place," Chase cried, sounding like he was giving up the fight. He usually did.

"Stop acting like it's the fucking end of the fucking world," Lee Earl said then pointed to the dog. "And quiet that little rat-looking son of a bitch up."

Chase sat by Scooby and took the dog's head in his lap, calming him. This incited Lee Earl for a reason he couldn't identify.

"Go ahead," he said, a hard cruelty in his voice. "I dare you to call them. See what happens. All the dirty things you done? They'll just give you to someone else. And they aren't gonna let you take Scooby with you. That's how it works."

Chase picked Scooby up and pulled him close. "Why? He's mine."

"I don't know why, shit-for-brains. That's how it is. Now tell me something. So we don't have any more fuckups. When someone asks, what do you say your name is?"

"Chase."

"Son, one more chance," Lee Earl said fiercely. "What's your name?"

"It's Chase!"

Lee Earl threw his beer to the floor then grabbed Scooby by the scruff of the neck and tossed him hard against the wall. Scooby squealed in pain, but he landed on his feet. Lee Earl got Chase in his grips and squeezed his cheeks, forcing him to look him in the eye.

"Your name is Alex Adams, and you're from Tucson, Arizona. Repeat it." Lee Earl squeezed Chase's face harder. Chase cried, and Lee Earl loosened his grip so the boy could speak.

"My name is Alex Adams," he sniffled. "And I'm from Tucson, Arizona."

"I'm Eugene Adams, and I'm your dad. I'm a security guard."

"You're Eugene Adams, and you're my dad. You're a security guard."

Lee Earl let go of Chase's cheeks. "See, that wasn't so hard now, was it?" He collected Scooby and held him tightly, letting the boy know he had total control over the pup's life or death. One wrong word… "Now let me hear it again."

"My name is Alex Adams, and I'm from Arizona. You're Eugene Adams, and you're my dad. You're a security guard."

"Again."

March 1984

Bobby didn't know how the fight started. Something he failed to respond to that Gwen said, something she thought was important. True, she had put forth that she wanted to move in together, so perhaps that wasn't the best comment to ignore. It wasn't their first fight, but it was their worst. It had started with reasonable debate but ended with her unfavorably comparing his disposition to that of a drunken hermit crab, then throwing a bottle of whiskey that shattered over his head. As such, Bobby showed up at the Snappy Turtle smelling of hard liquor. Wanda wouldn't pour him another drink until he proved his story by combing shards of glass from his hair. He felt bad about Gwen, but at the same time, she didn't care for the trouble or burden on his emotions.

The thing was, he knew she was right. He was resisting her. Having people meant losing people. It was simple as that. He didn't need a VA counselor to tell him he was afraid of losing another person. The more he needed them, the less he wanted them around. The whiskey never failed him, though. He nodded when Wanda threw a look at his empty glass.

"Hey, bud. Glad I found you." A hand landed on his shoulder.

"Mayor," Bobby said. He had always liked the mayor. Bailey Reed was from one of Sandy Beach's older, better families but didn't put on airs. He was elected time and again because he was just like the rest of the people of the town, meaning not afraid to tie one on in public or forward an unpopular opinion.

They exchanged pleasantries. Bobby thought that would be the extent of the conversation and was happy for it. Then the subject of the Sandy came up. Any other night, Bobby would have begged off. But now he welcomed the distraction, the way kids like cartoons when their parents fight.

"Okay, let's hear it," Bobby said, ordering some clams to coat his belly.

"You see," the mayor said, eyes gleaming. "What people don't know, or what they do know and don't want to acknowledge, is that it's an artifact of our history. And Sandy Beach's history, well, it hasn't always been pretty."

"If you're going to start on some curse…"

"No, now hear me out, Bobby."

"Do I have a choice?"

"Forget the curse stuff for now. But it's a fact that the hotel was built on the blood of a crime committed almost a century ago."

"Here it comes." Bobby grumbled before downing his bourbon. "Wanda! I'll need another before hearing this," he said, holding up his bare glass while thinking of Gwen. *At least their conversations dealt with reality even when drinking.*

The mayor chuckled. "Look, long and short, two innocent women were killed, with one being hung by her neck after the fact, no less, for reasons only a raging mob can explain."

"That's the thing about mobs, Mayor. Their actions do all the explaining."

"Well, nobody paid, and interest has accrued. That's not a curse. It's just a fact."

"You're speculating, what, that the place is haunted?"

"Look, don't get me wrong. I'm no hysteric. And I don't believe in ghosts, but I do believe in bad energy. Any weatherman will tell you about the power of things not visible to the eye."

"Fair enough, Mayor. But a hurricane didn't cause Ricardo Nunez to shoot his wife or exploit immigrants, nor did it cause Bartholomew Payne to do what he did."

"Payne…now there's a real topic of conversation."

"Mayor, if you don't mind…"

"Okay, okay, I get it. You deserve your time away from the job. You're doing a hell of one, I don't mind saying."

"Thanks," Bobby said.

"I'm just saying, if any of this needles you, check in again with me."

"I'll just do that, Mayor."

"All right then. Enjoy your clams, Bobby."

The next day, Detectives Bobby Justice and Jack Cutler were at the station doing a roundup of open cases. Bobby was glad to have put the prostitution ring behind them.

"So De'Ron Goodman, aka Goo-Man, is working where now?" Jack asked.

Bobby looked up from a witness statement toward Jack. "At the seafood diner near our favorite hotel." The detective shook his head at the thought of De'Ron working a regular job.

"Sorta seems like a variation of bullshit to me."

Jack nodded in agreement. "Placate the probation officer, right?"

"That's the safe bet," Bobby agreed. "Even though I don't think placating people is generally Cordale's style, but he's smart and slick enough."

Jack thought for a moment. "How are CG and Goo related?"

"I can only tell you that Cordale is not his real father, but he raised the boy," Bobby said as he sat back in his chair, recalling what little he knew of two Goodmans. "If I had to guess, I'd say he is De'Ron's uncle but is possibly his older brother, depending on sleeping arrangements."

"Bang-up job raising him, I see," Jack said.

"He has no school records—none. That life he has with CG is all he knows."

"Damn, that's a cryin' shame."

"Yeah, well, don't forget, that boy is dangerous," Bobby reminded Jack.

"Where's his mother?"

"Dead, if I'm to speculate. In any case, she has never been around. You can draw your conclusions on that one," Bobby declared.

"You think Cordale Goodman did something to her?"

"I don't know, Jack. I'm sure either directly or indirectly, he did, yes, but it's not something I've looked heavily at. Throw a theory at me, and I'll say it's possible."

"I got you."

"Speaking of dangerous, the older Lovell boy gets out of the correctional facility today," Bobby mentioned.

"Killed a cat, right?" Cutler replied. "Tick said there was barely anything left."

"Its head was pulverized," Bobby recalled. "Tickerrman told me its collar was just sitting there in a pool of blood and bone."

"As if his parents don't have enough to deal with," Jack stated.

"Don't remind me. Every lead on Elwood has dried up. We don't have squat."

"We could recirculate their pictures. Maybe we can look at putting a reward out," Jack said.

"Rewards have a way of turning every batshit crazy person into an eyewitness," Bobby said, frustrated. "Plus, who's fronting the money for it? The Lovells don't have a pot to piss in."

"Gotta save up for Hunter's misdeeds," Jack joked.

"Let's hope not. All the same, I'll keep him on my radar," Bobby said.

"It just feels like doing something is better than doing nothing."

"I agree with you. Yet until we have some credible evidence as to where he is, we would be spinning our wheels. Remember, this grub worm is not even from Florida. He's got roots going back to Albuquerque and Texas."

"Yeah, well, why do they call it the long arm of the law if it doesn't reach that far?" Jack said. All Bobby could do was shrug and keep thumbing through the paperwork.

*****

Todd and Kate picked Hunter from the correctional facility, waiting in the station wagon for him to appear through the gate.

"Don't be nervous," Todd said, taking her hand. "It's only been five months."

"You're nervous too," Kate said. When the gate opened, Kate gasped at how her boy had grown. He looked leaner, walked more rigidly, less like the child she missed so much. Hunter got in the back seat and simply nodded at his parents. They hadn't hugged, but nobody called attention to that.

While driving back home, Kate decided they should stop to get some food. She had planned on macaroni but suddenly didn't have the energy to cook.

"Why are we stopping? Can't we just go home?" Hunter asked.

"Well, we haven't done anything as a family for a while," Kate said. "It will be like a celebration."

"What's to celebrate?"

"You, sweetheart," Kate said. She meant it, but it somehow sounded insincere to her ears.

"Why this place?" Hunter groaned.

"Have you been here before?" Todd asked.

"No," Todd's eldest son replied.

"Then why you judging it so quickly?"

"Because it looks old and nasty. Looks like the kind of place old folks go."

"Well, we're old folks now," Kate said. "Worrying turned us old."

"It's been around a long time, which means the catfish and burgers are done right," Todd said, hoping to cut off any argument.

"Means the food's *old* too," Hunter sniped.

"You'd think after being in an institution, you'd want some good home cooking," Kate said.

"This ain't home, and the food wasn't all that bad," Hunter replied.

Despite his protestations, Hunter followed his parents into the restaurant. After being seated and skimming the menus, a waitress approached their table.

"Hi," she said. "My name is Tara, and I'll be your server today. What would you like to drink?"

"Sweet tea," Kate said.

"Same," said Todd, looking her over. Kate hit him on the shoulder, as if to say, "Jail bait."

Hunter glared at the waitress from behind his menu. "Cola," he finally answered.

"Okay," Tara said, still smiling. "And are you all ready to order?"

"Not just yet," Kate said. As Tara walked off, Hunter's gaze followed her. Todd gave his son a smile, glad he was interested. To heck with Kate.

"Don't be starin' at that girl like dat!"

Hunter startled at the voice of Goo-Man grinning down at him.

"Oh shit. You scared the crap out of me," Hunter said. "What's up?"

"That's Tara." Goo-Man looked over his shoulder to the waitress. "She fine as hell too, huh?" Goo stood there, looking almost proud of his food-stained worker's smock.

"Um, De'Ron, these are my parents," Hunter said, ignoring his friend's comment.

"What up?" Goo-Man said. Todd stared at the boy while Kate gave him a nervous smile.

"So you working here now?" Hunter asked.

"Yeah, dawg. I *run things* in the back room."

"Dishwasher!" a voice called from the doorway of the kitchen.

"Aw, shit. I gotta' go, man. Look, you know where I am. Come find me and we can hook up," Goo stated.

"Aight, my dawg," Hunter replied.

"Later, bro," Goo said, heading back toward the kitchen. Only then when Goo showed up did Hunter realize he had picked up on his friend's speech patterns. It was like they had a different language that bonded them. This pleased Hunter.

"Hunter, who was that?" Kate asked, leaning in, her face creased with concern.

"A friend, yo," Hunter answered.

"Yo?" Kate asked, looking puzzled.

*****

Hunter met De'Ron at the arcade a week after seeing him at the Surf Side Diner. Goo was playing Pac-Man while Hunter stood watching over his shoulder.

"Goo-Man playing Pac-Man, huh?" Hunter joked.

"Mr. Comedian over here," Goo responded.

"The only good part's when they turn to ghosts," Hunter said.

"You probably like Ms. Pac-Man," Goo said. Hunter shrugged.

"You still at the diner or what, bro?" Hunter asked.

De'Ron chuckled. "No. Why?"

"I stopped by there," Hunter admitted.

"I'm sure yo big ass did, and I'm pretty sure it wasn't for me," Good-Man said, his eyes still studying the screen.

"Whatever, bro," Hunter mumbled as he watched De'Ron play. "So you quit?"

"Nah, that fine ho got me fired."

"What? For real, bro?" Hunter asked, his brow arching.

"Yeah, man. Fuck that bitch."

"What happened?" Hunter asked.

"Just got me a little feel, was all. She was actin' like she didn't want me to."

"Fuckin' bitches, man. They piss me off!"

"Aw, damn, little ass nigga ghost," Goo-Man said as he slapped the side of the game console. He turned to Hunter. "Man, why they always be pissing you off?"

"Because they just—" Hunter shook his head. "They avoid me for no reason and act all stuck up because they have a damn pussy."

"Da fuck!" Goo-Man tilted his head sideways with a grin. "Calm down there, big dawg. I got something for her little ass," Goo-Man declared, grabbing his crotch.

"Fucking right." Hunter nodded.

"It's probably what you need, bro," Goo-Man said. "Get ya cherry popped. Might calm yo ass down some, nigga."

"Maybe you right, bro. So you looking for another job or what?"

"Man, that shit was just a front anyway." Goo-Man swatted his hand sideways. "Big blood got shit straight with my probation officer and has some real work for me."

"Oh, no shit."

"Yeah, my bro. I'm takin' a ride with one of the main guys to bring some of that good shit to a seller. I got to have my guy's back in case any crazy shit goes down."

"Where?" Hunter asked.

"It's called like Frisbee or Butbee something. Fuck, I don't even know, bro. I'm just ridin' and be ready if needed."

"Frisbee?" Hunter repeated. "Well, fuck, man. Let's hook up when you get back. I think you're right about the cherry thing."

"For sure, my brother," Goo-Man said, laughing.

*****

Bisbee, Arizona

Chase played with a limp fry from the takeaway burger fun box Lee Earl had bought him for dinner. He imagined it was a caterpillar or inchworm hanging from his fingertips, trying to dip its mouth into a ketchup pond.

"Either eat that or toss it in the trash," Lee Earl told him. "I don't want no more stains on this interior. We're clean people here. Not animals."

Before Chase could answer, a white van pulled up to where they were parked on a dirt road that led off into the desert. "Okay, put that food down and come on."

D-Dog, one of Cordale Goodman's men, and De'Ron Goodman got out of the truck. Both had the butts of handguns sticking from their belts.

"What's the guns about, guys?" Lee Earl asked. "I mean, we're all friends on the same team here, aren't we?"

"You got our money?" D-Dog said, looking at Lee Earl. "Ben Franklin's only teammate standing between you and this," he said while stroking grip of the gun with his fingers.

"Don't I always?" Lee Earl shook his head. "You boys never wanna trust the White man."

D-Dog waved him over. "It ain't about White. It's about green. Bring it here."

"Here, Alex," Lee Earl said, looking to Chase. "Bring the nice man that money."

Chase grabbed the bag from Lee Earl and walked it over to D-Dog.

"Talkin' about trust, and you got a kid doin' this shit. Fuck you," D-Dog declared as he counted what was in the bag. He then pointed his thumb to Goo-Man, who opened the van's back doors.

"Come on, Alex," Lee Earl said to Chase. "Those packages ain't gonna carry themselves."

"You fuckin' kidding me, old man?" Goo-Man let out. "I ought to shoot yo ass just for that."

"What the fuck is your problem!" Lee Earl yelled.

"You lucky yo ass be making money for us." Goo-Man pointed the gun at Lee Earl, who instinctively raised his hands, then chuckled. It was like the old West.

"Goo, give me the gun," D-Dog said, holding forth his hand. "Help the little White nigga out. We not trying to be here all fucking day."

"Fa sure," Goo-Man grumbled as he handed D-Dog the gun. "Sup, little man?" he said to Chase before grabbing a few packages from the truck. He leveled his gaze at Lee Earl as he walked past him.

"What? Can't a man take precautions? Never know who's watching," Lee Earl said, referring to the boy.

"Word. It's just this seems a little light." D-Dog held up the bag.

"Don't start that shit with me." Lee Earl pointed at D-Dog. "I have an agreement with the big man. Ask 'em if it makes you feel better."

"Oh, I will," D-Dog responded.

De'Ron and Chase each threw their last package in the truck.

"Either way," D-Dog said to Lee Earl. "I'll be seeing you soon."

"Can't fucking wait," Lee Earl uttered, and he looked to Chase. "Come on, Alex."

Everyone returned to their respective vehicles.

"I should whoop his ass," Goo-Man said, his eyes fixed on Lee Earl.

"Somehow, I think it's been whooped plenty," D-Dog said as he started the engine. "Trust me, this boy ain't learned shit since last time."

"Yeah, well, some people just need an extra helping."

*****

Lee Earl and Chase got back in the van. Chase suddenly wished he hadn't guzzled his entire Coke with dinner. "I'm thirsty," he said. He flinched when Lee Earl tossed a water bottle at him. "This is hot!" Chase cried out, though his real offence came from being pelted with the bottle.

"Well, aren't you just a fucking bright one?" Lee Earl said. "Either drink that or shut the fuck up until we get home. Then when we do, you can continue to shut the fuck up."

April 1984
April 13

Hunter was waiting by his house's front window for De'Ron Goodman. Getting out, away from his parents, would make him feel better, and Goo was like a lightning rod for excitement. Even his Atari bored him these days. Kid's stuff.

The shiny new truck Goo showed up in set the mood. It was a candy-apple red GMC, lights on the top. "Bro, your new wheels are fucking awesome," Hunter said as he circled the vehicle, checking out the rims and personalized license plate that read *187 MAN*.

"Damn right. No askin' for fuckin' permission to ride some fuckin' where," Goo confirmed, sporting the kind of parachute pants Hunter had seen on MTV.

"That a custom license plate?" Hunter asked.

"Yeah, man. Something D-Dog told me 'bout' in the Cali area. I thought it was tight," De'Ron explained.

"Dude, I'm so pumped to take it for a spin."

"Patience, bro. It's still is kinda early yet." Goo knew Hunter was talking about their plan to get some action. "Imma hook you up, Killa."

"Don't you have all kinda girls after you? Why don't we just get one of them," Hunter asked.

"Yeah, but fuck all that tonight. I don't have my own crib yet. Besides, I don't want you fallin' for some bitch that hangs out with us at big man's castle because it's your first time getting some snatch. We gone do this quick and easy," De'Ron explained.

Hunter laughed. Goo made it sound like going to the dentist, except fun. "All right then, you sure you can get us a room, or you too broke now?"

"Yes, nigga." Goo-Man held up a roll of cash. "I can get a room for yo ass!"

Hunter's eyes widened. "Fuck, I need to work with you!"

"Down the road fa sure. You have to meet the big man first."

"I'm ready whenever you say."

De'Ron gestured toward Hunter's house. "They ain't gonna come lookin' for ya, huh? I ain't in no kinda mood for fuckin' parents, especially when I'm 'bout to get my dick sucked."

"They won't even notice I'm gone. And if they do, fuck it. I'm already the black sheep."

A few hours later, De'Ron and Hunter arrived at the Sandy Beach Hotel. De'Ron used a fake ID to check in.

"Okay, Mr. Jones, here is your key, and it's room number two," Sally Bilbo, the front desk clerk, said.

"What yo cute ass doin' later?" De'Ron asked Sally as he tucked the ID back inside his wallet.

Sally, a blond the age of Hunter's younger teachers, looked up. Hunter wondered how far Goo would push it. "Um, I'll be working late, sir," she responded.

De'Ron laughed. "Well, how late does that be, because I'll be here all night, sugar. You can be sho the bed is comfortable. A place to rest your head, if you know what I mean."

The clerk smiled.

"Come on, Goo. Let's get the room," Hunter said. Goo gave him a harsh look for using his name then turned back to the clerk.

"Have a nice night Ms. Sally."

"Have a nice night, sir," Sally Bilbo said.

An hour later, both boys were kicked back on the bed, smoking a joint, sipping from the case of wine coolers they'd brought. Hunter thought they might just let their plan slide. The hotel had a soft porn channel, and the joint relaxed him. But no, the urge was too strong, and he knew Goo-Man could make it happen.

"So how's this work? They just come here?" Hunter asked.

"Damn, you gots to pay the bitch first. But yes, stop fussing. You pussying out?"

"I'm not, man. Just checking," Hunter grumbled.

Goo-Man chuckled. "Checkin' for the damn hundredth time."

Hunter gave Goo a playful shove. "Whatever, bro."

De'Ron shoved him back. "I just gotta make sure you don't get mad and scare the damn hoe off."

"Well, she best not give me a reason," Hunter said, laughing. He like the idea of having somebody there he could tell what to do. Whom he could decide to punish, like his parents punished him.

"You a damn killa," Goo cracked.

"You know, man, what I always wanted to ask? Why weren't you tougher on me in juvie? You could have made it really rough for me."

"I don't know, bruh. You was the new cat, and I just wanted to see what yo ass what was about first. Turn't out, we a lot alike."

"I'm glad you did. You the only person I got left," Hunter said. The pot made his mind loose, detached from his words. But there was something else. An energy that gathered in his gut. That wanted to be felt in the world. He suddenly wanted to strike out, at anything, but instead he took another drag, tamping the feeling down.

"Damn…that's fucked," Goo responded. "Maybe I just felt sorry for your ass."

"Maybe so, but if someone fucks with you, they are going to have to fuck with me. I still think about that bitch at the diner getting you fired."

"I feel ya, bro. Bitch did me a favor though really."

"Hey, why in the hell did you choose this cursed-ass fucking place?" Hunter said.

"Where the fuck you think we was gonna go, muthafucka? The Ritz?" De'Ron said as he grabbed another bottle. "Plus, they don't be looking too close at who checks in round here."

"Fuck, this place is old as hell." Hunter looked around the room.

"I brought you here to get yo dick wet, bro. So stop worrying 'bout what the walls look like because a ho sho ain't. They just goin' to worry 'bout that cash, and then they just gonna look at the ceiling or the pillow, the way I see it." Goo threw a hundred-dollar bill on the bed.

"Fuck…can I just keep a hundred and just wet my own dick by myself?"

"No, goddamn it. This shit is happenin'! Something goin' bump in the night, and that something you!" Goo proclaimed.

"For sure. Still, I know some bad shit went down here recently," Hunter recalled.

"Sure the fuck did. Some hoe was shot or some such shit. Maybe in this very room. Hey, what's that stain?"

"Aw, stop fucking with me." Hunter was giddy now. "That's wild, but I know more than that has happened at this joint. It's, like, historical."

"Yeah, that be like forever ago. Yeah, some shady shit went down…always different stories."

"I believe 'em," Hunter said.

Goo nodded in agreement. "Fa sure. Got to believe in history."

"Hey, how was the run to Butbee?"

"Shit was a trip, dawg. Almost had to knock some nigga out. Not even lying. He lucky I didn't."

"No, shit? That's awesome." Hunter laughed. "Why didn't you?"

"D-Dog held me back, bruh. That's the only reason."

Hunter got up from the bed. He felt the energy circulating in his limbs, in some savage third arm that had a mind of its own, like when he killed that cat.

"You know how Jabba the Hutt had Leia on a chain? That's how I'm going to have every bitch in this city."

"Man, we smoking the same shit? You're higher than the space shuttle," said Goo.

"What if the hotel hallways were like the Pac-Man maze, and there are ghosts coming after us?" Hunter said, laughing.

"Holy shit, you trippin'."

"Fucking ghosts, jumpin' in us, pulling us down."

"No more for you, Killa."

"Fuck that. When's this going down?"

"Patience. We got all night. I just gotta make some calls, Killa."

"Hmm. Let's go get some food first," Hunter suggested. "Because we're going to need it. Tonight's gonna be my first."

"Aight, nigga. You got someplace in mind?"

"I do," Hunter replied.

*****

The next morning, Kate told Todd to forget about waiting for Hunter and go to work. Things could only fall apart only so much, she thought, as she flipped through unpaid bills. The school had finally stopped sending reminders about Chase's summer school possibilities, at least there was that. And Hunter…she guiltily wondered if he hadn't been better off in state care. At least they could control him. As if summoned by her thought, the boy burst through the front door.

"There you are! Gosh, dang it!" Kate said, placing one hand on her hip and pointing her finger at him accusingly with the other. For some reason, he had no shirt on. "Why do I even bother with you?"

Hunter shrugged. "I don't know. You tell me. Why do you?"

"Because I'm your mother!"

"Great. Can I go to my room now?"

"Hunter, where were you?" she asked. "And what happened to your shirt?"

"What difference does it make?" Hunter said, agitated. "I spilled something on it."

"Tell me where you were, Hunter!" Kate shouted.

"Out with a friend!" Hunter shouted back. "I can't be locked up in this fucking house all the time!"

"Hunter." Kate took a deep breath. "You're sixteen now, and you have to start being more responsible."

"I'm so sorry I'm such a disappointment to you."

"Hunter, don't try and turn this back on me," Kate said as she took a few deep breaths to calm herself. "I was worried about you."

"Yeah, you look *so* worried," Hunter replied. "You're just yelling as usual."

"Well, I am very much worried, and don't act like I don't have reason to be upset."

"Bullshit!"

"Hunter! Stop! You can't speak to me that way."

"I can take care of myself."

"Can you? You just got out of the correctional facility last month, and you're already on a path to head back."

"Why? Because I went out with a friend?"

"Speaking of, who is this friend of yours? What's his name?" Kate asked.

"Goo."

"Seriously, Hunter?" Kate rolled her eyes. "What is his *real* name?"

"That is his real name!" Hunter said loudly.

"I don't trust anybody with that kind of name. You haven't even finished the hundred hours of community service you were given as part of your release."

"I only have fifty hours left, and I did some time yesterday."

"You should have been finished already. It was your idea to take a bus instead of letting me take you. Every time I trust you to do the right thing."

"I just fucking said I'm almost done," Hunter spat.

"It doesn't matter now that your school isn't letting you back in this year. And you know the agreement. It's going to double your community service hours unless we show them you're getting homeschooled."

"They don't want me back at that school anyway."

"I have to start going to work again, Hunter. I can only take so much leave."

"Fuck school. I'd rather just work anyway," Hunter said. *Work with Goo.*

"You belong in school, but you can speak with your father about all this when he gets home."

"Fine. I'm surprised y'all even noticed I was gone."

"Why wouldn't we notice, Hunter?"

"Y'all don't even notice anything else about me."

"I'm tired, Hunter. I don't want to fight with you anymore."

"I'm fine, Ma. Don't worry," Hunter said as he went to his room.

"*All I do is worry,*" Kate whispered to herself.

*****

With schools in the north going on spring break, The Sandy had filled up a bit. Sandy Beach didn't get the college traffic of Daytona or even Sarasota, but sometimes families passed through or decided to see a less touristed part of the state. A small portion knew the Sandy by reputation, and now that it reopened, they wanted the thrill of staying in the notorious hotel. The new chambermaids were kept busy but still had the luxury to leave a room or two unturned for some days as they attended to other work. Elena, a Guatemalan who had replaced Isabel, was attending to the breakfast room, refilling cereal and bread for toast, when Ms. Kerrigan called her over the walkie-talkie system. The sudden appearance of a voice still made her jump. In the Sandy, you never knew.

"Elena," the hotel's manager radioed. "Elena, come in."

"Yes, ma'am," Elena replied.

"Can you check room six, please? Guests in adjoining rooms are complaining of a bad smell."

"Yes, ma'am, but I didn't think we had anyone in room six recently."

"Yeah, we try not to rent it out, and I don't have anything recent on the register. Maybe one of the maintenance men had lunch there and left something in the garbage."

"I'll go now," she said, dreading the nauseating smell of old clam shells.

"Thank you, Elena."

Several minutes later, Elena was running down the corridor in a panic. She brushed past a guest and only stopped when she found her boss in the lobby.

"Ms. Kerrigan! Necesito tu telefono! I need your phone!"

"Elena, what's happened?" Ms. Kerrigan asked coolly.

"Muerto. It is a dead one, Ms. Kerrigan. Un cadáver."

"Okay, keep your voice down," Ms. Kerrigan said. "These things happen. Now go have a seat and let me take care of this. It's important that you let me do it, Elena."

"Okay, thank you." Elena went and sat in the chair across from the desk. She was glad Ms. Kerrigan would handle the matter, but she also wondered why her boss didn't seem concerned. Maybe pills, Elena considered. She saw a girl there, splayed and unmoving like somebody tore a starfish down the middle. Naked, looking somehow more naked in death. *Violated.* Elena never wanted to smell that smell or see that sight again. She put her head in her hands to cry then blew her nose.

*****

Another one, another missing kid. This one was older, a girl. Her name was Tara Hill. Bobby was convinced they had just found her—the girl whose picture he had on his desk—though they had no confirmation yet. The family would ID the body later. Bobby swore to himself.

The detective was just about to grill the medical examiner when Captain Curry showed up. Guests still came and went, studiously ignoring the police at work. Nobody wanted their vacation ruined.

"Detective!" Captain Greg Curry yelled out.

"Yes, sir," Bobby said, turning to face Captain Curry.

"Give me the rundown."

"I'll start at the top, Captain. Officer Jonsey arrived at the scene at eight thirty this morning after responding to a 911 call then waited for backup. Officer Tickerrman followed fifteen minutes later. They performed an initial walkthrough of the scene for evidence. Then they secured the perimeters and determined that the entire crime scene was inside room six of the hotel. Detectives Cutler and I arrived on the scene at approximately nine fifteen. I then called for forensics. Once Jeff and his team came, we canvassed the area but were unable to produce any witnesses. Detective Cutler is currently with the manager, getting all the names of guest who checked in over the past month."

"It shouldn't be too long a list," Curry said in a droll tone.

"Detective Cutler spoke with Elena Guzman, the maid who found the body. I have officers Pac, Jonsey, and Tickerrman interviewing staff members currently here, which includes the owner who made the 911 call plus all other managers, clerks, maids, and custodians. *Especially*," Bobby mumbled. "And we are also working on getting the names of all the other employees not working today."

"Have you spoken with Webb yet?"

"I was on my way to do that now."

Detective Justice and Captain Curry made their way to the room to speak with Jeff Webb, MD.

"Just a brutal assault," Justice posited. The words were easy to say, but the girl's body, splayed there, eyes bulged out grotesquely like a pug dog, defied any label.

"I will need to do the autopsy before I can confirm anything," Webb stated matter-of-factly. Bobby always wondered if Webb dipped into the hospital sedatives. How can you keep that kind of calm around so much death?

"Yes, Dr. Webb. Just give us your impressions of what you have. We're not here to hold your feet to the fire," Curry remarked.

"Initial guess is the body has been here for about a week. I see indications that the victim was forcibly held down. I strongly believe the body was moved from a different location. There is nothing in this room that suggests a struggle took place here. My guess is the body was placed on the bed after she was already deceased."

"The physical wounds?" Bobby questioned.

"Seems to be just sheer brutality. No gunshot wounds or stab marks that I can see. Cause of death looks to be compression of anatomical neck structures. In cop speak, she was strangled."

"Damn it to hell," Curry lamented.

"Thank you, Jeff," Detective Justice said.

"Let's take a walk, Bobby," Curry implored. The two let Dr. Webb get back to his grisly work. Bobby lit up a cigarette despite Curry's disapproving look.

"What do you think?" Curry said.

"Well, if it didn't happen here, then we need to find the actual crime scene," Justice stated.

"Goes without saying, Detective. But no one noticed a body in a room for a week?" Captain Curry asked, confounded.

"According to the hotel manager, no one has rented this room in over two months," Bobby stated. "It's not a room they tend to use, seeing as there's a trapdoor dead center leading to the ocean. So its extra money, and guests have to sign a waiver since anyone can fall through. The room door should have been locked, yet there aren't any signs of a break-in. Cleaner said last week, another room suffered some damage. Broken desk leg, missing sheets. Kids, she said."

"Let's get in there and see what we can find."

"We're on it," Bobby said.

It was only moments after they pulled the zipper over the girl's face that Bobby saw the news truck pull up.

"Got damn it, here come the cameras. All right, everyone, gather around me," Bobby called out to those who were still left at the crime scene. "First off, don't worry about the reporters. They ask, we say *no comment*. Let the captain handle the media. Eventually, DA Eldon Grey will be involved, as will Mayor Bailey Reed. The moment they arrived is the moment this case went high profile, more than it already was. Now this is what's happening. We are going to proceed as if the victim is Tara Hill, an eighteen-year-old female from Sandy Beach. The body is on its way to the morgue, and we have been in contact with Hill's mother, Lucy Hill, and both parents are on the way to the SBPD as we speak." Bobby turned his attention to the lead medical examiner. "Jeff, leave some of your people here to finish gathering evidence from both rooms and get down to the station. Find a picture you like for the identification. Prepare them for what they are going to see the best you can. Officer Pac, go with him to get any type of statement when the victim is, in fact, confirmed."

"Yes, Detective," Webb said.

"Yes, sir," Pac said with confidence.

"We are going to keep some of you stationed here by the hotel. This place is secluded enough that there will be no doors to knock on, no neighbors to interview, which frees us up to make a thorough search of the surroundings. That said, we do need to canvas nearby convenience shops, gas stations, and the like for statements."

A collective "yes, sir" rose from the assembled officers.

"Jack, we are going to keep going through those hotel registers. We will start making phone calls and doing background checks. See if we can't turn up a lead."

"Let's do it, partner," Jack said.

*****

De'Ron and Hunter didn't talk for a few days following their night at the hotel, but Goo called him one afternoon as though nothing had happened. Hunter felt lucky he got to the phone before his parents, who would have made up some lie or just told Goo he couldn't talk. Now he was waiting for Goo outside, not asking permission to take a ride in the red pickup.

"Where we going?" Hunter asked.

"You'll see," Goo said, tearing around a corner.

De'Ron smiled as he pulled into the driveway of his home, a good-sized split-level ranch house in north Sandy Beach that made Hunter feel embarrassed about his small bungalow. They walked through the living room, Goo barely nodding to a table full of older, scantily clad women smoking joints, not even hiding the spoons and mirrors with lines of coke portioned out like cat scratches. The many half-empty bottles gave the impression of a party that had been going on for days. In Goo's room, his friend pulled out a joint and turned on the TV.

"What's up with all the girls in here, Goo?" Hunter asked.

De'Ron smiled. "All? Shit, that's just a few bitches that hang out to get high and shit."

"They just hang out and get high?" Hunter repeated, amazed.

"Well, they do other shit," Goo-Man said as he rolled up another joint. "Basically, whatever big man wants 'em to do."

"What about what you want them to do?" Hunter asked as he stretched out on De'Ron's king-size bed.

"My nigga!" Goo let out a laugh. "Let them get some more of that powder in their nose. We won't have to be asking them hoes for shit."

Hunter got excited at the thought. "Seriously, Dawg?"

"Just wait, bruh," Goo-Man answered.

"Damn, this a nice room, bro. We should hang out here more often," Hunter said.

"I don't see why not. Big man always at the shop. No moms be fucking with us here neither."

"Where's your mom?" Hunter inquired.

"I have no fuckin clue. I ain't seen that no-good bitch since I can remember. She just another hoe," De'Ron said, gritting his teeth.

"Fucking hoes, dawg!" Hunter said, mimicking Goo's attitude. It felt good, being carefree in the face of things you should care about.

"Look at ya," De'Ron said, seeing a more confident Hunter. "You a brand-new man since you got you some snatch."

"I feel like one," Hunter mentioned as he realized how accurate Goo's statement was. *He was a new man.*

"I can tell for sure."

"We got to do that shit again. I got someone in mind that I want to ask out next time. I think she will like me better now."

"Oh, you do, huh?"

"Yep, forgot about her ass, but I saw her when I was doing my community service bullshit."

"How much of that shit you got left?"

"Like half."

"Well, I gots to handle some biz for CG that will prolly take a few days, and then we can take care of dat," De'Ron said.

"Hey, turn up the volume," Hunter said, gesturing toward the TV. A news anchor came on after the Breaking News graphic flashed. Goo worked the remote control.

"We are sad to bring you the news that, after a nearly week-long search, the body of eighteen-year-old Tara Hill has been found."

Footage of police and medical personnel at the Sandy Beach Hotel filled the television screen, but it cut back to the anchor before showing the body.

"Right now, the police have no leads. If you know anything, please call the hotline you see on your television screen." The station cut to a commercial, and Goo switched the TV off.

"Them pigs don't got shit nigga!" Goo-Man shouted.

"Po little pigs," Hunter said.

"You a stone-cold killa!" Goo said, laughing.

*****

After Tara Hill's identity was confirmed, evidence gathered, and possible witnesses questioned, the police working the case met in the headquarters conference room.

"Mrs. Hill also stated that her daughter got along with everyone, so she was not aware of any enemies, particularly someone capable of this. She also mentioned that Tara wasn't dating anyone recently," Officer Pac said, reading from her notes.

"At least anyone her parents knew about?" Jack surmised.

Pac shrugged. "Well, we have spoken with friends close to her, and that is the same info we got back from them. Of course, we will continue to follow up."

"Thank you, Officer," Detective Justice said before turning to his partner. "Jack, did we get any leads from the car?"

"Nothing was found inside her vehicle, the 1978 Ford Fairmont, four-door green, Florida license number 111XXX. What we do know was she never got inside of the automobile after she clocked out. The car was still outside with the doors locked when the night crew at the diner finished closing up four hours later. They were concerned, but no one heard or saw anything."

"You mentioned an incident the victim had with one of our favorite characters... De'Ron Goodman," Bobby said gravely. "At the Surf Side Diner."

"Yes, I looked into that. I guess Goodman, aka Goo-Man, worked there for about three weeks after being released from juvie. He wasn't spotted in the restaurant that evening."

"I wish I could have seen that kid slinging dishes. I would have made a trip there just to see that mope working a regular tedious job."

"Maybe he was actually trying?" Jack ventured.

Bobby threw Jack a sideways glance. "No, I highly doubt it. It was all for show."

"I guess that's more than likely the case," Jack said with a chuckle. "We did follow up. It seems it was a minor incident with the victim."

"So what happened?" Bobby said.

"He touched her inappropriately."

"Inappropriate in what way?" Bobby asked.

"He slapped her on the ass, apparently."

"I see," Bobby said with a blank expression.

"She reported it, and he was fired. The manager said that Goodman didn't seem the least bit upset by the termination," Jack said as he closed his notepad.

"No, I don't guess he would be."

"I tried to track him down personally and ended up speaking with another pal of ours, Cordale Goodman," Jack mentioned.

"Jack, that man is no one to fool with," Bobby cautioned.

"Understood. I was there to get some information. That's all," Jack said.

Bobby nodded. "If we tangle with Cordale, we need all our ducks in a row. What did CG have to say?"

"He said the boy has been working at the auto repair shop since he was terminated from the Surf Side Diner. Also noted that De'Ron was out of town running an errand for the shop when all this went down in the news."

"I'll take that statement for what it's worth, considering who it's coming from."

"He does have a record for sure, but nothing that indicates this level of violence," Jack said as he tossed his pad and pencil on the table.

"Violence isn't a trait you're born with, like blue eyes. It builds in people. Let's be sure to follow up," Bobby said.

"Absolutely," Jack agreed.

Bobby sighed. "Meanwhile, I haven't gotten past anything worse than unpaid parking tickets for the guests who stayed at the hotel. Most are out-of-towners on vacation."

"And these damn kids!" Jack said.

"What do you mean, Jack?"

"I almost forgot to say. Turns out Fred Jones stayed there this past week."

"Fred Jones?"

"Come on, man? Scooby-Doo?"

Bobby sighed. "I forget I work with a child sometimes."

"Thanks," Jack said with a smile.

"Jesus. So I guess our perp had a fake ID," Bobby said, frustrated.

"Yes...unless you know where Crystal Cove is?"

"Fuck...did the receptionist or the manager remember him? A description, anything?"

"No, it was a different set of people who worked that night. An assistant manager and a part-time desk clerk who, of fucking course, has gone on a vacation with her boyfriend. The assistant manager had no recollection of who signed that name into the register. According to her, she only goes to the front desk if called."

"And the part-timer?" Bobby queried.

"Ms. Kerrigan said she didn't know when"—Jack flipped through his notes—"Sally Bilbo, the receptionist from that night, will be back or if at all."

"Sounds about right."

"It would be nice if they had a spy camera installed, at least around the front entrance. It is the eighties, last I looked," Jack bemoaned.

"And cramp their style, please," Bobby quipped while rubbing his forehead. "Look, we will need to follow up with Ms. Bilbo ourselves. These assholes aren't getting off the hook that easy."

"I will work on getting her down here," Jack said.

"That would be helpful," Bobby said, lighting up a cigarette.

"Maybe we'll get lucky next hurricane season and that spook house will get washed out to sea," Tickerrman chimed in.

"Let's hope so," Bobby replied grimly.

June 1984

Bobby's apprehension about the meeting was palpable on the ride over to city hall. This made Jack nervous, rattling off jokes, clearly getting on Bobby's nerves. To create a kind of peace, he quieted down and let Bobby pick the music. Chet Baker calmed Bobby, but it also made him quiet and moody. Jack sipped his coffee and braced himself for a rough morning.

Mayor Bailey Reed, along with the District Attorney Eldon Grey, had called the meeting. Captain Curry would be there as well. It would be Jack's first time in the mayor's office. Much like seeing the principal, he wasn't sure it was an honor.

"Well, let me just say upfront, boys," Mayor Reed exclaimed once they'd all been seated and pleasantries exchanged. "I know this has been an unusual past year with these three high-profile cases. Starting with a kidnapping almost a year ago, then the prostitution bust, and now this murder. Bobby, I think you have been on the television more than me lately."

Bobby nodded but gave no particular reaction. "Maybe so, Mayor, but no one is asking for autographs yet, nor should they."

"Well, commendation is in order, because I know you guys have put every effort into solving these cases. Stopping the pay-for-sex scandal before it could get any worse was fine police work," the mayor boasted, playing up his Southern accent. "Even the Feds were impressed."

"Someone died that day, Mayor," Bobby replied.

"It's horrible and certainly not something we want to get used to. Yet that was out of your control." The mayor looked Bobby in the eyes. "You have my full support. As do all of you."

"Let me jump in and say I echo Mayor Reed's remarks," said District Attorney Eldon Grey. "Regarding the other cases, the unsolved ones, well, I've kept in contact with Captain Curry, and I know that you continue to pursue all leads. Dead ends happen when no one is willing to come forward. If you need anything, my office is ready."

"Yes, that's why I asked for everyone to be here today. I want you to know we are here, and we understand the pressure you might be feeling," said the mayor.

Jack could see Bobby breathe a sigh of relief. It was the needless deaths that weighed on him, and he assumed the world was going to be as hard on him as he was on himself. Jack was glad to be his partner.

"Thank you, Mayor. Thank you, Mr. Grey," Captain Curry said.

"Detective Justice, while I have you in front of me, can you give me a summary in your words for both those unsolved cases?" the mayor asked.

"A summary?" Bobby asked.

"Yes, if you don't mind. Your words, I always get it secondhand. No offense to Greg and Eldon." The mayor looked to both men then back to Bobby.

Jack watched Bobby gather his thoughts before speaking. "As far as Chase Lovell, that's been as tough on me as anything in my sixteen years at the SBPD. We know who has him—Lee Earl Elwood. We just have no clue where he is. We continue to monitor Elwood's mother, along with past known associates such as Roy Boutte and Otis Redgrave. He has not contacted them to date. Detective Cutler did get a lead that he's had dealings with Cordale Goodman in the past, but that's nothing we can prove, and Goodman certainly isn't going to just come forward with information willingly. We continue to keep the word out and have faxed updated artist sketches of what Chase could look like now throughout the state as well as other states that Elwood has had connections too." Bobby reflected again before continuing. "Tara Hill, we have details but no witnesses. We do believe the murder happened at the Sandy Beach Hotel inside of one room, then the body was dumped in another. Not the smartest move or entirely thought over, and most likely, whoever it was rushed into moving it to the second location. With it being a hotel room, there are enough fingerprints that could take months to go through, and it only shows you were at the hotel at some point."

"Any other leads, Detective?" asked Eldon Grey.

"It's a ruthless murder and feels personal. One of our leads is the use of a fake ID to check into the hotel room where we believe the assault happened. It certainly fits the timeline. My partner over here knew it to be a cartoon reference. Fred Jones. Makes sense this might be a younger assailant with said alias and amateur cover-up."

"Thank you, Detective," Mayor Reed said directly. "I'm sure you will continue to do great work."

"Thank you, sir," Bobby responded.

On the way out of the office, Jack was surprised when the mayor pulled Bobby aside and spoke closely into his ear.

"What was that about?" Jack inquired in the car.

"He wants a little side meeting with me later tonight at the Turtle."

"Why's that? You know you can trust me by now."

"It's not you. It's Eldon. The mayor wants to elaborate on some theory about the Sandy and doesn't want to speak on anything off-kilter around potential opponents in future elections."

"Politics," Jack commented.

"Always. In fact, you are coming tonight. Hear me?"

"Loud and clear, partner."

Later that night, Bobby found Mayor Reed at his usual booth. He was working his way through a pitcher of daiquiris. Bobby declined when offered a glass, preferring his beer and chaser. Jack was on his way, but he was surprised to hear that the captain was also coming.

"Sorry about earlier," Mayor Reed said. "Eldon took it upon himself to invite himself, so I couldn't speak freely."

"No sweat, Bailey."

Curry walked in looking uncomfortable. Bobby hadn't seen him out at night since his promotion to captain, and he wasn't sure he liked his appearance in the bar. He downed his shot while his boss was ordering a drink and put the glass on the neighboring table.

Curry sat, light beer in hand, followed by Jack, who just strolled in.

"Gentlemen," Bailey Reed said after some small talk. "I'll cut to the fine print. Now I don't mind Sandy Beach having a reputation. We're permissive when it comes to some things. It's live and let live here. But when it's kill and let die, things bear closer oversight."

"Agreed," Curry said. "If the budget allows."

"It doesn't right now," Bailey Reed said. "We need to work with what we got."

"Why don't you just go ahead and tell us what's on your mind first?" Curry said. Bobby sensed a reservation in his voice. Curry sensed what was coming. So did Bobby.

"Thank you, Captain Curry. This is important for the detectives to hear."

"Get ready, men. Hope you aren't scared of ghosts," the captain said, smiling and leaning back.

"Ghosts, sir?" Jack asked with a confused tone.

"Boys, you were both born in Sandy Beach, correct?" the mayor asked.

"Yes, sir. We are both from Sandy Beach," Bobby responded.

"How old are you, Bobby?"

"I just turned forty-one. Jack's twenty-eight going on twelve."

Bailey Reed nodded and gave a sly smile. "Ever heard the name Sandy Guinevere?"

Bobby looked up to the ceiling in thought. "Perhaps. I can't quite put my finger on it."

"No, never heard of her," Jack said.

"Boys," the mayor began. "Class is in session. This city didn't get its name from the beach. It got its name from its founder, Sandy Guinevere."

"Oh, hell!" Bobby exclaimed. "I always forget it was named after an actual person and not the beaches. My father told me that when I was a kid."

"That is very interesting," Jack added, clearly sucking up to the mayor.

Captain Curry looked over to Jack. "Oh, it's about to get more interesting."

"I can't blame you lads for not knowing. It's not like you read this in your high school history books. Plus, Sandy Guinevere died eighty-five years ago."

The mayor opened his attaché case and exhumed a manila folder. The officers looked on as Reed pulled out a yellowed newspaper article sealed in plastic for safety.

> Sandy Beach, Florida, was named after its founder, Sandy Guinevere. She was the second woman to found an American town. Juliana Tidwell, who was the first woman to establish an American town, owned the property on which Miami, Florida, was built. Juliana Tidwell was also the original owner of the land Sandy Beach, Florida, was built on, giving it to Sandy Guinevere.
>
> In 1892, Juliana Tidwell's husband, Roderick Tidwell, sold his metal casting factory in North Carolina. A year later, Mrs. Tidwell found out that her husband sold it due to bad investments and gambling debts. The monetary deficits left the Tidwells in dire financial straits. For extra income, they turned their four-story home into a boarding house and tearoom for young ladies. Help was needed subsidizing the venture; alas, they did not borrow from the bank. Anxious word would rise about how Mr. Tidwell lost their savings. All this put a strain toward the Tidwells' marriage.
>
> Juliana Tidwell traveled from Asheville, North Carolina, to Biscayne Bay to seek help

from her father, Isaac Thomas. On her arrival, he explained to her that his money was in property assets and some recently made investments. Mr. Thomas had the notion to introduce his daughter to the beautiful eighteen-year-old Sandy Guinevere, whom he met when she married his friend Alfred Alcock. Mr. Alcock, Mrs. Guinevere's much older and wealthy husband, had recently passed away and willed all of his belongings to Mrs. Guinevere.

In 1895, Juliana Tidwell's father died and willed his land in Florida to Juliana, including 1,060 acres across the Miami River. She kept 800 acres toward the north side of the river where the town of Miami, Florida, is now located. To settle her debt with Sandy, she granted her 260 acres along with a two-story house built by the Franklyn cotton slaves some 35 years earlier. The land and home were a day's travel away.

The Tidwells sold their home in Asheville, North Carolina, and relocated to Biscayne Bay, moving into Juliana father's home. Juliana Tidwell and Sandy Guinevere each decided to take a leading role in the movement to establish towns toward the Miami River. Still, they knew that decent transportation was important to attract development. Mrs. Tidwell and Mrs. Guinevere tried to induce Elmer Howarth to extend his railroad to Fort Dallas (Miami) and offered to divide their sizable real estate holdings should he accomplish this.

The pair wrote numerous letters to Mr. Howarth. Finally, Juliana made the trip to St. Augustine and made the offer personally. Her efforts were of no avail at that time; alas, providence favored them.

The great freeze of 1895 that lasted all through the month of December devastated the corky orange belt of central and northern Florida, destroying valuable groves and wiping out fortunes overnight. Mrs. Tidwell alerted Mr. Howarth that the freeze had spared the Miami River, sending as evidence a bouquet and oranges. He finally granted the decree to extend the Florida Coast railway. On February 10, 1896, the vanguard of the Howarth forces arrived. Under the agreement struck, Mrs. Tidwell would supply Howarth with the land for an inn and a railroad station at no cost and then split the remainder of her 800 acres north of the Miami River in alternating sections.

On April 22, 1896, the train office of the Florida Coast Railway befell the area. On July 28, the male residents voted to incorporate a new town, Miami. The town steadily grew from a fishing village into a metropolis. Juliana Tidwell and Elmer Howarth were considered the matriarch and patriarch of Miami, Florida. Women from all over adored Mrs. Tidwell for advancing women's place in the realm of business.

Finally, in July 1897, it was voted to incorporate another new town that became Guinevere Beach, Florida. Neither Sandy nor Guinevere Beach became as widely known as Juliana or Miami, as it grew at a much slower pace.

In January 1899, tragedy struck. Juliana's husband, Roderick Tidwell, had become jealous of Juliana's fame and obsessed over the younger and prettier Sandy Guinevere during this time. Mr. Tidwell mistook Sandy's kind nature as flirtation. When she turned down his plea to leave with him, he became angered.

The infatuated Mr. Tidwell started a campaign of letter writing and uninvited visitations to Sandy's home. Residents of both towns took notice, so after months of trying to shun Mr. Tidwell, Sandy finally told Juliana about her husband's behavior. On January 13, 1899, Juliana confronted Roderick and told him she wanted a divorce. He shot Juliana dead during that heated argument. Mrs. Tidwell was thirty-nine years old. According to authorities, a maid witnessed the murder and alerted police. Roderick Tidwell then killed himself to avoid capture. Yet rumors rapidly spread that Roderick Tidwell and Sandy Guinevere were in love. The townsfolk believed it was plotted to kill Juliana to be free of her, yet the police found no proof that such occurred.

July 13, 1899, six months after Juliana's death, women from all over felt government leaders failed to resolve the murder of Mrs. Tidwell. They continued to believe that Mrs. Guinevere conspired with Roderick Tidwell to murder Juliana despite there being no evidence to support this claim. Hence, a mob of women went to Guinevere Beach to find Sandy. They found Mrs. Guinevere walking along the beach near her home. Without warning, they pulled the woman into the water and drowned her. She was 25 years of age. They also hung her from a tree and burned her house to the ground. None were charged for the murder of the woman, though there is a photograph published in the papers of the woman rejoicing in front of Sandy Guinevere's home as it burned. The picture also depicts the drowned and hung body of Mrs. Guinevere.

The local officials who ran the town after Sandy Guinevere's death sought to change the

> name of the town to Sunny Beach. Residents signed petitions to keep the name of its founder, because they feared the vengeance from the ghost woman, who was believed to haunt the beach. Ultimately, the town council agreed that Sandy Beach, Florida, was a name that had appeal for the hospitality industry and honored times past, but not the dark deeds committed there. In their estimation, "Sandy" referred to the shoreline.

"Okay," Jack said. "Give me the *Reader's Digest* version."

"It's like this," the mayor said. "Our town is named to cover up a near century-old murder. The victim, Sandy Guinevere, was wronged twice by the town. Once in her death, then again in trying to erase her memory."

Bobby took a long draught of his beer then whispered, "Fuck."

*****

Marina Kerrigan thought she had struck gold by reopening the Sandy. There were already any number of cookie cutter hotels on Florida's coast, even in Western Florida. Resorts where people ate from buffets, swam in ultra-chlorinated pools just yards from clean, clear ocean water. But hotels with character, with a history, these were rare. She couldn't believe they hadn't torn the old structure down. It was ugly enough from the outside, spooky. But that's what she was counting on. She'd stayed at the Crescent Hotel in Eureka Springs and the Cecil in LA. These places had a constant stream of business from curiosity seekers—men mostly, who liked crime scenes, liked their danger with a well-stocked minibar. The Sandy, with a history well-documented in the press, was clearly such a location. Not that she believed buildings could be the source of bad energy, much less be haunted. If anything was haunted, it was money. A piece of paper made people do things, *anything*, it asked.

Still, she got a strange feeling from room 6, even before the body had been found. Marina couldn't say why. After the murder, she raised prices across the board. This kept some people away, but she was slowly rebuilding with wealthier or more obsessed clients. She had toyed with the idea of leaving traces from the killing—a strand of hair, a fake blood splatter. But ultimately, she decided she had her limits and left it as it was. In terms of having a creepy feeling, the room was doing fine on its own.

Marina smiled at the sound of the reception bell. Another guest with a pocketful of that powerful paper.

*****

Jack hadn't been to the Sandy Beach Library since returning from Tallahassee. He had checked out a few horror novels to quiet his mind before bed, but he only read a few sentences before putting them down. The books had sat on his bedside table until he returned them late, using the night deposit bin to avoid the fine.

The place had the same luxurious scent of old paper. *Kind of like how the smell in a restaurant gets you hungry*, he thought. The place was mostly empty. A homeless guy—Jack had seen him around town—with a pointed red beard was taking refuge in the night. The man was reading a thick leather-bound book, but Jack somehow felt he was observing him. Jack shrugged off the thought and approached the counter.

"Can I help you?" a young Hispanic woman asked.

"Looking for some info, ma'am."

"This is the right place then," she said. *Is she flirting?* Jack smiled.

"Town's history. Woman named Sandy Guinevere." Jack wanted to read up for the next time he met the mayor. He wanted to distinguish himself, and these were easy points to score.

"She wanted?"

"Might be," he said.

He let Raquel, as she introduced herself, guide him through the process of looking up old articles using a microfiche reader, which enlarged film copies of old papers.

"There we go," she said, scrolling through until she found what he was looking for. She left him there to read at his leisure. What he found made him wince. A photograph of *Sandy Guinevere* hanging from a banyan tree. Jack pulled some film from 1903. In an edition of the *Sandy Beach Times* from late in the year, he found an article that summed up a crime wave—three murders, a suicide on the beach. In a passing comment in what looked like the journalist's attempt at sensationalism, the writer made note of the curse put on Sandy Beach by Sandy Guinevere. Jack took a deep breath then jumped when he felt a hand brush his shoulder.

"Find what you're looking for?" Raquel asked.

"I suppose," he said.

"Well, we're closing up soon. If you want to pick out a book, you should hurry. Microfiche stays here."

"I'm okay for now," Jack said, though he was anything but. "Say, can you get me a print of this?"

"What do you have there?"

With an apologizing look, Jack showed her the picture of the hanging woman.

"I'm sorry. The microfiche doesn't copy photos well," she said. "And I don't have time to find the paper in the archive."

"No problem," Jack said. "But while I'm here, maybe you can recommend a book for a man who's got a lot on his mind and plenty of energy." He winked then let her close up.

The next day, Jack woke to find that a copy of the photo of Sandy Guinevere's execution had been slipped under his condo door. At first, he thought Raquel had done it, but how would she know where he lived? It was his day off, so Jack called the mayor's office, asking Reed to meet him at the Snappy Turtle in the evening. He invited Bobby along, knowing he wouldn't pass on the company.

"Okay," Jack said, breaking a peanut shell between his finger and thumb. "I appreciate the history lesson from the other day. I've just been doing a bit of looking into it on my own. As interesting as all this sounds, I am just not sure what it has to do with Tara Hill or any of the cases we're working."

Bobby nodded at Jack.

"Well, I only hit you with the opening act. That's what I am getting at," the mayor said, clearly pleased to have an opportunity to further discuss the town's history.

"We're not kids here, mayor. Feed us at the adult table," Bobby said.

"Okay. Let me be blunt. We can't act like what's happening isn't eerily similar to Payne."

"Bartholomew Payne's incarcerated," Bobby said.

"It's not the point," Jack said, catching on, nodding at the mayor. "It's not Payne we're looking at. It's the pattern."

Bobby cleared his throat.

"Here, look at this photograph," Jack said. He pulled the copy of the photo and passed it around. "See there? All those women screaming at Sandy Guinevere's hanging corpse while watching her home burn."

"That is a frightening photo, Jack," Bobby admitted. "There is no denying that."

"Yeah. Some helpful stranger slipped it under my door," Jack said. "Mysteriously, there was a myriad of deaths of women over the next few years. The one thing they had in common was they all told of being there when Guinevere was killed."

"Jack," Bobby said. "This all sounds a little harebrained for me. If I'd known you were so interested in excavating the past, I'd have brought you my wedding photos, and you could investigate what went wrong with my marriage."

"Come on, Bobby."

"Gentlemen. We're not to create a story for the *National Inquirer*, just to talk out some things. Keep an open mind here, Bobby," the mayor stated calmly.

"It's open. To a point, anyway. I'm just trying to get a handle on what we are discussing," Bobby said.

"There are too many similarities to turn our heads to this," Jack expressed.

"In death, murder, and the Sandy Beach Hotel," Mayor Bailey Reed noted.

"Break it down for me in concepts I can understand," Bobby said. "Meaning crimes and the people that done them."

"Okay, let me paint you that picture," Mayor Reed said, sipping a tequila. "November 13, 1942, Meredith Darling was found by her husband hanging by her neck from a belt at the Sandy Beach Hotel. Then on August 13, 1943, a woman was found dead with her throat cut at the Sandy Beach Hotel. He killed three more women but was never apprehended and would infamously go on to be called the Sandy Beach Murderer, active from 1943 to 1945."

The mayor leaned forward, putting his elbows on the table before continuing.

"Twenty years later, we have Bartholomew Payne, aka the Sandy Beach Slasher. Who was apprehended by your boss, Captain Curry, in case you didn't know. On September 13, 1963, a woman later identified as Bartholomew Payne's girlfriend was found dead from a drug overdose. Then again, on December 13, 1963, a woman found at the Sandy Beach Hotel with her wrists and throat slashed open with broken glass. Forward to March 13, 1964, and November 13, 1964, same MO. But this time, he killed them inside their homes. He also raped all his victims. Now here we are again. Twenty years have passed, and we have another killer. Twice can be a coincidence, but three?"

Bobby looked at the mayor. "Coincidence for what? A hotel with really shitty luck?"

"The Sandy Beach Hotel was built in 1940 in the same spot Sandy Guinevere's house burned down forty-one years earlier," the mayor answered. "Let me ask you, Detective Justice. When was Valentina Nunez killed?"

"January this year," Bobby responded.

"January 13, to be exact," Jack added.

"Yes, but Nunez's killer is locked up. He had nothing to do with Tara Hill or Chase Lovell for that matter," Bobby countered.

The mayor nodded. "Yet here we are with another murder at the Sandy Beach Hotel, very close to or on April 13 of this year. I guess that evil doesn't care who performs the actual killing as long as the end result is death."

"Okay," Bobby started. "Let me keep this straight in my head. So we have Sandy Guinevere unjustly killed by a mob of women. Then all these women who were, by their own admission, part of said mob, died in a relatively small short amount of time after."

"Yes, in a nutshell," the mayor said.

Bobby let out a laugh. "So Guinevere is happy for forty years. The curse lifted until she gets pissed off again because the city built a hotel where she used to live forty-one years ago?" he finished."

"That is one hell of a grudge," Jack said. "I'm going to need another beer to swallow this down with."

"Mayor, don't get me wrong. I'm enjoying this. It's interesting to pursue. But a person did this crime, and I fully intend to find whoever it is," Bobby declared. "We're not hunting ghosts. We're not… Fred Jones."

Jack let out a laugh and lifted his beer.

"Yes, Detective. No doubt, whoever murdered Ms. Hill needs to be caught and brought forward. I'm simply trying to help. That hotel…always seems to be involved. I'm also saying more is coming."

"I know you're the mayor," Cutler said, "but how do you know all this?"

"Son, I was born in Sandy Beach in 1922. I've been working for this city before you were even a pain in your mother's ass. Besides, in my line of work, it pays to know some history."

"Yes, sir. But why keep a building where so many deaths have happened, and continue to happen, then keep specific facts about the city from coming to light? Wouldn't it just be easier to get rid of the place?"

"No. It's a landmark, for one thing. And like it or not, people still stay there during the summer, which keeps it busy enough, which means employment. Plus, you don't just get to keep the favorable parts of your history, son. You don't discard old stories or places because you find them distasteful. Trying to forget this episode is part of what got us in this mess. The present isn't static. Things bubble up from the past."

"Greg has mentioned other history there too," Justice cut in. "About things happening to people who have tried to have the place condemned."

"I can't say that doesn't contribute to the lack of motivation by others. But it's not like the building itself is responsible. It's what beneath it, the foundation of the story. Energy never stops being energy, even if it's evil."

Bobby swished down the last of his beer. "Well, Mayor, as I said, I appreciate the history lesson. It's been an interesting talk."

"I guess my point is that we aren't unique because we have crime. We *are* unique because our most high-profile cases might be on a twenty-year schedule. I only bring it up to educate my local authorities."

"We appreciate you trying to educate us on our skeletons, Bailey," Bobby said, getting up to leave.

"Hey, where you going?" the mayor asked. "Look, I promise, no more spooky talk."

"I'll leave you with Jack," he said. "I've got some things to chew over."

"Okay, Detective Justice. I do appreciate you entertaining my theories. You got some time, Jack?"

"Nothing but," Jack replied, relishing the thought of time alone with the mayor.

Back home, Bobby looked at the phone like it was a sleeping snake he didn't dare to disturb. Still, it wasn't going to magically ring. Gwen wasn't going to do the hard work anymore. He sat wondering why it was so easy to let arguments rise then take over. Who knows, maybe ghosts *were* real. Things we given energy to have power over us if we feed them enough. They don't need physical form. Bobby rubbed the flesh on the arm that had his Green Beret tattoo, like a lucky charm. Gwen once told him he needed to open his mind to things. She burnt incense, had him sit in a lotus position, and close his eyes. He felt silly doing it, but it did bring some calm. He liked that hippie side of her, though he never told her so.

Bobby took a last sip of beer, sat on the floor, pulled his legs beneath him, and closed his eyes.

Scenes from the war tried to surface in his mind—men he had known who didn't come back. He saw their faces, these ghosts of the past. Bobby thought of them, permitted them to visit, then let them go. For a moment, Bobby felt peaceful. He inhaled deeply, as Gwen had instructed him, and then Bobby Justice fell asleep.

*****

"Can you tell me what the fuck we are supposed to do with all this historical ghost hunting?" Bobby asked as he loosened his tie, neck aching from sleeping on the floor. He wanted to put an end to the turn the investigation was taking, know how much of the interest in the city's past was just politicking, and how much his boss actually believed. And he wanted Jack in on it. "No need to find whoever killed Tara Hill. Sandy fucking Guinevere did it."

"Look, to be fair, I don't think that's what the mayor was saying," the captain said somewhat sheepishly.

"I thought it was spooky, honestly," Jack added.

"Well, enlighten me, Captain. What was he saying?" Detective Justice inquired. "What I heard is we have an annual twenty-year visit from our founding ghost."

"Bobby, I'm not sure what I believe. It's easy to dismiss spirits. Sounds like crazy talk, but it's also hard to deny the way the facts line up."

"Whoever killed Tara Hill is still out there, and we need to find them before they do it again," Bobby said.

"The mayor knows that. We all do. The only thing you should take away from it is that yes, we have a murderer we need to find. And just maybe, possibly, we should have known something bad was coming."

"I don't buy that. We don't have twenty-year clocks in our heads. Besides, what's the trigger that sets it off in motion? Was this a discussion back in '64?"

"Good questions. I don't have an answer for the first one. And yes, the mayor was just a city councilman back then. But believe it or not, he showed me the same letter you all heard a few nights back, and I have to admit as much I may have acted like it didn't bother me. Now it hit me a little differently."

"Is there any way someone could be trying to copycat the previous killers?" Jack asked.

The captain shook his head. "I don't think so. Not all the details about those murders are public, but I guess you can't ever discount crazy."

"I think they should just take the damn hotel down. Put a statue up or something," Cutler said.

"I think I'm starting to agree, Jack," the captain conceded. "That hotel never became what they imagined it to be. Instead of being one of our main attractions, and not for the right reasons. It's a place where teenagers and singles can get a cheap deal or where one goes to hide. But that's not my decision to make."

"Say, Captain, is Payne still alive?" Justice inquired.

"Last I heard, he was, yes. Osceola State Pen is where he'd be."

"That's not far at all. I'd like to talk with him. I have a few questions."

"Why is that, Bobby?"

"So I can put this curse theory to rest, once and for all. At worst, I'll get some insight into his motives and the motives of whomever is taking up the reigns on the killing spree."

"That sounds reasonable," the captain said. "I'll make a call."

"Captain, there was another thing that I wanted to ask," Cutler confessed.

"Yes, what is it?"

"The mayor mentioned Meredith Darling. Is that any relation to the doctor. And if so, what happened?"

"I think we should discuss that another day, Detective. Let's get back to the present day for now."

"Yes, Captain."

*****

Feathered hair. Heavy mascara. Guess apparel. All the models looked skinny and starved (*but in a good way,* Amber considered).

The articles were all about the same people: Brooke Shields and old men like Tom Selleck. Still, she'd flipped through the pages twenty times at least. Magazines left her hungry. She couldn't say why. She yawned.

Amber's mother was in the kitchen prepping a salad. New diet or something. Amber wanted something *now.* Something that had lots of flavor. A new magazine and a pack of Starburst—the perfect afternoon.

"Mom, I need something to read," the girl declared, knowing reading material scored more points than the latest issue of *Seventeen.*

"Maybe you should go to the library," her mother said as she cut up some vegetables.

"Only old pervs hang out at the library, Mother. Thank you," the girl said in mannered tone.

"Well, goodness gracious," her mother said sarcastically.

"You said you want me to read, so that's what I am doing."

"Don't kid me. I know all about you and your magazine addiction. Pictures of Boy George aren't reading."

"There's text too, Mom. You know, *stuff you read.*"

"Sure, sweetie."

"So can I borrow five dollars to get something from the Stop-N-Go?"

"I don't know, sweetie," her mother said. "I don't want you riding to that area alone, especially with what happened last month."

"It's the middle of the day, Mom," Amber said.

"Maybe you should just wait until we can go together."

"Mom, you act like I haven't gone a million times," she said, rolling her eyes. "I can't stay locked up because something bad happened." She knew she could wear her mother down like this. Indeed, her mother sighed and told her to ask her father. *Victory!*

"Okay!" She pivoted and shouted into living room. "Daddy! Can I have five dollars for a new magazine?"

"Yes, baby!" her father shouted back.

She grinned, ran to the living room, and hugged her father around the neck as he pulled a bill from his wallet.

"Come right back, okay?" her mother called.

*****

Goo picked up Hunter at the time and place they discussed the night prior after he finished some community service work. Hunter's parents had given him bus fare, but he preferred to ride with his friend and spend the money on a joint.

"Thanks, man," he said as he climbed into the cab. "Had enough of that bullshit for the day."

"My nigga," De'Ron replied. "What's they had you doing today—"

"Community service bullshit."

"No shit. But like what, though?" Goo asked again as he looked at himself in his rearview mirror.

"Like cleaning up litter off the interstate or helping at some dumb fucking soup kitchen. That type bullshit," Hunter said as he noticed Goo checking himself out. "You gonna kill us one day if you don't stop looking at yourself," Hunter said, laughing.

"Fuck you, Killa!" Goo also laughed. "I can't help that I be so damn fine." He looked at himself again.

"Yeah, you a trip, Goo!" Hunter professed.

"I know, my nigga, but shouldn't you be already done with that shit by now?"

"I would have been, but since I'm not in school, they added more hours to my ass."

"They be some motherfuckers, man!" Goo said, shaking his head, annoyed. "Like, what fucking school gone do for you anyway?"

"My dad didn't even finish college, so he can't tell me shit, right?"

"That's the damn truth." Goo looked at the dashboard. The light on the tank was flashing. "Fuck, I needs some gas again. This fuckin' thing looks fly, but it does guzzle the fuel."

"That Stop-N-Go has gas," Hunter said, pointing to the side of the road.

"No, shit? Let me stop before my ass runs out." Goo pulled into the lot and parked by a fuel pump.

"I'll pump, bro. How much?"

"Put thirty in that bitch." Goo ran inside to pay, returning soon thereafter with a pair of bottles in bags.

As Hunter pumped the gas, something caught his attention. "Bruh! No fucking way!"

"What, nigga?" De'Ron asked.

*****

Three corrections officers escorted the man in belly chain restraints through the barred door that had just buzzed open. They let him pass through first, knowing you can never be too careful. The prisoner comported himself with the air of somebody important, even though he had been housed in a barren cell for twenty years. The guards kept a watchful distance. He was in his own dark world.

Bobby Justice waited with his back turned, looking out the window at the prison tower guards.

"You can leave him, gentlemen," Bobby said, still staring out the small window. The man nodded to his escorts like personal bodyguards he was dismissing.

"We'll be right outside, Detective," a guard said coolly as he finished loosening the chains around the prisoner's wrists.

"Thank you, Officer," Bobby said then pointed to one of the tower guards. "I did that for a while, right after coming back from Nam. It's your own little world up there. Peaceful in some way."

"Seems like a shit job," the man said brusquely, a heavy everglades drawl in his accent. "Nobody should be in this place by choice."

Bobby nodded then turned and looked directly at Bartholomew Payne, a fifty-year-old with a strangely low hairline that gave him a simian look. He had alert eyes that were wide open as if he was looking at everything in the room at once.

"I remember hearing about you when I first got back to Sandy Beach. You had everyone in this city worked up. *The Sandy Beach Slasher.*"

"That's what this is about?" Payne asked. "Nothing new to tell, Officer. Why are you here?"

"That's a good question," Bobby confessed as he sat down across from the killer. "Keeping an open mind, I guess you could call it."

"I killed those three women, Detective. I never denied it. So I'm not sure what it is you're lookin' for."

"Not sure yet myself, Mr. Payne. But if you don't mind, I'm hoping you will talk to me so I might find out."

"Yeah, fuck it," Payne said with a broad smile, revealing a gaping hole where his front teeth should have been. "I don't see why not. I ain't got shit else going on."

Bobby nodded. "I looked at your rap sheet," he said with his hand on top of a folder. "Kind of a mystery, isn't it? Drug charges and some domestic disputes. You didn't have a violent history, record-wise anyway, until 1963."

Payne relaxed into a toothless grin again. "Hell, I guess I had me some good times in my day."

Bobby shook his head. "So you were thirty when you first killed? Or had you before?"

"Nope, but I sure as hell wasn't a fuckin' saint by any stretch." Payne let out a chuckle. "I've been in plenty arguments with some gals I wish I woulda killed. But no, never did kill anyone before then."

"So why all of a sudden? And so violently?" Bobby asked as he opened Payne's investigative file. "You tied them down. Shattered their bathroom mirrors and used the glass to slash both wrists and their necks, then raped them."

Payne gave a quick shrug of his shoulders. "I had to," he stated simply.

"You had to?" Bobby asked.

"Well, I was pretty angry after my girlfriend overdosed on them fuckin' goddamn pills. I knew I shoulda never bought 'em. But hell, she wanted the fuckin things."

"What happened?" the detective persisted.

"Ah, fuck, we were at a hotel partying. Then next thing I know, she's laying on the floor, foaming at the mouth like a rabid dog. Nothin' paramedics could do for her."

"I see. Sorry to hear."

"What the hell for?" Payne said with a raised eyebrow. "You weren't the one who made her dumb ass take anything she didn't wanna."

Bobby looked to Payne, finally comprehending the nature of the man he was speaking to. "I guess you're right. I spoke too soon," he said with a dry tone.

"I killed one of the bitches, I'd say maybe two months after," Payne said calmly.

"So you killed three women after your girlfriend's death?"

"Yeah. It's fucked up, huh?" Payne chuckled again. "Funny thing is, she was actually more like someone I knew. Just a girl from around, really, that was letting me bang her for some cocaine and pills. She was a good gal."

"You were upset about your acquaintance dying?" Bobby tried not to let his judgment of the man show on his face. The more Payne smiled, the more monstrous he seemed. "Then subsequently killed three women?"

"Pretty much. I'm not sure what had me so angry like that. Rage is more like it. Like I said, I had to," Payne said in a matter-of-fact way.

"Your first victim was Ms. Lovelace, correct?" Bobby showed Payne the woman's photograph.

"I guess she was the first one." Payne looked at the photo with no particular expression. "It's still fuzzy in some ways, but if that's how the cookie crumbled, fuck it."

"How did you feel after you killed her?"

Payne sat back and scratched his head. It occurred to Bobby this might be the first time he had talked about his perspective, that the man was enjoying the interrogation. "Not as angry, but that didn't last long."

"Why her?" Bobby asked.

"I couldn't tell ya." Payne shrugged and gave another laugh. "I was at the hotel, and something about her pissed me the fuck off."

"The same with Ms. Brown and Ms. Anderson?" Bobby asked after making sure the names and order were correct. "Your second and third victims."

"Yep. You know, I always end up feeling kinda shitty about losing my temper with folks. Not these two." Payne snickered. "I still don't feel anything for them. Not then and not now. You know the feeling, don't you? You musta seen some shit."

Bobby felt an agitation rise in him but kept his voice even. "So you were apprehended not long after you killed Ms. Anderson."

Payne's head twitched. "Yes, I was fucking messy. I didn't know what the hell I was doing. No fucking thought-out plan. I just followed both women back to their homes and killed them. I didn't care if anyone noticed. I could have exercised more self-control, thinking back on it."

"I'm not the parole board, Mr. Payne. You can just be straight with me," Bobby said.

The man eyed him with an air of interest. "I answered all these questions before. Why am I answering them again?"

"Well, you can always go back to your cell."

"You're overestimating the pleasure of your company," Payne said.

"Mr. Payne, as the Sandy Beach Slasher, you have a place in our history. Do you agree?"

"Why, yeah, I never thought of it that way."

Justice noticed a smile form on the man's face. "Well, we just want to have the story right, for future generations."

"So they remember me," he said. "For, what's the word... *posterity*."

Bobby could see he liked the idea of being remembered. "That's right. So can I continue?"

"Suppose so," Payne said.

"Now you spotted Ms. Lovelace at the hotel, correct?" Bobby asked, pointing at her photo.

"If she's the first, then yes. Their faces have blended together somewhat since."

"What about Ms. Brown and Ms. Anderson?" Bobby asked.

"Local bar somewhere. I went back to the same bar twice." Payne slapped the table in self-reproach. "You can see why it didn't take them long to find me. Creature of habit, I suppose."

"Do you remember the name of the bar?"

"Don't you have this written down somewhere?"

"Probably so, but I'm asking you," Bobby said in a stern tone.

"No, I don't fucking remember the name of some shitty ass bar from twenty years ago. One's as good as the next. Like women, I reckon."

"Did you know that both women lived alone?"

"Nope. Then again, they weren't at the bar with anyone that I can recollect. Probably wouldn't have made a difference. I guess that part was lucky."

"Lucky for who, Mr. Payne?"

"Well, being that I'm the motherfucker in here for life," Payne said as he leaned over the table, putting his face closer to Bobby. "No matter if I killed three or three hundred people. Then it seems to me that anyone not inside the fucking house was the goddamn lucky ones." Bartholomew leaned back again and put his hands behind his head. Indeed, this was entertainment for him.

Bobby stared at Payne. "Would you have killed anyone else living or staying in the victim's homes?"

"Not sure. I never have given any thought to it. I mean, a few had pets, but I'm not a monster. But yes, probably anyone who woulda got in the fucking way. I don't fucking know, but I wasn't there for anyone else."

"Tell me, Mr. Payne, would you have done it a fourth time?"

"Oh yeah. I wouldn't have stopped. I was already planning on finding another. It's the only thing that helped the rage I felt."

"Do you still feel that rage today?"

Payne smiled. "Sure, but not like that. Something about that time was different. It's a bit like when you go through puberty. It's you, but you are under the control of another force. The killings were like a second puberty. I grew from it."

"Really?"

"Yeah, and that's when I found my true identity as a homosexual."

Payne stared at Bobby for a moment then pounded the table and cackled loudly, the missing teeth reminding Bobby of a black pit or portal to some dark hateful world. "I'm fucking with ya, Detective!" Payne winked at Bobby. "To finish answering your question, Officer, once I got caught, I never did have that same urge again. So take that feather to your quack doctor."

Bobby rubbed his eyes. "One last question."

"Ask me all you want. I'm comin' to like you."

"Where were you staying during that time?"

"Still was at the same hotel room my bang buddy croaked in. The Sandy Beach Hotel. Lovely place. I recommend an ocean-facing room for your best experience there."

"*Fuck*," Bobby whispered.

*****

Kate was watching TV in the living room when Hunter burst through the door. His shirt was stained with dirt and sweat, and she could see an ink spot on his faded denim shorts, which she soon realized was blood. With only a foreboding look in her direction, he started up the stairs to the bathroom.

"Hunter!" Kate called from downstairs. "What happened?"

"Nothing!" Hunter shouted. "I had an accident doing this stupid fucking community service bullshit!"

"Let me look at you," she called then climbed the stairs and stopped outside the closed bathroom door.

"I'm fine! Hell!"

She took a deep breath and opened the door. Contrary to his assertion, she saw Hunter gritting his teeth in pain. His pants were around his ankles. Kate's jaw dropped at the sight of blood oozing from the inside of his leg.

"My God, Hunter! I'm taking you to see a doctor."

"No, I said I'm fine! Go away."

In pain, at least, she thought. *He sounds like the child I miss so much.*

"No, you're not fine. You may need stitches for that."

"Go the fuck away!" Hunter screamed.

"Hunter!" Kate cried out. But before she could demand again, the door was shut in her face.

*****

"Bobby!" Cutler shouted to Bobby, who had just returned to the station.

"Jack, what's all the yelling about?"

"Did you get my page?" Jack asked.

Bobby grabbed his beeper from his belt. "Got-damn new technology," he grumbled. "No, I didn't. It must have been the bad reception inside the prison."

"We have another missing girl," Jack said.

Bobby closed his eyes tight. "Fucking Christ!"

"Amber Callaway, sixteen-year-old. Lives in South Sandy Beach."

"Of course, she does," Bobby said, shaking his head. "How much do we know?"

Jack got his notepad. "I talked to her parents an hour ago. They said that she left home to go the Stop-N-Go to buy a magazine around noon. She hadn't returned home by two, so they went to look for her. When they didn't find her or her bike, they went straight back home and called the police. Normally, I'd say a teenager missing for a few hours, well, she's just off on a lark. But, yeah, these days…"

Bobby nodded. "Who do we have out looking for her presently?"

"Officer Pac is driving the area looking for the girl or her bicycle. Tick and Jonsey are questioning folks from the store and along the route she would have taken."

"Good job, Detective," Bobby said.

Jack smirked. "I'll take that compliment once she's found."

"Understood. Stop-N-Go in South Sandy. That's right by our favorite place," Bobby said. "Where does she live?"

"The White Pearl Subdivision, which is one of the few nice ones in that area. Good families."

"It's four p.m. Let's get out there and see what we can dig up," Bobby said as he got his car keys from his pocket.

"Let's do it, boss," Jack announced.

*****

Todd didn't see Kate when he arrived back from work, which kept him late. Everybody was putting in a deck these days or wanted platform beds for their kids. He was happy for the business, less happy with some of his shoddy work. He always thought that when he was building a deck, he was simultaneously building a future for himself and his family. He put his sweat into it because it mattered. It *had* mattered. Now he wasn't so sure. But he had to carry on. For Kate and, he guessed, for Hunter. Todd grabbed an Olympia from the fridge and climbed the stairs. No dinner on. He opened the door to the bedroom. Was she already in bed?

"You should probably go talk to your son," Kate said without even greeting him, propped up on a pillow, reading a paperback.

Todd sighed. Couldn't he even change out of his work clothing? "What? Why? What did he do now? I just got home."

"He came home today, cut up, bloody clothing. Said it was an accident of some kind. Probably another fight."

"I just walked in the door, babe," Todd said. "Can I get 'hi, how are you' or 'I'm glad your home'?"

"Well, I'm sorry," Kate said softly. "He was just so volatile. I thought you'd be interested."

Todd sighed, peeled off his shirt, and began toward the bathroom. "I'm going to take a shower."

He soaked for a few minutes, just letting his head hang there under the hot stream, only lifting it to take a sip of the Seagram's he placed on the sink. *A real luxury*, he told himself. *A drink in the shower*. Once finished, he toweled off, rinsed out the glass, and dressed. Kate was still up once he returned to the bedroom.

"I took a lot of Chase's old clothes to Goodwill today," Kate said, making it sound confrontational.

"I thought we said we wouldn't do that until we knew." Todd paused. "Well, until we knew he wasn't coming home."

"It's almost a year now, Todd," Kate said. "They probably wouldn't even fit anymore. He's had to have grown some."

Todd let out an involuntary chuckle. "I wouldn't count on that. He was such a little shit."

Kate sniffled. "How did we let this happen to us?" Kate asked.

Todd scooted closer to his wife and took her in his arms. "We didn't let anything happen to us. We did the best we could."

"This year, it's like a cell door shut behind us, and he's completely gone," Kate said. More than anything, Todd wanted to go downstairs and dig into the cardboard case in the fridge. But he stayed. Calming her would pay off later.

"A piece of crap sicko took him from us," Todd said. "And we still have memories."

"We have one that was taken from us and another that hates us." A tear rolled down Kate's cheek as she nuzzled into her husband. "And just about everyone else."

"Maybe we haven't exactly been there for him," Todd said.

"I know he thinks we blame him for Chase," Kate answered.

"Nobody's told him we don't. I think about that a lot, but I don't know." Todd rubbed Kate's shoulder. "I'm still angry."

"Me too," Kate said. "Angry for him not doing what we asked."

"I'll try to go talk to him," Todd said.

"He wouldn't even let me help him when he came home."

"I don't know that he will let me either."

"Oh," Kate said a moment later. "Before I forget, did you talk to Dr. Darling today?"

"Yes," Todd said. "I did. I'm meeting him Monday morning. I think he wants me to repair some steps behind his house and a few other things."

Kate nodded. "Yeah, that's what he said. He may have a lot to do around there. It's a huge place."

"Maybe so," Todd agreed. "That would be okay. I may need to find some more help with the other jobs I have going."

"Why don't you take Hunter with you?" Kate asked. "With him not in school, and it's not like we can afford someone to homeschool him. It would be good for the boy to make some money and not have so much free time."

"That's a good idea. He would probably just run a teacher off anyway. And besides, it's cheap labor." Todd winked at Kate. "I'm gonna go talk to him."

"Okay," Kate said.

Emboldened by their accord, Todd added, "And some cooking smells would make this place extra homey."

"Loud and clear," Kate said.

Todd made his way to Hunter's room. When he opened the door, he saw his son lying on his bed, captivated by a horror movie on his television.

"Hey, turn that down," Todd said.

"Wait for a second," Hunter said. "This is my favorite part."

Todd looked to the TV, and he raised an eyebrow at the disturbing imagery of a woman being stalked through a dark forest, a bloodied blade slashing at her back.

"A woman being assaulted is your favorite part?" Todd stood there a moment, watching the brutal scene, then walked over to the TV and turned it off.

"I was watching that," Hunter said.

"Son, you concern me." Todd looked down at Hunter. Video games where he shot things, TV shows where it looked like the killer was the hero, posters of heavy metal bands with blood streaming from the musicians' mouths. Todd couldn't think of one artifact from his own childhood that was gory or morbid. Had he indulged him too much? Is that how he shared blame? "I wanna talk with you," he said, taking a seat on the bed. "Look, you're going to start coming to work with me Monday."

"I would rather clean out more ditches, thank you," Hunter spat back.

"If you're not going to summer school or be homeschooled, then you're going to work. You're not a little boy anymore, okay? Your mother is worried about you."

"She just doesn't want to be around me. Period." Hunter looked away from his father.

"That's not true," Todd said. He sat down next to his son, still looking at the TV screen, even though it had gone dark. "We never wanted to make you think any of this was your fault, Hunter."

"Little too late for that, Todd," Hunter said dispassionately, as though reporting news.

"Don't get me wrong…we were upset that you didn't look out for your brother better, but we don't blame you for Elwood's actions."

"Could have fooled me," Hunter fumed.

Todd was silent for a moment. Hunter still wouldn't look at him.

"After dinner, maybe you should start getting to bed earlier." Hunter stood up. Had he always been this tall? "I have a few things I want you to help out with at work. I'll give you a couple of bucks when you're finished."

"Yeah? Am I gonna make some decent money, at least?"

"Oh, so living here for free isn't good enough, huh?" Todd teased.

"What?" Hunter raised his eyebrows.

"I'm just funnin' with you. Yeah, of course."

"Where we going?"

"Dr. Darling's first, then to another job that we will need to finish up," Todd answered.

"What type of job is it?"

"You'll see on Monday."

"So do I have to go every day?" Hunter asked, reaching over to turn the TV back on. "I'm just about done with the other crap I have to finish."

"We'll figure it out," Todd answered over the sound of eerie slashing sounds coming from the television as he left his son's room.

*****

Jack turned on the radio. Bobby reached over and turned it off. Bobby was in one of his quiet moods. Jack knew not to push it. His partner had his mind on something. Still, he ventured a question.

"How did the interview with the Slasher go?"

Bobby took a minute to respond. He was still deep in his thoughts. "Damn, that did happen today...didn't it?"

"Hell, almost yesterday now," Cutler said. It was one of those nights that seemed to be smothered in darkness.

"I can't think of when more crazy shit has happened in a year's time," Bobby said, restraint in his voice. "I'm completely drained."

"Same here, partner. I'm numb at the moment. What a damn day," Jack conceded. "Tell me what the slasher was like."

Bobby thought for a moment. "Fascinating," he confessed.

Jack looked to Bobby. "How so?"

"I don't know, Jack. I suppose when you have an image of someone, then it's different from that. You just have to reconcile that in your mind."

"I got you. But in what way was he different from what you expected?" Jack continued.

"I guess I expected someone more menacing and not the local bum at the park," Bobby said.

Jack again let out a small laugh. "I see. Of course, that was twenty years ago when he committed those crimes."

"I'll say this also," Bobby continued. "He didn't have any damn issues admitting it and sure as hell didn't show a bit of remorse for anything. Actually, he seems resigned to the fact he belongs in jail."

"A crazy that knows he's crazy. I guess that is a change of pace," Jack said.

"I mainly wanted to see what his motivations were for the murders."

"I am guessing he didn't say the ghost of Sandy Guinevere made him do it."

"No," Bobby said. "But he never killed until that month and even admitted he didn't know why he chose those three particular women. But he was arrested at the Sandy."

"We should just put bars over the hotel windows and save them the ride to jail. It sure would make things easier on us," Jack joked.

"Funny," Bobby said.

"That's me."

Bobby and Jack arrived at the station and went straight to the captain's office. They updated Curry on where things stood with the missing teenage girl.

"So there's no trace of her or her bike?" the captain asked. "That sounds eerily similar to a year ago."

"We still have officers looking," Cutler said.

"We will have foot patrols, their dogs, and volunteers first thing in the morning to start combing the woods around the area. Also, a news report ran tonight with her picture," Bobby said.

"I saw. Brief me again in the morning," the captain instructed as he grabbed his windbreaker from the hook.

Instead of going home, the two detectives walked to the end of a crabbing pier. They looked out at the horizon, though it was black as squid ink.

"What's up, Bobby?" Jack asked. "Want to go to the Snappy Turtle?"

"Nah, I think I've bothered Wanda enough for now."

"Kinda feels like a lot to take on, all this. I signed up for delivering speeding tickets and taking joints off teenagers."

"Maybe we were just fortunate for a while. Maybe this is what's natural, and people are just bad. I can't think of any other time where I felt so useless, and it just keeps piling on," Bobby said.

"I think you're too hard on yourself. We are working on every angle. You know as well as I do we can only go where the evidence takes us. Eventually, someone will say something, and we will get the break we need," Jack told his partner.

"I should be the one telling you all this," Bobby admitted.

"Hey, it's nice to be the one giving advice for one," Jack said. "Let me enjoy it. Now how about that nightcap?"

Bobby nodded and grinned. "Sometimes, you aren't such a pain in the ass."

*****

When Bartholomew Payne smiled into the mirror, he didn't see a pit or black hole. What he saw was a trapdoor. All he needed to do was part his lips to remember that beautiful night so many years ago. The trapdoor in the Sandy, where he had made a kill. A lot had happened, but his most vivid memory was gazing down into the water and feeling a sense of power and warmth. He liked the feeling of power over the women, but that was easy. Force, in the end, is easy to execute, and people are compliant, especially excitement-loving girls who don't know much about the world, or men like Bartholomew Payne.

He hadn't planned on killing her, not until he'd looked into the pitch black of the ocean and made peace with that side of himself. Killing was neither good nor bad. It just was, like satisfying an appetite. Hunger isn't a moral question. He laughed. He hadn't thought so much since school. Maybe he'd write a paper about it, send it to Detective Justice.

In his cell in Osceola State Pen, Payne remembered how he closed the trapdoor, feeling like he'd closed the door on his old self. Now the world was going to face a new Bartholomew Payne, starting with the woman tied to the bed. Lovelace, was that her name? He was glad nobody had saw him as they entered the hotel and meandered dizzily from the pills to her room. But now he felt sober as a bishop.

At first, she'd thought he was just getting kinky. But that was hours earlier. Now tears made her eyeliner run. Now she pleaded from a mouth hastily gagged with a torn pillowcase. The more she squirmed, the more convinced he became that she was there for a purpose—to be his sacrifice. A sacrifice to his new self. Payne went to the bathroom and looked closely at his reflection. He didn't just look at himself. He *beheld* himself. And then, in one quick furious motion, he hit the mirror with his fist and broke it into pieces. Goodbye to the old Bartholomew Payne. Hello to a shard of glass and the offering that waited on the hotel bed.

*****

Early Friday morning, with the rising sun warming the air and bringing color to the gray hues of night, Officer Pac was on patrol when she noticed a figure walking along the side of the road. As she approached, she was able to make out a teenage-looking girl wearing nothing but a pair of panties. Pac made a U-turn and slowly pulled alongside her then parked a few yards ahead of the girl, only then noticing she was bleeding from the mouth.

"Young lady, are you okay?" she asked, opening her door. The blood on the girl's face looked smeared, as if she had tried to wipe it away, but there was just too much.

"I…live there…" The girl lifted her finger, pointing up the road. Officer Pac reached back into her cruiser and grabbed the windbreaker she kept on the empty passenger seat for cold weather. She got out of the car and put the jacket over the girl's shoulders, noticing her flinch at the touch.

"I want to go home," the girl gasped.

"Okay, okay," Officer Pac said as she gently led her back to the patrol car. "I'll take you home. Just come sit down right here with me first."

The girl obliged, letting herself get eased into the back of squad car.

"Am I under arrest?"

"No, darling. I just need you back there for your safety. Now who did this to you, ma'am?"

The young girl looked at the officer with her bloodshot eyes. "I… I bit him," she said.

"Who? Tell me, ma'am, who?" Officer Pac implored.

"Eight-seven-M… Eight-seven…" The girl's hoarse voice trailed off as she quivered, wrapping the jacket tightly around her body. Pac knew protocol dictated she should have the girl taken in an ambulance, but this somehow felt personal. She didn't want her handled by men right now.

"It's all right. You're safe now. Pull that jacket over you and lay your head down." Officer Pac got on her radio. "Dispatch, I have a girl fitting the Amber Callaway description."

"Where are you now, Officer?" asked the operator.

"A few miles past the Sandy Beach Hotel heading toward North Sandy."

"Do you need an ambulance, Officer?"

"Negative. I'm heading to the hospital now. Call and give them a heads-up. I should be there in ten minutes," Officer Pac said. She took the risk of keeping the sirens off, wanting the ride to be smooth as possible. She saw the girl was traumatized, probably assaulted, but her injuries didn't look life-threatening.

"Copy that, Officer," the operator replied.

*****

Bobby and Jack were lucky their nightcap hadn't sprawled into a blowout as they were roused from their beds with the news Amber Callaway might have been found alive. The detectives met up at Sandy Beach Memorial and spotted Officer Pac sitting in the waiting area.

"Jane," Bobby called out softly. "Is it her?"

Officer Pac stood from her seat. "Yes, Detective."

"You were able to confirm it?"

"The parents' reaction was all the formal ID I needed."

Bobby gave a thumbs-up gesture. "That is the only ID I care about, Jane. Good job, Officer."

"Where did you spot her?" Jack asked.

Jane turned her eyes toward Detective Cutler. "About three miles past the Sandy Beach Hotel, walking toward North Sandy."

Bobby grimaced. "So she was heading in the opposite direction of her home."

"Yes, sir," Pac replied. "I suspect she may have been roaming the mangroves before making her way out or had been restrained and escaped. Honestly, I can't believe that she made it out at all in her condition."

"Damn it," Jack said through a clenched jaw. "We had search parties going in the opposite direction."

"Surveying near the home was the right play," Bobby reassured Jack while consolingly patting him on the shoulder. "Besides, there is only so much area we can cover in that short of a time frame with our resources."

Jack sighed. "Was she able to say anything?"

Pac crossed her arms. "Detective, she didn't even know where she was and looked like a Mack truck hit her."

"Understood," Jack said as his gaze fell to the floor. Bobby's did as well for a moment.

"Although," Officer Pac then mentioned, "she did manage to mumble what I think is a license plate number."

"Do you remember what she said?" Bobby asked.

"Yes, 87M. That's all she could muster."

Bobby exhaled slightly. "It's a start."

"We beggars can't be choosers," Jack said, glad to have any evidence to work.

Around forty-five minutes later, Amber's doctor, Dr. Dan Dominic, found the officers sitting in the lobby. Bobby got up and extended his hand to greet the doctor.

"Doctor, I'm Detective Justice, and this is my partner, Detective Cutler. Officer Pac here found the victim."

"Good to meet you, officers."

"How is Amber?" Officer Pac asked directly.

The doctor scratched his chin stubble. "We have her sedated. Honestly, she is fortunate to have made it away from her assailant alive."

"Dr. Dominic, what can you tell us about her injuries?" Bobby questioned.

"Where to start?" the doctor said rhetorically. "She has eye hemorrhaging and throat damage that is consistent with some asphyxia. Also, odd markings on her neck plus severe bruising all around it." Dr. Dominic pointed out areas on his own neck to illustrate.

"Odd how? From being strangled?"

"Yes, that would be my guess. There was something strong and forceful to the throat area."

"That's consistent with what we saw in the Hill investigation," Cutler noted.

"Whoever the attacker is, I'm sure he thinks she's dead. I would," the doctor affirmed.

"Any sign of sexual assault?" Bobby asked with a delicate tone.

"Yes, Detective. I'm hoping there isn't permanent damage."

"Permanent?" Officer Pac repeated as her chin quivered slightly.

"Yes, Officer. I hope she may be able to have kids of her own one day. This was a savage attack that may require some reconstruction."

"Has she tried to speak about anything, Doc?" Jack queried.

"No," Dr. Dominic said. "Her vocal cords are damaged. She also has some harm to the trachea, which is making her breathing labored and causing the throat to swell. Speaking more than a few words will be difficult or just about impossible for a while."

Bobby shook his head. "How long will she be sedated, Doctor? Maybe we can have her write something out or draw a description of who assaulted her…when she's ready."

Dr. Dan stared at the detectives, looking frustrated. "Even if Ms. Callaway wasn't sedated with her throat and various other injuries, I believe you will have to refrain from interviewing the patient today. It's not possible or ethical."

"Doc, it's vital that—"

Dominic cut off Jack. "Not to mention the vaginal and anal trauma, the bleeding, the pain, the severe dehydration, and concussion. Plus, whatever we may not have even found yet. All of which would be aggravated by the further trauma of recounting her story. Not that she can at this point."

"We have a job here," Jack said, meeting the doctor's frustration with his own. "Whoever this might be is still out there and will attack again."

"She's the only person that might be able to ID this person," Bobby added.

"I understand. I do. You want to get this guy, and I want to help. But my priority is my patient, and she's not ready. Neither her parents nor I will allow more than she can handle. So until she's able and, more importantly, ready to speak, you will have to be patient," the doctor said, looking between the policemen. "And I have authority inside these hospital walls. Legally."

"Gentlemen, please stop bickering. We all want what's best for the victim, Doctor," Pac said, calming the situation that had suddenly become tense.

Jack looked to Bobby, who nodded his resignation. They'd have to wait.

"Okay, Doctor. Look, let's keep this out of the media as long as we can. At least while she's here," Bobby specified. "I will send patrol officers to guard the room, twelve-hour shifts, and hospital staff personnel that only you allow can go in."

"That we can agree on," Dr. Dan said.

*****

It was a bit over the top, but Todd was glad to have Hunter exposed to places like Dr. George's house. The paintings, smudges of color that looked like they were done by a monkey, were a tad strange, but Hunter still took a few minutes moving from one the next. Maybe he had a mind for art. Also, the place was big—huge. Far more space than the old doctor needed. This showed Hunter you could aspire. You could get great things if you really worked. He didn't want the kid repairing other people's decks his whole life.

"Hunter," Todd called to him. "Have a look at this bronze horse and cowboy statue."

"Ah, I got that out of the back of the *New Yorker* magazine. You have good taste, Todd," the doctor said.

"Hold on," Hunter called. Todd saw his son now glued to the countertop TV, which was broadcasting the news.

"She's been missing for three days, and a major search is ongoing," the newscaster reported. "At this point, the cops believe the suspect related to the Tara Hill case, and now Amber Callaway, could be the same."

"So, Hunter," George began. "How old is a big strong-looking lad like yourself?"

Hunter couldn't take his eyes off the news report. "I'm sixteen," he mumbled, staring at the TV.

"Wow, a big youngster." George chuckled. "What are you feeding this kid, Todd?"

"He gets it from my side of the family. My dad was a big guy too." Todd was suddenly proud of his child, for no other reason than he was big.

As they talked, Isabel appeared from the kitchen.

"Welcome," Isabel greeted Todd. "I've heard a lot about you."

Todd gave her a good looking over. A lot of woman for an old man. He chastised himself for his thoughts. Why shouldn't the rich doctor score somebody so beautiful? "Oh, only good things, I hope," he said.

Isabel laughed, showing her radiant smile. "And who is this young man?" she asked, turning to Hunter.

"Hunter," the boy said with a low tone, staring at Isabel with a hostile expression.

"He's my oldest," Todd told Isabel.

"Very handsome young man, Todd," she said, offering a playful wink.

"Yeah, he gets that from me," Todd joked. He was glad to see her flirt a bit with Hunter. Get him interested in girls, finally. Or ones who weren't being stalked in some slasher film.

Hunter looked away from her. "Whatever," he said agitatedly.

"Oh, I think we made him shy." Isabel giggled with her hand slightly covering her mouth.

"He will be just fine." Todd laughed as Hunter gritted his teeth.

"Well, thank you so much for coming today," Isabel said politely.

Todd nodded, getting down to business. "Of course. Thanks for the work."

"I'll be upstairs. Yell if you need anything," Isabel said.

"Yes, ma'am," Todd said.

"Well, I'm off to work," George said as he kissed Isabel on the cheek. Isabel waved to them then headed to her room.

"So you're retiring on us?" Todd asked. "Start living on a yacht somewhere?"

George laughed. "No yachts, but the wedding date is mid-August."

"Good for you, Dr. Darling," Todd said excitedly.

"Thank you! Well, see you tomorrow, Todd, Hunter."

"Bye, Dr. Darling," Todd said.

"Later, bro," Hunter muttered.

"Bro? Seriously?" Todd asked after Darling had left the room.

*****

Bobby was glad his days off sometimes didn't coincide with Jack's. He appreciated his partner's enthusiasm, but his youth taxed him. He always wanted something, like a baby bird with its mouth perpetually open. Plus, he didn't want Jack around while casing the place. It would only put more thoughts in his head.

Nobody investigated the hotel when Amber disappeared. It was on the list, but only after more realistic locations had been searched, more likely witnesses interviewed. Now the girl had been found, but Bobby was determined the hotel played a role. Not in the spooky way the mayor insisted, but as a matter of common sense. Plus, Payne had him interested. With that in mind, he dressed in street clothes and parked down the beach from the Sandy.

Bobby strode into the lobby, looking at his watch. Just any tourist. No clerk. The desk was empty. *Nice security*, he thought. Bobby was struck by how dark the hallway was, considering it was daytime. It smelled of moldy wood and sea brine. He'd been in the hotel before, but that was in the rush of the prostitution sting and its confused aftermath. Now he felt the stillness of the place. Where were the tourists? It's like it had emptied itself out, knowing he was visiting. Did the hotel expect him?

He opened a door or two in the hallway, not really thinking he'd find anything. He wasn't disappointed. Beds were made to military perfection, with mints on the pillow. He closed each door quietly, as though trying not to wake the occupant, though he had seen with his own eyes that each room was empty.

Finally, at the end of the hallway, he came to room 6, where Tara Hill had been found. He opened the door again to discover a well-made bed. The room looked somehow older than the others. He entered and began to look around. Even though he realized the room was no longer in use, he still had that feeling he was disturbing somebody. A chill began to gather in his gut when he looked down. A trapdoor. He thought he heard a cry. Bobby felt a sudden surge of unexpected sadness, and a memory rose unbidden in his mind. "We'll call her Tess, after your mother," his wife had said right before the miscarriage.

Bobby braced himself and pushed the memory from his mind. He looked down at the floor, the trapdoor there. He was just about to bend over to pull it open when a voice came from behind him.

"Detective Justice, doing some research, I see."

Bobby spun around to find a man—a vagrant he'd seen around town—with a red beard and ratty clothing.

"Who are you?"

"Well, name's Bram van Brock. Friends call me Professor. 'Cept most have passed away by now."

"How do you know my name?" Bobby asked.

"Well, there's a lot to discuss. But not here. You can look all you like in the Sandy, but she keeps her secrets hidden. Trust me, I know."

"How's that?"

"Well, I'm a historian by trade. Used to draw a salary from Florida State before I began writing for the paper. Problem is, nobody wants to hear certain things, so now I just, well, freelance. Don't get me started on me. Come along, Detective. Let's take a walk."

That the man knew not only his name but rank got Bobby curious. He allowed van Brock to lead him from the hotel. Only now tourists came and went from their rooms, as though it had suddenly come back to life. As they strolled through the lobby, Ms. Kerrigan called from the desk, "Goodbye, gentlemen. Do come again."

Bobby nodded. *Creepy bitch.*

"Got a destination in mind?" Bobby asked.

"Just along the beach," Bram answered. "The fresh sea air keeps me young, if you don't mind."

"Sure," Bobby said. Then something struck him. "You were the one who put that photo under Jack's door, weren't you?"

"Indeed, I was," Bram said. "You have a good power of deduction. That's why you were in that hotel. That's why we're talking."

"I see."

"So, Detective, let's make good use of this time together. Tell me, after all you've seen this past year, what disturbs you the most?"

Bobby felt strange being interrogated by a vagrant, no matter what his credentials were. His ex-girlfriend, Gwen, had always implored him to open his mind to new things. Well, now he was trying.

"Chase Lovell," he finally said.

"That's admirable. I would have thought the idea of the undead or a town's damnation would keep you up at night. But an innocent boy. That's how I know you are a good cop—you attend to the good more than the evil. May I ask you what makes you think the boy is still alive and Elwood hasn't killed him by now?" Professor van Brock asked.

"We can't know for sure, but my gut tells me he still has him."

"Good. The gut is what connects us as people, you know. Not the mind or the heart, as romantics believe. But the gut. Trust it. Didn't Lee Earl Elwood live up the road from this spot?" the professor queried.

"Yes, but I'm not ready to make that leap," Bobby said. "I'm barely on board with what we are discussing now."

"Throw a stone in the water, you get ripples. Evil works the same way," the professor said. Bobby stopped and gazed out over the ocean.

"I looked into the two previous Sandy Beach serial killers, and if you're looking for patterns, you can find them," Bobby admitted then nodded toward the hotel. "But in this case, Valentina Nunez was the first to be killed there since the sixties, and her husband is locked up. So it's not him going on a Bartholomew Payne type of rampage."

"Ahh, outstanding, Detective Justice," Professor van Brock said. "I see you are open to the unknown after all."

"I would say I'm open to an occasional prayer, but I'm still not ready to go to church on Sundays."

"I completely understand," said the professor. "Yet you went to see Payne in prison. Not quite church, but—"

"How did you know that?"

"You're following a trail. He's a crumb. A mean murderous crumb, perhaps, but you needed to make that step."

"Yes, but it doesn't help solve who kidnapped Chase Lovell or killed Tara Hill or attempted to kill Amber Callaway. These are pretty spaced apart, I'd say."

"In my research, I have noted that there always seems to be a significant event that starts a string of killings. I would say the Nunez murder qualifies and surely Ms. Hill as well," Professor van Brock said.

"All right, I'll play along," Bobby said, suddenly craving a cigarette. "We know what happened in the sixties. You have the girlfriend of Bartholomew Payne overdose. We will call that a significant event. He then goes on to kill three women. One of them at the Sandy Beach Hotel. Correct?"

"Yes, Detective," said the professor.

"Okay, let's go back twenty years and discuss what happened," Bobby continued. "I heard talk of a husband finding his wife dead from hanging herself. Is the name Meredith Darling familiar?"

Van Brock nodded.

"Okay, and who was the husband? He had to have been the top suspect."

"George Darling? Dr. George Darling of the Sandy Beach Family Care Clinic, to be exact. I know him well. I think he's a great man," Professor Bram van Brock posited. "He came here from Miami during World War II after his infant child passed."

Bobby winced and silently wished a baby hadn't entered the picture.

"You okay?" van Brock asked then continued when Bobby nodded. "Well, he was staying at the Sandy Beach Hotel while looking for a home. He was taking medical courses at South Beach College here in town, which was doing its part for the military. They had expedited three-year courses at that time. Not long after moving into the hotel, his wife hung herself."

"Well, that's ominous," Bobby admitted.

"He never bothered with a home after. He stayed at the hotel until he graduated in '45 and worked as a military doctor until his return in 1950 when he opened the clinic."

"I know the clinic but wasn't aware of the doctor's past. Doesn't this follow the Sandy Beach Murderer timeline?" Bobby asked.

"Yes, absolutely, Detective. Four women from '43 through '45," van Brock recounted. "One woman in the hotel and the other three in their homes."

"Was Darling ever a suspect?"

"Not to my knowledge. Healers tend not to be killers. Darling was always just considered a grieving husband and father who was getting his medical degree amid World War II."

"What was the Sandy Beach Murderer's MO?" Bobby asked.

"The Sandy Beach Murderer would use a tonic to put their victims to sleep then slash their throats. Wrote a message on the wall with their blood," the professor recalled.

"What was the message?"

"*I'll find you again*," van Brock answered.

Bobby threw his hands up. "Jesus, we have enough going on currently unearthing the doctor's, no matter what it may or may not be, isn't something I can address right now," he said, annoyed.

"We're just having a conversation here, aren't we, Detective Justice? To pass the time, let's say. Now what do you see in this picture?" Bram asked, pulling a copy of the photo of a hung woman from his coat pocket.

"We've seen that before. Hardly a good postcard for Sandy Beach. Guinevere at her demise," Bobby said.

"Yes, that's what you *notice*, but there's so much more to *see*. Like that big lady in the crowd. That's Vasa Fionnghuala, one of the mob organizers. She was found dead in her home several months later. The cause of death is unknown. And as for the woman standing next to her, she was said to be the leader of it all. Her name would be none other than Eleanor Darling, grandmother of George Darling. She also passed soon in 1900, not long after giving birth to Margaret Darling, George's mother," the professor finished.

"Look, Professor, this isn't exactly helping. Fuck Darling, all of them for that matter, and Guinevere's goddamn eighty-something-year-old curse. We have an eighteen-year-old dead. We have another sixteen-year-old girl attacked and a ten-year-old who's been missing," Detective Justice insisted. "I'm not going to be arresting a spirit or a doctor that we have no evidence on besides a ghost story."

"But, Detective Justice, you were playing along so well before," said van Brock.

Bobby breathed in the warm Gulf air then relaxed. "Honestly, had I heard this before last June, I might have been more willing to discuss it. But right now, I just can't. Sorry."

"You don't have to apologize to me, Detective."

Bobby took another deep breath. He still had a strange feeling in his gut from being in the hotel, like something from room 6 stayed with him. He tried to put it down to lack of sleep but couldn't quite convince himself. Van Brock looked like he was waiting for Bobby to continue.

"Okay, fine. Let's say it is Darling along with Payne. How do you reconcile Nunez not being the killer now?"

"I'm not sure that part matters. It doesn't seem to be an impatient curse, if you will allow me to call it that," the professor said with a chuckle. "At least if you go back to the origin of all this. Roderick Tidwell shot his wife, and then two more women were murdered, but not by his hands. With Amber Callaway surviving, I think that puts another victim in jeopardy very soon."

"That would most likely be the case with any serial killer, Professor," Bobby said. "Curse or not."

"Very true, Detective. I guess to be more specific, look to next month as a target date. It's the anniversary of the Sandy Guinevere murder."

"I can't very well make all women, especially teenage girls, stay home now, can I?" Bobby rubbed his eyes. "This isn't *Jaws*. I can't just tell people to stay out of the water."

"Well, as you said before, Detective Justice, there is someone out there who still needs to be apprehended. No matter how it started, it won't end until you stop it."

"That's why we're talking. There are a lot of coincidences with the hotel and how things fall on specific dates. I'll concede there. I don't know what you expect me to believe or do after that," Bobby said.

"I know it's frustrating not to understand or not able to explain something away. It doesn't mean it isn't so," said the professor.

"Look, I'll put some personal beliefs aside if it saves lives. So if we are saying Guinevere's a ghost, and she is doing this, what does she want?" Bobby asked. "How could we make her stop?"

"I honestly have no idea," Professor van Brock said. "But like all of us, I'd wager she just wants what's right, and then maybe her spirit can rest."

"But how can I be expected to stop a ghost, or a curse, with godlike powers?"

"She's no god. Look, see that plane?" Bram pointed into the sky, where a plane sped across the horizon, a trail of exhaust in its wake. "Now from up there, that pilot has a much different view of the world. He can see much farther than the rest of us, but that doesn't make him Jesus or Lucifer or any type of god or for that matter, smarter than we are."

"Up in the sky? I'm not religious, but something makes me think Sandy Guinevere is closer to hell than heaven," Bobby said.

"Then that's where to start looking," van Brock replied with a wink.

*****

Later that evening, Kate was sitting in the living room watching the news, waiting for Todd and Hunter to return home.

"Authorities say they are following all leads in the cases of Tara Hill and Amber Callaway. They also ask if anyone has any info that could lead to an arrest call—"

Kate turned off the TV when she heard Todd's key in the door. She'd been locking it lately. Couldn't say why. "Hey," she said, standing from the couch. "How did it go today?"

"Might have me another full-time employee." Todd looked at Hunter, who shrugged.

"It was all right," Hunter said. "No biggie. Better than cleaning ditches."

"Maybe you can save enough in a few more months to make a down payment on a vehicle," Kate said, rounding the couch to hug her husband.

"You mean a truck," Hunter corrected. "Vehicle's a cop term."

"Do you have more work at Dr. Darling's tomorrow?" Kate asked Todd.

"Yeah," Todd said, setting his toolbox down. "But I gotta go meet Tommy at this other job Wednesday. This old lady, Mrs. Cross, is complaining to high heaven and back that he hasn't laid her new carpeting yet."

"Oh, okay," Kate said, nodding. "I just wanted to make sure my boss is taken care of, sweetie. That's all."

"I know, baby." Todd kissed his wife. "I'm just glad you smiled."

Hunter, still unaware Amber had been found alive, called Goo from the upstairs phone.

"This Goo," De'Ron answered.

"Hey, bro," Hunter responded.

"What up, Killa? How workin' with the pops went?"

"Sucked big ass. Whatcha up to?"

"Smokin' and hangin' with one of my side bitches."

"Dawg, you won't believe what I saw today," Hunter announced.

"I don't even wanna hear it," Goo replied with chuckle.

"Dude, this one is special, though," Hunter said excitedly.

"Yo ass fuckin' obsessed, bro. It's all you damn talk about. This ain't a business, Killa."

"What's that mean?"

"Means this shit ain't something you do every fuckin' day! You do realize that, right?" Goo asked, irritated.

"What the fuck is your problem? Aren't we partners?"

"Bro, are you not seeing what's goin' on? All the heat out there right now. We need to be layin' low."

"Fuck, dawg. Well, for how long?"

"Damn, nigga, what the fuck you tryin' to do? Be that Jack the motherfucka or whoever?"

"Let's just do this one last thing, and we can chill for a bit."

"The fuck, bro. Nah, we not doin' shit right now. Big blood will kill the fuck outta me, not fuckin' round. Legit kill my nigga ass if I bring any of this shit his way. Probably yo ass too."

"Fuck it then! I'll do what I gotta do on my own," Hunter said, angered.

"You do dat, Killa," Goo responded then hung up the phone.

"Hello… Goo?" Hunter slammed his telephone. "Fuck him then."

*****

Isabel stepped from the hot mist of the shower and wrapped herself in a towel. She liked a shower in the evening, the dampness of her hair keeping her cool though the night. George was already lying in bed. He rested his paperback on his chest so he could watch Isabel's every movement as she groomed herself, sitting in front of the bedroom mirror then brushing her hair with the mother-of-pearl handled brush he bought for her.

George looked at Isabel, admiring her. "You're so beautiful. Making you happy is all I think about."

Isabel glanced at George in the reflection and smiled back. "Such a sweet man," she said.

"Thank you, my love." George couldn't focus on his book any longer. Watching her was a story itself, every movement filled with meaning and consequence.

"What are you reading about?" she asked in an attempt to break his trance. George got up from the bed. "Oh, just something I found relevant," he said as tried to toss the book into an open drawer. It missed and fell to the floor, where Isabel was able to read the title: *Rebirth of a Soul: Living Inside Your New Skin.'*

"I see," Isabel uttered. "Okay, keep your secret." She let out a small giggle.

George appeared nervous for a moment. "Secrets, my dear?"

"Yes, keeping your book a secret," Isabel said.

"Oh, not so much. I just didn't think you'd be interested," George said.

"I'm just glad you have other interests," Isabel teased. "Sometimes you look at me like you haven't seen me in fifty years."

"*Forty*," George whispered. Sometimes his gaze shifted inward. He was still looking at her, but now he appeared to be lost in thought.

"What do you mean? It was just this morning." Isabel giggled.

"Was it?"

George's memory flashed to a woman's body, hanging lifeless in a hotel room closet like marionette. On the bedroom wall was a note written in blood.

I'll find you again.

"Are you okay, dear? George?"

"Yes, I'm wonderful," George said, focusing on her again. "I'm just anxious for our wedlock, my beloved."

"Do you think August was the right choice?" Isabel asked.

"Right now, tonight would have been the only choice that could have been better. I would have married you again the same day you walked into my clinic."

"*Again*? Are you sure you are feeling well?" Isabel joked.

George shook his head. "I just meant I'd marry you a hundred times if that's what you asked of me," he said uneasily.

"I think once will be enough," Isabel said. "I'm glad you did not mind planning it for the middle of August."

"If it's August that you want, then I do as well, my darling."

"Yes, I think it works out well because my mother will be here to witness it."

"It does, my sweet, and I'm glad she can make it."

"And I'm glad it will be cozy. I do not think it needed to be very big. Only a few of us," Isabel said, continuing to brush her hair.

"Yes, my dear."

"My sister and mother are so happy for us."

George sat quietly for a moment. She felt she knew George when he was talking, but when he was quiet, he became a stranger to her.

"What is it, dear?"

"I think I've decided to sell the clinic to Dr. Dominic," George said.

Isabel paused brushing, stopping mid-stroke. "Is that what you feel is best? she asked. "You may get bored being home every day."

George stood from the bed. "I want to spend every moment I can with you." He walked up behind Isabel, placed his hands on her shoulders, then gently kissed her neck. "You're the light in my life, and I am forever grateful that I found you. I would be lost without you now."

"Thank you, darling George," she said, trying to convey a pleasure she didn't feel. She suddenly saw the reality she was facing—day in and out with a man she barely knew and whose touch made her squirm. Again, in that moment, she weighed the pros and cons of her situation. She took a deep breath and tried to smile.

"I can't wait to be together for the first time on our wedding night," George said.

"Of course, dear," Isabel whispered as she sat motionless, staring into at the strands of dead hair in her brush.

July 12, 1984

Goo got a call from Cordale Goodman in the early afternoon. It was hot, and Goo wanted to stay indoors, smoking a joint and playing Atari, but Cordale couldn't be ignored. At least it would give him an excuse to get a pack of powdered donuts he'd been craving. It was a short ride to CG Auto Repair. He arrived with his upper lip dusted with sugar.

"What's up, my blood?" De'Ron greeted Cordale.

"Sit down." Cordale nodded toward the chair in front of his desk. "Jesus, boy, what you been dipping into?" Cordale involuntarily ran his tongue over his lip. Goo took the hint and licked his own lip. "Just some, what do they call it? *Brunch*. What you need done?"

"I need you to take a ride tomorrow," Cordale said and began to jot something down.

"Where to, and wit who?" De'Ron asked.

Cordale ripped off the part of the page he was writing on then handed it to De'Ron.

"Downtown and alone," he said.

"Damn, aight." De'Ron's eyes widened when he read the note. "Come back here with it?"

"Yes, knucklehead," Cordale grumbled, shaking his head. "Where else is yo ass gonna take it?"

"Fuck, just makin' sure, bruh," Goo said, irked. "So I don't need backup for this shit?"

Cordale waved his hand. "Shouldn't. These are businessmen. They are expecting us. And besides, you gotta learn to handle some of this on your own."

"I can handle it." De'Ron again glanced down at note, which included a large figure. "That be a lot of cheddar, though."

"It is, but it's not the product." Cordale lit up a cigarette. "I can't have you getting pulled over alone with that again."

"I feel ya, my dawg." Goo stuffed the note inside his pocket. "You got anything else for me?"

"Yes. Stop bringing all those little hoes to the house," Cordale stated as he blew cigarette smoke out of his nose.

"Why though?" Goo asked with a smile. "They all fine as fuck."

"It's not a fucking hotel. Plus, half them little bitches are probably underage."

"They not underage. Some older than me," De'Ron proudly confessed.

Cordale just stared at De'Ron. "Well, pick out a bitch, and then her ass can sleep over, but I'm tired of seeing six of 'em running around all coked out," he said, finally smiling.

De'Ron smiled back. "Fuck, aight then. Meddling nigga. You got yo hoes too."

"I'll leave it be when yo ass makes enough cheddar to get yo own place." Cordale leaned back in his chair. "Which is exactly what you gonna do if you get one of 'em knocked up."

"Shit, I said okay, nigga. Don't gotta get all upset, fuck."

Cordale pointed at De'Ron. "You just do what I need you to do tomorrow."

*****

Todd and Hunter had made good progress on the Darling deck. They'd replaced the rotted wood and were almost finished varnishing the new portions. Todd was glad to see Hunter, though showing little enthusiasm for work, was quite good with his hands and surprisingly strong. Having finished for the morning, they were eating lunch on the deck table when the porch door slid open and Isabel appeared, carrying a lemonade in each hand. At the sight of her, Hunter hunched his shoulders and glared.

"Hi, gentlemen. How are you today?" Isabel greeted them, placing the cold drinks on the table.

"Hello, Ms. Isabel. Just finishing up lunch, and we will get back to varnishing shortly," Todd answered.

"Oh, please, take your time. There's more lemonade in the kitchen if you want it."

"Yes, ma'am," Todd replied as his pager went off. He looked at the familiar number. "Ms. Isabel, may I use your telephone?"

"Of course, Todd. It's in the living room," Isabel replied as she headed back indoors.

After the door glided closed behind her, Hunter turned to his dad. "Ma'am? She's closer to my age."

Todd looked sternly at Hunter. "She's the boss, son. Be respectful."

Hunter crumpled his lunch bag into a ball and tossed it toward the pool garbage. "She's only with that old fart for money."

"Hunter! That's enough. I hope she can't hear you from inside, damn it," Todd said. "Now go grab that other damn toolbox out of the back seat of the truck."

"What the fuck, man. It's true. Don't gotta get all pissed about shit!" Hunter said as he stormed off.

Todd shook his head then went indoors to make his call. In the living room, the television had been left on. Isabel must have been watching soaps. He dialed, looking at the screen, his interest perking up over a bit of local news.

"And we may have some potentially promising news to report in the Amber Callaway case—"

Todd turned off the television as the phone began to ring. "That damn kid," Todd said aloud. "Hey, no, not you. Hunter," he told his colleague Tommy, who was on the other end of the line. "I don't know. It's always something with that boy. Anyway, what's up? Damn it, she's griping again? Did you tell her new carpet does that? Well, gosh dog-it, all right. I'll be by tomorrow. Okay, I got it. See you then."

Todd found Hunter back out on the deck, sunning himself, the toolbox at his side.

"All right, let's get back at it."

"Who called you?" Hunter asked.

"Tommy," Todd answered as he glared at the unfinished work. "We have to go back out to see Ms. Cross tomorrow."

Hunter chuckled. "She's bitching again?"

"That damn old lady can kiss my ass," Todd murmured under his breath.

Hunter tilted his head closer toward his father. "What? I didn't hear you."

"Nothing. Just hand me that dang bubble level," Todd said. Just then, Darling's yardman Jose walked up. He scanned the work then greeted them with a "Hi, fellas. How are you?"

"Hey, Jose, just fine. How about you?" Todd replied.

Jose shrugged and nodded. "I'm okay. Still fucking alive. Anyway, is the doctor around?"

Todd chuckled. "No, he didn't come back for lunch today. Ms. Isabel is home upstairs."

"That's okay. I will come back later. Thanks, Todd."

*****

The next day, Bobby was informed by Dr. Dominic that Amber Callaway was finally well enough to speak. Bobby had checked several times over the past month but had been put off by the on-duty staff who had grown protective of the teen. Amber's parents were clear on the phone—she would only talk to Officer Pac. Bobby grudgingly agreed and dispatched her on the same day.

Amber Callaway was propped up in the hospital bed, flanked by her parents and an array of multicolored bouquets.

"I appreciate this, Mr. and Mrs. Callaway. Especially you, Ms. Amber," Officer Pac said as she looked over Amber's healing face and arms. "I brought some Mountain Dew. I don't know if they let you have that in here. I can get you something else if you like."

"Not unless you can keep the press from hounding us," Cliff Callaway answered for his daughter.

"I wish I could, Mr. Callaway."

"She only began talking to us a couple of days ago," Jennifer Callaway confided, stroking Amber's cheek.

Cliff crossed his arms. "We're doing this because my daughter said she was ready. Plus, we all want this no-good coward caught soon before it happens again," he said.

"I understand. This case is a top priority," Pac said. "I have not slept in..." The officer paused. "I don't even remember the last time I slept through the night."

"That makes two of us," Jennifer Callaway remarked. "Do you have any leads?"

"We are looking, Mrs. Callaway. The detectives are following up on all leads. Your daughter is our first real opportunity to get ahead of this person."

"I bit him. Somewhere on the leg, I think," Amber divulged, proudly in Pac's estimation, without being prompted.

Everyone looked down at Amber. "Good for you, young lady. You're a fighter," Pac said as she pulled up a chair over to sit at her bedside.

"There was two of them," Amber revealed, resolute. "One drove and stayed in the truck. The other one grabbed me off my bike and hit me."

"So he has an accomplice?" Pac noticed the girl tremble. "You're doing great, Amber. Now I don't want you to feel any pressure or feel like you have to answer. Just tell me as much as you can recall about that day," Pac said, pressing the record button on the tape recorder.

"I remember riding home from the store when they pulled alongside me. The boy on the passenger side of the vehicle said, 'What's up, Amber?' I asked how he knew my name. 'He'll tell you if you go out with him tonight!' the guy driving shouted at me, laughing. Then the passenger side boy got out of the truck and said, 'You should be more worried about what I plan to teach you.' I told them goodbye and tried to ride past."

Amber paused, looking over at her father.

"Would you feel more comfortable telling me this alone?" Pac asked.

Amber nodded. Amber's parents reluctantly withdrew from the room. Pac checked to make sure the door was closed.

"It's only us now. Just know none of this is your fault."

Amber nodded.

"Okay, let's continue. And stop at any time."

"What I remember is that he pulled me off my bike by the back of my hair and threw me on the ground. I started to scream. Then he kicked me in the stomach. I couldn't breathe after. I was hoping someone would see, but it was as if everyone else in the world had disappeared, leaving me with just them."

"Do you want to take a break now?"

"No, I want to finish," Amber said. "I was trying to catch my breath when he lifted me from behind and threw me in the truck. They drove me into a wooded area far from the road. The one that kicked me yanked me out of the truck and dragged me behind a tree, ripping my clothes off. I screamed and slapped him repeatedly and managed to get away for a moment. He clutched me and threw me down again. He pulled his pants down and pushed my face toward his private area, so I bit him as hard as I could. That made him holler. Then he punched me in the back of my head a few times. Kicked me in the stomach again. I'm pretty sure I passed out then because I don't remember much after that."

"You're being so brave," Pac said. "Can you remember what they looked like?"

"I remember the one I bit was White, big, with shaggy black hair, and the Black guy had some tattoos on his arms."

"Had you seen them before?"

"I believe so. The one who grabbed me. I think I've seen him cleaning trash from the ditches and off the beach around my neighborhood. I feel like he knew me somehow."

"Cleaning trash?" Pac asked.

"Dad says we get people doing community service in the neighborhood. He might be one of them. Or maybe from the mall."

"That's interesting and something we can work with," Pac said, giving her a quick nod of approval. "Now this is very important. You said you remembered three numbers on the license plate?"

"I don't remember if it was a license plate."

"When I found you, you were repeating an *8*, a *7*, and an *M*."

"I do remember something with 8 and a 7. I think there was an M also. I'm pretty sure it was on the back of the truck. I just can't be sure if it was a license plate or not," Amber said, appearing more comfortable.

"And it was a truck? Not a car or anything else like that, correct?"

"I remember a red truck," Amber said.

"This is all so helpful. More than you may realize. Would you be able to identify the suspects if you saw them again?" Pac asked.

"Yes," Amber said without hesitation. "I will never forget his face."

"Thank you," Pac said. "You're one tough, courageous girl, Amber, and I promise we're going to do everything we can to find these guys for you."

*****

Todd could see Tommy waiting for them in front of the Cross house. When they pulled up, Todd flicked his cigarette into the gutter then got out of the truck.

"Have you talked to her yet?" he asked.

"Nope, the hell with that shit. I figured I'd just wait on you so we could all get bitched at together," Tommy said.

Hunter scoffed. "Nothing makes that old buzzard happy."

"Nothing. I swear, big guy in the sky could come down himself and do a job for this lady, and she would still complain. I have no idea why she keeps hiring us if she thinks we're so damn terrible."

"She's just lonely. And she probably thinks you're cute. Let's grin and get this over with," Todd said before mounting the steps and giving a solid rap on the door. A moment later, Mrs. Cross answered. "Hi, Ms. Cro—"

"You see this carpet?" the old lady said straight away, pointing at the floor in the living room. "It's supposed to be *flat*. It's not flat, it's *wavy*, and I'm tripping every time I walk on it."

"She needs a walker then," Tommy muttered.

"Ms. Cross," Todd pleaded, "we just laid it down. It may just need to settle."

Ms. Cross put her hands on her hips. "So I should break my neck waiting for new carpet to *settle* when it should already be *flat*?"

Todd knitted his brow. "Okay, Ms. Cross. We'll see what we can do to fix it." He turned to Hunter and Tommy. "Let's get it pulled up, guys."

Ms. Cross stood, looking them over. "I should get some kind of discount for this," she said.

"Well," Todd said. "It could just be the carpet—"

"It's not the carpet!" she snapped. "That's expensive carpet."

"*Bullshit*," Tommy cursed under his breath.

"I'm going to get my tools outside, okay?" Todd said, giving his hired hand a sharp look but keeping an even tone.

"Well, okay," Ms. Cross said. "I have a hair appointment. I'll be back in a couple of hours."

Out at the truck, Todd cursed the luck he was having that day.

"Dammit. I thought I'd put all my toolboxes back in the truck. You got anything with you, Tommy?"

"No," Tommy said flatly. "I didn't actually think we had anything to fix."

"Shit. I know where it's at." Todd turned to his son. "Hunter, take my truck and go to the house and find that rusty toolbox with the broken clip on it. That should have what we need. I think I left it in the shed. Or actually, it's probably at the Darling residence."

"All right," Hunter said. "Give me your keys."

Todd took his keys from his pocket, but he hesitated before handing them over. "You can drive this, right?"

"Yes," Hunter groaned. "I do have a license, you know."

"Yeah, but you learned on your mom's car. This is a bit different."

"Damn, Dad. Don't you trust me?"

Todd exhaled and decided he did, then he handed the keys over. He watched Hunter pull out, a little too quickly for his taste.

"Are we really about pull this damn carpet up?" Tommy asked.

"Look, we have to make it look like we did something, or she won't stop nagging," he said.

"If that ain't the goddamn truth," Tommy declared.

*****

Hunter took the interstate so he could test the truck's acceleration. The speed got him juiced; he could feel the vibration rise from the seat through his crotch. He blasted the radio, switching stations from his dad's classic rock to a rap station from Miami. *Fuck home*, he thought. He'd go to the Darling place first and see what was up. He sped the entire way. Once there, he parked on the street and walked up the driveway. Hunter let himself in though the porch door, which he knew was always left open. This time, he took scant notice of the paintings. Instead, he headed up the stairs. When he pushed open the master bedroom door, he saw Isabel in bed, sleeping. He kept his eyes on her as she moved restlessly in a dream. When he sat down in her vanity chair, the woman startled awake, seeming to sense his presence.

"What are you doing here?" she asked.

"Just looking around," Hunter said nonchalantly. "I forgot something."

"Well," Isabel stammered. "It would not be here in my bedroom. Please go."

"No," Hunter said, standing up and moving to block the door. "This is exactly where it is."

"You should leave, or I will tell the doctor," Isabel threatened, speaking firmly. She got up from the bed and appeared to be looking for a way to get around Hunter. Her negligee was something different than Hunter had seen before, like new a dessert.

"So you like old guys, huh? Or do you just have daddy issues?" Hunter taunted as he looked her up and down.

Isabel was now visibly trembling. “What do you want!” she shouted.

Hunter grinned and shook his head. “Sluts like you just care about money. Don’t even give a fuck about anything else. Stuck-up bitch,” he growled.

“Leave!” Isabel shouted, her voice cracking in panic. “Go now!”

“Oh, I will. But not until I get what I came for,” Hunter declared as he stepped toward the bed.

Isabel made for the door, slamming into Hunter and trying to squeeze past, but he was big enough to keep her contained in the room.

“What’s wrong?” he taunted, towering over her. “I don’t have enough money for you, bitch?”

Isabel threw her hands on his chest and pushed against him one last time, sobbing. That’s when Hunter grabbed her by the throat. *It’s the taking control that’s the satisfying part. The rest is just gravy*, he thought. She tried to claw his face as he walked her backward to the bed. When she attempted to scream, Hunter squeezed down harder on her neck, letting go only to punch her in the stomach before throwing her down.

Isabel gasped for air as she doubled over in pain, clenching her stomach. An arid scream left her mouth when Hunter flipped her over and pulled her to the edge of the mattress. His pants were already down as she thrashed with her legs to both kick him and squirm away, but her attempts were returned with fists. Hunter only became more incited by her whimpering and begging. Her tears ran dry as she heaved and choked each time Hunter slammed into her. Eventually, he felt all the fight fade from her. The deadweight of her body was heavy to Hunter as he grabbed her by the hair to throw her on the floor. She groaned in agony as she rolled onto her stomach. Hunter felt that black energy, the precious flow of his body and mind that only savagery could hold, and then it dissolved, and he was just a boy on top of a woman. He watched dispassionately as she made one last effort to crawl toward the door, a mouse crawling from a trap that had already broken its back. Hunter pulled his pants up and observed her almost clinically before he dragged her toward him and forced her onto her back. Isabel gave him one last weak plea before he stomped down on her throat, applying all of his weight, not stopping until the gurgling sounds of Isabel's struggle subsided.

Hunter washed his face and hands in the bathroom sink, putting the washcloth in the dirty hamper bin. It was the same kind his mom used, he noticed. He left the bedroom and headed downstairs and was almost out the door before remembering the toolbox. Sure enough, it was still in the same place it had been left a day prior. He picked it up and quietly left the Darling residence.

Hunter found his dad and Tommy in Mrs. Cross's living room.

"There, see?" Todd said, pressing down on the carpet with his hands. "That's gonna be much better."

"Not that much," Tommy said from where he leaned against the wall.

When Todd turned and saw Hunter, he stood up. "What the hell took so long?"

"There must have been an accident. Traffic was backed up a while," Hunter said. "Here's the toolbox, Pop!"

Todd stared at Hunter. "Pop? What's got you so giddy?"

Hunter pulled an expression like he was offended. "Nothing. Damn, can't I just say pop?"

"It's the tone, not the word." Todd looked closely into Hunter's eyes. "Are you on something right now?"

Tommy perked up. "If you are, don't be holding out on me. I'm going to need it when that old hag gets back."

Todd looked at his employee. "Tommy, you aren't helping, man. As usual."

*****

In the cloudless blue sky, the brutally hot sun cast its rays over the tourists just arriving on busses, set to join those already sunburned from sitting on the docks, crabbing or lazing on the beach. Northerners, probably. Like most residents, Dr. Darling was glad when they came and equally glad when they departed.

Darling was enjoying the day as he drove home to lunch to his fiancée. The stark white exterior of the house gleamed through the surrounding shadows of the palm trees and shrubbery. The picket fence gate was closed, and past the columns of the two-story porch, the wind chimes were silent. The Darling household gave no sign that a woman lay dead within its walls. Even a doctor, to whom death was no stranger, couldn't have guessed.

Dr. Darling pulled into his driveway, glad the workmen weren't there today, glad they'd be alone. He strolled the front door and called for Isabel. He hummed to himself as he began up the stairs, unable to help but pause and admire the large portrait of her he'd recently commissioned. Soon she would be his entirely. The bedroom door was partially closed. George opened it carefully in case his beloved was taking a midday nap. He hoped she would break that habit, but he also liked waking her with a kiss.

His gaze first went to the empty bed. Then it fell to the floor, where Isabel lay. At first, he presumed she had fallen, until the bruises on her naked skin came into focus. And the blood, a smear from her mouth down her chin, like she tried to swallow a scarlet-colored ribbon. *She isn't dead*, he insisted to himself. He held her in his arms. *No, not dead.* One of her naps. She was always napping, always asleep.

"Nine-one-one, what's your emergency?"

"I can't wake her! I can't wake her!"

"Sir? Who can't you wake? Sir?"

George could hardly speak. He hugged his fiancée to his chest as he rocked back and forth on the floor, tears spilling onto her knotted hair as her flowing blood stained his hands and clothes. His sob echoed throughout the house, as though succumbing to a fit. His stare rose to the ceiling. The phone slipped from his hand.

He laid his head over hers. "This can't be happening again. This can't be happening again."

"Sir," the dispatcher's voice sounded from the phone. "Please stay right there. Officers are on their way."

*****

A bit earlier, Bobby had been brooding over all that van Brock said. Lost in thought, he only picked up his phone on the third ring. "Justice here." His eyes widened as he wrote down the information. "Where are they taking him?" He listened for a moment. "Tell them not to touch a damn thing!"

"What's up?" Jack asked before taking a bite from his sandwich.

"Come with me to the captain's office," Bobby said with urgency. "Captain!" Bobby yelled as he burst through the door. "We got a break in the Amber Callaway case."

Captain Curry appeared startled for an instant. "Let's hear it, Detective," he said as he stood from his desk.

"In her statement, Amber Callaway described a red truck that had an *8*, *7*, and the letter *M* on the back of it," Bobby said between Captain Curry and Jack. "We've had officers on the lookout since, and wouldn't you know it, a red 1984 GMC crew cab with a custom license plate that reads *187MAN* just got into an accident." The detective slapped the note he'd taken down on the captain's desk.

"Son of a bitch!" Jack exclaimed as he threw the wrapper of his sandwich into the captain's wastebasket.

The captain took it in calmly. "That's excellent news, Bobby. Where is the driver and truck now?"

"Oh, the driver. You aren't going to believe who it is," Bobby said, shaking his head.

"Well, don't keep it a secret."

"De'Ron Goodman, a.k.a. Goo-Man," Bobby exclaimed. "Ghost my ass, but Cordale Goodman might make him one if he has a chance."

"Yes! Motherfuck! Got-damn!" Jack shouted as he pumped a fist. "Are they bringing him back here?"

"He's going to the hospital for evaluation, and the truck is being impounded," Bobby said then addressed Captain Curry. "We need to get a search warrant for that vehicle ASAP, Captain."

"I'll call the judge, Detective!" Captain Curry proclaimed.

Right then, Officers Alan Jonsey and Tim Tickerrman rushed into the captain's office. "Detectives!" Officer Jonsey shouted. "A 911 dispatcher just called with a potential homicide."

"Goddamn it! Can we catch our breath!" Bobby uttered then pointed at Jack. "Get to the scene. I'm right behind you. Let me coordinate getting someone to guard Goodman at the hospital and make sure that no one touches that fucking truck!" He then looked to the officers. "Jonsey, Tick, hang here a moment."

"Yes, sir!" they said in unison.

"I'm on it, partner!" Jack said as he headed out the door.

*****

A camera flash popped with white light, illuminating the interior of the master bedroom of the Darling residence. Police were moving about the room, documenting the crime scene when Detective Justice finally arrived. Jack assessed him of the situation.

"So we have a deceased female," Jack began. "Early twenties and no sign of forced entry or any type of burglary."

"Does it look like the same MO as Hill and Callaway?" Bobby asked as he stepped around Jack to get a better look at the victim, who lay sprawled semi-naked on the floor. He grimaced at the sight of her bloody and bruised face, but it was the pattern on her neck that caught his interest.

"Yes," Jack responded. "Savage assault, possible strangulation. This guy gets more brutal with each attack. It really is hard to fathom how Amber Callaway survived."

"Who found her?" Bobby asked.

"Jonesy said the owner of the house made the 911 call," Jack said. "Dr. George Darling. Says they are engaged."

Bobby nodded and then crouched down to get a better look at the woman's neck. "The doctor, huh?"

"So do you think this is the same perp?"

"I do, but considering some of the talk I've been hearing, we might want to make sure it isn't the guy downstairs," Bobby said, standing.

"You're joking, right?"

Justice shrugged, unsure himself. Right then, Officer Woodward stepped into the bedroom and approached the detectives.

"Dr. Darling still isn't talking," he told them. "I think he's in shock."

"Wonderful," Jack said.

"How does he appear otherwise?" Bobby asked.

"Well, if I hadn't seen Webb check his vitals earlier, I would have told ya we had two DOAs here," Woodward admitted.

"Have someone take him to the station," Bobby said. "We still have to try and question him. Make sure he has someone watching him too. I don't want him making that punchline a reality."

After giving orders to the team, Bobby and Jack consulted with the medical examiner.

"Some type of blunt force to the neck is what killed her." Dr. Webb cleaned his glasses with his shirttail, his gaze remaining on the body as he spoke. He put his glasses back on, only to frown at a smudge he missed on the lens. "The trachea seems to be crushed, but I still have to get a closer look during an autopsy to know for sure."

"It's him," Bobby affirmed.

"It's almost identical to Tara Hill," Webb continued. "The one change is that this is your murder scene. You can see the struggle happened here."

"What do you think that pattern on her neck is?" Bobby asked.

"Looks kind of like a shoe print to me," Webb said.

"Webb!" Jack said. "You're a genius!" He moved around Jeff and leaned toward the body. "In fact, looking at it now…hell, that looks like a sneaker print."

"Well, find that sneaker, and you may find your killer, Detective," Webb said sharply.

"Officer Pac," Jack said into his talkie. "Check Dr. Darling's shoes for me. Don't matter if he's wearing them. He won't make a fuss."

*****

De'Ron Goodman's truck was towed back to the precinct on a search and seizure warrant. The same afternoon, the Callaways brought Amber in to identify the vehicle. Officer Alan Jonsey picked up De'Ron Goodman from the hospital, where he was released with a few scrapes cleaned and bandaged.

"That shit wasn't my fault, Officer. That man cut me off," De'Ron said from the back of Officer Jonesy's squad car.

Jonsey looked at De'Ron in his rearview mirror. "From what I hear, that was indeed the case, and the good news is no one was hurt. Of course, there was some damage to your truck."

"That definitely be some very positive news, Officer," De'Ron said, playing up being the good citizen role. "I am glad no one got badly injured."

"Yes, that's not the only positive news," Officer Jonsey said as he parked his vehicle. "You see, that nice red truck of yours was identified with a violent crime in the area." The officer kept his gaze trained on De'Ron. He knew he should be letting Justice handle the questioning, but he couldn't resist. He also wanted to make detective one day. "You wouldn't know anything about that, would ya?"

"Fuck no. I don't know shit about anything violent, Officer."

Jonsey nodded and let him sit in silence for a bit.

Once they arrived at the station, Jonsey pulled De'Ron out of the back seat and marched him inside.

"Have a seat. You might be here a while. I'm sure you know how this works."

"I don't know why I'm in handcuffs when I didn't even do shit," De'Ron said.

Officer Jonsey nodded. "Well, hey, good luck with that," he said before leaving De'Ron with the on-duty desk officer.

"How long do I gotta be here, man? This is fucked up."

The admitting officer didn't even bother to look up. "You know the drill. Just sit there and keep quiet until the detective comes for you."

While sitting calmly, considering to just what degree of bullshit this was, Goo looked down at his shoes. One of his Adidas had become scuffed in the accident. *Damn.* He regretted this worse than the scrape over his eye. Turning his attention from the shoe, he began scanning the walls for something to keep him entertained. Then something struck him. There, on Sandy Beach's Most Wanted notice board, he recognized a face amid the photographs. "Hey, yo, I know that fool…and little man. That's who kidnapped my dawg's brother. Oh shit!"

The desk officer slowly turned and looked at the photo Goo had mentioned.

"You say you know this man?" he asked unbelievingly.

Goo hesitated. "Is that what I said?"

"Do you have info about him?"

"Well," Goo said, kicking his legs out to relax. "That all depends, don't it, Officer?"

*****

Kate sat on the living room couch. It was a good day with Hunter, by all accounts, doing well working with his father, taking on more responsibility. Todd had even poured him a few gulps from his beer at dinner and clinked glasses in a toast. Things were turning around.

"Sweetie," she said. "Maybe we can take a vacation this year. Go to the Keys or something. Barbados. Anywhere."

"I'd like that, honey," Todd said, looking at his wife. "Or we could just go upstate to Epcot and stop at your mom's on the way."

"She'd be thrilled. She never gets to see Hunter," Kate said, turning at the sound of a knock on the front door.

Todd stood from the couch. He answered the door to find Bobby Justice in uniform, two officers at his back.

"Detective? How are you? Come in." Todd stood aside and let Bobby enter their home. Kate rose from the couch.

"Where's Hunter, Todd?" Bobby asked with a serious expression.

"In his room. Why?"

"What do you want with Hunter, Detective?" Kate asked.

"Better let us take care of that," Bobby said and began up the stairs. But before he could get to the top, he heard a door close. He moved quickly, throwing the door open. Bobby got to see Hunter's back just before it dropped from the window.

"He's going out the front!" Bobby called down to his backup. The two officers, still at the open door, turned to give chase. It didn't take them long to apprehend Hunter, who had landed poorly on his ankle and couldn't do much more than hobble.

"Hunter! Oh my god!" Kate yelled, rushing out to her child.

"What are you doing, son?" Todd called.

"Hold on! Hold on!" Bobby managed to get down the steps and in between Todd and Kate and the officers. "Let the officers take him in, and I'm going to need you two to meet me downtown."

"What's going on?" Kate gasped.

"I'll explain everything when we get there," Bobby said.

"Is he under arrest?"

"Not yet. We just need to talk right now," Bobby replied.

"Then take the cuffs off. If he's not under arrest," Kate said.

Bobby looked at her. He thought of Chase and the increasingly difficult path Kate and Todd faced. They were good people. He nodded.

"Take 'em off, Tick. I'll keep my eye on him."

"You sure, boss?" Tick asked.

"It's what I said."

*****

At the station, Amber Callaway sat between her mother and Officer Pac. Jennifer Callaway clutched her daughter's hand as she let out a whimper and identified Hunter from a group of photos of similar looking teens, then confirmed it though the one-way interrogation room mirror. Bobby nodded, thanked her, and headed out to explain the situation to Todd and Kate.

"We haven't been able to see our son for almost half an hour now. What's going on?" Kate demanded as she stood up, Todd following her lead.

"What do you think he did?" Todd asked.

Bobby had them sit again then took a seat himself. "Amber Callaway gave us a statement that identified a red truck with a partial license plate number. We have confirmed that truck belongs to a De'Ron Goodman," Bobby explained.

"Oh Christ, is that the boy Hunter refers to as Goo?" Kate said.

"Yes, and he does have a red truck," Todd acknowledged.

Kate put her hands on her cheeks. "What has he got Hunter into?"

"Mrs. and Mr. Lovell," Bobby said firmly. "It's Hunter she's identified as the one who attacked her."

"What!" Todd cried out. "No way!"

"Have you seen any injuries on Hunter in this past month?" Bobby asked the Lovells.

"He may have come home bleeding a few weeks ago, but that was from an accident," Kate explained.

"May have?" Bobby arched an eyebrow.

"Yes, he did. But I don't see what that proves."

"Was there a wound on his inner leg? Near the groin area?" Bobby asked.

"Yes, but—"

"The victim claims she bit him there, trying to get away from him."

"That's bullshit." Todd shook his head.

"Plus, she's identified him."

"Identified him how?" Kate asked. "Detective, this is our son. You have to give us more."

"Okay," Bobby said. "When we spoke with her, she mentioned that a boy who had been doing community service work was the one who attacked her. She also said she saw him before but wasn't sure where. We went to the courthouse and looked into anyone registered for CS with a police record." Bobby took a deep breath. "There were only a few, and Hunter was one. Her reaction when she saw his picture told the whole story. They actually went to school together."

"Okay, but…" Todd froze midsentence. His body went numb.

"We have visual identification. Amber's in there with her family. But there is still evidence to collect. The best thing for everybody is for you and Hunter to cooperate. And if it all turns out to be one big mistake…"

Kate's head collapsed onto Todd's shoulder.

"Look." Bobby sighed. "This is what's going to happen. We are going to have our doctor examine Hunter's leg. We also need the clothes he has been wearing the past few days."

"Maybe we should get a lawyer first," Todd said, looking toward his wife. "I'm not sure if we should say anything."

"Yes, get a lawyer," Bobby said. "Because, guys, this isn't stopping with Amber Callaway. We have reason to believe now, through another witness, that Goodman might know something about the Tara Hill murder. And if Hunter has been hanging with this guy, then..."

"What is Hunter saying about this?" Kate asked. "I want to see my son."

"Right now, he's gone silent. And, Kate, Todd," Bobby said, leaning in. "Innocent people don't jump out of windows. Okay?"

"Oh, God," Todd groaned, turning away.

Kate shook her head. "I can't believe this is happening. There must be some mistake."

"Let us do our job," Bobby asserted. "If there's been a mistake, we need the space and time to uncover it. You can trust me. I'm not out to get Hunter. But I got the girl's parents in the other room who are ready to lynch him and De'Ron Goodman. And if you saw the girl, you wouldn't blame them—"

"How old is she?" Kate quickly asked.

"Like I said, they were in school together. She's sixteen," Bobby responded.

"May I see her?" Kate requested softly.

"I don't think that's a good idea, Kate," Bobby said.

Kate held firm. "I want to see her."

"Okay then," Bobby said with a deep exhale. "Let me ask the parents." He stood and walked to the room where the Callaways were waiting.

"Can we take our daughter home now?" Cliff Callaway asked.

"Absolutely," Bobby told him. "But I have a request from Hunter Lovell's mother...to meet you and Amber."

"She doesn't think she's going to talk this kid's way out of this," Jennifer Callaway said in a shaking voice.

"That's not what she wants," Bobby said.

"I don't give a damn what she wants!" Cliff countered.

"I think it could help expedite things if you let her come talk to you," Bobby told Mr. Callaway. "Hunter's parents' cooperation would go a long way, now and later."

Cliff shook head. "I don't give a—"

"Dad," Amber interrupted. "I want to meet her. It's okay. What's her name?"

"Kate," Bobby said. The Callaways both reluctantly nodded their assent. Bobby leaned out of the door and motioned Kate and Todd over. As soon as Kate walked in and saw Amber's still bloodred eyes and bruised face, she immediately broke down.

"I'm so sorry," Kate cried as she bent to hug Amber. "I'm so sorry."

Jennifer teared up too as she rested her head on top of her daughter's. Bobby noticed Jack waving him over, and he excused himself from the room.

"Bobby," Jack said, bringing him back to attention. "Look, Hunter Lovell isn't talking."

"I'm not surprised. But the night clerk at the Sandy Beach Hotel, Ms. Bilbo, identified Goodman, correct?"

"One hundred percent. No doubt in her mind that she checked him in that night. She even remembered him hitting on her," Jack said.

"Okay, hang on." Bobby returned to the room. "Todd, Kate? We'd like to search for Hunter's room."

"This is unreal," Todd said.

"Understand that asking is merely a courtesy now," Bobby said. "We don't need a warrant, but I'd just as soon have your blessing."

Sniffling, Kate pulled away from Amber and took another look at her face.

"Do what you need. I'm not stopping you. He has a hamper in his room. Check there for the clothes." Todd threw up his hands then crossed them over his chest, apparently resigned.

Todd accompanied the detectives back to the house and sat on Hunter's bed as they searched the room. Bobby opened Hunter's closet, and the sight of a duffle bag piqued his interest. He bent down and unzipped it, finding torn bloodstained clothes as well as a pair of bloody sneakers.

"Oh, I don't fucking believe this," Bobby whispered, using a pencil to dig through the clothes and flip one of Hunter's shoes on its side. "Look at this…and does this pattern look familiar?" Bobby glanced at Jack, who was peering over his shoulder.

"You have got to be kidding me."

"Whoa," Todd exclaimed from behind the bed. "What's all that?"

"Evidence, Mr. Lovell," Bobby said, zipping the bag up. "Forensic evidence."

"You mean you found blood on them clothes?"

Bobby nodded then bagged what he found.

"Look, Mr. Lovell," Jack began. "This isn't looking good. We're going to have to keep Hunter overnight."

Todd spoke, eyes cast down at the floor. "Can I ride back with you? I don't want Kate to have to drive home alone."

"I think that's a good idea," Jack said.

The three men exited the room. Jack began down the stairs with the evidence bag while Bobby stood at the landing with Todd, each waiting for the other to start down the stairs. *Two kids. One kidnapped, another likely a serial murderer. It isn't bad luck*, Bobby thought. It wasn't fate either. *It's just the way it is*, he concluded. All of a sudden, Todd seemed to lose his balance, going into a momentary faint, then recovering by grabbing onto Bobby. Bobby soon realized he wasn't letting go. It had turned into an embrace.

"All I ever wanted was a happy family," Todd whispered.

Bobby released him and looked him in the eye. "They still need you. Now more than ever."

Several hours after officially arresting Hunter Lovell, Bobby and Jack were sitting across from De'Ron Goodman in an interrogation room at the station. He hadn't called Cordale Goodman or asked for an attorney yet. The detectives were hoping to capitalize on the momentum and getting De'Ron to cave on what he knew.

"You want to talk with us or what?" Jack asked.

"I don't want to be here at all, but y'all ain't really gave a nigga a choice. So go ahead, but don't be recording this shit. I ain't ready for all that yet," De'Ron said.

"Let's not fuck around anymore. We have multiple witnesses now. You know that, right, De'Ron?" Bobby said as he leaned forward in his chair.

"It's Goo, mothafucka. And I'm sure yo ass probably does," De'Ron said nonchalantly. "It don't mean yo ass got proof of jack-shit, though."

Jack pursed his lips. "Never have cared for that term."

"I don't know. I think it's a pretty good one," Bobby commented.

De'Ron looked from one detective to the other. "What in the fuck you two talkin' about?"

"Let me explain something, Goo-Boy," Bobby said, staring hard at De'Ron. "Amber Callaway is alive. But you probably haven't watched the news lately, and I'm positive you didn't read about it."

De'Ron shrugged. "Who da fuck is that?"

"The young girl you and Hunter Lovell attacked and left for dead," Jack said.

Bobby placed a picture of Amber's beaten face and neck on the table. "She was in the hospital for close to a month because of what you two did." He watched De'Ron look over the picture. "But she remembered your face and those rockin' tattoos."

"You're not the only one she remembers," Jack added.

"Look, that was my nigga, bro. He's fucking crazy," De'Ron said, still looking at the photograph.

"You're going to put this all on your bro, huh?" Jack said. "Some friend."

"That shit wasn't supposed to go down like that with that hoe. I mean young lady. Hunter's ass gots a temper and gets so fuckin' pissed," De'Ron said, finally talking straight. "That killa likes the control, and I think he prefers when the bitches say no."

Bobby sat up straight. "What do you mean by *that one*?" he asked.

"Look, you know I gots some info that can help you police officers, right?" De'Ron said.

"I don't trust you enough to believe shit about what you say, you supposedly have," Bobby stated.

"Hell, I'd have to agree, partner," Jack said.

"In any case, you aren't going home tonight," Bobby explained. "So the sooner you start cooperating, the sooner we might start listening to your side of things."

"Now tell us what happened with Tara Hill," Jack told De'Ron.

Goo looked at the detectives for a second. "I'm no fucking Boy Scout, but I ain't neva did want to hurt those two girls. Maybe scare 'em, but my boy is lethal," he admitted.

"You are complicit, De'Ron," Bobby contended. "Accessory to murder."

"Maybe I'll tell you a little something, but this shit ain't leaving this office. I'll deny every bit of it, and yo little fucking kidnapped nigga can stay right where the fuck he is with that White trash Elwood."

Everything went still for a moment. Bobby and Jack exchanged a look.

"De'Ron, if you know something about that, it's in your best interest to tell us," Jack said.

"Don't be fucking tellin' me what my best interest is, Detective," De'Ron let out angrily. "Maybe I should go ahead and call that lawyer now."

"Give us something on Hill, and then we can look into what we can do on the other info," Bobby remarked.

"Like I said, I'll deny all this shit and claim police brutality or a forced damn confession," De'Ron spat out.

Bobby stood up. "You made your goddamn point. Now either stop wasting my fucking time or start talking, you little son of a bitch. And listen good. Nobody's going to go light on you. Think about it. Dropout from the wrong side of the tracks. Associated with known criminals. Meanwhile, Hunter's just an impressionable kid who has peachy sweet parents and a lot of goodwill over an abducted brother. Who do you think would be the convenient person to take the fall here?"

De'Ron, for the first time, looked shaken. He stared at Bobby then sat silent for a moment before he started talking. "All right, all right. As far as Hill, yeah, we killed her. I just wanted to scare her fine little ass for being a bitch, but Hunter, boy, I ain't neva did see some rage like that before," he confessed.

"How did you plan on scaring her and not get in some type of trouble for it?" Bobby asked.

"Man, look, we was drunk and high as fuck. Wasn't no planning nothin'," Goo recalled.

"Why didn't you two get rid of her body?" Jack asked. "Dumping her body at the hotel was amateur hour, to say the least."

"After she was dead, we went ahead and wrapped the body up in some sheets. We was gonna dump it somewheres by the beach. But the sun started coming up, and we could hear some damn people talking in one of the rooms. Plus some peeps was taking bags out their ride in the parking lot. Instead of going back to our own room, we saw the door next to that vending machine wasn't closed. We just decided to dump her dead ass in there. We figured it wasn't our room, so fuck it, we rolled her on that bed and took the sheets and walked out."

"Just like that. As if her life didn't mean anything," Bobby said.

De'Ron shrugged again. "I remember Hunter saying simple bitch got what she deserved before he ripped what was left of her shirt off."

Jack sat on the edge of the table close to De'Ron. "And why would Hunter keep her bloody clothes?"

Goo looked up at the detective. "His ass said he wanted to remember it. Like a souvenir or some shit. Keeping the clothes was almost the same type thing to him as like saving a ticket stub from a concert or movie."

"So now tell us about—" Jack started.

"Nah, we are fucking done for now. I want my lawyer before discuss anythin' else," Goo declared.

Bobby shook his head. "Yeah, De'Ron. Let's go find you a phone."

*****

Despite her grief—the kind that made it hard to rise and dress in the morning—Rosalina kept her eye on George. It helped her to focus attention and concern on somebody else. At the funeral, she watched him, not appearing to hear a word from the sermon, eyes dry and unblinking. *What is he seeing*? she wondered. Even when they moved Isabel's body into the above-ground mausoleum, George remained still, merely staring ahead. The mourning party took limos back to his estate, where George settled onto the couch, staring into the paintings on the wall. The gathering went on around him, but he made no effort to join. Rosalina was seated in between George and her mother, Emilia, and was looking after both.

"I'm so sorry for your loss," a friend of Isabel's named Alleta said. "Can I get you anything?"

"I'm fine. Thank you for asking," Rosalina said, forcing a smile, then repeated the question in Spanish to her mother. The woman, only in her fifties but aged by mourning, shook her head. "No, thank you, ma'am," Rosalina said.

Aletta turned to George. "George?" she asked gently. "Can I get you something?" She waited for a long minute, but George never answered.

"It's okay, Alleta," Rosalina said as she held George's hand. "I will take care of George."

"Okay," the friend said then headed into the kitchen.

Emilia leaned over and spoke a few words in Spanish. "Ahora no madre," Rosalina said quietly in response, but Emilia only repeated what she said, louder and firmer. Rosalina sighed in defeat and gazed into George's emotionless face.

"George?" she asked. "My mother wants to say that she only allowed this resting place in Florida because of the love you gave Isabel. But when my mother passes, she will want Isabel's body rested next to hers and our late father's in Cuba."

George slowly turned to look at Emilia. His eyes moved to Rosalina. First his eyebrow shivered, then his lip, as though his face were unfreezing, until it melted into an expression of raw pain. A loud sob escaped him, and his head fell into his hands as he openly wept.

"Mother!" Rosalina shouted as she embraced George.

October 1984

A couple months later, the detectives were still sorting through the evidence collected on De'Ron Goodman and Hunter Lovell. Hunter, already identified for the rape and attempted murder of Amber Callaway, was also the prime suspect in the homicides of Tara Hill and Isabel Dominguez. The information gathered pointed toward De'Ron Goodman acting as an accomplice in the Tara Hill and Amber Callaway cases and that Hunter had alone committed the murder of Isabel Dominguez.

Jack twisted his new Rubik's cube for a few minutes before putting it down. He wanted to say that it helped him relax, but really, it just got him frustrated. It wasn't the puzzle that was really bothering him. "I mean, is there any explanation in tarnation for having two kids get taken from a family like this? What kind of luck."

"Nobody said life was fair," Bobby intoned, eyeing the cube. "In Chase Lovell's case, it was a pedophile seeing his opportunity. In Hunter's case…"

"I mean, how is a serial killer created? Is it nature? Fucked-up parents? Or is it a mental abnormality? I guess if we knew that, we would be fishing on a boat somewhere," Jack figured.

Bobby leaned back in his chair. "I do know that the abduction of his brother and whatever his parents may or may not have said to him was not enough to turn Hunter into a serial killer."

"I'm just not comfortable with that term here. He just seems like a kid who's out of control. Not a Manson or anything."

"Manson wasn't a serial killer either. Never killed anybody himself."

"Yeah, but he seems like one. That's my point." Jack went back to twisting the cube every which way. "Speaking of the other child, Chase, what's the latest on that? You haven't mentioned anything in a while."

"Lawyers," Bobby said with a frustrated look.

Jack shook his head. "Of course. Man, the war must have been great. No lawyers, just decisions." Jack caught the look Bobby was giving him. "Sorry, but you have to talk about it some time."

Bobby cleared his throat and changed the subject. "Hunter and Goo will be incarcerated through the trial, and then a long time after that."

"Date been set yet?" Jack asked.

"Not yet. We have to keep working these cases and make sure they are airtight."

"Is what De'Ron knows holding things up with the court setting a date?"

Bobby nodded. "Yes, I think that's part of it."

"Have you told the Lovells?"

"No, not with everything that Kate and Todd have going on. They don't need false hope right now. Goodman will speak eventually. At least if Cordale doesn't have him killed first." Bobby chuckled.

"What was it? Fifteen thousand dollars that was found in De'Ron's truck again?"

"Seventeen thousand clams," Bobby said. "Or another way to put it would be an SBPD officer's starting salary."

Jack's eyes widened. "Hell, I think that might be my salary now."

"You make that much?" Bobby said with a wink.

"Buys one hell of a lawyer," Jack reckoned.

"Yeah, I suppose it does."

*****

It hadn't occurred to Kate and Todd that their son would not want their help or even want to see them. But that's what happened until he finally relented. Todd took work off, not that there was much anyway now. And they drove in Kate's car to the Sandy Beach

Juvenile Correctional Facility, Kate staring out the window, looking deep into the mangroves, as though they might offer some solution.

Once inside the facility, a guard let the couple into the visitors' center, where Hunter was already seated at a table. At the sight of his orange correctional uniform, tears formed in Kate's eyes. She circled the table to embrace him, but the guard instructed her to stay back.

"Can't she hug him?" Todd said, trying to sound tough for Kate.

"Security regulations, sir," the guard said. "Either have a seat or wait back in the hall. You have ten minutes. Make good use of it."

Kate wiped away the tears then took control of herself. She wanted to be strong for her son.

"Hi, baby," she said, struggling to form more words until she broke into sobs then fled the room.

"See now," Hunter told his dad. "I didn't want to deal with any of this crying bullshit."

"She's just happy to see you, son," Todd said.

"What about you? Are *you* happy?" Hunter asked his father.

Todd looked his boy in the eyes and laughed at the absurdity of the comment. "Of course, I am." The two stared at each other as though in a contest.

Kate returned to the room after collecting herself. She sat and addressed Hunter. "I hate seeing you in here," she said with a sniffle.

"I'm where I should be," Hunter said plainly.

Kate's lip quivered. "Why would you say that?" she asked.

"You sure you want to hear?" he asked.

"Yes," Kate said. "You are our son. You can tell us anything."

Hunter turned to Todd. "What about you?"

"Say your peace," Todd said, choking up a little.

"I'm not an innocent little boy. Not like Chase was, at least. I wish that motherfucker Elwood would have taken me instead." As he spoke, Hunter tightened his teeth, as though trying to bite down on the words. "He would be a dead bitch now too."

Kate felt the true violence of her son now for the first time. His language and his utter dispassion, as though his teenage angst had been solidified into something honest and deadly. "Why are you so angry?" she cried.

"Don't cry, Mom. You didn't break whatever's broken in here," Hunter said, patting his heart. "There's nothing there. I don't feel shit."

"Hunter, please, what can we do?" Todd begged.

"Time's up," a guard's voice sounded behind them.

"There isn't anything," Hunter said, standing from his seat. "Maybe get me some money for the commissary. That's all I'll be needing for now."

*****

Not long after Isabel's funeral, George Darling sold his practice to Dr. Dan Dominic. He retired to his residence, not allowing visitors but for Rosalina Dominguez. She came often at first, but her visits tapered off when she realized he wouldn't engage with her, sometimes leaving her alone at the kitchen table while he disappeared upstairs.

The only activity Darling outwardly indulged in were his regular visits to the mausoleum that he had purchased for Isabel. It was a five-mile walk there and back from his home, and neighbors talked among themselves about the red toy wagon he used to haul the flowers, stuffed animals, and perfume he left for her. George would sit by her grave and serenade her corpse with her favorite Cuban love song, "Como Fue."

No se explicarme que pasó
Pero de ti me enamoré
As was,
I can't tell you how it was
I don't know what happened
But I fell in love with you
It was a light
That illuminated my whole being
Your laugh like a spring
Watered my life with restlessness

"I miss you so much, my darling," George whispered to Isabel through the black wooden casket with gold-plated handles. "I've prayed for your spirit to return to me, and you have finally spoken," he said calmly and without tears. "Tonight will be the last night we spend without each other." The doctor looked into the wood of the casket, as though looking at Isabel, and smiled. "Oh dear, how dirty these clothes are. We just will have to get some new ones. Your closet is just as you left it. Our wedding has been delayed for too long. I won't stand for it anymore." George pouted his lips, as though in a kiss with Isabel's boney, gaunt corpse.

May 1985

Hunter Lovell went on trial separately from De'Ron for the murder of Tara Hill and the attempted murder of Amber Callaway in January. He was found guilty on both charges. Hunter received life in prison with the possibility of parole in thirty-five years and was still facing the long-awaited trial for the killing of Isabel Dominguez. Despite pleading guilty to first-degree murder, De'Ron Goodman only received thirty-five years and would receive a reduced sentence if the information he provided led police to the whereabouts and recovery of Chase Lovell. For this, they would need Cordale Goodman's cooperation to track down Lee Earl Elwood. Goodman had informed detectives that Elwood was constantly moving locations, so he would have to wait until he made contact to give them his whereabouts. Goodman, a man not to mince words, said he was confident he'd know soon enough.

Jack was sitting at his desk when his phone rang. "Sergeant Cutler here. Mr. Grey, how are things? Wow, that is great news! Let me go inform the captain."

Jack got up from his desk and strode into the captain's office. "Captain!" Sergeant Cutler said excitedly. "Cordale Goodman just gave up Elwood's location."

Bobby Justice—Captain Bobby Justice—stood from his chair. "It's about damn time," he said. "I guess Cordale does care about De'Ron in his own odd way. I began to lose hope this would happen."

"The last piece of De'Ron Goodman's plea deal," Jack noted.

"Only if it leads to Chase Lovell being found alive," Bobby added as he picked up his phone. "Let's get our newly appointed chief down here from city hall."

Jack walked out of the captain's office and looked toward Detectives Alan Jonsey and Tim Tickerrman.

"Sir, we have a pawnshop robbery and shooting," Detective Jonsey said to Sargent Cutler.

"All right, detectives," Jack said. "Get on that. Officer Pac, hold down the fort and keep in that study manual. You need to ace those exams next week."

"Done deal, boss," Jane replied.

"Yes, Sergeant," Detective Jonsey said.

Jack turned Detective Tickerrman. "And keep me posted, Tim."

"Yes, sir," Tick answered back.

*****

Tucson, Arizona

Nobody ever visited the small camper or tried to make friends with the man and boy. Neighbors could tell right away the two kept to themselves. But if you stood close to the abode, you'd make out a whimpering. It would be easy to mistake for the crying of a dog. Inside, in the dark fetid space, a boy slipped from the bed, wincing in pain. At eleven, Chase still couldn't get used the dull throbbing ache, as if the man were still inside of him. Elwood, with a cigarette dangling from his lips, zipped up his pants. It was over, *for now*. Still, the man stared reproachfully down at Chase, as though the boy had been the one committing the crime.

"What?" Chase asked with hatred.

"You are getting too big, too old, and that ass is getting too loose," Lee Earl stated with equal hostility.

Chase hobbled to the bathroom, putting on a shirt. "Good. Then leave me the fuck alone, you disgusting piece of shit!" Chase yelled as he slammed the bathroom door. He was angry at Lee Earl, angry at himself for now feeling rejected. Like now he was good for absolutely nothing.

"What have I told you about that damn mouth? Don't make me put the back of my hand to ya!" Lee Earl shouted. Chase heard Lee Earl shout, muffled by the sound of his own piss hitting the toilet water. He didn't flush but rather left it there for the man to see. Let him flush it. Lee Earl threw open the door.

"Get out. I fucking hate you!" Chase screamed.

Lee Earl backhanded Chase across the face, knocking him flat. "Next time, I'll use a bat on both ends of you," Elwood said, looking down at the boy. "Now I have to be at the lodge in an hour. Help me get this stuff in the truck, and get that fucking dog to stop barking!"

"Fuck you," Chase said, still gathering his senses.

Elwood strode to the dresser, grabbed his Colt 45, and pointed it at Chase. "Keep trying me, son."

"Do it! Anything would be better than this," Chase declared.

"Well then, let's kill that thing first," Elwood said and pointed the gun at Scooby.

"Stop it, you damn asshole!" Chase yelled. Then in a quieter voice, he said, "Okay, I'll help. Jesus."

"That always does seem to get the point across, doesn't it?" Elwood tucked the gun in his pants. "And fuck you too. I'm going to look for some fresh ass tonight."

"I don't care what you do," Chase retorted.

"And don't go touching my leftover Salisbury steak, you hear?"

"What am I supposed to eat then?"

"Here's some tomato soup," Lee Earl said, tossing Chase the last can from the pantry. "Should be enough for you two to share."

*****

Sandy Beach, Florida

Captain Justice sat gnawing off the sides of his Styrofoam cup, waiting in silence with Sergeant Cutler and Chief Curry for the phone call from Tucson Police Department.

"Bobby, staring at it isn't going to make it ring faster," Jack said. "And give the cup a break, you look like some mutant rodent."

"Jack, running your mouth doesn't make you sound smarter," Bobby responded, spitting a piece of the rim into the cup. He wished he had a cigarette.

"I'm just saying, buddy. Relax."

"Both of you are driving me crazy," Chief Curry said, rolling his eyes. "It shouldn't be much longer now."

"I'm glad you're here, Chief," Bobby stated. "Thanks for coming down."

The chief nodded. "Of course, Captain Justice."

"What about me?" Jack asked.

"Debatable," Bobby said with a smirk.

*****

Tucson, Arizona

The electricity was out again. Probably Lee Earl had forgotten to pay the bill or something. Chase didn't mind the dark. He knew where the monsters were and what they looked like. Dark meant cover, quiet, peace. He was enjoying it, licking the last of the cold soup from a spoon, when suddenly he saw red and blue lights running circles around the wall, coming in through the window. Scooby began to bark. Chase got up and risked a look through the window.

"Tucson Police Department! This is Detective Grant! Open up!" a voice shouted from outside.

Frightened, Chase stood from the tiny cigarette-stained couch and opened the door to see a tall plain-clothed man flanked by uniformed policemen.

"My name is Detective Grant. Are you Chase Lovell?" the man asked directly.

"No! My name is Alex Adams," Chase answered back automatically, picking Scooby up so he wouldn't jump.

The man turned to an officer standing next to him. "Give me that photo, Sid."

"Yes, sir."

Detective Grant looked at the picture then back down at Chase. "Is that you, son?" the detective asked, holding out an old photo to Chase.

It took Chase a moment to recognize the picture. Then it came back all at once. It used to sit in a frame by a picture of his brother. On the mantle. When he had a home, *a real home.* A lump formed in his throat as he nodded.

In an instant, cops rushed past him and began to search the camper bedroom and bathroom.

"It's empty, Detective," a police officer called.

"Where is Lee Earl Elwood?" the detective asked Chase.

"He's still at work," Chase said.

Detective Grant got on a knee to look Chase in the eye. "Where does he work, Chase?"

"He's a security guard at the Desert Lodge," Chase told him, still trembling.

"Officer, call the lodge and see if Lee Earl Elwood works there," Grant said over his radio.

"He will kill me if he knew I told you that!" Chase cried, holding Scooby tighter.

Grant stood back up and put his hand on Chase's shoulder. "Son, he's never going to touch you again. That's a promise."

Chase stroked Scooby. He began to comprehend his new circumstances and that helping the officers would be good for him. "He calls himself Eugene Adams at his job, not Lee Earl Elwood."

"Officer, correction. Ask about a Eugene Adams," Grant said into his radio.

Detective Grant sat Chase down at the table and waited. He'd seen mudslide victims, kids walk out of car crashes, and they all had this same glazed look as Chase. He knew the kid wouldn't process any of this until later. Grant had a lot of questions, but he let Chase be for now.

Before long, the call came in that Eugene Adams had left an hour earlier.

"Chase, what type of vehicle does he have?" the detective asked Chase.

"It's a tan truck. I'm not sure what kind," Chase answered.

"Pickup?"

Chase nodded.

"Get the word out that the suspect drives a tan pickup," Grant radioed.

"Copy that," the officer radioed back.

"Okay, son, let's get you to the station then back home."

"Back here?"

"No, son. *Home*, home."

Chase thought that over. "Will they be angry at me?" he asked.

"Your parents? I suspect they will be as happy as any parents alive, Chase."

Chase looked at his pet, who had begun to squirm under his embrace. "I can't leave Scooby!"

"He's coming too," Detective Grant said.

Not far away, a beige Chevy pickup began to make the turn into the trailer park. The driver, taking in the flashing lights in the distance, thought the better of it, righted the truck, and continued straight down the highway. Lee Earl Elwood decided it was time to leave Arizona.

*****

Sandy Beach, Florida

Bobby Justice was still in his office with Jack and Curry when the call came through.

"Is it confirmed?" He looked between the chief and Sergeant Cutler. "That's incredible, Detective Grant! Yes, Elwood is a slippery bastard. It is still wonderful news. I'll leave tonight, thank you, Detective!" Bobby placed the phone in the cradle and took a deep breath. "They have him."

"They have Chase Lovell?" Jack asked.

"Yes! Hell, yes!" Bobby exclaimed with a fist pump. "Let's get him back home before we talk to the Lovells," he said with a rush of excitement.

"Bobby, that's like a seven-hour flight," Jack explained. "Let me go, and I'll let you know when I board to come back home, then go tell the Lovells."

"That'll work," Bobby said. "Let's get this done."

"Careful, Bobby. Somebody might mistake that spasm on your mouth for a smile," Jack quipped with a smile of his own.

"What happened with Lee Earl Elwood?" Chief Curry asked.

Bobby's smile evaporated. "That piece of shit must have spotted the cops."

"Damn it!" Jack exclaimed.

"They are still searching for the son of a bitch."

The chief walked over to Bobby and put his hand on his shoulder. "Still, this is a great night. Congrats, Captain," he said with pride.

Bobby deflected the praise, knowing the job wasn't over. "You have a flight to catch, Sergeant," he said to Cutler.

"Yes, Captain. I sure do," Jack said.

*****

Kate collected the empties from the kitchen table. She didn't want Todd to see them, to see how much he put away the night before, wanting to protect him from his own shame. She knew he kept the Seagram's in the back pantry, behind rarely used boxes of Bisquick and cornmeal. She checked its status to find it half empty. He had been improving until Hunter's arrest. But that development, she saw, broke him. It would break *anybody*, right? He had been a good father or tried to be a good father. That should be enough.

But now what? Get a dog? Move to California? Get away from this town. Even her job was no longer keeping her happy in Sandy Beach, with Dr. Darling gone. The old man, ironically, brought more life and energy to the practice than his younger replacement.

Kate took some eggs and bacon from the fridge. But before she could start cooking, the phone rang. Why pick it up? Nothing will make anything better. But the ring aggravated her. She reached for the kitchen line.

"Hello."

"Kate?" It was Bobby Justice. Had she known the cop would call, she would have unplugged the line.

"I need you and Todd to come in. I have some great news."

*****

"You sure the flight arrived at eleven?" Todd asked for the second time. He was in the same thermal top he slept in. Kate didn't think to comment on it. They'd had plenty of time before Chase arrived, but they left as soon as the call came, out of some irrational fear they would miss the moment of his arrival. Now they'd had three coffees each, and the anticipation had turn to jitters.

"Don't worry. There's usually a touch of traffic on the interstate, but Detective Cutler will be using his lights. Like a little homecoming parade."

Kate smiled and leaned into her husband's shoulder.

Cutler radioed as he was pulling in, and the party met them in the station parking lot. Todd and Kate watched their boy get from the back seat of the cruiser, a dog trailing behind. Todd broke into a run, grabbing Chase in his arms. Kate followed and put her arms around both, Scooby jumping against them in excitement.

"You've grown so tall," Todd said, pulling away.

"I'm big now," Chase said.

Sobbing, Kate broke away from Chase to pet Scooby, who was trying to lick her face. "What's this little guy's name?"

"This is Scooby," Chase said.

"Hey, Scooby," Todd said, patting the dog's head.

"We can keep him, right?" Chase said, looking worried.

"Of course," Todd said. "He'll keep *us all* safe."

Justice led them back to the conference room, a box of Dunkin' Donuts waiting for the family. He closed the door to give them some privacy.

"I missed you guys so much," Chase finally said, looking at his parents. "I thought you hated me."

"How could you ever feel that way?" Kate asked, caressing her son's face. "We never gave up looking for you."

"Dad… I mean, Lee Earl said you gave me away because I made you mad, and you didn't have money for me," Chase explained.

"That piece of…" Todd gnashed his teeth to keep from cussing. "He stole you from us. I promise we would never give you to anyone," he said as he hugged his son again.

"We love you. There's nothing you could have ever done to make us feel that way," Kate assured him. "That sick man is a liar."

"I know he is," Chase replied. Then he suddenly thought of his brother. "Where is Hunter?" he asked.

Todd and Kate looked at each other. "You know your brother. Some things never change. He got into a bit of trouble and can't be here right now, but I know he will be thrilled to see you," Todd explained.

"Is he grounded?" Chase asked softly.

Kate measured her response. "Well, in a way. But please don't worry about that right now. We are so happy to have you back. We couldn't be any happier."

Todd stood and ruffled Chase's hair. "Your room is the same way you left it."

Chase gave a bashful smile.

A knock came at the door, and Justice poked his head in. "Kate, Todd, can we speak a minute?" he asked, gesturing for them to join him in the hallway.

"I'm sorry to interrupt, guys, but it's imperative to talk with Chase about Elwood while we have everyone here," Bobby explained.

"I don't know. This is all so sudden," Kate said.

"Elwood is on the run," Bobby replied flatly. "We need as much information on him as possible. I don't want him fleeing the country, or worse, trying this again with somebody else. Chase is the only person with some insight into the man."

"Can't we just get him home first, Captain?" Todd asked.

"We have a child therapist here now that he can speak with along with Jack and me," Bobby said.

"I'm ready now, Mr. Justice. I'm not scared anymore" came a voice from the door, which had been opened by Chase.

Bobby looked proudly down on the boy while his mother and father were still gathering their thoughts.

"Are you sure, Chase?" his mother asked.

"Yes, Mom. I want them to catch him," Chase declared.

Bobby sat down across from Chase Lovell. "Chase, I'm so happy to meet you, finally, big guy."

"I told him how much we looked for him," Jack said as he gave Chase a wink.

Bobby leaned forward in his chair to look Chase in the eyes. "I'm so sorry that we couldn't find you sooner, Chase. We knew Elwood had you, but we just couldn't figure out where he took you."

Chase shrugged. "I didn't know where I was either, so don't feel bad."

Bobby laughed. "Well, it was my job to find you, and I didn't. But I thought about you every day, and I never gave up hope."

Chase grinned. "How *did* you find me, anyway?"

Bobby chuckled. "I promise once your mom and dad have had a chance to be with you for a while, we can talk about it."

"Sure, Captain," Chase replied.

"Chase, my man, would you mind telling me how Elwood was able to grab you?" Jack asked.

"He didn't *grab* me. He worked sweeping the gym at my school. And one day, I was walking home with my bike because it had a flat tire, and he and Mr. Roy drove up and asked if I needed help. At first, I said no, but he said I could put my bike in his van. I got in too, but he never stopped at my house."

"Had you ever seen him down your road before?" Bobby asked.

"I don't think so."

"My guess is no," Jack said, looking at Bobby.

Bobby nodded at Jack then turned back to Chase. "Big guy, you're one brave kid, and I'm proud to know you. I know what a monster this man is, and we will get him. We got the deck stacked against him now."

Later that night, once the therapist had confirmed and recorded Chase's account of Elwood's crimes, the family ate out at the Calypso Shake Shack. Chase got a clam roll and a chocolate shake.

"No clams in the desert," he said.

"You can have as many as you can eat," Todd said, beaming at his son.

After returning home, they gathered in front of the TV. Kate searched the channels for something nonviolent, and they settled on a sitcom. But just when they were relaxing, the show paused for breaking news:

"We have some breaking and exciting news to report tonight. Chase Lovell, the youngest son of Todd and Kate Lovell, also brother to Hunter Lovell, now known as the Sandy Beach Darling Killer, was found and returned home after being abducted two years ago by sex offender Lee Earl Elwood. Hunter Lovell, set to stand trial in the murder of Isabel Dominguez next month, has previously been convicted and sentenced to life for the murder of Tara Hill and a concurrent thirty-five years for the rape and attempted murder of Amber Callaway. It would seem as though the Lovell family nightmare may have finally come to conclusion. Here is Captain Bobby Justice addressing the media earlier this afternoon."

"Yes, it's taken a long time for these parents to get some closure. To say Todd and Kate Lovell have dealt with a lot over the last two years would be an understatement. No one knows that more than me. Everyone knows their story, and I vouch completely for their character. They loved both of their children, and the actions of one shouldn't define who they are or their standing in this community. Going forward, I hope that you will respect their need for privacy."

"If you any information on the whereabouts of Lee Earl Elwood, please call the tip line on your television screen," the news anchor stated.

"Hunter is in jail for murder?" Chase said in disbelief.

Todd turned the TV off and faced Kate, who was trying to keep herself together.

"Oh, boy," Todd said, looking at Chase for his reaction.

"Holy cow! What happened?" Chase exclaimed.

"Look, buddy." Todd put his arm around Chase. "Can we talk about it a little later and just enjoy the fact that your here with us?"

"We are still pinching ourselves that your home, my sweet baby," Kate said, massaging Chase's back.

Scooby jumped up on the couch. Chase appeared to draw courage from him. "Well, I have to know, or I won't be able to sleep tonight," he told his parents.

"Okay, buddy, look, I'll tell you the truth, but I don't know if we have the strength to explain everything right now, all right?" Todd said.

"So he did it?" Chase asked, looking at both parents for an answer.

"Yes, your brother hurt three girls seriously, and one survived," Kate told him plainly.

Chase sat up. "Three of them! Why?"

Todd shook his head. "We don't know, and I don't think Hunter does either. He has always been angry. We were *all* angry at Elwood for taking you, but what Hunter did has no excuse."

"Those girls had families, and they were so young. And, baby, you should know he's never getting out," Kate explained.

"Can we go see him?" Chase asked.

"We can call soon, but it might be a little while before we can visit," she said.

"Chase?" Todd asked with some hesitance. "Do you know a person named Goo-Man?"

Chase looked lost in thought, struggling to remember. "Yes! He's a cool dude."

Bobby and Kate looked to each other. "Oh, boy," Todd mumbled.

June 1985

Lee Earl Elwood sold his truck at a small used car lot off the highway near the Mexican border. They paid cash and didn't ask questions, which was why he took a good deal less than it was worth. He had some of Goodman's product stashed in the pickup, which he was able to pawn off on some hippies at a rest stop. It gave him some extra money to live on. He bought another truck with a cab so he could sleep in the back if needed. Lee planned on hopping the border and had made it as far south as the crossing in Naco. The night before though, in a motel room, his plans changed.

He'd gotten to sleep fine. Didn't think too hard on the close call. He'd been wanted for so long. The stress was nothing new. But that night, he woke in a cold sweat. As though by instinct, he reached over to grab for Chase. But after a few hazy moments, he realized the boy was gone. At that thought, something opened up in him. He reached for the bottle of rum he'd bought the night before and poured a hefty shot.

It was a strange feeling for Lee Earl. He had picked up and discarded his playthings easy as throwing out a bouquet of flowers that had wilted or a donut gone stale. But now the image of Chase returned.

"Let it go," he said aloud to himself. But the feeling that had gripped him so strongly before he had grabbed Chase was rising, like a ghost set to possess him.

He looked at the back of his hand. The veins on his wrinkled skin popped out like a road map. Chase made all that bearable, the ugliness of his own withering self. Now he was what…a middle-aged man, alone. *Fuck it*, he thought. *Time to go.* Lee Earl packed his bag and took it out to the truck. He left the motel room key in the lock and headed out into the night, the high beams pointing his way east.

*****

Bobby and Jack were chatting in Bobby's office as the day was winding down. The jubilation of retrieving Chase had worn off over the previous month, overtaken by the anticipation of the Dominguez murder trial. Jack twisted his Rubik's cube, still frustrated at his inability to solve the puzzle.

"Hard to believe they are bringing this to trial," Bobby said, twirling a pen between his fingers. "Hunter just needs to plea and save everyone the time and effort."

"Lawyers," Jack stated. "That's all there is to it. As long as this case is in the news, there will be people trying to make a name for themselves from it. Even if it's off someone else's grief."

Bobby sat back and stopped fumbling with the pen. "Yeah, I suppose so," he grumbled.

"Well, at least it all worked out in the end," Jack said, taking a sip of his coffee.

"Worked out for who, exactly?" Bobby asked. "Not for the family of Tara Hill. And while Todd and Kate got Chase back, Hunter Lovell's life is over before he's eighteen. Chase, I'm sure, still has a tough road ahead of him dealing with what that perverted piece of shit Elwood did. You can say the same for Amber Callaway. And certainly nothing worked out for Ms. Dominguez or even the doctor, George Darling. He lost a fiancée and seemingly his marbles or what was left of them."

"True enough. Say, any word from those two? I've left messages, but that camp went silent."

"Darling's AWOL. We may need to do a welfare check. As for Ms. Dominguez, I can't say."

"Well, at least the bad guys are in jail, and Chase is back home," Jack said. "Things are getting back to normal, let's hope."

"Jack, this dance ain't over just because the music's stopped playing."

"Bobby, you need to be clear with me. I got this here cube if I want to scramble my mind."

"I'm saying it's too early to celebrate, and let's close that damn hotel one way or another."

"Captain, are you saying you are taking to this idea of a curse?"

Bobby topped off his coffee and finally told Jack about his meeting with van Brock, but he kept to himself the dark feeling he'd had in the hotel. Something about his experience there felt private.

"I agree with you, Bobby. But it's not our job to worry about that hotel," Jack said. "We have enough on our plates."

"I'm beginning to think the hotel *is the plate*, Jack. Again, I'm not promoting ideas about ghosts. I just want to suture closed this vein of Sandy Beach history before it spills more blood."

"I hear you, partner. You don't mind if I still call you partner, Captain?"

"That's fine, Jack."

"Well, I can tell you one thing," Jack said, shaking his head. "I'm never going to forget these past couple of years. Fucking crazy."

"Same here," Bobby agreed. "I'm not so old. Maybe I can retrain as a plumber."

"Why?" Jack asked. "You would still be cleaning up shit one way or the other."

Bobby laughed. It had been a while, and the laughter felt good. "True enough, Sergeant. I only wonder where our next mess is coming from."

Just then, Detective Jonesy walked up to Bobby. "Captain Justice, Rosalina Dominguez is here to see you."

"Well, something's still in the air. At least this mess smells nice," Jack quipped, hoping to keep Bobby smiling.

"Send her in, please," Bobby instructed. The demur dark-skinned sister to Isabel stepped into the office. Her time away from hotel cleaning had done her good. Long and lustrous red nails extended from a soft hand that clutched a Guess purse. She smiled at Bobby.

"Hello, Captain Justice and Sergeant Cutler. Nice to see you again."

"Ms. Dominguez, please have a seat." Bobby stood and gestured to the open chair next to Jack. "We were just saying how we haven't been able to reach you or Dr. Darling. We still need to talk about a victim impact statement and make sure he is ready to testify."

"Yes, I have received your messages," Rosalina said. "Sorry, but I have been coping with the death of my mother."

"Oh," Jack said. "I'm sorry. What happened?"

"It was not a surprise, Sergeant," Rosalina said. "Mother had been sick for a long time now. She just hid it well. After my sister's trial, I will have her remains moved back to Cuba to be buried next to our parents. The thing is, since George found out of my mother's passing, he has been even more difficult to get a hold of."

"*More* difficult?" Bobby rubbed the back of his neck. "We haven't been able to speak with him at all. When was the last time you contacted the doctor?"

Rosalina sat up straight with the posture of a ballerina. "I would visit almost every day after school and sometimes go with him to see my sister in the mausoleum, but even I can't go every day and night. In truth, it was too painful, so I have avoided going at all recently. Now I can barely get the doctor on the phone," she explained.

Jack and Bobby exchanged looks. "He still paying for your schooling?" Jack inquired.

"That has been paid for completely, Sergeant," Rosalina said.

"Well, as far as we know, he went on vacation, and some people have heard him rambling on about a honeymoon," Bobby said.

Rosalina shook her head. "He's not on vacation, Captain. He left a message yesterday from his house phone crying, begging me not to take Isabel from him. He had that classical music on in the background, so I know he must be feeling sad. This worried me. I'm afraid he's going to do something drastic, like move the body. Or worse."

"Can he do that?" Jack asked.

"He signed the death certificate. He purchased the space. He signs papers and gives money, so he can do what he wants. He's so quiet sometimes, but I can see there are terrible things going on behind his eyes," Rosalina said, almost shyly.

"So we believe the good doctor is at home then?" Bobby asked.

"I tried stopping by earlier, but Jose says he won't come out no matter what. That's why I need your help."

"Jeepers," Jack said. "Maybe he took a ride on the good ship lollypop there, huh?" He wiggled his eyebrows at Bobby, who glared back at him as he stood up.

"I don't know. Sometimes, I think you're on a permanent cruise," Bobby told Jack.

"Why?" Jack asked, standing as well. "What'd I say?"

"Relax, Ms. Dominguez, we are overdue for a visit with Dr. Darling," Bobby said.

Bobby and Jack followed Rosalina Dominguez in their cruiser to Dr. Darling's residence. Pulling into the driveway, Bobby noted a short man leaning against the fence with his arms crossed tightly. Rosalina told them that was George's yardman, Jose. When he saw the police car, he threw his hands up.

"Mierda! Did he call the cops on me?" he asked as the detectives approached him.

"Did who call the cops?" Jack asked.

"Mr. Darling!" Jose pointed to the house.

Jack straightened his tie. "Why would he have called the police?"

"Because I wait all day. I wait for my pay. *I need my money*!" Jose said sternly. "Hard work, hot sun."

"Well, Mr. Jose, I can assure you we aren't here for you," Bobby said then nodded toward the doctor's house. "Are you sure he's home?" he asked.

"Yeah, he's home!" Jose said. "I see him through the damn window curtains dancing around with some big doll. Plus, he's been playing piano music all day. I wait, but I can't wait forever."

"A doll?" Bobby said with a furrowed brow.

"I come yesterday, same thing. Dances behind the curtain, doesn't answer the door. I need to feed my family," Jose let out, pointing to his empty hand.

Jack squinted, trying to peer through the window. "I can barely see anything. Should we try to force entry?" Jack said.

"Detectives!" Rosalina called. Everyone turned to see her standing at the open front door.

"You have a key?" Jack asked.

"Yes…why?" Rosalina replied before stepping inside and disabling the alarm.

"Then why didn't you just go inside in the first place?" Jack asked, frustrated.

"It's not my house," Rosalina said tentatively.

Jack threw up his hands. "Then why do you have a key?"

"Isabel made them so when my mother or I came to visit, we could just come in if no one was home. With Isabel not being here, I won't do that now. But I have the police with me, so I opened the door."

"Okay," Bobby intervened. "Now that we have the key mystery solved, let's go see if the doctor is around. Jose, you wait here. You too, Rosalina."

"Oh, sure. Always wait," Jose said, crossing his arms again.

The first thing Justice noticed inside the stately home was the flicker of light coming from candles on the dining room table. He blew them out, noting they had been burned down to the end. Music sounded softly from a classical music station on the stereo. Bobby turned it off and listened, holding a hand up to quiet Jack. A shuffling came from above, somebody moving around. He signaled with his head for Jack to follow. They began up the stairs, looking uneasily at the portraits of Isabel. As they crept down the hall, Bobby became alert to the sound of moaning coming from behind the master bedroom door. Jack and Bobby exchanged a puzzled look. Jack made an obscene gesture with his hands, and Bobby rolled his eyes in return. But the closer they got to the door, the louder the moans became. The scent of perfume mixed with another strong, mulchy odor filled the hallway. Soon, the smell was almost overpowering.

Bobby gave a knock. "Dr. Darling. Bobby Justice here. I need to speak with you."

No response came, so he twisted the doorknob. It was locked from the inside, so Bobby stood back and nodded to Jack. The young officer loaded a kick, then burst open the door with a powerful strike. They both recoiled at the macabre sight before them. George Darling was lying on top of a greenish body, groaning as he pumped into it. It took a moment for Justice to apprehend that under him was Isabel's corpse. What looked like a wedding dress was hiked up over her flayed legs, and her face, turned toward them, was covered in a waxy mask, the black eyes staring into Bobby, as though challenging him to save her.

George, lost in his passion, was oblivious to the officers' presence, panting, drooling down on the body as he muttered to her, "Are you enjoying our honeymoon, darling?"

Jack covered his mouth, bent over, then vomited.

Forensic officers and an ambulance arrived at George's house soon after Bobby made the call. He had escorted Dr. Darling to the kitchen. The man was docile, unreachable, the smell of death and residual perfume wafting from him. He only mumbled to himself and asked for Isabel, who was left upstairs, under a blanket Jack had thrown over her. Bobby declined to cuff the doctor until he was led to the squad car, when it was procedure.

As Bobby sat contemplating the situation, Officer Pac, whom he'd dispatched to the cemetery, radioed in.

"It took some doing with the overseer, but when he noticed the clasps on the coffin broken, it wasn't hard to convince him to open it up. Nothing but soil and some stones. Darling must have taken the body long ago. Any idea why he wanted it?"

Bobby wrinkled his nose. "Jane, let's just say for now I'm still working that out in my head," he replied.

"Oh my," Officer Pac uttered before signing off. Right then, a young crime scene officer came rushing down the stairs. Once he spotted Bobby, he strode over. The captain noticed he was carrying a cardboard box.

"Gentlemen, I think you should see this," he said.

"If it's his pornography collection, I am pretty sure I don't want to," Jack quipped from across the room.

The officer put the box on the table for Bobby to open. Inside, he found faded Kodachrome pictures of women, before and after they met with what must have been a knife.

"Jack, get over here," Bobby called.

"What do you have?" Jack said, striding over to the table.

"Have a look," Bobby said, flipping through the old pictures. "Looks like these come from forty or so years back. You know what that means?"

"Yeah. From the cold case files."

"Looks like Darling's greatest surprise isn't just his love for dead women but love for making them dead," Bobby stated.

"Even though a theory pointed this way, I still never would have thought Darling would be a killer. You'd think doctors would have some kind of, I don't know, immunity to this evil cycle. But I guess, every twenty years, it's a new surprise," Jack said.

Bobby took the box back to the cruiser and placed it in the trunk. There was no rush with Darling in custody and another long evening at the Darling residence still unfinished. Bobby had just pulled out a thermos of coffee when the medical examiner, Jeff Webb, MD, came to find him.

"This is one of the more unique cases I've seen," Jeff said, sounding almost excited.

"Unique? You want to hear what's unique?" Jack retorted. "How about walking in on George Darling with his wrinkled ass hanging out while he's having sex or whatever the hell that was he was doing with Isabel's dead body? That's fucking unique."

"There's a kind of unique that it's fair to say is an acquired taste," Bobby expressed. "One I'd just as soon not get accustomed to."

"I understand," Jeff Webb said. "Let me get more specific in my wording. The term for this is *romantic necrophilia*. Where a person can't let go of the deceased and remains attracted to their dead body. It's just another disorder among many. Although I must say, a lot of love and care went into keeping this body together. Come, let me show you."

The three returned to the master bedroom, where the scene was still being photographed. The blanket had been removed, Isabel's body in full view. Now it looked to Bobby like some film prop.

"So…how did he keep the bones attached? She's been dead for a year now," he asked the doctor.

Jeff pointed to some of the knots fitted around the joints. "This looks like piano wire. And this, I believe, is coat hangers." The examiner continued to admire the doctor's work. "Very carefully done, too, if I may say so."

"What about her face? Was that a mask?" Jack asked.

"Yes, well, not something from a local costume store." Jeff held up some of the material. "As with everything else, the doctor went to great lengths to keep up Ms. Dominguez's appearance."

"What is that?" Jack asked, looking at the waxy substance.

"It appears that as the skin of the corpse continued to decompose, Dr. Darling replaced it with this silk cloth soaked in wax or plaster of paris. Good-looking stuff, huh? Oh, and then he fitted the sockets with glass eyes for that lifelike glimmer."

Bobby and Jack stared at Jeff with blank expressions, which only egged the examiner on.

"And you two are going to love this." Dr. Webb turned to pick up something from the table. He held up a bag of hair. "The wig Darling so fashionably made was her real hair. Rosalina Dominguez confirmed Darling collected the hair not long after Isabel's burial."

"Doc, I don't even know what else to ask," Jack said.

Bobby shook his head. "Jeff, I don't recall you ever being this giddy over anything. It's disturbing me."

"There's real artistry here. I'll give Darling that. I could work for the rest of my career and never see anything like this again," Jeff said, again looking over the corpse.

Bobby suppressed a gag. The stench of the perfume was almost worse than the body. "God, I hope so. I'd rather burn my eyes out than come across this again."

"Well, we talked about the hair and face, so let's move down a bit." Jeff set the hair down. "The doctor filled the abdominal and chest cavity with rags. I would think to try and help keep the original form of her body. He kept the remains dressed in stockings, jewelry, and gloves. I would guess it's all from her closet."

"Um…" Jack stammered, lifting his hands. "How did he…"

"Are you asking how he had intercourse, Sergeant? I guess you're also interested," Webb said with a wink.

"Try to keep it professional, Doctor," Bobby said.

"There was a paper tube inserted in the vaginal area," Jeff said.

"Jesus Christ," Bobby sighed.

"Why would he do something like that?" Jack asked.

"You want logic now? In my professional opinion, he suffered the worst of afflictions. He loved her," Jeff said.

Bobby covered his nose with his arm. He wanted out of there, lest he begin vomiting. "Anything else?"

"Only what you have already seen and smelled," Jeff said. "He used large amounts of perfume to help mask the odor and preserving agents to help slow down the effects of decomposition. Other than that, you'll have to wait for the report."

"Published by Stephen King," Jack joked.

"Title it *A Darling Obsession*," Webb quipped.

*****

Elwood avoided driving through Sandy Beach. Even though it was his destination, it was the last place he wanted to be seen. The town of Chickee Grove was close enough, and there was less chance of running into Roy or Cordale Goodman. Besides, it was inland from the water, and the motels were cheaper. He had any number of fake IDs he could use, not that they ever asked at the desk. Places like this were just happy if you didn't kick holes in the walls or draw the cops' attention. When he wanted to make his presence known in Sandy Beach, that's just what he'd do.

Lee Earl also had half a mind to turn himself in. This longing he had, for Chase and the others, while to him it was the most natural thing in the world, only brought hate and persecution his way. And it was exhausting. Like always swimming against the tide. Sometimes he just wanted to sink. If he could just drown this energy, this haunting. But that's not how it worked. He liked his freedom. And he felt he deserved Chase, who had been a bad kid sometimes, but mostly stuck by him. Who hadn't tried to flee once. That said something. If he could just get Chase back, he wouldn't have to search ever again to satisfy this feeling. The boy would be enough.

After checking in, Lee Earl went back out to pick up some Jack-in-the-box and supplies from the drugstore. He turned on the TV then turned it off again. He was agitated and had to figure out just what he was going to do next.

*****

"You stay off your feet today, and we can go out somewhere nice when I get back, okay?" Bobby said, staring happily at his fiancée. Late one night, unable to sleep, Bobby had taken a long walk, which ended with him knocking on the door of Gwen's houseboat. She'd let him in, and over something called Red Zinger tea, Bobby pled his case. He told her stories from Vietnam, of his platoon, of the carnage he had witnessed, the memories flooding back as he spoke. Gwen sat back and listened and continued to listen when he promised to be more *present*—that was the word she liked—if she took him back. He promised to try, *really try*. She told him no, but later allowed him to pack her a bag, wrap her toothbrush up with her toiletries in a towel, and bring her back to his condo. They were engaged within the week.

Gwen giggled as she stroked the side of his face. "Let's get out and do something. I can't sit around all day."

Bobby smiled. "Just relax and look through those reality brochures. We need to upgrade."

Gwen put her hand over Bobby's. "Are you sure, babe?"

"Of course, I am." Bobby kissed Gwen on the lips. "I'll be back soon."

*****

The chief had called a meeting to confer over recent events. Bobby and Jack strode into city hall to find the rest already gathered.

"Well, howdy, Mayor! Chief! Eldon! How is everything?" Jack said as he entered the room. He shook everyone's hands with more formality.

"Welcome to the party, Jack. How are you, Sergeant?" Chief Curry said.

"Great, especially now the SBPD is finally up to three detectives and added some new young officers who are ready to work."

"Well, I'm glad to see the new budget is treating you well, Sergeant," the mayor said. "Good work gets rewarded."

"All right, everyone, have a seat," Chief Curry said. "Are we missing anyone?"

"Looks like the gang is all here now," the mayor declared.

After small talk, they got down to the business of George Darling.

"Bobby, before we get into deeper matters, I have to ask you. Just how did Darling transport the body to his home?" the mayor asked. "You have reason to believe it wasn't in his car?"

"No. From talking to neighbors, I learned the doctor walked every day. It doesn't look he had been driving very much, and the graveyard was only a couple of miles away from his home."

The mayor raised his eyebrows. "Well, he certainly didn't carry it, right?"

"I wouldn't think so. There was a toy wagon in his garage. It had dirt on the tires, and neighbors say it's what he used to bring flowers to her gravesite. We believe that's what he used to get her corpse back with."

"Where there's a will, there's a way, Mayor," Jack said.

"I think in light of what happened, it's time to discuss this," Bobby said then placed the box that was discovered in George Darling's closet on Chief Curry's desk.

"Don't keep us in suspense, Captain," Mayor Reed said with his hands folded over his belly.

Bobby opened the box and spread before them the pictures of Sandy Beach women who were murdered forty years ago.

"We discovered who Sandy Beach Murderer is, and I don't think it will shock you."

"Here, Mayor. You are our resident letter narrator." Bobby handed some pages to Bailey Reed. "Do us the honors."

The mayor looked over a couple of the letters then cleared his throat and began to read:

> My darling,
>
> I have a small confession. Forgive this pouring out of my heart. I cherish the beach where we first met. The moment I laid eyes on you, I knew you were going to be a beautiful girl. Recently, I have begun to regard you as much more than just a beautiful girl. My feelings for you intensified when I saw you laughing in the moonlight. Your tremendous smooching skills further wowed me.
>
> All my love
> For
> Your Love Darling

> My darling,
>
> Your lips are like a sexy goddess, and you have the brightest eyes I've ever seen. When I look at you, I just want to grab you by the hair and kiss your neck. I know that to you, I'm only a stunning fool, but I think we could be happy together, dancing like two lovely dolls.
>
> Please never leave again, my darling!
>
> All my love
> For
> Your Love Darling

"Jesus, the man broke not just once but twice," Mayor Reed exclaimed.

"I wonder, why did he just stop?" Eldon asked.

"He found something that took the pain away," Bobby speculated. "His practice. Once he had that new love, he moved on. Now that he had lost both again, you see the results."

"And we don't need to get into *other* explanations right now," Jack brought up.

Bobby sighed. "Darling is currently at the Sandy Beach Institute for Mental Health, and if we can keep it like that, this doesn't need to see the light of day."

The mayor glanced at the district attorney. "Save the town the money of a trial, not to mention reopening old wounds. I like that. Eldon can see to it that the doctor never leaves that place."

"Are there any living relatives left from these victims?" Eldon inquired.

"I did some checking. None of these women had children and no siblings that live in Sandy Beach," Bobby revealed. "I don't like it, but as long as he stays there, I can live with it."

"In that case, I can make sure of that, Captain," Eldon assured.

"I'm glad we agree. I, for one, am looking forward to some vacation time. And taking it easy for the next twenty years," Bobby said.

"Good news. You will be too old worry about it next time, partner," Jack told Bobby, giving a hearty wink.

*****

Chase only peeked into his brother's room. Everything looked the same—the disarray, the dark from the shades being constantly drawn. Even though he knew he wasn't coming back—Hunter ultimately pled guilty in the Dominguez case, adding another life sentence to the one he was serving—being there still felt like an intrusion. Like the spirit or something of Hunter still resided there and needed its privacy. Chase didn't like being the only child, and even though his brother was sometimes rough with him, he missed that roughness too. He closed the door and bounded downstairs to talk to his parents.

"Can we go see Hunter tomorrow?" Chase asked.

"Are you ready for that, sweetheart?" Kate asked.

"Yes, I am," Chase said. "I've been ready. It's you guys who haven't been."

Kate smile at Todd then hugged and kissed Chase on top of his head. "When did you get so smart?" she asked while squeezing his cheeks.

Chase shrugged. "I don't know. Recently, I guess."

Kate put her hands over her mouth and giggled while Todd gave an affectionate laugh. "Well, at least one of us has," Todd said.

"Well, babe, what do you think?" Kate asked Todd.

"I think Chase is exactly right if we are honest with ourselves." Todd sighed. "He's been ready. We haven't."

"I don't guess I can disagree with that," Kate replied.

"And considering what we have decided to do, it makes even more sense," Todd said.

Kate nodded in agreement. "Also very true."

"The trial is over, Mom. You said once it was over, we could, and now it's over."

"I know, sweetie, I know. I will see if we can go tomorrow, okay? Happy now?"

"Yes! I can't wait!" Chase said, darting back up the stairs.

"Know what? Neither can I," Todd said. At that, he seemed to arrive at a decision. He went to the kitchen, took the bottle of Seagram's from the shelf, and poured what remained into the sink. Then he tossed the remnants of a six-pack in the trash. If Chase could be strong, so could he.

*****

Hunter was working out with another inmate, having set a goal of bench-pressing his own body weight. Hunter had some respect from the others, but he missed Goo, now at an adult facility, and had forgiven his old friend for acting as a witness against him. At the sight of a female correctional officer walking by, Hunter paused for a moment, observing her, then proceeded with his workout as another guard walked into the exercise area, informing him he had a visitor.

Hunter looked around the visitor's room, not seeing his parents. He was about to turn and call a guard when he noticed the mop of blond hair, the kid waving at him. "Jesus," he said out loud when he recognized his brother. He strode over and sat across the table from the boy.

"Chase! I didn't think I would ever see you again."

"Hey, brother," Chase acknowledged. Hunter knew of his kid brother's return, but seeing him was far more surprising.

Hunter shook his head in disbelief. "Effing Goo-Man. Of all the damn people to find you. Not the police, not the FBI, but De'Ron fucking Goodman. I can't even be mad at him for giving me up. It brought you home."

Chase laughed. "I never knew you cared."

Hunter paused and looked at his little brother. "I always cared in my own way. I just didn't know how much until you were gone. Then I realized you were my best friend and the only one who never judged me, just like right now."

"I just see my big bro, and I miss you. I even miss you bitching at me for fucking with your video games." Chase smiled, remembering. "When I was with Elwood, I thought about how I would do anything to have you bitching at me."

"Anything I have left in that room is yours," Hunter said, nodding at Chase.

"Oh, believe me, I got my sights set on some games and cassette tapes already."

Hunter chuckled. "Forget the video games. My blade is hidden under the mattress. You take that. I want you to have it. It'll make you feel better. Safer."

"I don't really like dangerous things," Chase said.

"Okay, then just leave it there. So how are you doing, bro? I can't even imagine."

"Umm, all right, I guess. I'm happy to be home. I started seeing a shrink twice a week," Chase said. "Some of the kids around the neighborhood call me a fag. I don't tell my mom and dad about it, though." He shrugged. "On the bright side, I finally got that basketball hoop I wanted."

Hunter twitched his head. "Call you fag? Why?" he said agitatedly.

"Some of the things that happened with Lee Earl got in the newspaper. It's embarrassing," Chase mumbled.

"So they catch that homo yet?" Hunter asked, angered.

"Hopefully soon," Chase said. "From what we hear from Mr. Justice, real soon."

"Hope they get the fucker," Hunter said. "Maybe he will end up around here."

Chase and Hunter sat quietly for a minute. "You bigger than I remember. Even bigger than Dad now," Chase said.

"I guess I take after Grandpa Lovell," Hunter admitted. "That's what Dad always said anyway."

"Yeah, I took after Mom," Chase said, rolling his eyes.

"Where are they at? I know you didn't ride your bike here."

"Went to get some chicken sandwiches or something. They wanted us to just say hi without them."

Hunter sighed. "I knew it. Confrontation never was their thing."

"They said it was best for us."

Hunter sized Chase up. "Well, I guess you grew a little bit."

"Grew where it counts," Chase said, grinning. "Of course, you wouldn't know about that, huh, half-inch."

"Fuck you," Hunter said with a laugh, bathing in his brother's attention. "Mr. Comedian now."

"How did you end up in here, man?" Chase finally got the courage to ask.

Hunter just shrugged. "Because I got caught, little brother. Didn't watch enough *Hill Street Blues* episodes, I suppose."

"It doesn't make any sense," Chase said, shaking his head.

"What obsession does?" Hunter confessed. "I'm just living like I want to live. That's what we're supposed to do, right?"

Chase looked like he wanted to ask more questions but kept them back.

Hunter turned serious. "Hey, bro, no need to lie about our folks. I know they're here."

Chase looked ashamed for a moment. "Yeah, they're waiting out front. They thought you wouldn't want to see me if they were here too."

"Fuck it. Tell them to come in."

Chase walked to the door, opened it, and gestured to his parents. Kate came in first, followed by Todd. They sat on either side of Chase.

Hunter waited for them to speak first. "Hey, baby," Kate finally greeted him. "I'm not crying this time."

"I'm glad you finally decided to see us again," Todd said.

"I'm surprised you would want to," Hunter said.

"Of course, we want to," Kate said.

"Never did get to finish our last conversation," Hunter said, folding his arms on the table.

"Help us out here," Kate said.

Todd twisted his wedding ring nervously. "We just want to know how this came to be," he finally said.

Hunter sighed. "You know I have also thought about this. And, well, the truth is, you all gave birth to a killer. And if Amber hadn't survived, I know I would have done it again."

"How can you say that?" Kate asked. "Maybe if you would have come to us, we could have gotten you help."

"And said what?" Hunter retorted. "'Hey, Mom. Hey, Dad, I thought killing a woman sounded like it would be a blast, and you know what? It was!' Something like that?"

"Fun?" Todd repeated. "Did you really find it fun?"

"I think you heard me say I'm where I should be," Hunter said.

"Is this our fault?" Kate asked. "Because of how we acted after Chase was gone?"

"It would be easy to say yes to that," Hunter said. "But the truth is, I've had these thoughts about doing things like this since I was seven or so years old."

"I can't believe that, Hunter," Todd said.

"Well, it's true," he told his parents. "So feel free to take yourself off the guilty hook."

"We are also worried about you," Todd said.

"You don't need to. You can just pretend I didn't happen and go on with your lives," Hunter answered.

"There won't ever be a day when that happens. You're still my firstborn. I love you," Kate said.

A guard approached to tell them they had but a few minutes left.

"The truth is, we might be moving," Todd said. "A new start for Chase. For us."

Hunter took the news calmly. "Well, in time, I guess they'll send me to Osceola State Pen, same as Goo, so you'll be able to write me there. Just be sure to send your address once you get one," Hunter said as he stood. "Take care of yourself, little brother."

Chase nodded, still in awe of his mighty big brother.

*****

"Do you want fried chicken for dinner?" Kate called to her men, sitting on the couch enjoying a Gators baseball game.

"Extra crispy!" Chase called out.

"Well, let's get hustling before it gets too late," Kate said.

"Mom! I gotta see Albert Einstein Gator once more."

"Let's just get takeout, honey," Todd interjected. "That way, I can start repairing the aluminum siding out back and work up an appetite."

"Fine. Just don't go anywhere without your dad," Kate instructed Chase.

"I'm waiting for Albert Gator, then I'll just chill," Chase said.

Kate laughed then kissed Chase goodbye and locked the front door She was glad Scooby would be in the yard with Todd. He'd keep the bad guys away.

After some few more minutes of play, the Gators won in the final inning. Uninterested in the news on TV, Chase got a popsicle and plodded up the steps. He stopped outside Hunter's room.

Then, remembering his brother's urging, he pushed open the door. He stood in the silent darkness. The place still smelled faintly like Hunter, which gave Chase a warm feeling. Wanting to extend that feeling, he picked up the joystick to Hunter's Atari. "Pew, pew," he sounded, imagining himself shooting down robots in Berserk. He didn't need to turn it on. He could play in his mind. But he heard Scooby barking at some squirrel, so he slipped a Galaga cartridge in the console and turned the TV on with the sound up. He slaughtered a squadron of attacking spaceships then let himself die, not wanting to play more. He sighed, content, but hungry for the chicken.

"Hey, buddy!" he heard.

Chase froze. It couldn't be real. He pushed the restart button and began firing.

"Finish up now. We don't have much time."

Chase slowly turned, still hoping it wasn't real. But there was Lee Earl Elwood, standing in his doorway, looking mean.

"Now get some clothes together and let's get the fuck out of here," he commanded.

Chase stared up at him. This horrible stranger in his dirty jeans. "Dad!" he called.

"Oh, that man in the back? He's taking nice ole nap right now. But we gotta hurry. Come on now, Alex."

"I'm not Alex," Chase spat out. "Get outta here!"

At that, Elwood started for Chase. He wasn't going to let him go this time. Elwood had staked out the house almost daily, parking down the street, biding his time. The father had been easy to take out. Too focused on his power tools to notice what was coming. Lee Earl took no pleasure in knocking him unconscious. But now he was fired up and prepared to take his child by force. Elwood grabbed Chase by the hair and dragged him into the hallway. The brat had already grown defiant. He'd whip that out of him soon enough. He smacked Chase on the side of the head to get him to comply.

Chase felt the pain and saw pulsing stars, then recovered. Kicking backward, the image of Hunter flashed through Chase's mind. The awesome power of his brother. Hunter would never let this happen to him. With a deft motion, Chase flipped to where he was facing forward and rushed at Elwood, biting him in the arm that held him. Elwood screeched and released the boy. Chase darted back into Hunter's room, slamming the door, Elwood following in long angry steps.

"Okay, you want it like this, boy? You won't leave this house alive!" Elwood called, thrusting open the door that had been shut in his face. There was Chase, facing him, arms behind his back. He sprang at the child, perhaps to embrace him, perhaps to put an end to him, he couldn't say. His body hit the boy with such force they both fell onto the bed. Only then did Elwood feel a pinch in his belly, a pressure, then warmth that spread over his stomach. He rolled off Chase… Alex…his son. He looked down to see the blade sticking from his stomach, the bone handle rising like a middle finger. Lee Earl felt his body begin to weaken.

"Alex," he whimpered, his vision blurring. But Chase's face, like a dark angel in front of him, gave him strength. He pulled the knife from his belly and tossed it aside. Then he strode toward the boy. "Alex!" he cried again. Then he felt a blow, and the wind get knocked from him. Elwood was flying, and fast. A strong shove had catapulted him past Chase, then into the pane of glass and out the window. Landing on his back, before he lost consciousness, he gazed up at the man he had clobbered in the yard. Elwood saw him lean from the window and shake his fist.

"My son's name is Chase, you son of a bitch," Todd said, looking down at the dying man with blood streaming from the side of his head. He spat on the dying criminal.

*****

"Shouldn't be allowed," Jack said. He lifted a beer and took an angry gulp. The Snappy Turtle was near empty that night.

Bobby put cash on the bar for Wanda. "We're the police, not city planners, not moral authorities on how people should spend their time and money."

"It's just that I get this curse is something we need to live with, but why should that woman go making money off our town's bad reputation? I mean, it's a good fucking town in the end. You could argue that even Dr. Darling saved more lives than he took. And when evil men like Bartholomew Payne and Lee Earl Elwood poke their heads up, we always beat them down again. We teach those mopes."

"Only thing Elwood learned was how fast body temps fall when blood stops flowing."

"No charges on the Lovells, I assume," Jack said.

"Charges? Awards, maybe. Prizes."

"What, an all-expenses paid stay at the Sandy? Compliments of Guinevere."

"Well, like I said, if people are coming to stay there, that's their business. The root of the problem's not curiosity seekers or even Ms. Kerrigan. Done the background check. She's clean as a whistle. You could even say she's a victim here. Drawn in by one big spiderweb."

"I don't know. I still vote for tearing it down and blaming it on a hurricane," Jack said.

Wanda walked lazily over and poured the men a shot on the house each.

"Hey, Wanda," Jack said, perking up. "I'll pay for my booze if you smile just once."

Wanda looked at him, blank-faced. "Drop dead, and I might."

Bobby let loose a peal of laughter.

"Man, I love this place. Only in Sandy Beach," Jack opined, shaking his head.

September 1985

The offer came as a surprise to Marina Kerrigan. A far larger sum of money than she paid for the place. Done through a holding company, acting via a lawyer, there was no name to the prospective buyer of the Sandy. Just a contract and the lawyer's out-of-state number. The only condition was that she depart the premises without delay and leave every item of furnishings intact, down to the last towel.

Marina took a rare drink—a martini poured from a minibar in room 6. It had become a habit, sitting in this room. She knew if she were to decide, she had to do it here, the place which she believed was the heart of the hotel. Though she couldn't say why. The truth was, something felt different to her about the hotel lately. She couldn't put her finger on it. The feeling was like that of a love affair dying. Instead of a living, breathing body, the Sandy felt like it was turning to material of the dead—dry bone.

"What shall I do?" she uttered out loud. From the center of the room, a rattling came. Marina went to the trapdoor. She couldn't help but imagine that there was some invisible flood in the room that was draining into the trapdoor, a trickle of energy departing. She thrust the hatch open and looked down into the blackness. For a moment, a hand seemed to rise and summoned her forth, inviting her to submerge herself in the water. Marina Kerrigan stood on the edge of the opening, feeling at once both trapped and free and unsure in which direction she would move next.

*****

Todd, Kate, and Chase were finishing with the last of their packing. Scooby trotted over to the For Sale sign in the yard and lifted his leg. They didn't have a destination settled on yet. The idea of just driving west appealed to Todd. They'd sold most of their furniture and belongings in a yard sale. Collectors who trafficked in serial killers' memorabilia had driven from great distances to pick over Hunter's toys and clothing. It was something that made Kate slightly sick. Still, they had raised enough money to move wherever they wanted.

"So where are we going?" Chase asked, setting a box down in the truck.

"Just somewhere different," Todd said. "Somewhere our name doesn't mean much to anybody else."

"Can we go to Kentucky?" he asked.

"We can drive through, honey. Why Kentucky?"

"I just like the name. And the chicken," Chase said honestly.

Kate laughed but stopped when she saw her son's face turn gloomy.

"What about Hunter?" Chase asked. "I want to see him again one day."

"He's not going anywhere, is he?" Todd said as he put his hand on Chase's shoulder. "Plus, there are telephones there, so we can always call and send letters."

Chase nodded, not looking convinced.

"How about California?" Kate said as she handed Todd a box. "You always like those Beach Boys songs."

Todd smirked at her. "Why, you want to start a band?" he asked as he took the load and kissed her on the lips.

"What if I do?" Kate said, putting her hands on her hips.

"Well, I guess we'll have to work on producing a few more members," Todd said, pulling his wife in for a hug.

"Maybe they will have some good therapists for you guys too," Chase said, looking away.

"Fair statement, my little honey," Kate said as she pinched Chase's cheeks.

"Ouch, Mom, stop," Chase groaned.

"With that son of a bitch Elwood rotting underground, I'll be just fine," Todd said.

"Hun, can we not bring his name up, please? Like ever again."

"I'm sorry, guys. Promise, never again." Todd pondered a moment. "California also has some nice beaches, I've heard."

Kate smiled and said, "It sure does."

*****

Bobby turned the pillow over again, trying to sleep. Sometimes, he wondered if the energy of Sandy Guinevere hadn't affected him too. If he didn't feel some dark force rising in his body, wanting to exert itself. Things should have been right in his world. The crime wave was over, wasn't it? Hunter Lovell was behind bars, and Dr. Darling was put away, getting help. And most importantly, Lee Earl Elwood was dead, and Chase was safe. That should end it all. Still, he couldn't shake the feeling the past wasn't done with them. Like gas bubbles in a swamp, dislodged things rose to the surface and weren't on any schedule. Perhaps the real curse, he considered, wasn't history but was how people destroyed their lives in their own way, with the bottle, with self-recrimination about the wrongs they committed, or by just neglect.

Restless in his skin, he could see Gwen getting irritated with his tossing and turning. She rose and, as if in a dream, said, "I need rest." Then she fell back onto her pillow. Bobby rose and went to the liquor cabinet. He reached for a bottle then stopped. *I need rest.* That phrase struck him as familiar. It was then that he recalled what van Brock said: *Then maybe she can rest.* Something in Bobby clicked. He called Jack and left a message, telling him to meet him at the Sandy Beach Hotel.

The captain sat in the living room, thinking until sunrise. He kissed his sleeping fiancée on the cheek then drove his cruiser to the Sandy. He parked in what was an empty lot. Walking to the front entrance, Bobby saw a piece of paper taped across the door: Closed Until Further Notice—Management. This he hadn't anticipated. He stepped back and noticed the storm shutters had been closed. Like the entire hotel had gone to sleep after a bout of strenuous activity.

"Damnit," Bobby said out loud. He walked around the outer deck, wondering if the boards always creaked this much or if he only noticed it because the Gulf was particularly quiet that day. Near the service entrance, he found what he was looking for. One of the shutters was hastily closed, left unlocked. Bobby pried it open with his fingers and slipped into the Sandy through the window, turning on his flashlight to make his way through an empty room and into the corridor. He shivered. The Sandy seemed to have sucked the warmth from the air. Bobby stepped gently, having the same feeling like after a hurricane, presided over by a watchful quiet.

Finally, he came to room 6. It was open, still looking pristine. He shined his flashlight around. Not a sign of life or death. He was alone, to the degree you could be alone in that hotel. Bobby went to the center of the room. Putting his back into it, he lifted open the trapdoor. Waves lapped up at him. From beneath, a blackness greeted him like spilled India ink. What was below was like another galaxy or a dark circle of some kind of purgatory. Bobby shuddered when he heard the distant cry.

Without thinking, the captain stripped down to his boxers, took a deep breath, and plunged headfirst into the water below. Cold surrounded him as he dove, reaching out in front of his body until he found the rocky ocean floor. Light from the emerging sun cast rays through the water like blades, but he could only make out shapes. Out of air, he emerged, breathed heavily, inhaled, then dove again. Then, like some undiscovered sea creature, he saw the shimmering outline of what appeared to be a woman rising from the ocean floor. She opened her arms then burst in golden light and was there no more. Bobby swam down to where she was, then dug furiously, running out of breath. He thought he felt arms closing around him, embracing him, before his hand came across an object with a smooth round surface. He lifted it, his lungs screaming for air, then turned and surfaced, bringing the skull back above water. Bobby floated there for a moment, unsure how he was going to get back up through the trapdoor. He swore, guessing he'd have to swim ashore, when a hand reached down toward him.

"Hey, partner," Jack called. "Strange place to take a bath."

Bobby laughed then let Jack take the skull before pulling him up into the room.

"I got your message. Figured you'd come to this room through the back."

"Are you saying you got inside my mind? Nice work, Sergeant."

"It's a dark scary place, that mind of yours," Jack teased. "But say, I thought you didn't like the ocean."

"Still don't," Bobby said.

"Did you fall in love with Isabel's older sister?" Jack quipped. "Not a great look for any hotel brochure."

"Here, you have our gal," Bobby said. "All we need to do is get the rest of her then give our friend Mrs. Guinevere a proper burial."

"I'll be damned," Jack uttered, looking over the skull.

"You sure it's her?"

"I'm sure," Bobby said.

"I'll call in a diving team from the station. No rush. I suppose we have another twenty years to get it done."

"I don't mind waiting for them to get here," Bobby said.

"I hear you, partner. I didn't think you believed in curses and such."

"I don't," Bobby said. "It's just that Gwen is expecting, and I don't care to tangle with history. There's just too much of it."

"I'll be damned. Congratulations. Bobby Justice, you're a new man."

"Thanks, Jack. Don't waste time about this, you hear?"

"You're the captain. Let's get it done."

"That's right, partner," Bobby said, allowing a rare smile.

Epilogue

September 13

George Darling was committed indefinitely to Sandy Beach Institute for Mental Health, where he was diagnosed with a posttraumatic stress reaction and placed in the top-floor wing where they housed the criminally insane. George was docile, only gazing out the window or sitting at a desk. He took his meds and was compliant when the staff needed him to be. He soon gained trust and was left to go about his business as the orderlies paid attention to more troublesome patients.

George Darling stood in front of his window, looked into the blue sky, lost in his memories, before sitting at his table. He slid a blank piece of paper in front of himself and picked up a crayon. Then he began to sketch. He paused for a moment, glancing up to look at his drawings of the four other women. The visions in his mind were alive on the page. He continued to draw Isabel.

He was putting the finishing touches on her hair when a nurse entered to let George know he had a visitor. Darling nodded. It was the same person who had come every day of his admittance. Dr. Darling continued his sketch, even though he heard footsteps behind him.

"George," the nurse said again. "Your visitor is here now."

Rosalina smiled at the nurse. "It's okay. He likes to be shy these days."

The nurse smiled back. "All right. I'll be around if you need anything."

"Thank you," Rosalina said as she stood looking at all the pictures spread out on the table that George had drawn. "Who are all these women, George?"

George looked up with a blank stare. She thought he might not respond. He looked back down his current drawing. "Which one?" he muttered.

Rosalina looked through the drawings and picked out the faces she didn't recognize. "These four women. Is one of them your wife? Do they work here at the hospital?" Rosalina questioned.

George stopped drawing then suddenly stood and swiped his arm across the table, sending the pictures flying. "They were all liars, but not my Isabel. Not my innocent one. She was the darling that came back to me." George sat down again then put his face in his hands.

Rosalina walked around the table and whispered something in his ear. George lifted his head and looked at her with an intense stare.

"I'll be back tomorrow, George," Rosalina said before kissing him on the top of his head and walking off.

Dr. Darling watched her leave. Once she was gone, he took a fresh piece of paper, picked another crayon from the box, and began to draw. "I found you again," he whispered.

THE END

A Darling Obsession
Inspired by True Events
S. R. Murray

About the Author

S. R. Murray is from New Orleans, Louisiana, but lives in Picayune, Mississippi, with his wife and two children. He always had ideas for characters and stories, and he finally decided to share one of them with everyone else.

Lightning Source UK Ltd.
Milton Keynes UK
UKHW010636200422
401787UK00001B/28